ONCE THE DEED IS DONE

ALSO BY THIS AUTHOR

The Dark Room
Field Study
Afterwards
The Walk Home
A Boy in Winter

ONCE THE DEED IS DONE

RACHEL SEIFFERT

virago

VIRAGO

First published in Great Britain in 2025 by Virago Press

1 3 5 7 9 10 8 6 4 2

Copyright © Rachel Seiffert 2025

The moral right of the author has been asserted.

All characters and events in this publication, other than those clearly in the public domain, are fictitious and any resemblance to real persons, living or dead, is purely coincidental.

All rights reserved.
No part of this publication may be reproduced, stored in a retrieval system, or transmitted in any form or by any means, without the prior permission in writing of the publisher, nor be otherwise circulated in any form of binding or cover other than that in which it is published and without a similar condition including this condition being imposed on the subsequent purchaser.

A CIP catalogue record for this book is available from the British Library.

Hardback ISBN 978-0-349-01416-6
Trade Paperback ISBN 978-0-349-01417-3

Typeset in Garamond by M Rules
Printed and bound in Great Britain by
Clays Ltd, Elcograf S.p.A.

Papers used by Virago are from well-managed forests and other responsible sources.

Virago Press
An imprint of
Little, Brown Book Group
Carmelite House
50 Victoria Embankment
London EC4Y 0DZ

The authorised representative
in the EEA is
Hachette Ireland
8 Castlecourt Centre
Dublin 15, D15 XTP3, Ireland
(email: info@hbgi.ie)

An Hachette UK Company
www.hachette.co.uk

www.virago.co.uk

In memory of Toby Eady and Dan Frank

and for displaced people everywhere

Character is just like a glove. There are good ones that last a long time. But no glove can last always.

BERTOLT BRECHT,
The Jewish Wife

To be truly alive means having to make choices. To be truly alive is also, quite simply, to love.

JACQUELINE MESNIL-AMAR,
Maman, What Are We Called Now?

At the start of 1945, up to 850,000 British and American soldiers were arriving at Germany's western border. Across in the east, one million Soviet troops were closing in on Berlin. Six years of fighting and twelve years of Nazi rule had already displaced millions of civilians – among them legions of forced labourers, mostly Poles and Ukrainians, brought to Germany from the lands it occupied and put to work in its war industries. As the Allies closed in, upwards of six million workers were still held there, scattered across cities and towns and villages, awaiting war's end.

Lüneburger Heide, 1945

March

1

A Town on the Heath

Benno

It was late, but he was wakeful. There was snow on the way again: a last fall. Benno could smell the cold of it as he pushed his face between the curtains. His breath fogged the glass, the dark was spread wide across the rooftops, across the heathland beyond too, and the night out there had him restless. The shadow-shapes of the Rathaus, the town hall clock spire and town woods.

Earlier there were sirens. At the town's far outskirts: at the munition works.

Benno had almost grown used to that wailing, rising from the pine trees, like he'd grown used to the flak thuds from the Elbe and the far Hamburg shipyards: to all the sounds of the war winter. The Rathaus clock marking the hour, and then the half. His brother's low snores; Udo's long-limbed sprawl in the bed beside Benno's own one. His Mutti and Vati downstairs in the parlour, listening to the gramophone, or to the Berlin programme.

Tonight, though, the siren had come later than usual – long after nightfall.

And now Benno's Vati had been called out.

Someone from the town had called him: Benno heard the telephone, loud at the foot of the stairwell; his Vati's short words and pauses, and then the door slam not long afterwards. And although he'd been dozing, these noises had woken him; they'd had him slipping to the window – just in time to see his father step out onto the pavement, cigarette turned into his palm to shield it, town police cap pulled against the cold night.

Benno's Mutti was still downstairs, the gramophone turning out its low song; his brother lay sleeping, one arm flung across the covers, breath coming slow and even, and Benno would have lain down just like him. Except his father had been called out to the munition works, he was sure of it. His Vati been gone a good while and Benno felt he knew why.

He'd seen a transport come, just that afternoon.

All these past war years, there had been trucks and van loads heading along the Heide roads, carrying machine parts to their small munition works, carrying armaments away again. So Benno had got used to this also: seeing these vehicles, in twos or threes, as he biked out of town along the Poststrasse. They'd pass him on his way to grammar school in the mornings, or when he was riding home again, pedalling behind Udo and the older boys after classes, after Hitler Youth duties, all in their shorts and shirts and neckerchiefs.

The boys knew when to watch for those truckloads. Stopping their bicycles, dropping their satchels on the verges, squinting along the heath road, the wide horizon. *Here they come now.* Benno watched at Udo's shoulder. His brother was taller; the other boys also. They were all classmates, all HY Kameraden in the years above Benno, and they knew more and better than he did: which transports carried shells and mortars, and which just the housings.

Mauser! and *Panzerfaust!* and *Tellermine!*

Udo listed the best ones, slinging his satchel back over his handlebars. The other boys listed the battle-lines the munitions were sent to:

Dünkirchen! El Alamein! and *Kharkiv!*

They shouted out the places as they rode onwards, calling them back and forth along the Poststrasse, all the way to the town square and the steps of the Rathaus – and Benno had to ride hard just to keep up, just to catch all the names.

Sometimes those transports had brought workers.

Ostarbeiter and *Polacks*: that's what Udo called them. So Benno knew they were *Fremdarbeiter*; they were workers and strangers, brought in from the East Lands, from all the new Reich territories. Udo said they were toilers, brought here to do war service: he said all Reich hands were needed for the war work, all Reich shoulders – even these new and foreign ones. Still, Benno wasn't sure of these worker-strangers with their work-rough faces; the patches they wore like a warning, P and OST, P and OST, stitched into the cloth; the way they were packed into truck backs under tarpaulin.

Worse were the ones who'd come just lately, though.

Whole convoys, driven across the heathland, grey under the grey sky.

These new transports had brought on the sirens – that wailing that told of their arrival – and Benno had been caught out twice now, both times on his home route. First he'd heard the alarm rise, then truck after truck had driven past him, all under guard, all along the Poststrasse.

Benno had been alone those afternoons.

All the older boys had HY drill or air raid duty, so he'd been the only one to see them: the flapping tarpaulins, the guards at every tailgate, the labourers crowded filthy behind them. Too many for the town works: Benno thought they couldn't be heading for the factory, surely; he hoped they were only passing through here. He didn't like to see those workers in any case, so close and out in the open.

Udo said they must be from other works.

– Larger ones. Nearer the front lines.

The other boys agreed that the guards would be wary.

– The fighting must be hard now.

– They must be driving the labourers elsewhere.

– But where though?

Benno had waited, alone at the steps of the Rathaus, for Udo and the others to come riding, and after he'd told them about seeing that transport, the boys spoke in awed tones:

– If all our factories are being cleared out, then this could be the endgame.

– Don't you think so?

– So will they clear out our town works also?

Benno had whispered this to Udo when they got home again – once the others weren't there to hear him – and Udo had shrugged, matter of fact, lifting his satchel off his handlebars:

– Most likely.

He said if the guards were bringing so many past here – whole truck convoys of Ost men and Polacks – then maybe they'd empty the small works in the process. Maybe the sirens were the signal to clear out.

– Who knows, though?

Udo laid his arm across Benno's shoulder as they walked up the back steps and inside.

– Little brother. They will do what they will do – and that's all.

Benno's Mutti didn't allow war talk.

– Not at table.

Not any longer. Even on his Vati's duty evenings, when it was just him and Udo there, she put a finger to her mouth if Benno asked across the dinner plates.

– But how close are they? The English armies?

– We still have to trust, *mein Sohn*.

That's all she told him.

– We all have to hold out.

*

Benno's Vati was milder.

He was slow and tired in the mornings, just a year from retirement, soaping his chin in the shaving mirror, his police cap laid out behind him, his cigarette balanced on the sink edge.

And when Benno lingered in the hallway before heading out for his school day, his Vati blinked at him, patient.

– *Na, mein Jung?*

Benno didn't like to ask him about the fighting, but maybe his Vati saw he was thinking about it anyway, because he put down his razor and took a draw on his cigarette.

– Soon you will be a grown boy.

He said it kindly. But also as though to caution him.

– Soon we won't have this war either. It is better you prepare yourself.

So Benno had tried, for his Vati's sake, if no one else's.

But still, the winter cold and the way the other boys spoke had made the days sound dangerous – and those worker-strangers all the more so.

– Where will the guards take them?

The boys asked this low-voiced. And:

– On whose orders?

And if they didn't whisper about the convoys of toilers, then they whispered about the forces: the fronts that were coming ever closer to the borders.

– The Russians are heading in from the East Lands.

– Yes, for the river Oder.

– And the Amis are at the Rhine, no? Or is it the English?

– Well, our bridges won't fall to them.

Hushed and fierce, the boys reported what they'd heard at drill practice, or passed sidelong from school desk to school desk. They didn't stop and watch for the transports any longer so Benno thought this too had become dangerous. All their murmurs were of the end days, and of the *Endsieg*.

– How soon will our Wehrmacht end this?

Benno had been alone again this afternoon.

He'd been riding homewards, knuckles cold on his handlebars, when he saw a new column on the heath road.

There were no trucks this time, just guards and labourers in the winter dusk light. Benno hadn't even been sure what they were at first, because it was hardly a column really, more just a straggle of workers: a line of shadows along the verge grass. A dozen, two dozen, at most, and only two men in charge of them.

The workers were all on foot, but not marching. The guards were pressing them to the roadside, as though they were supposed to rest there – or perhaps they were lost here? It was hard to tell in the half-light, but there was something wrong in any case, because the guards were ordering the labourers to crouch down – *Runter, ich sage!* – and the two men were arguing: *Scheiss noch mal.*

Benno heard them, voices fervent as he rode past – and he pedalled fast, but he saw the workers hunkered on the verge there: their too-thin shirts, their tatters and rags. Benno passed just close enough, also, to see that most wore shawls and skirts.

They were women – women labourers – and Benno had never seen women brought on such a transport before now. Or guards who argued.

So, tonight, when the siren had sounded, the sight of them was still there, odd and twilit, in his mind's eye – and then the telephone rang for his father.

His Vati had no charge over the munition works: that place was for the Werkschutz, for the guards to deal with, not for the town policeman. So why had that call come?

Benno's Vati had been terse when he'd answered. But after that first, he'd made another and then another call. And when Benno heard the door go, when he'd looked out of his window, already there were two, three, four more townsmen gathering down there on the pavement.

His Vati ahead, they'd strode together towards the town woods, towards the munition works.

Now all Benno saw was his own street and street lamps, the same gabled house-fronts as always; and when he looked out across the rooftops, looking for lights on in windows, for other watchers like him, he found none.

When Benno looked out further – towards the town woods – the dark grew too thick to look at. He had to catch his breath; he had to drop his gaze, wipe his fog from the window. The town street empty, his face close to the glass, he stayed and he waited, though – until he saw his Vati returning.

His father came alone, and Benno was glad of it.

He wasn't striding any longer, just coming slow and homeward along the pavement. This shadow shape of him was so familiar, Benno stayed to watch another moment, thinking just to listen for his father closing the front door behind himself.

Then he felt Udo take his elbow; Benno found his brother awake, and stepping up to the windowpane.

– Is that our Vati?

His brother was close and bed-warm, his palm on Benno's shoulder – but everything about him was cautious.

Down below them, the door was pulled open. The hall light spilled across the front step, across their father standing there.

Benno saw the shake of his Vati's head; he caught his Mutti's words in return.

– *Mein Gott.*

That's what he heard her say.

Hanne

Were those footfalls? She lifted her head from the pillows.

Hanne had been awake in any case; sleep yet to find her. She blamed the siren. It had come so late this time – well after darkness – and it had carried so loud on this cold air: out from the town works and across the heathland, even as far as their Hof walls. So although she'd shooed her chickens into their lean-to, as always, and although she'd pulled on her nightshirt and lain down, Hanne hadn't closed her eyes. She hadn't yet been able. Old fingers uneasy, old ears impatient, she'd gone reaching for the radio: turning the dial to find voices, just to hear word from beyond here.

All these past winter weeks – longer – there had been rumours of Allied advances, and under the eaves here, the signal was clearest, so Hanne kept the radio at her bedside: close enough for the kind of listening she did. Searching the dial for good news, through the crackle and hiss for English. *How much longer?* How far had their soldiers come now?

Hanne only listened after dark came, when there would be no one out to hear her. Between their Hof and the Poststrasse, the far town streets, there was only the Brandt yard, and then the schoolhouse under the lone oak branches – and neither the yard man nor the school wife would be out and walking the Heide tracks on a night as cold as this one.

Still, Hanne kept the radio low, or her Gustav would only come frowning.

– You're listening for defeat, aren't you?

Her husband didn't think it right to wish for enemy advances.

And besides – the Heide might be wide, her husband reminded her, but their town was a small one, and its folk grown small-minded.

– What if you're reported? You know how word passes here.

Gustav found sleeping just as hard as her. Ever since their Kurt had been called up, he'd been like this; ever since their Kurt had been wounded, he'd been all the more so. Gustav hadn't come to bed yet – he hadn't even come upstairs – so when Hanne heard footfalls, she'd turned over, knowing it must be her poor husband, restless and wandering.

And now, sure enough, she caught his tread on the back stairs: the stop and the start of his nightly roving. There had been too many nights like this just lately, both of them sullen in the mornings, pale with lost sleep hours.

Up until the winter came, Gustav had still been working.

Just the odd day here and there at the Brandt yard, but enough to keep him occupied. Now Brandt's joiners were all drafted, though, along with his bricklayers and his carpenters – and even his last apprentice boy – so he had no yard work to be offering. Brandt could have gone to the Rathaus to request assistance. But the town hall would only send old men like Gustav: *who else is left now?* Or he'd get Hitler Youth, most likely: *that'll be our luck, no?* The best Brandt could get would be a handful of town boys in uniform, sons of Rathaus clerks and shopkeepers. They'd come cycling out from the town streets, all bony knees and neckerchiefs and certainty, the only ones still sure of the Führer and his great purpose.

Well, Hanne thought, the Rathaus could keep them.

Just like they could keep their war effort, too, and their munition works. She scorned all those desk men in the town hall offices, still keeping on with their war talk, even now the fighting was a lost cause. *Must we lose more to this?* Since her Kurt had been wounded, Hanne found it hard to feel anything but bitterness.

He was her second-born. Her afterthought.

Just let him come home to us.

Hanne's first had been a daughter, and Hanne had thought she'd be her only, because the girl had married young and far from home even before Kurt's arrival. He'd come so unexpected, such a late and welcome comfort, Hanne felt they'd been blessed in their old years, she and Gustav – even if their boy went his own way, in all things.

Already in his school years, he'd cut and run from classes; making for the school wall, up and over, into the old oak branches. Send him with the day's eggs to the grocer, he'd come home with heath sand in his trouser cuffs, and cigarettes filched from the shepherd's huts. Kurt had squandered whole mornings at the Heide brook, or up on the high pass – and it was the same once he'd started his apprentice years at the Brandt yard. If there was sawdust to sweep, or tools to be sharpened, he'd get himself distracted, collecting wood curls with the school wife's two young daughters. And then, come evening, he'd head off to the town bar for dice games, winning coins off the back table drinkers. Or he'd go courting the baker's girl, standing under her windowsill, talking and charming into the small hours.

Still, Hanne wanted her son back.

And was that too much to ask for?

Let the Rhine bridges fall. This was her daily wish now. *Make the Amis come faster.* Hanne willed it as she punched the day's loaf into shape each morning, and while she split the stove logs come the afternoons. *Let the English breach the border.* Hanne urged them onwards as she dressed for bed at night and lay and listened to the radio. *Let the Russians come, even.*

Hanne knew she shouldn't wish that last part.

It was just that her Kurt should be here now, seeing out these last war days, safe and alongside them, but instead he was in the East Lands, and barely a word from him to go on.

If he fell, they would be told: that was certain. Getting no letter was hard, but far preferable.

Or let him be captured; that had become Hanne's next best hope: a Red Cross notice for the school wife to read out loud to her; Kurt's POW number on an envelope to stand on the mantelpiece.

But the fighting would be hard now, Hanne knew this: hand to hand and to the last man. And the thought that Russian troops might catch him – *no!* – this was too much to contemplate.

Hanne only wanted all of this to be over.

She was sure it was the same for most of the townsfolk also, and for their Heide neighbours up here on the heathland – or why no work for Gustav? He said they were waiting out the winter, hoping for things to turn again. Hanne knew they were waiting out the war, just like her, even if they wouldn't say as much. *They wouldn't dare.*

Now she heard a door bang, hurried murmuring.

This time it came from the Hof – was Gustav outside? What was he doing at this late hour?

Hanne turned over again, impatient. She pulled up the covers, just to be warmer, except then Gustav called out to her:

– Hanne!

He kept on too, as she pulled herself upright, hauling the blanket around her shoulders.

– Hanne – *komm doch!*

And when she came stumbling down the last stairs, she found the kitchen door wide, and Gustav on the Hof flags. He was standing in his woodshed doorway: she saw the nervous stoop of his shoulders.

– Komm nun!

He held up the lantern to hurry her – into the cold – into the night and the frost – and as soon as she was beside him, Gustav pulled her inside, closing the woodshed door behind them.

– You see this? You see this?

He held out his palms.

– You see what I have found here?' he asked.

All Hanne saw was a huddle of skirt and shawl and small limbs. Then a face, young and startled, turned to blink at her in the lamplight.

It was a child! *No* – a woman and a child!

Both pressed to the wall in the dark there.

Even before Gustav stepped forward, even before he tugged at the woman's shoulder, at the cloth patch stitched to her work shirt, Hanne had already seen the dark border, the dark P stitched to the cloth there. She already knew the woman was a worker: the woman was a danger here.

– You heard the siren?

Gustav whispered this.

– They must be runaways.

On and on he went.

– They must have run from the munition works. Or they must have come with one of those transports. Don't you think so?

The woman eyed her, too, from the corner.

Such a slight thing – reed-thin, and no older than Hanne's Kurt was. But she was hard-lipped for all that, her face tight and hostile; and she didn't like Hanne's eyes on her, only curling herself tighter in her worker's blouses.

She wore two against the cold, Hanne could see that now – and that the patch on the top one was coming away at the corner. The stitching picked loose there, the cloth was ripped along the near edge, blouse buttons left dangling. This woman must have done that tearing – Hanne thought she must have meant to disguise herself – because as soon as she saw Hanne's gaze land there, she lifted her shawl to cover her handiwork.

She kept a shielding arm around the child too, but Hanne could see it was a girl, and little more than a baby yet. A bare and curled head, a pair of child cheeks raw with cold, sore with grime, eyes large and tired and blinking. The woman had wrapped the shawl to carry her, now she tried to wrap the girl to keep her warmer, only her fingers were too raw to manage it.

– Where did you run from?

Hanne asked while the woman eyed her, while she began to rock the child.

– Was it from the Poststrasse?

Hanne tried another time, uncertain the woman understood her whispers.

– Or was it from the factory?

But they didn't have women working there – and in any case, this one was so wretched, Hanne thought she must have been on the road for some time.

– So did you come from out that way?

Hanne tried gesturing outside, at the heath around their small Hof, because she thought the woman might at least nod if she pointed the right way.

But the woman only rocked and rocked, back and forth.

Were there more runaways in the cold out there? Hanne pictured the guardsmen – Werkschutz with rifles. Were they out too, and running after them? This last thought had her turning, sharp, to Gustav.

– Keep that lamp low!

She gestured him – *away now!* – from the windows.

Even after he'd dropped his arm, though, the woman still didn't respond. She only watched them, shawl-wrapped and bone-tired, rocking and rocking the child she held.

The woman must have meant to find rest here – the night too cold, the child too heavy to carry further. Hanne thought she'd meant to tear off that patch, to cover her tracks – or just to warm herself, because the woman tried again now, lifting one grimy palm, tugging her shawl over the girl, only for it to fall from her shoulder.

– What do we do?

Gustav kept whispering, nervous.

– Will they send patrols? he asked.

And:

– Will they come out this far?

Hanne had to raise her palms; she had to take the lamp from his fingers. Turning the light low so she could focus, and so no one should see it from the Hof track, Hanne crouched down.

The woman shifted, her grey eyes flitting to the Hof beyond the window. It was closed in on three sides by Gustav's workshop, Hanne's chickens and her winter larder. Their house lay on the fourth, the light still falling bright from the kitchen doorway – and Hanne could have cursed herself for leaving it blazing, for leaving the door wide. She cursed this woman for hiding here.

But now the child's eyes were closing. Her fine lids flickering, her small mouth falling open: the rocking was doing its work. Her head was still bare, though; her thin neck, her shoulders; and the child looked so solemn and cold, even as she was dozing, Hanne couldn't help herself but reach forward.

The woman gave a start, lifting an arm to shield herself. But once she saw Hanne take the blanket from her own shoulders, once she saw Hanne raise it like a question, she relented. Dropping her elbow just enough for Hanne to reach over, the woman let her tuck the blanket around the girl.

Hanne gave a nod when she was done. The woman nodded in return – but guarded. Her face level with Hanne's own, her eyes so very close – and so very hostile also – Hanne had to douse the lamp wick. She had to stand up.

Casting about herself, Hanne motioned for the woman to stay down – *Stay low!* – and she pulled Gustav's work coat from the wall hook, laying it over her and the girl she held. *If only they hadn't come here. If only there were more to cover them.*

– But they can't stay!

Gustav started now.

– It's not safe!

But Hanne cut him short.

– They have to lie low. That's all.

It was all she could think for the moment. She pointed to the house and the Hof.

– We have to turn all the lights off, shut all the doors.

So they lay in their bed, she and Gustav, under the eaves and in silence – because what was there to say now? All they could do was wait, while the cold came seeping.

Hanne listened for noises from the track and the Poststrasse; she felt Gustav do the same, lying tight beside her in the darkness. Were there guards close? *Please, no.* Were there other workers? *How many more ran?*

The clock tower sounded the small hours, far off in the town streets. Hanne tried to picture the munition works, in among the pine trunks. But then – from somewhere – came the crack of small arms. And straight after, as if in answer, she heard the Elbe flak guns pounding. So Hanne closed her eyes, trying to close herself off – only to lose herself to night thoughts, endless, long and awful.

Werkschutz at the Hof gate: arrest and disaster. Men with patches on the Heide track, coming in through her kitchen doorway. Hanne wrapped herself tighter, but her dreaming mind was caught now: a confusion of works guards and munitions workers and voices on the radio. Of town boys and town woods, and English at the border. Of wide heath, and winter trees, and runaways among the high trunks.

And then – just like that – it was light outside.

It was morning.

The day started with slammed doors, with Gustav calling her. With snowfall in the grey dawn. Hanne lifted her head to see flakes blown against the windowpane; she hurried downstairs to find the kitchen door wide again, and Gustav outside again at his woodshed doorstep. Except he was alone this time, his shirt-back creased with sleep, and his arms raised heavenwards.

– *Verdammt!*

The doorway was open – the woman was gone. Gone!

Nothing left of her but a trail of footsteps in the whirling snow, and the tell-tale larder door left open, the empty ceiling hooks where the last of the winter sausages hung.

– She's taken the lot!

Gustav shouted as Hanne stepped outside, and he ran to the Hof gate, as if to give chase. But then he turned for his woodshed, looking for his winter jacket – only to find that was gone as well.

– *Verdammt nochmal!*

He pressed his old hands to his forehead.

The coat was worn, but thick and lined: brown corduroy. Hanne imagined the woman, tearing along the verges, zipped into that warmth. It'll come to her knees, she thought. But that was all to the good. It would cover the woman's torn patch, keep her from capture; it would keep out the cold too while she ran onwards – and the further she ran from here, the safer they all were.

The flakes were thick and coming faster; already the ruts in the lane were whitening, the woman's footprints blurring. Soon they would be smothered over: no one need ever know she'd been here. And the relief – the relief of it all! – Hanne felt it wash over her.

She ducked through the snowfall to her Gustav, not anxious any longer, just hoping for a Heide barn for the woman to hide in. For another woodshed – or a shepherd's hut, up on the high heath – just anywhere she could bed down with that small one while this snow fell. Now the woman had run, Hanne wished her a shelter. *Just let her be far from here.*

The flakes whirled in the woodshed doorway, landing cold on Hanne's cheeks and fingers, and on the furrows in Gustav's forehead.

– Good luck to her – no?

Hanne whispered this, grateful that they were safe again,

just the two of them. Hanne even smiled as she took her husband's shoulder, wanting to remind him that the war would soon be done too – that their Kurt would surely come home again – and then so many worries would be done with.

But Gustav looked at her, grave.

– We still have the other one, don't we?

And Hanne turned to find the child there.

Still wrapped in her blanket, the girl was solemn and sound asleep in the woodshed corner.

What now?

April

2

The Camp on the Outskirts

Ruth

– This is when the work starts.

Her father was first up, the day the letter came – finally.

He had it propped up against Ruth's teacup when she came down for breakfast, giving her a small nod in greeting, and then a small salute in its direction. And although she'd been waiting, it still threw Ruth to see it there, in their Highgate kitchen corner. The Red Cross on the envelope, her name typed beneath it: *Officer Novak.*

She'd been living in between-times – they all had – everyone counting down the war weeks, counting on a ceasefire. Ruth still did her ward rounds at the infirmary, and her welfare calls through Kentish Town and Archway: working through the last of the air raids, but all the while waiting on the all clear – and on where she might be posted.

Her father was always the first to wake; he would greet her with tea first, and then with war news. Always there was more news: another city fallen, or more land taken by the Allies. His old face smiling, beetle brows raised high in excitement, he'd sit with Ruth at the table, starting her day off with his gleanings from the morning radio:

– Our troops have crossed the Rhine.

Or:

– The Russians are over the Oder.

And:

– Can you imagine?

His old Poland: had the Germans been driven out of there entirely? What a thought that was!

In the evenings, they sat in the parlour. Ruth's mother knitting, her father reading *The Times* out loud to them, and then the *Chronicle*: all the reports he'd been saving. Ruth beside him on the sofa, half thinking about the next day's calls, mostly following his finger across the atlas. Where might the Allies reach next; where might the Red Cross send her? Tucked between the book-lined walls, and her father's piles of more books on the chair arms, the floor; his maps folded open on the rug.

Ruth knew her mother would have tidied, only too gladly. But she indulged him – they all did. *My family unit.* Her father enjoyed that English phrasing, smiling at how very English his life had turned out – his two children most of all. Ruth and her brother both long grown, and with radios and newspaper subscriptions of their own, they still listened to their father's reports. Daniel dropping by on his way home from Whitehall to keep him company, Ruth picking her way around his book and map maze at the end of each workday to slot herself in alongside him. They'd both long sat in the midst, too, of the Friday-night gatherings her father hosted here.

His émigré evenings. This is what Ruth and Daniel called them, when they were among themselves. Ruth was the younger; the one at home still; she spent most time among these visitors. Doktor Birnbaum, Pan Kowal, Doktor Nagel: *all the Herr Doktors.* Most of them medical men like her father: they were Frankfurt surgeons, Berlin internists, Warsaw students – all of them exiles. Stripped of their savings, their reputations; torn from friends and family, left to throw themselves on London mercy. They came visiting in their felt hats and once-good overcoats, worn threadbare at the cuffs, their brows furrowed with worry and loss – and then they were eased by the evening company, by this fellowship around the fireguard, behind the blackout blinds.

Ruth listened for the most part.

– Still nothing from your sister?

– Still nothing. Six months – almost seven – since I wrote to her.

Because what words did she have to help them?

– What can we do but wait, though?

– Really: I don't know.

Like everyone, Ruth had lived with sandbags and gas masks; she'd spent nights in the shelters; clambered her way to work through the rubble in the mornings. But for all that, listening to the Herr Doktors, she knew how very safe she'd been here. Twenty-six when the fighting had started – and didn't it seem an age ago? – Ruth was thirty-two now, and so aware of it. *What have I done all this time?* For all her ward rounds and her Home Front duties, she felt she had only been watching from the side lines – all the more so since talk had turned to war's closing. So when the Red Cross call had come, she'd sent in the forms.

Ruth had shown her father the announcement:

– Oh, that's my good girl.

He'd smiled his approval.

– You'll get to play your part now.

Still, Ruth had been slow to tell the rest of the family unit. Or she'd been slow to tell her mother, in any case.

This hadn't felt quite right to her – like subterfuge – but Ruth had known it would worry her. *Are you sure, child?* Her home girl, posted abroad, and for months at a time. It would have led to all the old questions, also, that Ruth had hoped they'd put behind them. *Will you not be lonely? I just don't like to think of you on your own, my daughter.* And: *Aren't you of an age, now, to find someone? To settle – yes? Don't you ever think about that?*

Of course she had. Didn't everyone? Before the war, when all her cousins and college friends were marrying, Ruth had felt this especially – and that she didn't fit the mould somehow. She was never lonely. She had so many wards and charges – all those mothers and babies, their families and neighbours, spilling from their kitchens into their front rooms. Ruth had all the new welfare girls also: each year, another group was assigned to her. And if she married, wouldn't she have so much to forgo there?

Not that offers came thick and fast at her. She was tall – enough so to turn heads – but perhaps too angular? Ruth often found herself wondering about this as she checked her collar in the mirror before her shifts started. She could hold her own in meetings, and at parties – Ruth always liked to be in the midst of talk, in among that back and forth – but perhaps too much so for most men? Ruth had a hunch that she was just too forthright. Even with her brother's friends, she saw this, and it irked as much as it hurt her, because wasn't it in the midst of life that all the best of life might find you? And why should she forgo that either?

All men her own age were at the Front now, so it didn't come up like it used to. Ruth could name any number of other London girls just like her, left to their own devices. It was only now the war was nearly over that she'd begun to look about herself, that Ruth had begun to wonder about time passing, about missing out on chances. *Don't you ever think about that?*

– So you've set your mind on this?

– I have, yes.

After Ruth told her brother her Red Cross news one evening, he'd nodded, much the same as her father. But then he'd shaken her hand in parting – oddly formal – holding on to it on the doorstep.

– But you'll take good care, though – you hear me?

– Of course, Dan. Of course.

Ruth had squeezed his palm in return: hard, to make him laugh. Even so, she'd felt it inside then – a strange lurching.

Ruth set store by her brother's word, by his civil-service caution. Daniel was War Office staff, after all; he'd read reports that were still classified, so he knew better than most what might lie ahead of her.

– I know you'll have your reasons. But you will see things.

This is what he'd told her.

And she knew what he meant. Maybe they didn't know the worst of it yet; maybe there was only so much a Jew can take.

The morning the letter arrived, her mother shook her head, disbelieving.

– You didn't think to say a word to me, Ruth Novak? Not a word of this?

Belted into her dressing gown, she stood, wounded, in the kitchen doorway, pointing at the envelope.

– This is how you let me know?

After Ruth opened it came more:

– You will be posted to *Germany*?

Her mother pressed her palms to her forehead, and Ruth felt it herself: that same lurching. *To Germany.* Of all the places the Allies had taken this past year. She took her mother's hands in hers.

Ruth's father, though: he held the letter up and nodded.

– It's the right thing for her.

He smiled, too, as he spoke:

– Our girl will be where she's needed.

And wasn't that the right place always?

– She will be at the heart of things.

Joining her unit at Caen – as soon as she'd landed, straight off the boat from Portsmouth – Ruth spent her first night in billets with scores of nurses, and all her first days pressed inside service transports, with little time to think further.

They crossed through France, then Belgium, setting out each dawn, only pitching their field tents as dusk fell, following the path of the invasion – the liberation! – mile upon shattered mile. The farmland they passed through shocked her: blighted with tank ruts and craters. The towns and villages were pock-marked, house walls scarred, roof tiles torn off by mortar fire – but they were safe, at last. Ruth was grateful for each sight of an Allied flag. She tried to remember where she passed them, to write to her mother, to reassure her, and to her father, so he could follow her path across his map rugs in the parlour.

Crossing the border, though, left her nervous.

Now they were on German roads – and with no word yet of a ceasefire. Ruth's first sight of the Rhine was a stark reminder: all the bridges blown by the retreating Wehrmacht; all the buildings left blackened on the approach roads. *They'd destroy their own land sooner than have it fall into Allied hands?*

Her convoy passed few Germans.

Lone farmhands in winter-bare field rows; housewives with half loaves in their ration baskets; old men and young boys. They all stopped for the convoy as it passed; they lifted their heads, pausing at their tasks, and Ruth thought surrender was so close now, these last Germans must know it was upon them. Hadn't they seen their own retreating soldiers? When she looked into their faces, though – so closed and stony – she didn't know what to make of them – or of the way they turned their eyes away. And each mile further, or so it seemed to Ruth, took her deeper into the heart of this.

*

She was riding passenger when they sighted it: a small town on the horizon. A clock tower and a cluster of steep-roofed houses, rising among the treetops.

Ruth's convoy had been skirting the rail tracks since first light: troops ahead, welfare corps following, early sun falling in slants across the dashboard. They'd been taking the wheel in shifts, one hour on, one hour off – always on the watch – and this town was the first they'd come to: this huddle of pine and silver birch and gabled house-fronts.

– Nothing to fear from this place.

The quartermaster pointed, and then Ruth caught flutters of white there, in the distance: bedsheets hung as flags from upstairs windows.

– At least we'll have nothing here to detain us.

But they had to pass through the town woods as they approached the outskirts, and here the road darkened – here, they found otherwise.

A high factory wall, topped with barbed wire. A pair of high factory gates by the roadside.

The whole convoy slowed now, pulling up at the verges. Soldiers and welfare corps alike, they began spilling, apprehensive, from the jeep doors.

The gates were chained shut, guard posts deserted. But when Ruth peered through the railings, she began to make out forms and faces.

– There are people inside here!

The soldiers began calling, pointing through the gates at the labourers.

Some were ducked at the edges of the courtyard, others crouched in the machine shed doorways; all of them were fearful, all of them worn out. They were men left grey with working, with patches stitched to their jackets and jerkins, and at each wall and window, Ruth saw more of them. Toil-worn and held captive; civilians with prison badges. Men and more men; misused and then abandoned, and all hunched as though to hide themselves.

– God almighty.

The sergeant had come to a halt beside her, along with a handful of his supply boys, all held by the sight of these workers. Their quiet had Ruth cautious; this place among the trees, too. What more might they find here?

But the labourers stared first at the soldiers – at their khakis and rifles – and then at the convoy they'd arrived with. They saw the Red Cross on the truck doors, and then on Ruth's welfare officer uniform.

Their relief spread in murmurs in the morning sunlight.

3

The View from the Schoolhouse

Emmy

When it came to Berlin, and to the government, she and Arnold had been of the same mind. That brown crowd wouldn't last long. In parliament? The thought was laughable. Those blowhards and hardliners, they'd burn themselves out. Or they'd fall on their faces like they deserved to.

Emmy wouldn't let them concern her, not in those early years. She'd taken this as a matter of principle. The Party men were low sorts: braggarts and social climbers, drawn from among the worst kind, and she had no time for their rallies and marches, their machinations. She had far better things to fill her days in any case, with the schoolhouse and Arno's gardens; with the town and heath children in their classrooms; with their Freya, and then in time their little Ursel.

Arnold, though, he found this harder.

He always had. Right from the first, when those Party men had installed themselves – and not just in Berlin but all over: even out here on the Heide. Their own Bürgermeister, Otto Paulsen – *Otto Paulsen!* – had stepped straight from the Brownshirts and into the Rathaus.

– Must we have that dolt in charge? That loudmouth?

Emmy's Arno had been born earnest, born straightforward; a natural schoolmaster. It was there in the way he stood and spoke and held himself: clear in his instruction, always correct – *just so* – in all his dealings. He was a man of the Kaiser times; this is how Emmy saw him: a man of older and nobler days. And although the last war had put paid to them, along with the hunger that came after, she still felt he carried the best of those years somehow. It had his young pupils sitting up straight at their school desks, and their parents tipping their hats to him on Sunday walks across the Rathausplatz. People had respect here for their schoolteacher, and so did Arno's colleagues on the school board. In due course, they'd assured him, he'd be lined up for preferment; in time, he'd hoped he might even serve at the training college in Hamburg – because hadn't he proven himself scrupulous, always with an eye on the right way of doing things?

Except – this was also the part of Arno that worried Emmy most of all.

Ever since '33, that disaster year.

She shared his disdain of Otto Paulsen – how could she not? – and of all those others at the Rathaus who'd scrambled into office alongside him. Just a year before, these men were no-hopers, back-table drinkers at the town bar who no one took seriously. But now they were in charge here and throwing their new-found weight around, and Emmy worried this might become too much for Arnold. He might overreach himself, overstep a mark and come to regret it afterwards. Because she saw how it rankled whenever he got word of new men promoted.

– Such upstarts! Such puffed-up Nazi appointments!

Or when he heard of old colleagues forced into retirement, their views too plain-spoken or their wives too Jewish for the new authorities to tolerate.

– After all their years' service! And who will replace them? That's what we have to ask ourselves.

For a while there, it seemed that there were always new petty edicts to provoke him: books to replace the old ones, dubious unions to be joining, Führer portraits to hang on the wall above the school desks.

– Does the man mean to keep watch over every classroom in the country?

It had Arno pulling at his beard, his shirt cuffs, his good eyes smarting behind his glasses – and Emmy knew he was a proud man, not just scrupulous, and not just a throwback to the old order; sooner or later, he would have to speak his thoughts about the new rules, because who in their right mind could do otherwise?

When the portrait arrived at their own schoolhouse, he'd left it wrapped in string and paper in the entrance hall.

After lessons were over, Arno had walked straight past it, hanging up his teacher's frock coat, rolling up his shirtsleeves. Instead of fetching a ladder, he'd weeded his borders and consulted his botanical volumes. Or he'd taken himself out along the Heide paths with his easel.

Arno had long done this with his classes. *A child should know the place that forms him, after all.* Heath and town child alike, he'd taken them to draw the dolmens where the Heide ancients lay at rest now, and to sketch the bark swirls on the lone oak by their own school wall, its gall and acorn, its moss-covered branches. Botanical studies were a hobby from his student years, and heath landscapes another that that he worked at perfecting in his spare hours, taking on whole series: small and watercolour, fine and thoughtful, just like he was.

The weather was so fine that year – and that portrait delivery such an insult – Emmy couldn't begrudge him his time for painting. And also, although Freya was still small then, he'd taken their daughter out with him along the Heide slopes. Starting to school her in the heath shrubs and grasses, their habits of budding and branching; collecting leaf and rock and lichen, teaching her the Latin terms and the common names and their origins – and Emmy liked this. Better that Freya should know this side of her father, rather than the angry one, glowering at the newspaper over the breakfast plates.

But Arnold took her further too, up to where the gorse grew and the shepherds parked their huts for summer grazing. He roamed the slopes with her, hours at a time, carrying her piggyback on the home route, returning sun-brown and smiling – and this was so unlike him, Emmy began to wonder: was it the view and the child that buoyed him, or was it his own defiance of the new authorities?

Because that portrait stood a week first, then another, and a further. Long enough that it began to nag at her.

Emmy hadn't wanted Arno to get a visit from the Rathaus, or to be called in front of the school board – because who knew what he might say there? He might not be able to help himself. So, in the end, she'd taken it into her own hands, heading up to the yard while Arno was out and roaming. Emmy had called on Achim Brandt, asking him to send Gustav Buchholz, or one of his other workers.

– With a hammer, please, and a ladder long enough. And can you make it soon – yes?

The big man had nodded, sage and neighbourly. Then he'd come himself that same afternoon, striding down the lane they shared from the Poststrasse, his cap pulled low across his forehead, ladder balanced on one high shoulder.

Emmy hadn't meant to shame her Arnold, but then she saw how it galled him when he stepped inside the doorway, little Freya still on his shoulders, only to find his wife had instructed the yard man on his behalf – and in such a task!

Their neighbour had already unwrapped the portrait, wordless; he'd hung it high on the wall above the desk rows – and Emmy couldn't think what to say then, how to help her Arno.

It was Achim Brandt who'd done that.

When he'd seen the defeated look of him, frowning up at the whitewashed rafters, the man had shrugged and pointed:

– I've hung the damn thing here, Schoolmaster – right where you can turn your back on it.

*

They made unlikely friends: the yard man and the schoolteacher. It took Emmy a while to get used to it: the sight of the work cap and the frock coat, standing and talking in the lane they shared at the end of their workdays.

She wasn't too certain if it was the wisest of friendships either. Because there were others like Brandt among his workers, and they all stood and smoked in the lane there at the end of their yard shifts, mulling over this and that and laughing among themselves – mostly about the Rathaus men, and all their new cronies among the townsfolk.

– Who knew we had so many crawlers here?

The yard men were scornful of their lapel pins and newfound Führer loyalty.

– You've seen the way they stand outside the town bar, rattling their Party tins under everyone's noses?

– Unless the nights are cold.

– Oh yes, unless the nights are cold, Schoolmaster.

– Then they get themselves schnapps-warm at that back table, and they leave their sons outside to rattle those tins for them.

Arno didn't grin with the yard men; that wasn't his way.

Still, Emmy saw how their grinning helped him – especially since those same sons sat on the benches in his classroom.

First it was the grocer's eldest, then the policeman's two boys; and then, with each term, there were more dressed up like Brownshirts in the desk rows, coming in single file behind Arno as he dismissed them at the school gate: a column of junior Kameraden. It went against the grain for Arnold – Emmy knew – to see children trussed up like this, drawn in to this mess of adult making. She couldn't make it right for him – no one could. But at least with the yard men, he found a little fellowship. Sharing glances as the brown boys passed, and then watching them head off town-wards along the Poststrasse.

– *Ach*, you're building a fine little troop there, Schoolmaster.

The yard men gave Arno fair warning too – and here, Emmy couldn't fault them.

Those times were angry; there had been street fights – and worse – in Hamburg, and the word that came out to the Heide was of Brownshirts at all the harbour corners, looking to recruit, looking to strong-arm. Each new journeyman arriving at the Brandt yard carried news from along the Elbe, via Harburg, or Maschen or Stade – and some of it alarming.

One told of a welder. A bold one – a cousin of Achim Brandt's, in fact – who'd run with the Communists in the hunger years after the last war. The man wouldn't be told; he wouldn't be leaned on, certainly, so he was never going to like the Nazis. But he'd never learned to keep his voice down, either. So he'd been taken one morning. Hauled from his bed at dawn, thrown down the tenement stairwell, his brow split open, his two thumbs broken in a Gestapo cell.

– Those bastards.

Already they'd made such places. Already such things could happen now.

Brandt didn't like his workers to talk of it. Emmy thought that was understandable. But Arno heard more anyway from old Gustav, because the Hof man had seen the cousin afterwards – first hand, and just by chance – when he'd driven over to Hamburg in the yard van to pick up a timber order.

– The cousin was a sight, Schoolmaster.

Still grey-faced after his detention, his hands still swollen; Gustav said this former master of his craft was reduced to standing on harbour corners, waiting on day wages.

– And who'll give him work now? They're all too frightened.

The cousin said they were right to be – perhaps that was the worst part: *Only fools aren't frightened of this lot.* Gustav and the yard men nodded, serious:

– And he was just a loudmouth, remember. They do plenty worse.

– Yes – if you're a Red.

– Or if you're a Jew now.

– Oh – if you're a *Jew*, Schoolmaster.

The men shook their heads and looked over their shoulders – and then they whispered such Dachau stories. Arnold wouldn't repeat them all to Emmy; he couldn't bring himself.

He wandered the Heide more after this. Before and after classes, drawing and painting and walking, mile upon heath mile. Days could pass while Arno left the post to pile up; at breakfast he shunned the papers, looking instead at the view through the open windows. And it was the same when he was removed from the school board.

Emmy never knew the full story there, but Arnold must have known it was inevitable. Because letters had gone back and forth; there had been arguments behind closed doors; and then he'd been given notice – he'd been struck off the promotion list. More: Arno had been relieved of his school board duties.

With regret.

His colleagues wrote notes to him.

You left us no choice, dear Arnold.

He read them and burned them, dropping them into the stove flames in his classroom.

Those letters hurt him – those colleagues deserting him – just as much as the demotion. Arnold had seen – perhaps for the first time – what life might hold now under these new rules. But when Emmy asked, all Arno told her was that he'd have to wait until better times and better rulers.

– And I don't see an end yet. Do you?

So Emmy had decided: better not to know about those arguments.

Better Arnold stayed his own man and stayed out of it.

This was all still before the war.

If Emmy thought of those years, she saw Arno with his daughters. Freya, tall and growing taller in her Heide girl pinafores; Arno with his pencil behind his ear and his glasses on his forehead. Or all of them in the shade somewhere, a rug spread wide, and Ursel, baby-fat and content with life, sitting on her father's knee. The times had confounded him; his life had turned inward, not as he'd imagined it. He'd given up hopes of advancement – given up on his colleagues too – even on his old trust in others' decency. But family was family still; they were sufficient unto themselves.

And there were still folk who turned to him, looking to the schoolmaster.

Heide shepherds with a letter that needed writing, or heath neighbours calling by with cuttings to swap for bean seeds or seed potatoes. Or Hanne Buchholz, pulling her son behind her.

Young Kurt had just started his apprentice years. The boy didn't cut and run from the Brandt yard like he had from Arno's classroom; he was still the same Kurt, though: smiling and guileless, and so maddening. Doing just as he liked, too. Drinking beers with the journeymen at shift's end, then calling on Christa Heinrich at the bakehouse – standing and talking under her window at all hours. She was a fine girl, with her plump cheeks and strong calves and forearms; Christa was her father's pride, moreover, and not intended for a Heide lad. But if what Emmy heard from the town wives was anything to go by, this is how those evenings started: the bakehouse daughter climbing down from her window, unbeknownst to Heinrich. And this is how they ended, too: up on the high pass, under the gold of the gorse, passing the dusk hours, Kurt's palms inside Christa's blouses.

That was in the last summer before the war started.

Everyone knew it would be called – it was just a matter of time – and maybe some of that restlessness had caught the lad. Because Kurt went out further too. To Maschen or Stade, to see his married sister, or just to drift along the Elbe shore. He took himself off – and who knew where? – for days at a time, sleeping out under the stars, or under a shepherd's hut if the rains came. Arnold would come upon him some mornings. Setting out with his easel in the early light before classes, he'd find the boy striding his way back along the high pass – and only just in time for his yard shift.

But Kurt fell into trouble also.

First it was with Heinrich, after the baker caught him bringing Christa home one night with gorse snags in her blouses.

Then Kurt had fallen upon a new place in his wanderings. A bathing spot at the millstream, up above the town woods and the old factory. Kurt had found a circle of stones there that the town sons had built themselves. He'd camped out beside it – and he swore it was only for the one night – but he'd built himself a fire there with the twigs and branches that the town boys had been gathering and piling, and then he'd been asleep by the embers when they found him.

When Hanne pulled him up at the schoolhouse doorway, Kurt's lip was split, his front tooth chipped. But he was grinning for all that, showing his new gap to Arno and laughing.

– You should see the other boys, Schoolmaster!

It turned out one of them was the policeman's eldest.

– And what can we do now?

Poor Hanne Buchholz.

She'd stood and worried in their parlour, that the sergeant might call on Gustav – or worse: that he might haul Kurt in for questioning. She knew the whole Heide was on edge, waiting on war news, and the townsmen were especially short on patience.

And all this while, her boy had sat on the front step, chatting with Freya and Ursel.

Emmy had watched him through the window: how he'd grinned as her girls came to blink at his bruises. Kurt had plucked blooms and stalks from Arno's borders, winding them into rings for their fingers, and crowns to adorn their young heads – smiling wide at their delight, as though untroubled by his injuries, and what was passing inside.

– Could you speak for him, Schoolmaster?

Hanne asked if Arno could go to the Rathaus.

– Might you do that for us?

It had been hard for Arno to refuse her.

Hard to tell her, also, that he wasn't much in Rathaus favour. Not these days. That his word might not do her son much good.

– Better – perhaps – to try the sergeant?

This is what Arno asked Emmy afterwards.

Because the policeman didn't drink at the back table – did he drink at all? He was known for his sober conduct. And for keeping his counsel. Hadn't he'd kept his job under the new crowd, although no one could say what he thought of them?

Arno had gone to see the man in private. In his parlour out there by the town woods. The way Arno described it, the man had closed the door and heard him out in silence – father to father and off the record. Even so, the whole idea had had Emmy frightened. Because was there such a thing any longer? Didn't all things get back to the Rathaus? Wouldn't the man have to act now – even just to cover himself?

A week went by while they waited – and then another and a further – while the sergeant didn't call at the Buchholz Hof, or the schoolyard, and Emmy fretted, trying to guess at his thinking. Wasn't he just as cowed as the rest of them? But in truth, by that time – and already it had been a long Third Reich meantime – she'd grown accustomed to such worrying. This is how life was now: ordinary and awful, and always so much more of it.

And then came September, and wartime, and no one could think of anything beyond that.

For months, it was all the boys in the schoolyard could

talk of: regiments and papers and postings. Whose father had been called up, whose uncle had fallen. Each draft letter arriving brought the war closer: too close to home here. And then, even before the second war year dawned, the town works were turned over to armaments – over to the government – bringing the war right to their Heide doorsteps.

The high gates came with the handover. The high wall also: the old farm works expanding along the Poststrasse. Guards came at the same time: now it was a war works, it had to be guarded. The same went for the works trucks and works vans: they all had men from the Werkschutz riding inside them.

Soon enough they didn't only guard the munitions there, either, but also those who made them. Because by that time, the Wehrmacht had already pushed through Poland, the Reich claiming new land beyond it, and new workers. In the queue at the bakehouse, the town wives passed word of this among themselves:

– It won't be Heide men at the factory any longer.

– Yes, I heard we'll have strangers – from the East Lands!

– Can you imagine?

When the first trucks came with that new workforce, some shook their heads, disbelieving.

– They don't belong here.

Others pulled their mouths tight: the less said about the munition works, the better now.

– Just keep them behind that high wall.

And Emmy found herself thinking – not for the first time – perhaps it was better if you didn't know.

*

And still, the days passed and kept on passing, the wartime weeks and wartime months. Yard man after yard man coming along the lane to bid a grim adieu to the schoolmaster – *we'll be seeing you – well, let's hope so* – sent off to do the bidding of the Führer.

Arnold resented this.

– Why should they fight in a war they wouldn't have started?

He grew worse when his old pupils were drafted – Kurt included.

– Why should he be called at all?

The youngest in his unit – only nineteen – and his troop train had dropped him directly at Kiev – right out in the midst of those East Lands.

The boy couldn't write, of course: he'd never sat long enough in Arno's classes. But letters came anyway, written by his commander, his Kameraden, delivered to the postbox at the corner. Arno took these to the Hof to read out loud for Hanne and Gustav, and then he reported to Emmy afterwards – out of earshot of Freya and Ursel.

– Every page appalling.

Tales of the miles falling under their tank tracks and the folk coming out to greet them; all the pastures to be staked out, and farmsteads to be freed up for settlement, workers to be taken to Germany.

– So that's soldiering? So that's our Kurt's duty?

The boy had rolled like that almost to the Don – almost a full six months – before the shell had caught him. His unit had pulled up at a crossroads; they'd just parked their vehicles and then the blast had come. Not from a soldier; not from a Russian, even, but a villager. A Donbass partisan, in the knee-high grass, had sent a single mortar.

A jolt and a rip and it was over. Kurt had been thrown off his feet, off the truck bed he'd been unloading. His left arm torn off, clean at the shoulder.

Arno read that letter in silence.

He took Emmy with him to the Buchholz Hof that morning.

– *Mein armes Kind!*

Hanne pressed her fingers to her forehead, sitting down hard in the chair that Emmy pulled up for her.

And then Arnold sat with the two old folk each week that followed, at their Hof kitchen table, looking through all the letters that began arriving. Notice of Kurt's field hospital, his transport dates, his military pension entitlement. Reams of bone-dry civil-service German: Arnold clarified it all for them. Out of schoolmaster's duty, Emmy thought, but perhaps also because he saw he was caught now. His own draft papers would be in the postbox before long: next month, next year, or as soon as tomorrow morning. And you couldn't stay your own man, not in wartime, not when all men would be called upon. Not when others were losing their limbs and their livelihoods.

When it came to it, Emmy knew they'd been fortunate.

Arno was called, but only to France, and only behind the lines. He'd had to bow to war service – he'd had to leave Emmy to take over his classes – but at least he'd seen no fighting, and at least when he was captured, it was only by the Americans.

Arnold's own letters were spare. He drew instead. Because

what should his girls know of soldiering? He filled the pages with heath trees and grasses – *for my Freya, my Ursel* – sketches of all the places he would return to. He only had a pencil stub to work with, a single thin sheet of Red Cross paper, but the lines he drew were just as careful as any of his paintings.

When the late snows came this last winter, they covered everything.

Emmy had no post, no pupils. The drifts were too thick along the Poststrasse; the mercury dropped too low to think of opening the classrooms. She didn't open them when the thaw came either – the fighting had drawn too close by that time. So Emmy spent all those last war weeks in schoolhouse solitude with Freya and Ursel.

And then the end – when it arrived on the Heide – came without gunfire, without mortar rounds. It passed across the heath so quietly, coming in with the spring winds and the clear skies, Emmy didn't even notice it passing.

No tanks came rolling, only another and then another spring sunrise.

She was hanging out the wash with the girls one such April morning when they saw their first English soldiers. Emmy was just pegging her way along the clothes lines, as normal, when a pair of patrol jeeps passed the lane mouth.

Ursel pointed:

– *Mama! Soldaten!*

And Freya turned to look up at Emmy, startled; the sheets and blouse sleeves blowing around the three of them.

May

4

Everyone Has Their Lost

Ruth

They found 112 men here, all told.

Ruth counted them on arrival: her first task so simple and so daunting. As soon as the soldiers broke the yard gates open, she went wherever she could find workers: crouched beside the lathes in the work shed; heads in hands between the bunks of their sleeping quarters.

– Can you stand? *Woda?* Do you need water?

Going by the patches stitched to their jerkins, she tried Polish with the Poles – searching out the words she'd been brushing up on with her father – relying on gestures with the Ukrainians, and noting all in need of medical attention.

– Doctor? *Lekarz?*

Their thinness alarmed her, but that was only the start of

it. Many were toothless, although most were younger than she was, their limbs slack, faces exhausted. At each man she came to, Ruth had to swallow her shock, not to let it show. The men gazed up at her as she spoke, as though grasping for words – as though still not sure of what had befallen them. And not a guard, nor an overseer, in sight.

– Not even one bastard left, sir.

The sergeant sent his soldiers searching, combing the machine sheds, the guard block – but all had fled. The last trace of them a pair of braziers in the courtyard, the fires inside both already cold; the ashes of the factory paperwork heaped in piles on either side: charred remains of order books, personnel files.

– Tommy Englander!

By then the workers had begun calling.

They'd all seen the soldiers, streaming in through the gate posts, and they started calling out for food, for news – if the war was over.

– *Krieg vorbei – no?*

They asked Ruth the same as she came counting.

– *Angielką?*

– *Ty anhliyka?*

The men blinked at her uniform, at her Englishness, pulling themselves up to standing, confused at these new arrivals, and to have a woman here.

– *Dama?*

– *Ofitserka?*

Those that could searched for English words; others spoke in broken German, following her to the next man, and the next:

– *Wir gehen – bitte.*

– We go with you?

– *Czy możemy wyjść?*

Ruth didn't know what to say to them; she couldn't gather her thoughts. What she saw here, it hardly seemed possible.

Everywhere that spring, the troops had been falling upon such places.

The vast camps had come first: all the horrors inside them. Each new report had shaken Ruth further, but she'd read each briefing, and she'd steeled herself, knowing there might be more yet. Hadn't the Red Cross warned her? There could be many more such cruelties – in barracks and brick yards and munitions works. Still, this place unnerved Ruth. The way they'd found it, hiding in plain sight. The way it had been deserted, too, paperwork left to burn.

She'd never thought she might be among the first in.

The town was placed under curfew that same morning; each former worker here was taken under Allied care and custody. Ruth passed on the numbers to the sergeant; he made requests for more trucks and further orders, radioing up the chain of command; and then she tried her best to reassure the men as she gave out blankets and canteens.

– *Prędko, prędko.*

Soon, soon. It wouldn't be long before they could join the convoy, before they could leave this place behind them.

Come the afternoon, the Bürgermeister had been arrested, along with the police sergeant, and the town hall had surrendered – all in short order – and Ruth was sure she'd be gone by day's end, driving away from here with all these workers. But when word came from command, it was that the munitions works should be impounded. More: the factory was to be requisitioned for Allied purposes. It was a DP camp now, each man inside a displaced person – and Ruth was tasked with their welfare.

– I'm to stay here?

– You're to stay, Officer Novak.

– All these men too?

That spring evening, as the rest of the convoy departed, she found herself left with the quartermaster sergeant, his staff from the Royal Army Service Corps, and their one-hundred-some charges.

No cars passed in those first days; all was quiet, oddly becalmed.

The gates were left open – as a symbol – this felt important while the men were still kept inside them.

– Temporary. *Tymczasowy.*

Ruth found herself repeating this, for each DP who came to stand and stare beyond the gateposts.

– Just until the ceasefire.

She found herself saying the same words when the men looked past her to the high walls, to the soldiers on guard:

– *Tymchasovyy.* Only there until the fighting is done with.

Ruth tried to reassure them – in her halting Polish and in her even more halting Ukrainian – that the camp would give them food and shelter, and safety from any last skirmishes. Although no one had the least idea how long these might yet last – or how long these men might be held here.

Around them lay the town woods, and beyond these the town roofs, outlines sharp in the spring light. It was all under the Allies: this heathland, as far as the horizon; such great swathes of Germany, all newly taken. But while the DPs came to the gates to look beyond them – or just to see them standing open – few stepped into the road there. None showed interest in venturing further, out among the Germans.

Still absorbing the shock of this English arrival, the three meals served daily, and the long rest hours they could take now, the men seemed to settle in – for now at least. Sitting with their backs against the high wall, against the machine shed they no longer had to work inside, they dozed for the most part, their faces turned to the sunshine.

Ruth was still working through her own shock, and she knew it was the same for the troops around her.

She had to inspect the bunkhouses with the quartermaster, Sergeant Farley, leading the way with one of the supply lads; the three of them stepping into the sour dark, the air thick inside, the bedding grimy, mattresses foul with use.

– They're only fit to burn.

Ruth lifted one corner with her fingertips, appalled, and the supply boy beside her nodded:

– You throw a match one night; I'll tell no one.

But then Farley turned such a look on the two of them, they continued the rest of the inspection in silence.

A bit of a sod is what the supply lad had called him, leaning in to whisper to Ruth as they stepped outside again. *Don't you mind him too much, Miss.*

She already knew the quartermaster was close-mouthed; he could be surly; Ruth wasn't at all sure he liked being stationed here. But then she didn't much like it either.

At least there was no slacking on his watch.

Farley had the bunkhouse doorways boarded over, moving the men out wholesale, ordering tents thrown up to house them, and all in little less than an afternoon. He called in more tents by field telephone – as many as he could muster – along with sets of clean service sheets from the army clerks newly stationed at the town hall. Then a small team of medics arrived, also on Farley's initiative: all Durham Quakers, a whole crew of Friends Ambulance Service that he'd diverted here from Bremen.

Their first task was delousing. Each DP was dusted in fine white powder. It cleaved to their shirt seams and their eyebrows, riming the creases in their palms; they lifted these to gaze at them, still dazed, or as though diverted by this newness, the way it clung in the curves around their fingernails.

The two doctors listened to chests and shone torches into eyes while the auxiliaries marshalled the DPs into the lines, and by the time Ruth and the supply lads were helping all the DPs back under canvas, the new tent rows already ran the full stretch of the long side wall.

Come evening, Farley was still at work too. Hammer in his fist, nails clamped between his lips, he was kneeling in the dusk, laying the last slats of the duckboard path that ran along the front entrances.

The next morning, Ruth began making the rounds of them: her own duties starting in earnest.

Each man they'd found here had to be registered – properly – their identities confirmed, as far as was possible. Ruth had already pulled the factory books from the braziers; what remained of them. Now, once the breakfast rations were done with, she began building up her own lists.

The DPs at the first tents greeted her politely. Most with nods and tipped caps, their old gentlemanly manners re-emerging, some even with small smiles, starting to recognise her:

– *Ofitserka.*

Sitting outside their tent flaps, on the grass and on folding chairs, they showed her their passes, all the work cards she asked for. The men gave her their full names, their dates and places of birth, slow and patient while she wrote. And then, in stop-start conversations, in Polish she half-understood, in Ukrainian and in German translated between them, these first men told her what they could about how they came here.

Balanchuck, Jerzy – b. 17.02.1919
I am from Pila; I am from Poland, yes? The Germans, when they came, they lied to us. You come to the Reich! they say. You come to earn! they say. Ha! You think we have earnings? For all these years we have been here and working?

Bagan, Taras – b. 01.06.1923
My home is at the Don. Just at the river. The Germans, after they chased away the Red Army, then they came to my farm, to round up my family. They took my father first. After, they took me and all my cousins.

Kowacz, Adam – b. 20.09.1920
I tried to run. My two brothers, they tried also. But the Germans took us anyway.

So many stories. Tent by tent, morning by morning, Ruth set about recording them; the places these men been taken from, and the people.

In the afternoons, she tapped out their index cards – one for each DP. Typewriter on her lap, sitting on her field cot, in her field tent, pitched by the factory courtyard; notes and maps and dictionaries piled beside her.

For each man she spoke to, she tried to find a name to match in the factory paperwork. But it only took an afternoon or two for her to realise: these records the Germans had kept – even burned and incomplete – showed there were many more workers here over the war years. These DPs had seemed a multitude when the convoy arrived here – so many and so weary. But the place had already been half empty.

– The others?

Ruth began asking the next morning:

– Where did they go?

– Oh – they were taken.

Taken. Ruth heard this at each tent she came to. She asked each DP before she moved on, and it was always the same answer. The men said:

– Zabrani.

And:

– Z dala.

Gone.

They held out their palms – open and empty.

– *Z dala!*

– All gone from here.

But Ruth couldn't work out yet: were the labourers evacuated? Taken by the guards when they fled the place? Transported elsewhere?

The last tent she came to was one of the largest; she sat talking with the half-dozen men inside it, long into the afternoon, and they all met her with that same gesture: pointing empty-palmed towards the factory entrance, towards the rail tracks, along the Poststrasse – waving their arms in all directions.

– *Gdzie?*

It was all in the cold time, they told her.

– *Zima, na mrosie.*

In the last winter weeks.

– *Koniec zimy.*

That was the worst time.

– *Ach*, but the Germans were always moving workers.

One Pole spoke in English. Grey-haired and tired, he shrugged when she turned to him to hear more:

– I was moved – so many times – in my years here.

The men around him nodded their agreement.

– *Tak, tak.*

Yes, yes. They shook their heads over the Germans. Still, Ruth looked to the same Pole:

– But where, though? I have seen the paperwork.

With his English, she hoped he might be able to explain things further. But the man had already turned to the other workers, because the DPs closest were frowning and speaking among themselves – and now those at the back began calling, offering more thoughts.

– *Zapamietaj?*

– *Vzymku – tak.*

– Wait, wait.

The old Pole kept offering translations, as best he could, in fits and starts, and it was hard for Ruth to follow most of it. But what she heard was about winter transports.

They came in truckloads. The men said how guards and soldiers had come in convoys. *Yes, in that cold time.* They'd brought whole transports of labourers. *So many – too many for this factory.* The men said they must have been workers evacuated from elsewhere. *From I don't know where.* But each time, there were sirens:

– *Syreny! Syreny!*

The DP closest to Ruth threw his palms up, describing the dread sound of this, and the whistles the guards blew shrill outside the barrack block.

– *Karabin!*

– *Strilyayut!*

The man next to him joined in, raising both his arms, miming a rifle held up to terrify – and the old Pole told her:

– That was how it was in those last weeks.

When the Werkschutz conducted the roll call, they'd fire their rifles skywards, before hauling the men from their bunks and into the courtyard.

– Or the guards would come through the machine sheds, blowing their whistles, pulling workers from their stations. Selecting men to be taken away from here.

He said this didn't happen with every transport, but often enough that they learned to fear the siren – the sound of whistles and rifles – and even of truck engines.

– *Tak!*

– *Tak – huchno!*

– When we heard your English convoy arriving, we thought – now it's our turn.

– *Niemcy!*

– We think – no! You are Germans! We think – no, no! Now you take us.

They paused a moment, turning to each other and murmuring, as though to calm themselves – as though to remember more for her. So Ruth asked:

– Those convoys – those soldiers who came then – where did they mean to take the workers?

But at that, the DPs could only shrug, falling quiet again between the tent sides.

Who could guess at German reasoning? Who could fathom why the Germans did anything?

All through the next week, more DPs began arriving.

Some came walking into the compound of their own accord, off the surrounding heathland, having walked off the farms where they'd been sent to work.

– We see you English! We follow your jeeps here.

Others were picked up by the night patrols, found camped out in hedgerows along the heath roads, or making ground in the quiet hours before dawn, trekking eastwards.

– You can let us keep walking, no?

Ruth allocated tents to house them, and blankets and

rations to keep them comfortable; then she led them across the compound, busy with supply trucks, supply corps and further tents of all kinds.

There was now a mess for the soldiers, with a field kitchen behind it; then the medical station, and the ration station, too, outside which sleepy Poles and Ukrainians came to queue. Beyond them, the tent lines started. And beyond those – deeper into the factory grounds – there were piles of more tents waiting to be thrown up, and the supply boys making ready for more arrivals.

– More will come here.

This is what Ruth told the new men, hoping they might feel the comfort of numbers – and that she might also. But while they nodded, thankful for their rations and blankets, these new DPs also brought new questions.

– And my two cousins, please? How shall I find them?

– Where is my brother? You can help me? I have to know.

Almost every man who arrived had an uncle, a neighbour he had been taken with, someone from home that he worried over: his health and whereabouts.

– He is somewhere like this, you think?

The new DPs gestured at the tent rows extending around them.

– Maybe he is with other English? With Americans?

In the evenings, when Ruth added their cards to her index files, each had to have another clipped behind it: a missing Taras, a missing Osip or a Jozef.

Always more names to add to her records. Each a dear friend, or a grown son, or a neighbour to someone.

Everyone has their lost.

Ruth wrote this in her first dispatch, last thing and longhand before lights out.

She wrote it home too – to her father – although he already knew this from the exiles in his parlour. Doktor Nagel's sister – where was she now? Where were Doktor Birnbaum's young brothers? Ruth had seen from them how hard it was to live with such questions – caught between fear and hope, day by slow day, week by slow week. Here, she felt this anew, and just as sharply.

Whenever a patrol brought another group of workers through the high gates, Ruth would be called from across the compound to receive them – three blasts on the sentries' loudhailer – and the DPs in the tent rows soon came to recognise this signal. As soon as it sounded, they followed Ruth along the duckboards to the courtyard, lingering at the edges while the jeeps or trucks were parked up – and then she saw how they watched and watched. Would a cousin climb out? Would a nephew appear from among the soldiers? Or at least someone who might have news?

The men looked, and they looked, and they found only strangers.

– *Zavtra, zavtra.*

Tomorrow, tomorrow. Maybe.

They murmured among themselves, drifting back again among the tent sides.

How to help them?

Ruth knew there were holding camps and transit centres and field hospitals being set up all over: wherever the troops came across forced workers. She would send on her lists to the

Red Cross offices in Hannover, and then they would distribute them further – to other camps like this one, and larger. But recording all these people, reporting them – it didn't feel like enough. Finding them, reuniting them – that could be the work of months – longer. Of many hands. Where do you start?

And then there was the matter of the missing workers, those winter transports. Where had the Germans scattered them in those cold weeks?

Writing her dispatches, sitting on her army cot, under army canvas, Ruth found her mind running on and on beyond the high wall, the town woods, the wide heath, to wherever those workers might be now.

Why had she thought she might be able to help here?

But the end of that first week was wonderful. News arrived from the town hall:

– Berlin has fallen!

The army clerk who delivered it came tearing into the compound, jeep top open, waving his cap around his bare head.

– At last, at last!

The DPs emerged from the tent rows to see why the English were shouting.

– It's over?

– All over!

– *Prawda?*

First came disbelief – then, oh, the rejoicing!

Ruth was hugged, over and over. By the doctor officers, the auxiliaries, the supply lads. And when the DPs found her, they took her by the elbows and danced her along the duckboards.

– *Ofitserka Novak!*

– *Ofitserka!*

Extra ration tins were distributed, the mess tent spilling over. Flags were found in supply trunks, or stitched together and hoisted: the red and white of Poland joining the Union Jacks above the tent rows, and the blue and yellow of Ukraine too, improvised from shirtsleeves and coat linings.

Towards afternoon, Ruth found Sergeant Farley, leaning uncharacteristically still against a truck side in the service yard. His hands in his pockets, the quartermaster made a strange sight.

– Officer.

He gave her a short nod – awkward – and then he rubbed his broad forehead.

– I had no idea what this would feel like. I still have no idea, if I'm honest.

The next time she saw him, he was calling the supply lads to order. Upright again, impatient to be off about his work, he was gathering his troops outside the field tent that doubled as his office.

Farley reminded them they could celebrate.

– Of course you can.

But only once their duties were over.

And then, as night fell, the Ukrainians lit a bonfire.

It turned out they had been building it most of the afternoon: tearing boards from the walls of the old bunkhouses, aided and abetted by a handful of supply lads – and under Farley's blind eye? Ruth had to wonder. She made her way through the tent rows with the auxiliaries to take in the spectacle.

The flames rose high into the night; an accordion was brought out. The Poles sang and sang, the Ukrainians talked and talked, and Ruth sat in the warm dark among them, listening to their voices. Their tones so like the exiles' in her father's parlour – but joyful.

Ruth hoped her old dad felt this joy too, and she thought to write this scene in a letter home before she turned in. The smell of the woodsmoke; the pine-dark woods around them; those voices, carrying off into the night. It was so satisfying – so long in coming, that triumph; Ruth wanted her father to know this, her mother and Daniel – but all the Herr Doktors most of all. *You must read this out loud to them.*

For the moment, she watched the sparks rising, floating over the town woods and the town roofs beyond them, and she closed her eyes. And then – for the first time that day – Ruth thought of the townsfolk. So close by. She thought of how they had been there, this whole time.

And now?

They should see this also. Her thoughts hardening, so clear behind her closed eyes, Ruth wanted the townspeople to see those sparks, to hear these songs. *Let them be wakeful in defeat.*

I hope that none of them can sleep.

5

Town Word

Benno

Udo had found apples for breakfast. Benno ate with him, outside. Sitting by his brother on the kitchen steps, the two of them elbow to elbow in the shade between the coal store and the alley wall.

When they'd come downstairs, Udo had opened all the cupboards in the larder, looking for more food.

– You know the English won't honour our ration cards?

He gave a short laugh, closing all the doors again.

– They won't honour our Reichsmarks, that's for sure.

His brother would have heard this from one of the other boys; Benno knew this. He saw how they came passing down the alley here on their bicycles, out of sight of the patrol cars – that's how it worked now.

Or Udo would have got it from the neighbour wife across the back wall – *Junge, tell your Mutti, you hear me?* – who'd have heard it from her neighbour in turn, all along the town street and round the corner.

Benno's Mutti wasn't up yet. This was how it worked with her too since the English arrival. The day the soldiers had driven in from the Heide, the day they'd come for his Vati, she'd gone upstairs and closed the bedroom door behind her; she'd drawn the curtains inside there. Ever since, it had fallen to Udo to wake Benno in the mornings, to see that he washed and dressed himself, rummaging in the drawers and the ironing basket. *Here – you wear this now.* Udo told him they couldn't wear their uniforms, so Benno pulled on shorts with holes, or old trousers, and they wore their father's shirts, rolling the sleeves up to their elbows. Udo rinsed them in the sink at night, draping them over the line to dry; he spread the bread when they got hungry; and it had gone on like this until the neighbours came to the back gate.

– Is your Mutti still there, child?

Benno thought his Mutti must have heard them.

She must have known she was talked about. Because now, even if she didn't wake him, or set out his clothes and his breakfast like she used to, she buttoned herself into her dresses, and she brushed her hair again. And when Rathaus wives came to the back door, his Mutti showed them into the parlour.

The women held her hands there; they clasped her palms in sympathy, speaking with her in murmurs:

– What a way for it to end – no?

Benno knew this because he'd come upon his brother in

the hallway the first time the wives came. Udo had been listening in at the parlour door, and he'd pressed a finger to his lips, pulling Benno closer, draping an arm around his shoulder, so he could listen further:

– *Not a sound, little brother, yes?*

Benno hadn't known what Udo was listening out for; most of the parlour talk that morning had been of the day the English arrived here.

Who had hidden from the soldiers. *The grocer; he shut himself in his coal store.*

Who had hung out their bedsheets to greet them. *So many! Who would have thought?*

By the time the jeeps drove across the Rathausplatz, there were towels and eiderdowns hung from half the town windows. *Those surrender flags. At least they didn't fly from our Rathaus.*

Udo had stood up straighter when talk turned to the Bürgermeister; he'd let go of Benno, edging nearer to the doorway.

Frau Paulsen was inside there; Benno had seen her arriving with the other wives, their arms linked in hers as she came up the back step. Now, she told them her husband had got up *just like any other morning.* Herr Paulsen had dressed and set out for the Rathaus, *just as normal,* only to find a pillow slip hanging from Heinrich's bakery. *From Christa Heinrich's window. Right there at the corner! And her Kurt still at the Front too.*

The further he'd walked, the more such pillow flags and tablecloths he'd seen along his familiar route. *Not just from the usual suspects' houses. But from families he'd been sure would hold out – and to the last. Even if only for their sons who had fallen. Because who wants to lose a son to a lost war?*

Before he'd knocked at those doors, she said her husband had taken off his hat, holding it to his chest, so those inside could see this mark of respect. But he'd got no answer. *No door opened to him that morning.* Benno heard how this took her aback: her husband left stranded, alone on the pavements to face the English convoy.

Herr Paulsen was arrested at the Rathaus. *But at least he was at his desk. Yes, at least he was at his post when the English came for him.*

Benno heard his Mutti being told this, and his Mutti saying nothing.

Although his Vati had been arrested that same day – his Vati had been arrested at home here – and Benno thought the Rathaus wives must know this.

He'd washed and he'd shaved, and he'd dressed himself as always, lighting a cigarette at the front door. But then he hadn't gone out to start his morning's duties. Instead, he'd pulled a chair out of the parlour, and he'd sat himself down in the hallway. So when the English came calling, that's where they'd found him: his coat buttoned and his shoes tied, his cap on the chair arm, like he'd been waiting for them.

Benno's Mutti was silent without him; Benno didn't know what she thought.

He knew his brother was angry, though. Even when Udo laughed it felt that way. His brother's eyes were hard as he'd listened that morning, his mouth also, as though daring the town wives to pass comment.

*

Udo picked up town word on the English – he made it his business now, collecting it from the other boys and elsewhere – and then he passed it to Benno.

– There are soldiers on guard now at the Rathaus – that's the latest. Except no one knows how long they'll stay there. Or keep this curfew.

He'd heard they had soldiers at the town works also:

– You know they've taken that whole place over?

The boys said the English had taken over the workers at the same time.

– They're keeping them behind that high wall. Or that's what it looks like.

The way Udo spoke – all in second-hand report and rumour – it sounded like no one could say what the English might do next.

– They're just waiting on orders, most likely. Before they can leave here.

Udo had told him this, just this morning, as he threw him his apple portion. It seemed to Benno that no one knew what to think now, or what might come next.

There hadn't been a knock at the door yet; Benno hadn't heard his Mutti stirring. He hoped it would be just him and Udo here; a day without visitors or rumours. But once they'd eaten, his brother threw his apple core over the alley wall, and when Benno turned to look for it landing in the nettle patch beyond the gate rungs, he saw Udo's bicycle, already leaning outside.

– Not a word – yes?

His brother put his finger to his lips again.

*

The English passed through the town streets, morning and evening, to mark the start and the end of the curfew. But Udo still rode out between times, even if the English didn't like it; even if their Mutti asked him not too. *Must I have another of mine arrested?*

Udo didn't say where he went. Maybe it was to find the other boys, or maybe it was just to be out and riding; Benno didn't know what he did.

He'd gone out with Udo once – once only – since the soldiers arrived here. Just to stay close to his brother's shoulder; just to see what the town looked like under the English. Udo had known Benno was nervous, so he'd waited until the jeeps passed and then a few more minutes afterwards, before pedalling out with him into the alleyways. Udo had assured him this much was allowed now:

– Little brother, we are allowed out of our houses.

But then, at the Rathausplatz, they'd found no one.

None of the other boys had been out yet – or anyone. The empty square had had Benno silent, riding tight behind Udo across the wide flags. The sun hard on the paving, shadows falling sharp across the house fronts; shutters bolted at the town bar, sheets and pillowcases all pulled back inside.

At the Rathaus itself, they saw only one soldier. Sitting behind a desk, behind a typewriter, just inside the main door. Was he dozing?

– You know our Vati is under guard now?

That's what Udo said when saw him.

Their Vati was in Bremen; Benno knew that the English were holding him. Still, it gave him such a sting to hear it spoken – and to see how angry it made Udo: the silent town and the sleeping soldier, but mostly their Vati. That he'd sat and waited. That he'd given himself over when the English came.

Cutting back home again along the side streets, they'd seen their first townsfolk.

The grocer, come out of his coal store to wash his wide shop window; Christa Heinrich, tying her apron strings and yawning in the bakehouse courtyard. Every few houses there was someone. A town mother Benno had seen calling on his Mutti; another he hadn't, but who was familiar to him anyway. And then a handful of old wives in mourning, just come to stand outside – their skirts dyed black and their blouses, their fingers still grey from the rinsing, like the rings under their eyes.

How many had hung out surrender flags? How many had wanted the war to be over?

Benno tried not to stare – but it was like he didn't know who was who here, not any longer.

No one called out; few heads lifted as they passed. Benno saw, though, how those few turned to them – and then he felt that same sting again.

How many knew about his father? How many were angry, like Udo was?

He'd been glad to get home that morning, out of sight of town eyes. And if his brother rode out now to be away from them, Benno thought his brother should be allowed that; it shouldn't matter what the English said. So when Udo stood to go, he watched him leaving – *not a word* – like his brother had asked.

Still, the house would be quiet now. Udo would be gone the whole day; it would be just him and his Mutti here until curfew, or even afterwards. And Benno didn't want that. Just sitting here and waiting, hoping for no more callers.

Had the patrol jeeps passed yet? He hadn't heard their rumbling. Benno stood up anyway, he pulled his bicycle, quiet, from the outhouse and into the alleyway.

Freya

For Freya, this was all new.

The sight of English patrol cars, the sound of English voices, English big bands on the radio.

When she tuned the parlour set to music, it was such a bright noise, she had to put her ear up close; Freya had to lift Ursel, her sister's young arms reaching to do likewise. And when they climbed up into the old oak, they heard the same notes rising faintly from the Brandt yard, drifting like the stove smoke from the far Buchholz Hof, out across the Heide.

So the war was over. And the war was lost, too. Yet every day there was sunshine.

Freya didn't know how it was – or if she was just being foolish – but when she climbed into the branches above the schoolyard, the sky did seem all the wider. High among the oak leaves, she pulled her sister up beside her, Ursel breathless and pink-cheeked and tousled, her fat plaits coming loose of their bindings. They both lay belly down on the rough boughs, and let their arms and legs go dangling, and then this all felt so fine and new to Freya, but so confusing also; she didn't know how to describe it. Like something come loose inside.

*

– *Mädchen!*

Their Mama called them to work in the garden.

Pulling weeds, on their hands and knees, Freya showed her sister which to pluck, which to leave. She and Ursel made their way along the bean rows, while their Mama dug the soil for new ones – and for peas too, and potatoes. Each new peacetime day that passed, their Mama dug over more of the flowers from their Papa's borders.

Since the English arrival, they'd been eating peas from last year's jars, all the leftovers in the larder; Freya's Mama had been cooking up the winter potatoes to substitute for bread flour until the bakery re-opened. And if she wasn't digging or boiling or planting, then her Mama was cleaning the windows, running dusters along the skirting boards. Working room to room, she took down all the curtains, hauling them all outside – laborious – laying them across the grass in the garden, giving everything a good airing.

– Out with the old.

She said.

Or:

– That's that, then.

As she dusted off her palms.

Freya's Mama slept in the afternoons.

Downstairs, on the sofa, with the radio on low, and all the windows open.

Those hours were the longest. Freya thought they should have been the best too – because the war was over, and all their chores were done with – but the afternoons spread so wide around her, Freya thought she would never fill them.

She rode the lane ruts with Ursel on her handlebars. Or she rode them out to their old haunts, pedalling along the Heide paths, Ursel slipping down to collect gorse sprigs and red thorn.

Ursel collected these for their Papa – for the next time they wrote to him – Freya knew this. She knew, also, that there was no post now: not under the English. Still, Freya let her sister gather her apron pockets full, finding snail shells and curls of sheep's wool. Freya let her climb onto the saddle, too, for the downhill home ride, taking the last slope fast, the way Ursel liked it.

In the grass under the parlour windows, they sorted through Ursel's best finds. Placing shells in rows the better to admire them; choosing petals for the blotting sheets in their Papa's bureau, ready to press them between the pages of his encyclopedias. Ursel hummed along with the English tunes; Freya waited for their Mama to wake again.

Few townsfolk came out this far, even fewer with the English curfew in force. Freya did see one or two in those first days of no war: how they passed with their heads down along the Poststrasse, on foot and on bicycles – and how they turned to look at the yard and the schoolhouse when they heard the radios.

Herr Brandt was their only visitor.

The neighbour came to sit on the garden wall, speaking to Freya's Mama while they kneeled and weeded in the borders.

He shook his head over the lost war.

– What was it all for, then? I ask you.

But Herr Brandt grinned, too – Freya saw this – when he told her Mama about the town surrender.

– Our bedsheet capitulation.

This is what he called it: the day of the English arrival.

– Our Christa – that fine one – hanging out her pillowslip for the soldiers. I bet she has half the town furious.

It seemed to Freya that he enjoyed this, not just because he grinned so, but because he couldn't say it enough times.

– Our Kurt's girl – just think of it!

Herr Brandt grinned most, though, when he spoke about the men at the Rathaus:

– You know the English took the place at gunpoint?

The yard man laughed at the thought, soft and hoarse. Still, talk of guns had Freya listening harder.

– It was only a last few hard cases they found there.

Herr Brandt waved his palm, as though waving those men good riddance now.

– The English pulled down the banners in any case, and the Führer portraits – all of them. And then they pulled out the Party lists from the bureaus, finding all the right addresses to call on. You know they unscrewed the name plates from the doors, even? Just think of that now: all those names set in brass – all those functionaries of these past years.

This made Herr Brandt laugh again, and then shake his head at his own laughing.

– Oh, it's just too good – no?

His big face turned to the sunshine, he sat and let himself enjoy the thought: the Rathaus men arrested, all the Party men who might be next now.

But then he dropped his chin, newly serious.

– You know the English are coming for more men?

He told her Mama:

– They've been knocking on doors, handing out papers. They stopped me while I was out driving. I hadn't gone far – just along the road here, and they handed me an envelope. Right through my van window.

Freya saw her Mama sit back on her heels when she heard that; and how she looked to the lane mouth and then the Poststrasse. Was she looking for English soldiers?

– They gave me pages and pages.

Herr Brandt said he had to write down so many things.

– Any lapsed Party membership. Any dates in the Brownshirts. Any military service – and mine was only in the last war, but I still have to put it on paper, though, before they'll clear me for work again.

He pushed back his yard cap and rubbed at his rough cheeks.

– It's the same for Heinrich. He told me.

Herr Brandt said the baker had to complete the same paperwork before the English would supply him with flour rations for the townsfolk – and Freya saw how this set her Mama blinking, like she was thinking, or like the news had surprised her. Her Mama looked to the lane again, the road there.

– So will they call on all of us?

While she was out and riding with Ursel, Freya tried to imagine what it might look like when the English came calling. Did they stride house to house, checking who'd had sheets out? Or did the soldiers come in through the doors? Did they search through the desk drawers for Party books? Along the walls for portraits?

When Freya came home again, her Mama wasn't on the sofa.

She wasn't cleaning either.

Freya went looking from kitchen to bedroom to parlour; she looked upstairs, while Ursel looked downstairs, but their Mama was nowhere. It was only once they'd walked the bean rows that Freya thought to look in the schoolhouse.

She found her Mama had unlocked the school door. It must have been the first time since the snows, the first time since the schools were closed, because the place felt so empty, the air stale and full of dust motes.

– Mama?

It was Ursel who saw her. They found their Mama inside the classroom, hands on hips and looking up at the portrait – on-high and dust-rimed under the rafters.

– How do I get at the damn thing?

Their Mama had to stand on a chair to reach high enough – and then stand the chair on one of the school desks to reach further – and even so, she could only get at the corner with the long pole for opening the windows.

Freya watched while she shoved at it and pushed, until she nudged the thing off its hook, and then it made such a crack when it hit the floorboards! It gave Freya such a start – and Ursel also. Her sister slapped her hands to her mouth, hard, like she wanted to laugh, and Freya had to squeeze Ursel's arm so she would stop. Their Mama shouldn't think that they were laughing – or not at her in any case.

The frame had broken where it landed; it lay face down and in cobwebbed pieces on the floorboards, and the way her

Mama looked at it – the way she let her breath out – Freya couldn't tell: was she happy now? Was she furious?

Her Mama wouldn't be helped down. She shoved away Freya's fingers. She did the same when Ursel crouched to help her gather up the remnants.

– *Lass doch!*

Her Mama scolded them, filling her apron, in a hurry to get it over with, fitting the pieces into the classroom stove for burning.

She struck the match – once, twice – and dropped it inside.

That's that, then.

Except there were still things that bothered Freya.

They kept her watching those flames dance, thinking and wondering. Mostly about what her Papa would say now.

Because that same portrait had hung in her grammar school – in the foyer with its parquet, and in the headmistress's offices – and Freya had known her Papa didn't like this. But even so, before she'd started, he'd worked to prepare her for her new classes. He'd sat her in the parlour, each morning, with her Mama's old schoolbooks on Latin and algebra, his finger marking her place in each exercise.

– Just so. Just so, yes.

Her Papa had never been one to show much. But Freya knew when she'd met his approval. It was just in his nod, or in the tilt of his head, especially when the pages got harder. Freya had seen him give the same nod, the same tilt when she sat in his classes, especially when he'd seen her keep pace with the town sons on the benches reserved for the oldest.

– *Genau so.*

The day he'd gone to the Wehrmacht, her Papa had told her she'd be just fine at the new school – *you'll hold your own, child* – and Freya had felt his pride then.

– *Mein Heide Mädchen.*

But when September came, and her first weeks started, there had been so many girls in the hallways, all of them talking around and across her as though they'd known each other always. It was the same inside her new classrooms: so many good town daughters, from places far and wide, and all in good town shoes and blouses – in German Girl skirts and neckerchiefs. Freya, in her Heide apron, sat quiet in the desk rows.

And shouldn't her Papa have known it would be like this?

He'd taught town daughters. He must have seen that starting at grammar school wouldn't just mean harder classes, it would mean signing up for German Girl duties. Her Papa had even taught Erna Paulsen, who strolled the lunch hall in her uniform.

All that autumn, Freya had seen Erna at the Rathaus steps on market days, smiling at the townsfolk, tilting her pretty shoulders, rattling her Party tin for the war effort. It made Freya shy to find her there – but it made her want to keep watching too somehow: Erna's dark skirts wide, her blouse tucked so neatly into her waistband.

– *Na, ihr Kleinen?*

When Erna spoke, it had Freya in a tangle, wanting and not wanting the older girl's attentions, flushing as she patted Ursel's parting.

– *Oh – schau mal!* Our schoolmaster's daughters.

Seeing Erna's father was worst though, the way he watched

all this from the Rathaus steps, in that Bürgermeister's way of his. Freya could feel him, taking in her tallness, her pinafore. She could see what he was thinking: that she should have a tin and a skirt and a neckerchief, just like his own child's.

But when the Rathaus sent the enrolment forms at New Year, Freya's Papa wouldn't hear of it.

Not likely.

This is what he'd written, in his very next letter home.

Not my daughter.

He would not bow to pressure from Herr Paulsen – he would not put her in uniform – even if this left her Mama frowning, and Freya dreading the new term.

– It's your Papa's pride, child.

This is all her Mama could tell her, as if in apology.

So that was that then, also.

There were others like Freya at the girls' school, but just a few. They sat far apart in classes, and when she passed them in the stairwells, they pretended not to notice. Freya learned to do the same: she saw the looks they got. She felt the same scorn from the desks around her own one. Some school mornings, Freya shut herself in the bathroom; she took her Mama's headscarf, put it around her neck and held it there – just to see what it might feel like. The mirror was old and spotted, and she looked at herself for a long time.

Was it the same at the boys' school?

Freya didn't know.

Back when they were all her Papa's pupils, they'd played the same running games as her across the schoolyard. In summer they'd climbed the oak branches; in winter, when the puddles froze, they'd come early to slide on their boot soles, just as Freya had with Ursel. There was Klaus, whose uncle was the station master, and Niklas and Thomas, who were cousins and both lived just beside the Rathaus. And then there was Udo. He was the tallest and the finest – at least to Freya's eyes. But after they went to grammar school, she hardly saw him. Or only on the home route after classes. On that last long stretch before the yard lane turning, pedalling his way ahead of her.

Already Udo seemed a good head taller, his legs long and loose as he rode, and when Freya saw him, it was like a tumbling inside her, or like pins and needles: sore but not sore – but still, she was not sure. Especially when it came to those other boys. When Freya saw them, she would slow down. It was better to slow than to pass them, because if she passed them, they fell silent. They watched her legs, her calves, her ankles; they looked at her arms, her nape as she rode past – and Freya saw the looks that passed between them; she saw the grins they shared. Her old schoolyard companions turning to one another and laughing – this hurt far worse than anything the girls did.

And would they go home and tell their fathers?

Some days, when she'd rounded the corner and found the boys there, Freya had slowed to a stop entirely. Pulling over to the roadside, getting off her bicycle, she pretended – even to herself – that she had to retie her shoes, or pull up her socks. Or, if that didn't take long enough, she would re-arrange the school bag in her basket, keeping her head down and her eyes on that task – but so aware of the boys ahead of her all the while. Grammar school classmates, HY Kameraden; Freya thought they could keep their laughing, their stupid neckerchiefs and stupid duties. Still, the way they wound down the road so slowly, they'd made her feel so lonely.

She'd been grateful when the snows came, when the schools closed.

When the post stopped was best though.

Freya knew it wasn't right – it wasn't nice – or what a good daughter should think about her father. But she didn't want to write to him. Or open another envelope of his drawings. *For my Freya, my Ursel.*

All these new peacetime mornings, when her sister asked to go to the postbox, Freya lifted her onto her handlebars and bumped there along the lane ruts. And each time they found it empty, she felt the same hard twist inside herself. Her own angry pride, stubborn and satisfied.

Now Freya was glad to see the portrait burning – and glad at the same time that her Papa wasn't there to enjoy it.

She watched until Ursel tugged at her fingers.

– *Komm doch!*

Until her sister pulled her out into the schoolyard, wanting to play again, not to be staring at stove flames. But while Ursel ran ahead of her to the garden, Freya was still caught in her own thoughts.

Her sister didn't seem to mind their Papa not writing. She didn't seem to mind about this new peacetime, either; this new Heide wideness and stillness. The days when Freya rode her to the old ford to go wading, or across the rail bridge at the station, or just along the tracks and paths – they could ride for hours and see no one, but did Ursel even notice?

Just this afternoon, Freya had ridden further than usual. By the time they'd started on the return route, it was already getting close to curfew. The Brandt yard roof tiles, the oak and the school wall, they'd seemed so far; and then, when they'd passed the Buchholz Hof, old Hanne had been outside, shooing her chickens into the lean-to, her apron flapping white against the Heide.

The neighbour wife had cried out when she saw them.

– Oh!

Old Hanne had shouted – loud – as though they'd startled her, or as though they'd caught her out somehow – and Freya had been just as startled: it wasn't like the neighbour wife to be angry at her and Ursel. She'd had a child on her hip – a small one – and this too was unfamiliar: the little form held tight in the crook of the old wife's elbow.

– Ach, Kinder!

Old Hanne had shouted another time. She'd had been so urgent too, shooing them on their way again, back to the schoolhouse before the curfew – and yet Ursel had only waved to her, just like always.

But now there had been that whole business with the portrait.

And this must have set Ursel thinking too, in her own way.

Because later, in the bathtub, when it was just the two of them, her sister sat and puzzled in the water. Watching the evening turning blue beyond the windows, and the sparrows come home to roost along the schoolhouse ridge tiles.

Ursel murmured:

– When Papa comes home again, will the English still be here?

And:

– Will they let him across the border?

And then:

– Freya – will the war still be over?

She looked so earnest, too – and so Freya saw it was all just as new to her, and just as confusing. The curfew, this lost war. Seeing the roads quiet, and the rail lines, and a child at the Buchholz Hof, where there had only been old Hanne and old Gustav for such a long time.

When would their Papa come home again? Freya didn't know. She didn't know what she could tell Ursel.

Instead, she took the bath jug and filled it, pouring it warm over her sister's shoulders. Freya poured it over her own, too. And then she emptied the rest over her forehead, splashing and gasping, so Ursel would laugh – and so she wouldn't ask further.

– We'll look again – in the postbox – tomorrow morning.

This is all Freya told her:

– We'll see when a letter comes, won't we? We'll see what our Papa says.

Although she didn't know when he would write next. Or that she wanted to hear what their Papa said, either.

Freya had long stopped thinking he knew best. And in any case – what did he know about the English? He'd been gone such a long time, what would he know about anything?

June

6

The Winter Child

Hanne

How long had she been with them now?

Hanne hadn't dared mark time, at least not in those cold days after the child was left here.

No one had passed the Hof. The drifts had lain thigh-deep across the Heide. She and Gustav were snow-bound: cut off from the schoolhouse, the Brandt yard and the Poststrasse – from the whole world, it felt like. Long may it last.

The fear, though, had taken longer to pass.

In that first shock, in the woodshed corner, Hanne had picked up the girl and held her – because what else do you do with a cold child? The girl had been out there all night, and now snow was falling, so Hanne carried her inside – just because both of them would be warmer.

And when Gustav had caught up with her at the stoveside, and he'd whispered:

– We could be up to our necks – you know this?

Hanne had taken up a wash-cloth instead of answering; she'd pressed it to the girl's cheeks, her fingers, because she couldn't let that thought go further.

The rags the girl wore were so dirty, Hanne sat down to peel them off – just to keep her fingers working – just to keep herself from feeling frightened – anything, anything rather than feel that.

And then, there in the chair at the stoveside, naked in Hanne's lap, the girl had cried for the first time, her small face crumpling. So Hanne had rocked her. Because the woman who'd run had rocked her also; and because she was a child – just a child – left behind in this cold time. Her limbs so narrow, her skin so pale, her eyes so grey and startled.

Gustav had turned and gone back out into the yard. And Hanne had known he was scared – just like her – more than he was angry. But she couldn't follow him; she couldn't let her own fear show, or she'd be lost to it. She could only think about this girl child that needed quieting.

What else could she do but hold her?

Outside, the snow fell – on and on – while Hanne's hands set oats for soaking; while her legs carried the child upstairs to search out the baby clothes in the bedroom trunks: all the small things she'd knitted for her own two children – so many years ago now. Her daughter's little cardigans, Kurt's little woollen caps: they were just about the right size. And at least Hanne's fingers knew to work still, pulling the small arms into the sleeves, socks onto the small feet. Just keep the girl warm now, just keep her from crying.

Night fell, eventually.

Dawn rose on the snow again; thick and white beyond the windowpane.

And there she was still, this winter child. *Impossible, impossible.*

Gustav watched her, mute with fear, mute with confusion, and Hanne felt much the same way, staring and staring at this small weight on her lap, that was no weight at all.

– We're looking after her.

Hanne whispered this – because she had to say something. To herself as much as to Gustav.

– We've been asked to do this.

Once the words were out, Hanne even felt like they might be true somehow. The woman had run to them, ragged and cold and grimy, unable to carry the girl further, and then the woman had left the child with them to care for – hadn't she wrapped her in Hanne's own blanket?

– It's only for a short while.

Hanne said this because she hoped so.

Although she feared – at the same time – that the woman might yet be captured, somewhere up on the heathland. Or that the woman might return here – *please, no* – after hiding out in a Heide barn. And then – dread thought – she and Gustav would be found out. They would be hauled off to the Rathaus – and then to some place far more frightening.

And what would happen to the child then?

If Hanne could have said how long they would need to hide her. Or if she could have said it was right – it was right to do this – clear and simple, without also knowing it was reckless – without also fearing the knock at the door in the small hours – then that might have helped her.

Sooner or later, Hanne felt the woman would come to claim her daughter. Because any mother would do that; she would have to, surely. *Not now, though*, Hanne pleaded, inward. *Not yet.* She hoped the woman would see reason, wherever she had hidden, wherever she had run in Gustav's yard coat. *Let her be gone to ground, please: gone to earth, where no one would think to look.* Even the thought of her ragged form at their Hof door was too frightening. Her torn patch, her buttons hanging from her blouse front.

Hiding her child was madness – it was madness – but it was the only thing they could do. That was the impossible truth of it.

The girl was here now; it was already too late to do otherwise.

And although Hanne tried, she could find no words to explain this to Gustav – to herself, even. Or none that made it anything other than strange and dangerous.

Gustav couldn't hold the child: that was a step too far. He could only watch while Hanne held her, and Hanne saw how he turned the same fearful thoughts over:

The girl wasn't theirs – and what if someone from the town or the Rathaus came calling?

The girl wasn't German – and didn't it show in her

smallness and her thinness? Or just in her grey eyes? Her narrow palms?

The girl was a quiet one. After those first tears, she did no more crying, so at least there was that. She only eyed them both in grave and watchful silence.

But the girl was a worker's, a stranger's – wasn't it obvious? – wouldn't anyone know this?

The Heide was wide, but their town was a small one: hadn't Gustav always told her so? You couldn't do anything – anything – without somebody noticing.

So Gustav couldn't see that the child was cared for: he couldn't bring himself. But at least Hanne could do that without thinking: feeding the girl when she was hungry, rocking her when she needed sleep; sewing her a change of clothing – and then another one – out of the scraps in the linen basket. It was the work Hanne was born to.

It didn't stop her feeling frightened. At night especially, Hanne listened for the siren, sleepless in the silence. But because the child had to be cared for daily – hourly – regardless – it was this work that got her through it all.

The thaw came, a dripping from the icicles, a rippling in the gutters under the Hof tiles. The snow retreated from the roof above Gustav's wood store, then from the track and then the Heide slopes.

Still they'd kept the doors closed, the shutters across the windows.

They'd been so careful – keeping the curtains drawn, even, whenever the child was in the room with them – and that way the days had become weeks, become a month, and longer. Until the first warm morning, when Hanne opened the upstairs window, letting in the new sun.

The girl was so very quiet still, Hanne sat her on her lap while she peeled the potatoes, on her hip while she swept the floorboards. If she had to fetch water from the yard tap, or eggs from the chickens in the lean-to, she sat the girl at the stoveside, between cushions and blankets: *you sit tight there.* Or she left those chores for nap times, tucking the girl into the big bed, in among the eiderdowns.

And then, in among that dressing and holding and feeding, in among that secrecy, they'd grown so used to her there.

Little Ditte.

They even named her – half by accident.

They gave her a German name – perhaps that was safest.

The child wasn't theirs to be naming – they knew this. But the girl had begun crawling by that time, edging careful across the kitchen tiles behind Hanne's striding. She'd started looking into Hanne's face, too, when she held her; reaching for her old cheeks, small fingers growing curious. And then Hanne had sat her on Gustav's knee one mealtime, just while she dished the soup into their soup bowls, and the child had looked startled at his large palms, large fingers that held her for the first time. So then, stranger's child or not, he couldn't just call her *Mädchen*, or *Dirn*. Gustav couldn't just call her girl.

Ditte had been his sister, and so this is what Gustav called the child that afternoon, without thinking:

– Hanne – can't you take her? How can I eat with Ditte on my lap here?

And Ditte must have been right for her, because Ditte she was then.

The first to see her was Gerda.

This was still before war's end, when Hanne's eldest had come to the Hof – unannounced, and all the way from Stade. By bus, and then on foot and farm cart.

Gerda had come for eggs, as usual. Ever since the war rations started, their daughter had taken to arriving every couple of months or so, during laying season anyway. Then she'd carry home two good basket-loads, nestled inside dish-cloths to protect and disguise them.

Gerda traded those eggs with her neighbours. Against work shirts for her Jost, who wore his way through plenty at his work furnaces; or against scarves and socks for his father, who lived with the two of them and complained of the cold, even when Gerda kept the fires lit.

Except this time Gerda came earlier than usual: it wasn't even April yet; the hens had only just started laying again after their winter rest. Hanne hadn't been expecting her.

When her daughter arrived, Hanne heard her before she saw her: Gerda's voice, loud in the Hof, telling her father the Americans were on the way to Münster.

– They're heading north and west now. And so fast, I couldn't wait, you see? Not any longer. We might all be under the Amis soon. And who knows if visits will be allowed then?

On and on she talked.

About Jost and what he'd heard of the fighting from the other forge workers.

About her father-in-law, who simply would not believe that the war was as good as over.

Sight of the child stopped her, though – when Gerda stepped into the kitchen and saw Ditte at Hanne's skirt hems.

– *Was ist das hier?*

The story of Ditte's arrival kept her silent – unsmiling – while Gustav explained to her. While he tried to, in any case, about the woman in the woodshed corner, her shawl-wrapped bundle and torn blouses.

– *Nein, nein.*

Gerda shook her head at them.

– *Nein, nein.*

Their daughter was beside herself.

– It is too much – just too much – don't you see that?

She'd come all this way only to find them harbouring disaster?

And then Hanne had to tell her there were hardly eggs left for her to take home either – not just because the laying hadn't properly started, but because Gustav had been trading their winter-stored ones. He'd been tramping across the high pass to the dairyman – a little more often than was usual, but not so often as to draw attention – and then he'd come clanking back again with two full canisters, bringing the milk that Hanne would usually have soured or made into cheese, had everything been as normal, but which they'd been giving to the child here.

And see how plump her cheeks are!

This is what Hanne wanted to tell her daughter. But she found herself unable. The look on Gerda's face said she didn't want to talk more – not about the winter girl – not about this stranger's child, sitting and watching her from the floor tiles, a little more plump-cheeked but still as solemn as always.

– Is there word from Kurt?

Gerda asked after her brother instead. Only to shake her head about him also, as she always did – while Gustav joined in.

– None at all, my girl. None at all.

Father and daughter, they turned to one another, leaving off from the child for the moment to fret over Kurt's war wound, his dim prospects. Because whoever had need of a one-armed apprentice? Neither could imagine him doing Hof work either. A wound like Kurt's – that only made sense among soldiers – and Hanne thought probably the boy felt that too, because he'd stayed on at the war hospital even after his discharge, learning the trolley-and-mop duties of an orderly. Doubtless he'd learned to play dice again from the other wounded, to deal playing cards one-handed, roll a cigarette. For all Hanne knew, that's where he was still – over in the East Lands.

– And how can he get home from there now?

Gustav was certain he'd be captured; Gerda sure the Red Army would already have him.

– They'll be taking all the hospitals, all the Wehrmacht places, won't they? My Jost says so.

She frowned at Hanne in warning:

– Mother, you ought to go to the bakehouse – you know this. Call on Christa. Show we're keeping her in mind, yes? When was the last time you did that?

She said Christa couldn't wait for always.

– That girl will have her choice of townsmen, once they start coming home from the front line. My Jost says this also.

So then Hanne had to pull her own mouth closed.

She had to remind herself that Jost was a rough one, much like his father. And it must be impossible for Gerda to live with the two of them and not have some of that roughness rub off on her.

Hanne said:

– Your brother will be back. The Russians can't keep him. They won't want to.

Although she wasn't at all certain she believed this, and neither was Gerda – Hanne could see this from the way her daughter met that thought with silence.

Still, as that quiet fell between them, Hanne saw the worry lines at Gerda's forehead, the grey at her temples where there used to be blonde, and she felt a little tenderness returning.

So they'd left it at that – almost.

Gerda had kissed the two of them on their old foreheads – still disapproving, still worried for Kurt too – and then she'd headed off town-wards with her empty baskets.

She'd glanced at Ditte once more, though. After Hanne had picked up the small one to see her off at the kitchen door, Gerda had looked back at her and Gustav:

– At least the Amis should be here soon.

She told them.

– So you can give that child over in a week or two.

That child.

Hanne felt a stiffening inside herself. Was that any way to talk about this small one?

And besides – why should she give the child to Americans? To soldiers? To anyone who didn't know her?

Gustav was slower – as usual – turning this idea over in the hours after Gerda departed.

Hanne saw how it occupied him, trying to think what was right here. And also – how might he explain the child to an American in uniform?

What could he say about that night, the siren, the munition works in the town here? What could he say about the woman too – that worker and stranger – because hadn't she run again?

The woman hadn't run from them, of course. But the Americans wouldn't know that. All they'd hear was that she'd arrived at their doorstep and then gone again: she had disappeared into the Heide snowfall. And what might that sound like to a soldier? When every German was an enemy, and every German word ought to be regarded with caution?

While they lay in bed that night, with Ditte sleeping between them, Gustav told her what he had decided:

– We should wait – yes.

They should not be too quick to come forward.

– The woman might come back yet. Especially once the fighting is over. And if she can take the girl, that would really be easiest.

And if they took the child to the Americans?

– Well. You don't know what the Amis might make of such a story.

*

In the end, it was the English who'd come to the Heide in any case.

It was peacetime – finally.

They had English at the Rathaus, English-issue ration cards, and no soldier had come knocking yet or asking. Already June had started, and Gustav had said nothing further. So now Hanne gave as little thought as possible to taking Ditte anywhere.

7

Only Just Getting Started

Ruth

For a while, there was hardly chance to catch breath.

Now the Germans had surrendered, DPs were being brought in daily by occupation soldiers: driven in from market gardens; from canning factories that lay north and west along the river Elbe; and from endless munitions works.

Most were still Poles and Ukrainians. But there were a handful of Italians on her camp register, three Czechs too, and a lone Belgian. None had been moved from the works here in the end days. Still, Ruth asked each new man arriving, hoping for word of the missing workers, or even just of those winter convoys. Where had those transports been taken?

She filled out forms for medicines, for shoes and shirts; but what the DPs needed most was sleep and food, sleep and food. So Ruth saw to it that they were dusted, given field cots and blankets, and then she assigned them to tent rows where they would be among their own countrymen.

Each dawn came as blue as the last – and just as fast – and each evening, the canvas roof lines stretched further under the summer sky; already the duckboard paths reached almost to the back wall.

– There's no way to get everyone accommodated.

Farley stopped outside Ruth's tent flap one dusk.

– We already have canvas on every spare inch of this compound.

He pulled up sudden and blunt at the threshold, in the lamplight, as she was starting in on her typing.

– Where are we to keep them all?

It wasn't like him to make conversation; and it wasn't in Ruth's gift to issue orders that might solve these problems, so she wasn't quite sure what he'd come for. She could feel the sergeant wasn't yet sure of her either, the sod in him still dubious of this Red Cross stranger he'd been thrown in with, and all her Red Cross duties. He gestured to the forms and clipboards and record cards that Ruth had spread across her field cot beside her; all the names and DP numbers.

– Tomorrow there will be more of them – you know that? And you know our tents are insufficient as it stands. Not to mention the latrines.

Once he'd said his piece, though, Farley only looked at her, weary, like he didn't expect her to answer. As though he might simply be too full of work thoughts to turn in yet – just like her.

A major was due any day now, to take charge at the town hall, and to oversee the camp as it expanded. Farley said:

– I've put in a request – just so you know – ready for when the new man arrives. I'm thinking we should have Nissen huts built here. At least a few.

No one had told Ruth – perhaps no one had worked it out yet – if they were still a holding camp, or becoming something more permanent. How long the medics might be staying on here; if she might get another welfare officer to guide her, or at least someone to work alongside. Ruth had heard a little about the new major, though. That he was an old hand at soldiering, not just an army functionary; that he'd fought his way up through Italy, and even spent time in captivity – according to the supply lads anyway – so Farley's Nissen request seemed promising. Maybe even part of a longer game? Ruth asked:

– So you think we'll be here a while yet?

Because if anyone had an inkling, she thought Farley would.

Except he just gave her another one of his army-issue shrugs, the sod in him returning:

– Ours is not to ask, Officer Novak, just to put our shoulders to the task here.

Over the next days, more factories were impounded. More DPs were brought in for Ruth to register, and to make requests for from the supply boys. But among them came two young Frenchmen: two young miracles. Both escapees from a labour detachment – and both of them Jewish!

Romain and Bernard.

They only stayed one night. Still, Ruth sat up late with them, in the medical tent, helping to change the dressings on their sores and bruises, and listening while they recounted their war's end, the two of them talking to each other as much as to her – as though they still couldn't believe it.

– The Germans are done now?

– Truly?

They'd been in the same labour camp.

– Yes – up at the Baltic.

– Yes, it felt like so long.

They said it was a year, perhaps longer, before the order to evacuate.

– Before the Red Army came – you understand, yes?

Ruth thought events must have come so fast then, because the two men spoke and then broke off, before starting from scratch again, as though trying to get everything straight in their own minds.

– We were herded into the transport yard, that's what I remember.

– All of us labourers – the whole camp – all cleared out.

– And we all told ourselves, *the Russians, the Russians* – now they are coming for the Germans.

The workers were driven for days across country, past checkpoints that were guarded, and others that had been abandoned. At each stop they'd whispered, feverish, among themselves, passing news and rumours of Slav and Steppe reinforcements, townsmen and villagers recruited along the way and coming after them.

At the rivers, those stops were longest. All the currents winter-swollen and the crossings rendered treacherous. The bridges at the widest points were still guarded. First had come the Vistula and then the Oder.

– The Old Reich border.

There, among the mines and barbed wire, Romain said they were divided into work gangs. Set to digging tank traps and trenches before they were driven onwards to dig more of them, along road and rail lines, further and further back into Germany.

– First we were with soldiers.

– We were in SS convoys.

– Yes, but I remember Wehrmacht also.

Bernard said they'd crossed the river Dahme and then the Havel – so they knew they'd crossed half of Germany on their flight westward.

– And then it was just police, you know? To guard us.

The two Frenchmen told of soldiers with rifles, calling out orders, and then of old men in police coats, pulling on armbands.

– The Germans, they must have had no one left then. We saw that.

Their guards went knocking on doors, calling all the old men out of their houses, up from their cellars and their shelters.

– Police, and old soldiers from the last war.

Their labour gang had been near the Elbe when a daylight raid caught them. Romain told Ruth how all the prisoners had lain down at the roadside as the bombers flew over, too weak to do otherwise. But their old guards had run.

– Run!

The two Frenchmen lifted their arms, faces open with the

surprise of this. They even smiled as they told Ruth about the old Germans, fleeing under the bombers' roar.

– And then they were nowhere!

– *Disparu!*

– Vanished!

– Just think of that!

Bernard said the workers fled just as fast.

– As soon as we realised.

The two of them had struck out across country, spending a whole night walking, the next day hiding in a woodshed, waiting for dark to come. That second night was the hardest: spent cold and hungry, and walking the riverbank. They'd watched the mortar flares across the water, fearing how bright and near they were, just above the reeds where they'd sought shelter.

But as the light rose, they'd come upon a glasshouse, of all things, and a half-walled garden. They'd found themselves in the grounds of some grand pile, just above the Elbe shore.

– So beautiful, you know? So gracious.

– So much not what we'd expected.

The big house was dark, the owners gone who-knows-where; the two Frenchmen could walk no further.

– No further.

They'd stayed in the kitchen garden, digging up the remnants of the winter vegetables and sleeping out the last war days, under the glass roof of the greenhouse, in among the pots and ferns.

– It was you English who found us.

One evening, there were English soldiers in the doorway. Come to requisition a German house, only to find two French hideaways.

– And so hungry!

Ruth brought them soup to eat in the medical tent; she found them new boots and clean shirts for their onward journey. And then in the morning, she was at the gates when they were collected by an ambulance crew, heading for a larger camp at the French border, where they'd be given rest and care with other survivors.

Ruth helped the two men climb inside, spreading blankets across their laps, seeing to it that they had water in their canteens; and then she watched as they waved their adieus to her through the open side window, driven away again along the Poststrasse.

– *Courage!*

– *Bon courage, Mademoiselle!*

Brief visitors. No time to talk more.

But there are survivors. Ruth had the evidence of her own eyes. People can be found again.

More flags were stitched and hoisted: Italian and Bohemian and Belgian stripes. Ruth began to find comfort in their fluttering, and in the DPs' company: watching the way they met on the duckboards that marked out the borders; passing on the camp latest, any news from beyond too.

– Hitler?

– Dead now. Dead.

They spat in the dust.

– Himmler same, same.

– *Na ha!*

Ruth was glad to see them laughing.

– And Stalin?

– Stalin? Is he king of the world yet?

– Spare us!

They bartered their rations all the while – soap for chocolate, chocolate for corned beef and packets of black tea. Coffee was the hardest currency – and cigarettes. Even American brands had started doing the rounds, although where they came from, Ruth couldn't imagine – and the supply boys in the ration stores claimed they couldn't either.

– On our honour, Officer Novak.

– You won't tell the new man – the new major?

– Please, Miss?

The major's first inspection was too busy for reporting anything – even if Ruth had been inclined to.

The man arrived early, driving himself into the courtyard, parking up and starting before Ruth and Farley could arrive to greet him. They saw his empty jeep first, then they found him at the side of the machine sheds: a lean and spare man, older than she'd imagined: his face creased, his uniform loose across his shoulders, or was he just war-worn? He was already at work, taking notes of the lathes left by the Germans.

– Just getting myself acquainted.

Farley had to show him everything: the supply yard and medical station, the mess and the barracks and all the tent rows.

– You can see tents are not ideal, sir.

Ruth had to go through the numbers of DPs housed inside them; the numbers they'd found on arrival; the many still arriving.

– The Germans had more workers here. I have the lists, whenever you need to see them.

The major gave nothing much away through all of this. Ruth caught no surprise at their task here – at the sheer numbers they were charged with, or at the news about missing workers – more just a grim and tired acknowledgement. He surveyed her dispatches, the provisions she and Farley had made so far, and she thought of how many places like this he must have seen, making his way up the country.

– How many huts do you anticipate, sergeant? Any last corners to show me?

The man took them aside before he departed, speaking to Ruth and Farley at his jeep door in the courtyard.

– I can't give you answers yet.

He couldn't say about latrines, or Nissen huts, or about how long they would all be here:

– That rather depends, you see, on the Higher Ups.

He said nothing, either, of how he might help with tracking down the labourers missing from the factory.

But he said Ruth should get a desk:

– A proper place to work while everything is decided.

The major told Farley he should see to this:

– High time she was moved out of that tent, sergeant, into a room of her own.

The only one available was in the former guard block.

– Sorry about that.

Farley told her, deadpan, while he led her up the back stairs, so lately occupied by Werkschutz. The supply boys had taken over the ground floor; the dorms down there were cleared out, made companionable with bunk beds and card tables. Ruth's room was on the first.

– So you'll be alone up here.

Farley stood to one side in the doorway, to let her step past him.

The room was small and at the end of the corridor. But it was spick and span, the floor still damp with supply lad mop-swirls, and it had two windows.

The nearest overlooked the Poststrasse and the factory wall; stepping to the other, Ruth could see the town woods beyond – and she saw it wasn't just pines out there, but birch too, and beech trees, all in full leaf, fresh and green. Spring had sprung without her noticing. She had been so busy here; how long since she had written home?

Farley cleared his throat, pointing to the sink in the corner.

– That's in lieu of a washroom.

He gestured towards it, a little uncomfortable.

There were showers: Ruth had seen them downstairs, in passing. Farley's tour of the ground floor had been perfunctory – both of them were short on time and long on duties – but he had told her, pointed, *those bathrooms are to serve the supply troops*, and Ruth had guessed it did not sit right with the sergeant: a woman digging in with soldiers.

– There'll be more troops on the way soon. The major has seen to that much.

This is what Farley said now, telling her those new supply boys would fill the remaining bunks in the ground floor dorm rooms.

– They'll be Royal Army Services and medical auxiliaries.

He even named the divisions, labouring the point a bit, as though he couldn't let go of it. Then he lifted his chin at her:

– We can't have you sharing, Miss.

When they were first left in charge here, Ruth had seen how the supply boys looked her over: no ring on her wedding finger, but older than most of them. She was too old to flirt with, and a good rank too high: a spinster-officer in uniform trousers. Ruth had taken this in her stride, though: she was still adjusting to being around soldiers herself; to this new working life. At the infirmary, they'd been all girls together on the wards: nurses and welfare staff in the canteens and the corridors; even her house calls had been to mothers left on their own because of the war. Here, the supply lads were all rough banter when left to their own devices, then sudden and exaggerated politeness when she entered the mess tent, and they were forever switching between *Officer* and *Miss* and *ma'am* – a friendly confusion, awkward but affable. Farley's manner had been different from the start: all business; if her dealings with him were brisk, at least they'd been simpler for it. But his manner was different again now, and that last *Miss* had irked her: so deliberate. It was enough for Ruth to turn to him.

– Might some of the new supply corps be female, Sergeant Farley? Or the longer-term medical staff? Then I'll have company.

She felt how much she'd like that, also: a few nurses, other Red Cross girls up here on her corridor. She might even find comfort in spinster numbers.

But then Farley lifted his chin again in answer:

– Even so. I don't think that you'll be comfortable, Officer Novak.

Still in the doorway, he watched her, only not with his usual sergeant's briskness. He was cool this time, even disobliging – and then it began to dawn on Ruth: there was more about her that didn't sit right with the man.

It's as old as time. That's what her mother said about this feeling. *You'll get to know it. We all do.*

She'd put Ruth wise, already in childhood, telling her as gently as she could: *you'll grow accustomed – I'm sorry, but you'll have to* – and she'd been right too. Still, Ruth hadn't reckoned on this from Farley. She had to fight a moment, inside, against the disappointment. Always worst when it was unexpected.

– I'm looking into rooms for the major.

The sergeant was still talking, telling her:

– We're finding him a place in those villas near the town woods.

Like the medics, Ruth thought, and the army clerks: they were all housed away from the camp – and Farley would have her do the same; she could see that now. If all things had their proper order, he'd have her billeted at arm's length.

But Ruth did not want to be billeted with Germans.

Or to be away from her work here – she was only just getting started.

So she turned her back on him, looking out at the view again, across the tent rows and the treetops, before she stepped past him.

– The room is just fine. Thank you, Quartermaster.

*

Farley gave her the office the major had ordered: four walls of planed boards that the supply boys knocked together in the old factory courtyard.

The sergeant assigned her a DP, too, to help with her duties. Or anyway: he told her a man had volunteered.

– It was a Stanislaw. From that near tent row.

It turned out to be the grey-haired Pole from the first week.

– Pleased to meet you.

The man gave a small bow to introduce himself, this time as a translator, outside his tent where Ruth went to find him.

– Maybe you can call me Stanley?

His English excellent, his manners impeccable, he was among the oldest there, but still he got up from his folding chair so she could sit – *you sit* – while they went over his new duties.

Stanislaw could speak Ukrainian from his Lwów childhood, as well as German from his time here.

– I had to learn enough to get through.

Small and professorial, more suited to desk work than a lathe, at home he'd been an engineer; Ruth had already noted this on his record card: he'd taught mechanics, at a technical school.

– Yes, I was at the university. And then here, I was a labourer. A machinist. Like everyone.

Stanislaw lifted his fingers, regretful at how thickened they were, and he told her he'd been in munitions works dotted all over Germany:

– I was called on to fix things. And to blame, of course, when they did not work.

But he would like to be of camp service.

– Please: if I can be.

*

So then Ruth had company. Stanislaw coming out with her on her morning tent rounds, translating Polish to English to Ukrainian and back again. He took notes, too, so Ruth could compare them with her own, and he found places on maps for her, unfolding them on her desk in the afternoons, whenever a DP had mentioned a new one.

– There it is. Just there – you see?

This task seemed unending: remembering the many towns and villages and regions. The borders had changed – and changed again – under different occupations, the place names changing with them, but Stanislaw said he was used to this.

– It was done to my own home. So I know it.

He shrugged, a little rueful, while he told Ruth:

– It happened, so many times over.

Even just in his own lifetime.

– When I was a boy, then it was Lwów, because my city was Polish. Then it was Lviv – you see? – under the Soviets. And after the Germans rolled their tanks in – well, then it was *Lemberg* on the tram stops, *Lemberg* on the city courts, and on my old university. On everything.

It was Lemberg on the German maps the guards had left behind here; Stanislaw showed Ruth – *you see now?* lifting his grey eyebrows. Then he took up a pencil and wrote LWÓW along the map fold, neat and defiant.

Already Ruth liked the man.

He took to bringing maps out with him, too.

Each morning, while Ruth conducted her duckboard interviews, Stanislaw unfolded them on the grass between the tent sides, in the sunshine. First, the DPs gave their details, dutiful, listing all the names they could remember: the farms and the factories, all the German companies they had worked for – and they tried their best to find these, crouching before the German maps with Stanislaw.

But the maps of their own countries were what they held out for.

When Stanislaw laid those out, the DPs just gazed a while – at all the rivers and the roads and the rail lines. Then they started pointing, pointing with their work-knotted fingers:

– *Tam – tam! Ojczyzna!*

Home, they said. *Home!*

– Oh, look!

– My home is there. There it is!

They turned to Ruth delighted:

– But when can we return?

They looked at her so expectant, she did not like to lie to them.

– *Prędko.*

Soon.

– Soon. I hope.

It was all Ruth could say for now.

– I am sorry.

The men smiled – a little sorry too – as they repeated:

– Soon, soon.

– Soon, soon.

They were learning English words from listening, and from Stanislaw. *In a fortnight* and *in a few weeks* and *maybe.* They tilted their chins as they tried them out loud.

– Repatriation.

This became a favourite.

– Re-pa-tri-ay-shon.

They sounded out the syllables, tapping them out along the map folds with their fingertips.

But Ruth looked at those maps, too, while they did so, and she saw that it would be quite some journey. So many hundreds of miles – all of them bombed and blasted – and the DPs would have to cross occupation zones. Some would go through the American, but most would have to pass through the Russian – all the Poles here, and all the Ukrainians. And no one had told Ruth how that would be organised. Would the DPs go straight from here, or via other holding camps? Would they be held up in the Russian zone? Did the major know?

There was so much work still ahead of all of them.

Over their mess-tent lunches, Stanislaw took to teaching her Ukrainian basics, and more Polish verbs and phrases. Unfailingly courteous, but strict too – pedantic – he got her to practise on the Eastern surnames they were collecting, insisting she repeat her vowel sounds: *Not so flat; it is better not so flat.* Hard not to smile at that.

He was inquisitive also – gently so.

Stanislaw blinked at her one lunchtime:

– May I ask?

– Go on.

Ruth couldn't help but smile again as he leaned in across their tin plates:

– You are a Novak?

– I am, yes.

Stanislaw leaned back after she'd answered; he gave a small

nod, as though satisfied – and then he gestured to the morning's lists and maps between them:

– So. You are one of us – no?

With her broken Polish? *One of us* had Ruth laughing:

– Oh, not me. Oh, not really. It's my dad's name – if you must know.

Her father was a Lublin boy. *And my own father before me, etcetera, etcetera.* He'd sung old songs to Ruth in childhood, he'd told old stories; all the Polish words she knew before she'd come here, he'd taught her. So Ruth told Stanislaw:

– It's my dad you should talk to, really. My vowels are his fault entirely.

He laughed at that also, and the two of them sat a moment.

But then Ruth didn't know what to say next.

Because while her dad had sung old songs to her, he'd told her also: *Lublin was no place to be one of our kind.* And how to tell that to Stanislaw? Ruth didn't know him nearly well enough. Only that he was from Lwów; only that he had no sympathy for the Germans. Once they'd rolled their tanks in, Ruth knew Lwów would have been no place for a Stanislaw – for anyone. But still, she wasn't ready to find out if he were another Farley.

So she was grateful when he didn't ask further, just giving her a nod, raising his tin mug of army tea to her:

– To all our fathers.

Stanislaw gestured beyond the mess tent, at the canvas maze out there:

– What would they say to this mess – I ask you?

Ruth grew to like this about him especially: his gentle humour. He did not pry; she did not either.

Although she looked up his records that evening – just to remind herself, just to feel that *one of us* thought again. Ruth pulled out his index card, and found another clipped behind it.

At the top was a name: *Barthos*. Then an address too, for a Lwów apartment – all in Stanislaw's neat print. He'd written *brother* and underlined it.

He has a brother, Ruth thought. And he hadn't told her. Although he must have meant her to find this. Or for the Red Cross to try and find this Barthos in any case. Perhaps Stanislaw had offered his translation services in hopes that he might speed the process?

Ruth started a tracing request that same night, so it could be added to the others, sent in the next set of dispatches. And then, at the bottom of the card she found a further address, this time for a university – this brother's old workplace maybe? Or it was Stanislaw's? Ruth found herself wondering: had they shared college lecture halls, college machine labs? Did Stanislaw hope – in private – that this brother was there still? What did he think of, when he folded out those maps?

The June heat set in early. The sun strong in the mornings, the pale tents blinding, their white sides throwing off the rays. Inside, they were baking, already long before midday.

With Stanislaw to help, though, Ruth's morning rounds grew easier. She could talk to the DPs for longer, write more of what they told her; she could go back and talk again to the ones she'd already registered.

Ruth took their record cards with her, and the ones clipped behind them, because she'd got to thinking that perhaps with more details, her dispatches might match up with others more easily, with those lost brothers and cousins scattered across the occupation zones. They might be found yet, in other camps like this one.

Ruth grew to hope.

Once the interviews were over, the DPs lay outside, in the shade cast by the tent rows, moving with the path of the afternoon hours.

– Like sundials.

Stanislaw gave her a small smile.

He wasn't one for lying in the grass. Once his translation duties were done with, he walked a circuit of the camp – or two, or three – as though to take in its boundaries. Ruth saw how he looked out across the wide reach of the meadows, and then up at the low slopes, scattered with pine trunks, that marked the start of the town woods. Was he thinking himself beyond them? Imagining his way home again; imagining his brother there? Ruth couldn't say.

But on one of these circles, Stanislaw came across the supply lads sorting through the guard block remnants: all the shoes and shaving mirrors and dressing gowns left behind by the departing Germans. Stanislaw saw there were radios, and he came to Ruth to request they be spared for him.

– Please, yes? You can put in a word?

Some of the sets were working, most were not, having been dropped or dumped or kicked to one side when the guards were evacuated – and then dropped and dumped a second time when the supply lads cleared the guard block. The lads were only too happy to hand them over, and to lend Stanislaw pliers and screwdrivers.

Now, his camp circuits completed, he sat in the sunshine outside his own tent and tinkered: taking off the backs, taking out the parts, cleaning them with oil and rags, replacing them with others. Ruth saw his new contentment when he reported to her office for duty, and the new brown across cheekbones. She liked the delight he took also, in all the small luxuries afforded him by his new translation services: bringing an extra coffee that one of the supply boys had poured him, or – even better – a slice of buttered toast to share.

– Such indulgence!

He smiled as he chewed.

There were even fresh bread rolls some mornings: a mess-tent sensation.

The town baker had been vetted by the army clerks: he'd been found clean enough to be charged with baking the rations for the townsfolk – their 400g daily bread. This new loaf allocation granted them by the English was small enough to leave room in the baker's ovens; it was a fact the major had decided to make use of, ordering rolls for the town hall, and for the DP camp staff on Fridays.

– You have to wonder what the baker made of that – don't you?

Ruth asked Stanislaw while they watched the man, parking up his van in the courtyard one morning, just across from her office windows.

It was the first time she'd seen him. He'd been sending his daughter before this, the young woman driving in through the gates here, unloading her father's bread crates. She'd been turning the sentries' heads as she did so, with her round calves, her wide hips, and her apron tied neatly around them. She went striding into the mess tent, and then the supply boys' eyes followed her as she strode back to the van again.

Her father was balding, a stout and small man. He'd come later than his daughter, Ruth noted, and he unloaded his crates, bent-backed, head down, as though he might be reprimanded for his tardiness – as though he knew he was watched too. And then he spent so long patting down the pockets of his overalls, looking for his paperwork, he even started to pain her. Ruth had to look away: she did not care to feel pain for a townsman.

Stanislaw, though: he kept watching. He let himself take in the baker's discomfort, his haplessness; this ordinary little man in his ordinary work clothes. Ruth didn't know – was the Pole enjoying it? She wasn't sure what she saw there.

Late one afternoon, three blasts on the sentries' loudhailer called Ruth to the camp gates.

Instead of finding a jeep or a truck there, and men to house in the tent rows, Ruth found two women standing there in farm skirts and aprons.

Both of them were Polish, both had worked at the same market garden, at the edge of the Heide.

– Our farm wife, she said to come here. She can't keep us.

– She showed us to the road and told us to keep walking.

After them came more – almost daily. Along with more men arriving, there came Martas and Janinas and Polinas: all farmhands and dairy girls, left to find their own way across the heathland.

– Our foreman, he said *Go! You go to the English!*

– Our farmer, he said he can't feed us. Not on his new rations.

– It's up to you English now – that's what he said.

They smiled, relieved, when the gates were opened. A few were Czechs, most were Poles and Ukrainians like the men here – but little more than girls still. Just nineteen, just twenty: young women, with young and shy ways about them, excited to be here now.

None had been evacuated in the end days.

– No, we were on the farm then.

– Oh, no: we were working still.

So at least they'd not had to suffer that.

None were sisters or cousins to the men here either – but they would be sisters and cousins to others, Ruth told herself. She was grateful to send word of them in dispatches, to be able to write in her report to the major that they hadn't been badly treated – and she was glad to be greeting Sofias now, as well as Jakubs, as she came along the duckboards in the mornings.

There was still room – just about – to house them; the male DPs made sure of this. As soon as they saw there were women arriving, they began to make space for them among the tent rows.

The men began coming to Ruth with requests too:

– You have paper? *Koperta?* Envelope?

– A pen for me to write, please?

Sight of the women had them thinking of sisters, of wives back at home still.

– I can send a letter now? Is there post?

– Your Red Cross, your English army, they can send my letter for me?

They offered their help in return: moving cots and tarpaulins, going to Farley to say they could pitch more tents; the army clerks arranged for more to be sent, and with some shifting here, some shifting there, women's quarters were founded, the camp folding itself around them.

And then, one midsummer evening, just past sundown, a Josefa was picked up by a jeep patrol.

She was found sitting by the roadside, her shoes unlaced beside her, her heels chafed open, soles bloodied with walking.

Older than the other new arrivals, she was a Pole from Silesia, and she'd left the farm up by Cuxhaven where she'd been working a few days after the surrender. Told to go to the English, she'd been trying to make her way east ever since.

– You will let me? Please?

Her feet were in ruins, ankles swollen, but she sat with Ruth in the medical station, and she asked to go further.

– I can rest only one day. One day only. I've been in Germany for two years. Too long. It is too long for anyone.

Josefa said when the Wehrmacht had come to her district, she'd been packed into a truck back with all the women, all the girls from the villages around her own one – and she'd thought that was the worst they'd do.

– But when we got to the border, they took my daughter. My Elizabieta. You understand me? They put her in a different truck, they drove her away from me. I have been waiting two years to find her. Two years! You have to let me try now.

Ruth persuaded her to sleep; she sat with her until she did.

She entered Josefa's name in the records that same night – and it appalled her anew, to see the woman's words as she typed them.

Dudek, Josefa – b. 14.07.1909
They took my daughter. Put her in a truck and drove her. She was thirteen, just thirteen. It is more than two years, I have not seen her.

Over the next days, there came others. Along with more young farm girls, there came more mothers.

Janik, Ana – b. 02.12.1911
From Wroslaw. 1943, I was taken with both my children. They were nine and six, only nine and six. Where are they?

Krupa, Natalia – b. 11.02.1913
I have a boy. Twelve years old. Before, I had him with me. Now, I don't know – I don't know!

Everyone had their lost; Ruth had almost come to expect this. But now these mothers had arrived without their children – and it floored her.

– *Kde je muj syn?*

– Where is my son?

They asked her this, in whispers, in Czech and Slovak, and in Polish.

– They took my daughter.

– *Moja córka?*

– Where did they take her?

The women looked to Ruth for answers. They'd been holding out for war's end, telling themselves their children would be safe then; as soon as the fighting was over, they'd vowed they would find a way to reach them. Now these women had been brought here.

– But my daughter?

– My boy, he must be with the English?

It was hard for Ruth to see their confusion.

– So then he is with the Americans – maybe?

Ruth started new index cards: missing sons, missing daughters; names and ages, and places last seen. She clipped each child's card to its mother's, wiring Red Cross dispatches, and requests to other holding camps, marking them urgent – *urgent*. She asked that records be searched – *as swiftly as you can manage it* – and that requests be forwarded – *as soon as possible*. She sent word to the major at the town hall; he would know who best to turn to; and then she told the mothers the Red Cross had been alerted – all the necessary authorities – so they should stay and rest and recover here. But Ruth knew they'd have to wait for replies – and for how long?

The women looked to her in the meanwhile. When she was out on her morning rounds, they asked:

– You have no word? None at all?

Josefa came in the afternoons, to sit in her office. Her feet bound, yet to heal, she murmured between her tears, between Stanislaw's soft translations. Ruth saw how her eyes searched his face as he was talking, as though looking for clues; she felt how Josefa watched her too, as though the woman thought they must know more than they told her. The English authorities, the Americans, they must have a plan – surely – where or how her daughter might be found again.

Ruth stayed late at the end of that week, writing out a further request to the major; if he could see that word was sent faster. *These women were forced here to work; their children were taken from them.* Could his Higher Ups make this a priority? There were missing children among the missing workers. *If we aren't already searching, then we ought to be.*

Stanislaw stayed with her as she typed. They'd been working and working, hardly talking, but Ruth could see how much the women's stories shocked him. Normally so neat and straight-backed, despite his years of toiling, tonight he sat with his head bowed, face grave, his good fingers folded. He could see, just as she did: there must be so many more missing children, scattered across Germany.

Stanislaw lifted his eyes when she was done.

– This country.

He shook his head.

– These people.

They let all this happen right under their noses?

8

The Sisters by the Town Woods

Brandt

He set out straight after breakfast, as soon as the curfew jeeps had passed, driving out of the lane mouth onto the Poststrasse, then letting the van roll to save on diesel. Brandt let the hill do the work, heading for the Berger place: the two old Berger sisters, on the town's far side.

They'd called on him to make a repair. Since the English had allowed him to work again, Brandt could count the jobs he'd done on his fingers: a chimney that had fallen over the winter, a drainpipe come askew at Heinrich's bakehouse, a barn door leaning on its hinges. Small work, and time consuming – but he was glad enough of any calls, and just to be out in his van again. His foot light on the pedal, eking out the quarter tank left him; his toolkit on the passenger seat, alongside his morning bread and margarine. If the roads were empty of cars, as they so often were now, he could roll as far as the Rathaus, almost.

Today, Brandt had to brake for an English jeep first, and then for three town boys flitting into a side street on their bicycles. At the Rathausplatz, he had to slow a third time as he passed the grocer's; since it had re-opened, the ration queue stretched round the corner, spilling off the kerb there. Still, Brandt's engine caught in third gear, despite it all, and he idled through the back lanes to the Bergers', arriving with the fuel gauge hardly a tick lower.

– *Ach, da sind Sie.*

Hilde Berger already had the door open as he came up the front path; her old wrists trembling, she pressed her two hands around his:

– I knew we could rely on you.

The Fräulein Bergers were old money; Lüneburg money. Hilde and Trude: the last branch of a once-grand family tree. Neither had ever married, and now they lived like old birds, on little or nothing, their grey hair plaited and wrapped about their foreheads like they were girls still.

Hilde was the younger; it was always her who greeted Brandt at the front door: warm and formal, her eyes closing as she spoke, as though with the effort of talking, her chin held inclined, gently shaking. Now she led the way through the ground floor, putting her fingers to the panelled walls to guide her, asking after the yard, and after his joiners and apprentices: *alle Ihre Jungs da*. All his boys and workers still not returned from front-line duty.

Since the English had passed Brandt's paperwork, Hilde

had called on him already once – no more than a week ago. The lock on the back door hadn't been working right; the key wouldn't turn for her old fingers, and she'd wanted an extra bolt fitted too – *zur Sicherheit*. For security.

This time, she told him it was about a cracked window, and she took him out onto the back veranda.

– There, see? The bottom pane in the scullery. Does it look like a new break to you, Brandt? I've only just noticed. Goodness only knows how it got broken.

Hilde stayed while he knocked out the shards and measured up the new glass, the old girl lingering on the veranda flags, blinking out across her gardens, as though puzzling something out for herself.

– Goodness only knows, yes.

But Brandt was already used to this. It had been the same with Heinrich, when he'd been called to the bakehouse. Brandt had gone to clear the guttering, so the baker had footed the ladder while he climbed to the top rung, and the whole time he was working, Heinrich had stood and sighed down there, fretting out loud about this delay to his day's labours, and about the English also. *They come with my flour sacks; you know I have to wait hours some mornings? But they set the rules now, don't they?* He blew his cheeks, like he didn't know what to make of this. Most of Brandt's regulars had taken to keeping him company: he worked, they stood alongside him, at a loss as to what to do with themselves. The war had ended, but life had yet to start again. Any sort of life they recognised.

Hilde Berger was no different. She stood in the shade of the house wall, looking at the sun falling across her lawn and borders, all rank and overgrown.

– But there you have it.

She sighed, and pointed.

– You see what's become of us?

The school wife would dig that whole lot over, Brandt thought, and in little more than an afternoon. Where the schoolmaster had grown his lupins, she'd planted cabbages, potatoes – and she'd started digging over the schoolhouse lawn too. She'd told Brandt this was to keep her girls fed through the autumn, but he knew it was also to keep herself occupied. She'd give her right arm for this garden here – especially for the Berger orchard.

At the far end, just before the town woods started, the Bergers had plum trees, pear and walnut, the moss-covered trunks at least as old as the sisters, the grass between them grown knee high since their gardener had been enlisted.

– And who can say when he'll be returned to us?

Hilde sighed again at the state of her gardens – at the state of everything – and then she pointed behind herself, in the direction of the Rathaus, a little anxious.

– How long until the soldiers go again, do you think?

Heinrich had asked this also – just yesterday. He'd said:

– Are they settling in here? I do wonder, Brandt. Because that's what it looks like.

There were soldiers at the hotel: the English army clerks had taken rooms there in their first days, just opposite the Rathaus. Heinrich told him there were others, too, in summer houses at the edge of the Heide. It was the new English major that had the baker wondering most, though. Because this new man in charge had chosen a villa for his residence. One of the closest to the town woods and the town works, right next to the Werkschutz commander's old apartments. The English had requisitioned that place on arrival – of course they had. They'd taken the villas either side also – and now one of them had a new English occupant. There would be no hotel room for the major, nor Heide summer house; the Englishman's choice seemed to be clear: he would be settled here a while yet.

– It just doesn't sit right with me.

Hilde made no mention of her new villa neighbour – not directly. Still, the old girl hovered, distracted, while Brandt cut the new glass for her scullery window.

– Do we need so many soldiers here? I ask you. Does our Rathaus really need guarding?

She addressed her questions to the lawn more than she did to Brandt.

– Why do the English have to stay in the town at all? They're in Hamburg, aren't they? Isn't that close enough? Goodness knows the Russians are in Berlin now.

Brandt didn't think he was required to answer. He set the new pane in place, smoothing the putty around it, just letting her talk. He wasn't too sure of the soldiers here either. The English were better than the Party men of the past years – unbearable – but why so many of them? And why the damned curfew?

The day the English had given him his papers, he'd only gone out for the sake of a first drive in peacetime. He hadn't gone far from the yard; Brandt hadn't even thought he was out beyond curfew – or if he was, it was only by minutes. And then it had been humiliating to have to explain himself to the soldiers. To a pair of English boys in uniform! They'd made him step out onto the verge to search him, rifling through his toolkit, and then his van too: peering inside his footwells, inside his glovebox – and with torches. Awful. They'd taken note of his yard name on the van doors, on the pocket of his overalls – as though even this was suspect. So Brandt felt it all the time now, when he was out and driving: a back-of-the-neck, pit-of-the gut discomfort that he had no name for yet. Like Heinrich said: it just didn't sit right. It was the kind of thing that could get to you, if you thought about it too much. So instead of responding to Hilde, Brandt turned to sweep up the last few shards of her broken window, thinking he would go soon.

Except, when he turned to pack up his tool bag, he found Trude Berger had come to join them.

Older than her sister, she was thinner also, standing propped on her stick at the back door.

– You've been talking about the English.

It wasn't a question. It came out impatient: an accusation, aimed at her sister – the old girl's ears were sharp, for all her apparent frailty, and her tongue as well. She gave Brandt a curt nod in greeting before she turned again to Hilde:

– You talk and talk, sister-mine.

– All right now, all right.

Hilde stepped forward, offering her an arm, flustered at her abruptness; she fussed to distract her, and Trude allowed herself to be helped out into their garden. But once she had both feet on the paving, she batted away her sister's fingers:

– You know why they've stayed here – the English. We both do.

Trude gestured to the end of the garden, raising her stick to point beyond the orchard – towards the town woods.

– It's because of that place. It's to work out that mess.

It took Brandt a moment to understand her – that she was gesturing towards the munition works. Trude shook her stick beyond the trees again, as if in emphasis, and then at her sister:

– I said that they would do that. Didn't I? Even before the English arrived, I said that to you.

Hilde gave no reply. Her old head still tilted, still standing with her sister, but her face was a little less mild now; she only blinked at her gestures. So Trude turned her eyes on Brandt:

– It makes my sister angry when I talk about the town works.

She spoke to him low-voiced, conspiratorial:

– Because she doesn't like it, you see? That camp the English have made there.

– Well, you don't like it either.

Hilde countered:

– You don't like it any more than I do. Don't you always tell me so? That the English should be sending those workers home?

But Trude ignored her, planting her stick in front of herself.

– My sister doesn't feel safe – you understand me? Hilde thinks it's one of the Polacks from the camp who broke that window. She insists it must have been one of the workers the English are holding there. She tells me they come into our garden.

– Well – I have seen them.

Again, Hilde put her side:

– You know this, Trude. They come after dark – I have told you – or early in the morning.

– So you say, yes. But we saw those workers before, too – didn't we? We saw them all through the war. And in any case: I want to talk to Herr Brandt here. I want to ask him while he's with us to be asking.

– But Herr Brandt has to go soon.

Hilde took her sister's arm again; she tried to take charge again:

– Herr Brandt has work to do, Trude. And anyway: we never liked the munition works. We never knew why they had to take over our factory here in the first place – the authorities. And that's all.

Still, Trude only raised her eyebrows.

– Oh, well, yes. You never did like anything these past years. Of course not.

Was she mocking her? Brandt couldn't quite make it out.

– But, sister-mine: you must remember. If the Werkschutz commander passed us? Or one of the men from the Rathaus? Didn't you always hold your arm up? Quick smart. Even if it was only halfway.

Now it was Hilde's turn to raise her eyebrows.

She pulled her mouth tight at her sister's bluntness. Dropping her arm at the way her sister spoke to her – and in company. Hilde turned to her lawns again, and Brandt would have turned back to his tool bag, only too gladly, except Trude's words had left him wary. He knew nothing about that camp, or the workers: what did she want to ask him?

– You worked for the Klebers.

This wasn't a question, either: Trude was just stating facts for the moment. Or that's what it felt like, as she turned to point again beyond the orchard, towards the munition works.

– You built those machine sheds with your joiners.

Brandt nodded. Because he had indeed built the first of them, when it was still the Kleber Werke. But that was before the war – long before all of this – when the Kleber brothers still had charge of the place. So he couldn't think quite why she would be asking.

– How many can they house, then? How many workers?

Brandt could only lift his shoulders:

– I couldn't tell you, Fräulein Berger. I didn't build the barrack blocks.

He hadn't built those hovels for the labourers; that was well after his time.

– Well, my sister says it's full now, that English camp. There are too many workers.

Again, Brandt lifted his shoulders. Still thinking of his machine sheds, and now of barracks alongside them – what a thought that was. He didn't like it. Or that these old girls would know what that looked like: from their villa wall, their villa windows, Brandt thought they must have quite a vantage.

Trude said:

– The Werkschutz. Or the authorities. They set about clearing the works here, before the war was over. They brought all those trucks – yes? – last winter. They sounded those sirens, when they came clearing workers from here and elsewhere.

She moved her fingers in a wide arc, describing the run of the Poststrasse, the path of those convoys beyond her gardens. And Brandt had heard the sirens, of course he had; he'd even seen some of those truckloads evacuated across the Heide – but Trude asked now:

– So where were they taking them?

How should he know? All Brandt remembered of those weeks was cold and no yard work, and end-days nervousness.

– They must have been taking them somewhere.

Trude continued: on she went, and without mercy:

– And all these workers here now – they could be taken somewhere else too, surely? If my sister is right, and there are too many in that camp at the munition works, then if the English can't send them home yet, perhaps they can find another place to house them. Somewhere bigger, with barracks large enough. No?

– If you say so, Fräulein Berger.

– Well, I do say, Herr Brandt. And I wanted to ask you because I thought you might have heard more.

– About the camp, Fräulein? Or the convoys?

He really didn't know about either. All he knew about the factory was from years and years ago now. But Trude was not to be halted:

– About the convoys, Herr Brandt. And the Werkschutz – or the guards who drove those transports. They made such a commotion, with those whistles and sirens, and firing off their roll-call rifles. We lived so close to that. Bad enough that we lived with that munition works, with those workers so close to us. You didn't hear where the Werkschutz were taking them?

– No. Did you, Fräulein Berger?

– No. But you heard about the convoys, though? You must have – because of the night they brought that foot transport.

A foot transport? Brandt shook his head now: he had only seen trucks pass.

– You saw workers on foot here, Fräulein Berger?

And at night time? He was doubtful, and the old girl shook her head too. But she frowned as she did so – as though frowning at being doubted – and then she narrowed her eyes as though to help herself remember rightly. Who had told her? What had she been told exactly?

– Well, we only heard the siren. We only heard the whistles blow. But we were told more afterwards. That there were workers on foot – yes. We heard there were women workers. And in any case, there was trouble that night with the Werkschutz – because didn't they call in more hands? Didn't they call in townsmen?

Townsmen?

This was news to Brandt now – and it must have shown because, for the first time, Trude looked uncertain. She glanced to her sister to confirm this.

– That's right, yes? We heard that Herr Paulsen was called out, and more too. Because we heard about the police sergeant – and that he made the call to Heinrich.

Heinrich? This was news to Brandt also: the baker hadn't said a word to him. He looked to the old girl, waiting for her to say more – but now Trude looked at him and faltered:

– He didn't tell you?

– Me? No.

– Oh.

She faltered further:

– I thought Heinrich would have done that. Or I thought someone would have told you in any case. One of your other customers.

Who to trust here? Brandt could see her turning the question over. Whose word to rely on? Town word could only tell you so much, and Trude Berger wanted to know the whole story. Who was called to the munition works, who did the calling; she'd thought Brandt might be the one to ask – except she saw now: he didn't know the half of it either.

– You must excuse me.

She looked to her sister, then to their lawns again, their orchard; then she turned her frown back towards the works again – that puzzle among the pine trees.

– No, you must excuse both of us.

Hilde stepped in there, stepping towards Brandt, reaching her palms out to take his.

– Our apologies.

She squeezed his hands with her shaking fingers.

– We've taken too much of your time, Herr Brandt. We mustn't take any more now.

Then she took him by the elbow.

– What good does it do, in any case – all this talking? All this wondering? It's as bad as having all these soldiers here. Really.

The old girl pulled her door keys from her pocket, ready to show him through the house again – ready to lock up tight once he was gone – and she asked:

– What good does it do to keep those workers here? That's the real question – don't you think so? Why must the English hold them under our noses when they should be sending them all home?

Back in his van, Brandt drove again, slowly.

Still frowning over the Bergers and their arguments; those winter transports; the idea of townsmen called out.

Hilde had seen him down the front path, handing his payment through the van door, pressing it into his palm: old notes, soft from folding, and the last of a bag of sugar cubes. But this hardly helped him. Those Reichsmarks, as good as worthless; those sugar morsels, dug out of a jar at the back of their kitchen shelves. And then, at the Poststrasse turning, Brandt only frowned all the further when he found himself looking towards the munition works.

It was years since he'd been inside there. Brandt still knew the place from old, though. Not just the machine sheds, but also the factory courtyard, the factory offices that looked out across the compound.

He thought of Kleber senior at his desk there. Solid and suited, and just about as old as those two sisters. Brandt's yard had been young then, but Kleber had offered him good terms, the man rising to his feet, in his waistcoats, ceremonious, sealing each of their agreements with a handshake after Brandt had signed his yard name in the factory order books.

The last war just over, and the hunger years only just passing, Brandt would have taken any and all work – but those Kleber orders had been important. Each one an endorsement, bringing in further work from townsmen and heath farmers. They'd allowed him to take on more hands. In time, he'd begun to have standing. More than this: Brandt had known, for the first time, the kind of pride this brought a man. Having his yard name painted on the van doors, machine-embroidered onto his apprentices' overalls.

After Kleber senior's passing, his brother took over. Just as solid as the older man, but with new ideas for the new era – or this was what he'd told Brant, the first time he'd called him into the factory office. Young Kleber had been sent to school in Lüneburg, to university in Hamburg, and he'd managed the works at arm's length, along with others he'd bought with his brother's inheritance. Still, if building repairs were needed on the town works, he'd seen that Brandt was called. *For old time's sake.* He'd smiled. Or: *in memory of my brother.* Always some sentiment along the same lines.

After the war came, though, and young Kleber had turned the factory over to armaments, it was other yards he'd called on to build the new machine sheds, the barrack blocks. It was men from Lüneburg, from Hamburg, who'd got those contracts.

– *Ach.* They'll all have Party badges. Won't they?

That's what the schoolmaster had told Brandt. To ease his disappointment; to show his disapproval too, as they stood at the yard wall, talking things over at the end of their workdays.

– Those other yard owners, they'll all be the same kind.

And probably he was right too.

Young Kleber was known for his low Party number; salutes had long replaced handshakes in the factory offices; Brandt had had to brace himself before each of his visits to the works – and there was a time, not so far into the war, that he'd gone almost monthly. Swallowing his pride, and his discomfort, requesting that his yard be reconsidered as a supplier. *For old time's sake?* He'd even got the ferry to Hamburg, to see young Kleber there in private. But no contract had come out of it.

– Better it's other fingers that are dirtied.

The schoolmaster had shrugged his shoulders.

Except Brandt hadn't been able to shrug it off so easily.

It had annoyed him, even, that his neighbour could just dismiss that loss of business. Lines were fine things to draw, especially when they left you feeling on the side of the righteous. But food on the table was a fine thing also – and unlike his neighbour, Brandt could ill-afford such high-mindedness.

Didn't he remember hunger years?

Brandt had been a journeyman after the last war, paid his day's work in his day's bread – and no more than that – because even his masters had been hungry. And now it was wartime – again, again, it was wartime – so Brandt could hardly afford to lose orders, not when he was already losing men to the Wehrmacht. It was only yard work that paid his way in life; only his yard contracts, and perhaps – in the schoolmaster's eyes – this made him a small man with a small man's outlook. But his neighbour had seemed naive to Brandt: too satisfied with his own rightness, like a boy still.

Besides, the yards that had got those contracts were all larger. They could work at a scale Brandt simply couldn't match. Those other yard owners had the command he'd always lacked. And so – Party badge or not – Brandt knew he'd been surpassed. He'd been too wounded to drive past the Kleber works for some time after that.

Now, making the turning, he looked at the road stretching long beyond the Bergers', flanked by the town woods and that high wall. And then he glanced at it again, in his rear-view mirror, unable to shake the place. Brandt saw the high gates – unmistakable – and a jeep parked outside them. And then that jeep had him thinking of soldiers. Of English boys in uniform. Searching through his footwell, his glove box; digging out the Party lists in the Rathaus.

Lists just like those would be dug out all over now, Brandt told himself: everywhere the English came to, including the offices at the works there. Those Lüneburg timber yards, those Hamburg brick merchants: their names would be inked into the Kleber order books – and had the English already found them? All those true believers – and all those others who'd raised their arms in the interests of business – were they somewhere on an arrest list?

Then Brandt thought of his own arm raised – only halfway, but raised all the same – in all his last meetings with young Kleber. It could have been his own name inked on those pages, his own fingers dirtied, so easily.

And what would the schoolmaster say to that? Brandt had to ask himself.

That he'd got off lightly? That he'd been saved by circumstance? Saved from himself, even?

He and Hilde Berger: both cut from the same coward cloth. Saluting whenever salutes were called for, and yet still pretending – even to themselves – that they weren't the kind to do that.

And what about the townsmen called to the works there?

Brandt would rather not think about that if he could help it.

He'd rather not have heard any of what the Bergers had told him this morning. Still, the old girls had one thing right, he decided. The English should close that camp of theirs, take the workers far from here. They should leave that factory to rot, he decided; the roofs to fall in, the walls of the machine sheds as well as the hovels alongside them. Let the trees grow tall around the compound, the trunks and branches of the town woods, the ivy. He'd like to see the place emptied and silent.

Nearing home again, the head of the lane in sight, Brandt saw the schoolmaster's daughters. The two of them in the long grass, one on each side of the letterbox at the corner.

Young Freya would have ridden them there; Brandt saw her passing the yard almost daily, checking for post from their father, and then riding home again, empty-handed. The same was happening again this morning, Brandt thought, because Freya began lifting her sister onto her handlebars as he drew closer, bumping her back along the lane ruts.

So then he had to rouse himself. Brandt had to pull over, push the van door open.

The children gone again, he took the Berger sugar bag from the seat beside him, opening the mailbox, placing it inside there. And then – for all his own heaviness – it was good to imagine those young sisters when they found it. To think of eyebrows raised in surprise, not scorn this time, or disbelief.

Brandt thought of the schoolmaster's daughters, each with a cube in her cheek, smiling and riding homewards.

And then, climbing back into his van again, Brandt told himself – at least their father hadn't been cowardly. When it came to it, hadn't the schoolmaster kept his daughters out of this? It was the one small good he could point to, in among the rest, in amongst this mess.

July

9

Good News

Ruth

– The back wall will have to be knocked down.

Farley gave Ruth the news over breakfast, pushing a map of the compound across the mess table, tapping at the pencil lines he'd crossed through the rear boundary.

– The major has given the go ahead. We're to take out that whole stretch. Make room for more hut rows.

Since he'd made himself plain in her new quarters, he'd been giving Ruth's office a wide berth, speaking to her only on the duckboards, on her tent rounds, or like this at mealtimes. Farley had kept his distance since the women arrived especially, giving Ruth charge of them while he got on with the rest of the camp business, relaying orders only in passing – even important news like this.

– So it'll be gone by tomorrow evening.

He tapped the lines on the map again, already impatient to be on his way, so Ruth looked up at him, delaying him a moment.

– Won't the factory owner object?

Farley had to know she wouldn't be passed over so easily. He let the supply lad answer for him, though, giving only a brief raised eyebrow.

– Well, he might. Won't do him much good.

The soldier gave Ruth a grin as Farley turned to go again.

– Good thing prison walls are thick, ma'am. Good thing we don't have to listen to him in any case.

The owner had been tracked down in Hamburg; he'd been arrested. Ruth found the dispatch from the major when she got to her office.

– He'll be sitting in a cell there!

She held out the page to show Stanislaw as he arrived for duties. Good news to start the day with.

Once the back wall was down (to much loud DP cheering!) the camp opened onto the water meadows beyond it – broad and welcome, bright with flowers and grasses. Farley had Nissen huts thrown up, the new land wide enough for whole rows of them. *A small town's worth*, he called it.

For days, there was sawing and hammering, until Ruth could follow the duckboard paths beyond the old line of the factory wall, all the way to the millrace that marked the new boundary. Its waters came running down the slope above the munition works – cool from the shade of the pine trees, from the town woods. The early summer days all unfailingly beautiful, the DPs crouched at the banks, washing their shirts and trousers, and then they spread them out to dry across the new curved hut roofs, the corrugated iron warm under the sun's rays.

The Poles took the near quarter, the Ukrainians the far one; soon there were flags hoisted, or tacked to the hut entrances. The Czechs and the Italians spread themselves between the tents that remained, agreeing to stay under canvas so the women might have their own Nissen row, as the major had ordered. To Ruth's eyes, it made a fine sight, this new and larger camp: like a continent in miniature.

An expanded camp meant more arrivals, of course; the major sent word to be prepared. He had the first set of medics returned to Bremen, to be relieved by a new group on their way to replace them. But a few days passed first, where Ruth and Stanislaw had no one new to register.

They spent these with the mothers, in the women's hut row, at the border between the Polish and the Ukrainian quarters. Making the new huts homely: stringing washing lines from wall to wall inside, draping tarpaulins over these at intervals, marking out small cubicles. The rooms these made were rough and improvised, but at least they offered some peace, some privacy.

The men in the surrounding rows kept a respectful distance at first. Raising their hats as the women passed along the duckboards, or leaving gifts at the hut entrances. Spare pillows and blankets, or sugar portions and tea leaves, skimmed from their rations and wrapped in twists of paper.

The young women who'd been here longest gathered

wildflowers from the millrace. *So it will make the huts nicer, yes?* Ruth helped them scrub out ration tins to serve as vases, and after they'd put the sprays on the mothers' bedside lockers, it did make the cubicles a little cheerier.

When the younger women saw that, they wanted to gather more. Tucking up their skirts, they went splashing through the waters to pick at the far side of the millrace: bellflowers from the meadows and quaking grasses; late violas and celandines from the edge of the town woods. They climbed up and up the slope in the afternoon, passing into the pine trees, and Ruth watched them disappearing between the trunks there, pleased by their chatting and gathering.

But when she finished up in her office, and they hadn't returned yet, she found herself watching the slope for sign of them.

Ruth caught herself glancing at the trees, too, from her guard block windows, after she'd retired to her room there, the end of her day turning anxious. Until she heard voices:

– *Ofitserka! Ofitserka!*

Ruth opened the casement to find all the young women gathered below on the courtyard: a cluster of smiles in the evening light, calling up to her, delighted.

– Good evening, our Officer Novak!

They'd spent the whole long afternoon exploring, and now they'd sought out Stanislaw, pulling him along the duckboards to relay their findings.

– They found the old mill wheel.

He smiled up at Ruth from the crowd there, as though the excitement had caught him also.

– It's just at the top of the millrace, among the pine trees.

Too old to be working. But the place has a mill pool, and a weir too.

And that wasn't all.

– *Bil'she.*

– *Bil'she!*

The women urged him, trying to speed the translation, their voices calling across his own, in Polish, in Ukrainian.

– Not so fast; not so fast.

Stanislaw had to laugh; he had to lift his palms.

– They say they found a mill stream too.

– *Strumok!*

– A stream – *tak!*

They called out, still calling over him, while Ruth leaned on the sill to hear more.

– The water is warm like a bath, they say. They swam and swam half the afternoon – and not a soul from the town in sight.

– *Tak! Piękny.*

– *Tak!*

– They want you to know it is wonderful. They will go again tomorrow.

– *Zavtra!*

– *Won-der-ful!*

In the morning, the young ones set out early, heading out to paddle in the waters, to eat a ration picnic at the stream banks – only for a foot patrol to turn them back again.

– We found them in the pine trees.

Farley stopped Ruth on the duckboards:

– Your new Polish girls. They have to be told. They can't

stray all over. Just because the back wall is down, doesn't mean they can go roaming. Just because the stream banks are empty of townsfolk, doesn't mean the place is theirs now.

Then a jeep patrol, out early in the morning, found a pair of Ukrainians – male DPs this time – on the Poststrasse.

– At the bend where the town villas start. You know the one?

The major came to the camp to meet with Farley, and Ruth was called in to attend. Both men were already deep in talk when she arrived with Stanislaw, the major telling the sergeant:

– They had their pockets full of chocolate bars, your Ukrainians. More in their jacket linings.

He'd brought their haul in a gunny sack; he placed it on Farley's desk.

– I'd say those Ukrainian boys were out trading: swapping this lot for American cigarettes – wouldn't you?

Packets were bartered now among the townsfolk; the major told them, weary:

– Only so much my patrol teams can do. I'm sure you have your share of trading in the camp here.

There was no need to answer; no point in pretending either: the man would have seen enough in his years of soldiering; he'd know how things worked when supplies were short. Now he went on:

– Those Ukrainian lads. I'm told they were waiting at the roadside, so they must have a contact. Outside the camp, I mean. So do you know anything, sergeant? Because either it's a townsman – or it's one of mine at the town hall.

Ruth could see which one the major would rather.

– I'll look into it, sir.

Farley nodded, but offered no further comment.

Ruth thought it wouldn't be unheard of: one of the army clerks seeking ways to top up his wages. But didn't the same go for the supply lads? She glanced at Farley, to see if he knew more than he was letting on, but the man's face was unreadable.

The major turned his gaze on Stanislaw:

– Have you heard, perhaps? Who brings in these cigarettes?

– Me, sir?

Stanislaw was taken aback – Ruth also, to see the old Pole addressed so directly.

– I am afraid not, sir. I haven't. I really can't help you.

The major nodded, short.

But then he looked to Ruth a moment, as though for a signal: should this translator's word be trusted? She saw a first flash of impatience in the man – not just war-weariness: who to rely on here?

He told Farley:

– The DPs. Everyone in the camp. They just have to know who is in charge. At the moment, I'm afraid they're making us look like amateurs.

He turned to Ruth, too, before he left.

– If we are to believe them, Officer Novak, those Ukrainians only went out to pick flowers this morning. And all for your new female arrivals.

– Flowers for the new women, my arse.

This was what Farley said, after the major had gone again, and it was just him and Ruth and Stanislaw.

– Those lads are making up claims and nonsense. That they only got up at dawn, for one, so the flowers would be dew fresh. *Dew fresh.* They told my patrol boys the chocolate was for your women as well. Saved up from their rations to surprise them.

Ruth wasn't sure which part annoyed him more – being given the run-around by the Ukrainians, or being pulled up by the new major. But the DPs were getting the brunt of it.

– Hearts of gold, they have. Butter wouldn't melt, and all that.

He shoved the sack of bars across to Ruth, gesturing to her to take them, and then he lifted his chin to the doorway, sending her and Stanislaw on their way again.

Ruth divided the chocolate between the women's huts, placing half a bar on each bedside cabinet, and she took the few weeds and grasses the Ukrainian men had picked, adding them to the tin vases. The mothers sat up from their blankets, smiling at these offerings, and at the story of their origin – Ruth's Polish just about good enough now to relay it all.

– They got up early? And for us?

– Well, that's what they *said*.

– Oh! So kind, so *kind*, those boys.

Stanislaw kept to one side.

Ruth wasn't entirely sure he approved of her joking – or perhaps it was the major's impatience that still sat uneasy. Because when he and Ruth left again, some of the younger women were outside: the would-be swimmers and explorers, sitting barefoot in the warm grass, passing an American cigarette between them, and Stanislaw murmured,

– They'll have to get better at hiding that.

*

But the next afternoon brought the best news.

Two trucks turned in through the yard gate, and Ruth was there with the supply boys, with Stanislaw, to receive them. The first was open-sided, full of farmhands, men in their forties. But when she lifted the canvas from the second, Ruth found two young faces at the tailgate.

A boy of seven – no more than that – looking out at her. A girl of sixteen, seventeen beside him.

Two children among the labourers!

Stanislaw stepped up to the truck back, turning to Ruth as he did so – *Look!*

She felt the same prickling shock, the same sudden lift inside her. *We found some. We found some!*

Each with an OST badge stitched to their clothing; each with freckles across their cheeks and forearms. They were brother and sister, these two young Ukrainians, Ruth was sure of it. Hair like sand, eyes dark like wood – each like a version of the other. But it wasn't just their sand and freckled likeness that struck her, it was the way the sister held the boy, her fingers gripped to his young shoulder.

Farley was giving out orders; the labourers were climbing out of the truck back with their bundles, but the children hadn't stirred yet. DP after DP pressed past them, and the girl kept holding back, mistrustful – gripping the shirt cloth between her brother's shoulder blades, as though she thought someone might snatch him.

Then Ruth heard the calling:

– Dzieci?

– Dzieci!

She turned and found women coming into the courtyard.

– *Ofitserka?*

Josefa was the first one. Hurrying out of the hut rows, imploring.

– *Moje dziecko?*

Somehow she must have heard there were children, and now she was heading straight for Ruth with her palms raised.

Is she here?

– *Moje Elizabieta?*

My daughter?

Ruth had to take her hands and hold them; she had to press her fingers to still their trembling. But already more and more women were following: Natalia and Ana, and so many others behind them. How had word spread so fast?

The boy and his sister were still in the truck back, but even they turned now, to see the women pressing their way along the duckboards. The news had pulled them from their Nissen quarters, from their beds even, as swift as their bare feet could walk; their faces so hopeful, eyes searching.

– *Moje dzieci?*

They only stopped when they saw the two children – and then they stared and stared.

10

A Camp Son and Daughter

Sasha

None of those women was his mother.

All the looking and the asking, it got too much for Sasha.

First he was in the courtyard with all those strangers, crowding around him and Yeva, looking hard into both their faces. Then he was led away along wooden pathways, but with the women keeping stride. And even after they'd been taken out of that crush – after he and Yeva were brought to a hut with two short bed rows and no one else inside it – still there were new women coming all the time. Pressing themselves into the doorway, at the windows; calling out in Ukrainian, but in words he did not understand too; speaking and shouting in all languages.

There were so many people watching them and whispering.

Listening to everything they were asked; everything Yeva answered:

– We were with our mother.

– When?

– Until last year, when they took her.

– Who did?

– The overseers. The Germans that came to the garment works. I don't know. I don't know where she is now.

Ne znayu. Ne znayu.

I don't know when, I don't know who.

Yeva had to say this – so many times – while the soldiers watched them, while the women came and went at the doorway.

The tall one with the Red Cross uniform – the *Ofitserka* – she stayed with them the longest. She spoke quietly – but in words that did not sound right. She had to turn all the time to the man beside her to get her words straight – to the one with the grey hair who Sasha wasn't sure of. The man could speak Ukrainian: at least he could do that. But he'd lifted Sasha from the truck back without asking, although anyone could see he was with Yeva – that his sister was there and holding on to him.

Now the tall *Ofitserka* and this grey man, they stayed and stayed, and they asked and they asked.

Not just about Sasha's mother – not just about overseers and Germans – but also about all the places Yeva said they'd been taken.

– Where was this?

And:

– Do you remember?

And:

– Did you see other children there? How many mothers? How many sisters and brothers?

It made Sasha angry.

He sat with his sister, on the bed where they were to sleep now. Sasha kept himself pressed into Yeva's straight back and her stillness while she gave her answers, while the doorway women stared at them. Those women stared at all of him: his arms and his fingers; his knees and his ears. Sasha kept his eyes turned away, but he could feel them. What did they want? He tried to sit patient – to sit as still as Yeva, and as straight as her also – until he just couldn't any longer. Until he had to crawl behind her where no eyes would be able to look.

Sasha crept under the blankets. He'd have crawled under the bed, too, if he'd thought Yeva would let him. He would have pressed himself under the floorboards, under the grass and the earth and away from here. Far from this new place they'd been brought to.

When Yeva pulled off the blankets, the women were gone again. Even the *Ofitserka*.

There were two plates of soup, two spoons, and Sasha was hungry.

But before Yeva would let him eat, she took the blankets and hung them from the wall hooks; she hung them all around their new beds – and then it really was just the two of them.

It was getting dark by that time; even darker once their bowls were empty, and Yeva had used a damp rag to wipe Sasha's face clean and his palms. They'd been left a wash bowl, wide and blue enamel, and the water was cooling, slopping over the sides onto the floor each time Yeva dipped the cloth. The soap smelled like medicine, between his fingers, behind his ears, even after she'd wiped it away again. When Yeva crouched down to wash herself, to comb her plaits out with her fingers, Sasha undressed like she told him, folding his jerkin, his shirt and trousers like their Mama had taught him, laying them ready for the morning. His sister would fold them again later, properly, smoothing out the creases with the heels of her hands, Sasha knew this, because he had watched Yeva do this most evenings since their mother was taken. And when he saw the creases she'd made in his shirt earlier – still deep in the cloth from when she'd held on to him in the courtyard – he thought Yeva would have to smooth hardest there.

Sasha had been given his own bed to sleep in. But the sheets were stiff and cool against his bare toes; he didn't know yet what to think of this place. Or even what kind of place it was. So once Yeva lay down, he slipped across the floorboards and climbed in next to her.

She was elbows and knees and shoulders; his sister was all angles. But she allowed it. Yeva even put one arm around him. And it was good then, in the quiet just before sleeping.

Beyond the blanket walls, Sasha heard women coming in through the doorway. Footsteps soft and careful, so as not to disturb, they climbed into the beds all around them.

Sasha didn't know how long he and Yeva would have to stay now – but he knew they would not have to work. Yeva had told him it was the End of All That. She had promised him there would be No More Germans.

*

Time was, there had been three of them. Sasha and Mama and Yeva. They had been moved on and moved on, in trains and on trucks, to different places, always different bunk-houses and dormitories. But at night, he'd had his sister and his mother, and Sasha had always slept in a bed with one or the other.

One place he remembered, they'd had bunks under a sloping ceiling. A warm stovepipe, too, that ran into the rafters next to the bedstead. There, his Mama had been the one who'd hung the blankets, so that the warm of the pipe and the dark of the woollen walls surrounded them.

Around those walls there were others: so many sisters and mothers. Sasha could hear them as he lay in bed at night: talking and settling and snoring. Women who were young like his Mama, or older like aunties – or even older, like grandmas. There were bunk rows and bunk rows: a whole dormitory.

Yeva slept on the slats above, Sasha with his Mama down below, curled into her breathing. He didn't remember, though, how they'd been brought there. Sasha didn't remember too much of what had been before that. Or before that, either: he was still too small then. He only knew there was war with the Germans, and until that was over, his Mama and Yeva had to do war work for them.

They sewed uniforms for German soldiers.

All those mothers and sisters did, who'd lived in that dormitory; all the aunts and grandmothers also.

The overseer came for them in the mornings, to take them to the big halls with the sewing machines. But he would not take Sasha. If his Mama tried to slip Sasha past, the man spoke harsh words; he cut their evening rations, too. So his Mama buttoned Sasha's shirt in the mornings; she rubbed the wash-cloth across his cheeks and fingers; then she and Yeva, they went working – and Sasha, he stayed in the dormitory all the long day.

There were three of them left there: Sasha and two girls – both small like he was. They swept with the twig brush where their mothers had told them: where the overseer had ordered. They swept in all the nooks and the corners, crouching and crawling, and all along the spaces between the bunk rows.

It must have been summer then, because it was hot. The days were much longer than the sweeping work. So when the twig brushing was done with, Sasha and the two girls, they hid in the cool dark underneath the bedsteads, tying cat's cradles with their laces, or watching for the spiders that crawled up the bunk legs. They let them crawl along their fingers, across their palms – as far as they dared.

The sunlight from the high and small windows, it crawled across the floor too, but so slowly, and it got so stuffy in there under the rafters.

Those windows were not for opening. But if Sasha climbed up to one of the top bunks, he could just about see out of them. The two girls didn't like to do that: climb onto other mothers' beds, over other grandmothers' clothes and blankets. So they stayed on the floor and watched, while Sasha said what he saw. Clouds and chimneys, city rooftops; tram wires and trams and people inside them; church spires and birds flying. He didn't remember: while they were there, did he ever go outside?

When the factory whistle sounded, then Sasha knew the

mothers and the sisters would come soon. They came from their factory duties, from the ration queues; he remembered the rush of them through the doors, their faces tired and hard in the evening light.

There were only three stoves for all of them in the dormitory. The mothers and the older girls were meant to take it in turns, except it didn't always work that way. Sasha saw mothers who shoved and shouted, mothers who cursed. *You should be cursing the Germans!* His own Mama kept clear of them, kept her back turned. She warned Yeva to do the same, and Sasha. His Mama peeled potatoes while she waited; she and Yeva, crouching over the pot, always in the stove queue that was quietest, and she turned Sasha's face away, firm, with her fingers, so he couldn't even look at the ones who swore.

Sometimes his Mama brought back extra rations from lunch. Food that the German workers had left. A slice of bread that she'd slipped up her blouse cuffs; the end of a sausage, wrapped in a cloth scrap and buried in her pocket. His Mama cooked for them, whatever she had brought. Then she hung the blankets back across their bunk row and they ate, straight from the pot, sitting around it on the floor.

Sasha didn't know how long they were there for.

His Mama kept their bags packed, their spare clothes folded.

Last thing at night, she laid out their clothes for the morning, smoothing and folding – and then she tied everything else into their bundles, even the cooking pot, rinsed out and dried. Because all the time, they had new bunk neighbours; new women with hard and tired faces; new grandmothers and sisters who went again.

The two girls Sasha swept with: they were gone one morning, and their grandmother also, and then he had no one to sweep alongside him.

– We have to be ready – always.

His Mama cautioned him and Yeva.

They might be moved on to another place, another factory, without warning. So she knotted their bundles, she combed and plaited Yeva's hair each night with swift fingers, and said:

– We will go together, yes?

When it happened, their whole bunk row was chosen.

They were taken outside, across open concrete, told to climb into trucks that drove them. Sasha's Mama kept him on one side, Yeva on the other, their bags held tight on her lap, while the guards drove through the city roads first, and then even further: out to where the buildings stopped and there was farmland. Sasha peered with Yeva through the truck slats, blinking at the fields they passed, high with wheat, with potatoes.

– Are we to help now with the harvest?

The women around them whispered and murmured, because those fields were full of crop but empty of workers.

– All the German farmhands – think of it. They must have been sent to be soldiers.

The woman nearest Sasha grumbled at the thought:

– First we sew their uniforms. Now we do their farm work for them.

But others told her: *no, no* – this was good news.

– Think about it – think harder!

– If they have to send their farm boys to the fighting, that must be bad news for the Germans.

– Yes, yes: it means their war is going badly for them.

But all the talk stopped when the trucks did.

They had come to a square full of people: lines of Ukrainians with patches; huddles of Germans gathered at the edges, most in farm overalls.

The Germans in uniform started going from truck back to truck back with their clipboards, calling names out, pulling women out also. Sasha's Mama had their bags on her lap still, and their bundle; she'd laid out their papers, open and ready on top of everything. Now she took hold of Sasha's shoulder, hooking her elbow into Yeva's so they would go together – *yes*.

But when the truck back was opened, when her name was called, it all fell out of her arms. Their papers and their bundle, the cooking pot: all of it sent tumbling.

This is how Sasha remembered it.

His Mama was taken by the elbow – his Mama was taken without them – and she was hauled out so fast, Yeva had to hold on tight to his jerkin to stop Sasha falling after. He almost tipped over the tailgate and onto the paving – clang! Like the pot had. It was only Yeva who saved him. And then by the time he was upright, he couldn't see his Mama – not anywhere. Only the crowds and crowds of workers; only their bundle spilled open, their papers blown about the place, the cooking pot still rolling.

Sasha could feel his sister still holding him.

Each time a new farmer came that afternoon, a new German in uniform, Yeva gripped him tighter between his shoulder blades. The Germans came looking into the truck back, but none of them brought Sasha's Mama back, or took them to her, and he couldn't understand why not. *We go together – yes?* That's what his Mama said. She would not go without them. But the farmers who came to look them over, and the Germans who called the names out, they took only the older ones. Hour by hour, they took all the women and the older girls.

It was Herr Maas who took Sasha and Yeva – eventually. He came and looked at them with his old face, lop-sided.

– *Die beiden?*

He stood in his drooping overalls, blinking his drooping eyelids. And he asked the guards:

– *Was soll ich mit denen nu machen?*

Like he didn't know what he was supposed to do with two children.

But he took them in his farm cart; he kept them through the harvest, the winter, and even when the summer came again. Was it only one summer they were with him or more than that?

They worked in his milk parlour, slept in his barn – again they were under rafters, this time on straw mattresses with wool blankets to cover them. When it was cold, Herr Maas climbed the ladder, stiff and slow, to bring more. He spoke so stiff and slow as well, Sasha began to understand the few words he said. *Junge* was boy. *Nein* was no. *Iss nun* meant he should eat up. They ate in his kitchen, and it was always just the three of them. His wife was a black-rimmed photo on the wall; his grown son in the photo next to it, in uniform.

When Sasha saw it, he thought his Mama might have sewn that tunic. His Mama must be sewing somewhere else now. Sasha thought his Mama might come to the farm, even, that she might just be there one morning. But she never was.

And he cried so much there at first, Yeva had to keep him close at all times. When she collected the eggs, when she cooked Herr Maas his breakfasts, even while she did the milking. Her forehead pressed to the cow's flank like Herr Maas had shown them, she pulled Sasha down to crouch next to her, turning his face away, firm, from the old farmer, who worked at the cow's flank in the stall opposite.

– Don't you let him see that crying.

This is what Yeva whispered.

– Don't you make him angry – you hear me?

Because if Herr Maas got tired of Sasha's tears, he might send them away again, that's what Yeva thought.

– We might get sent anywhere.

So Sasha had to press his eyes with his knuckles, crouching in the cow stall beside her, trying to press the tears back hard enough.

Sasha didn't like to remember that.

Even now, while he lay in the new bed with Yeva, he didn't like to think of it. Only of what Yeva always told him – that their Mama was here still.

– She is in Germany.

Yeva had said it at the farmer's place, on nights when Sasha lay wakeful; if he crawled across the straw to press himself against her, then she whispered that their Mama would find them.

– You'll see.

It's what she'd told Herr Maas, too, when he'd said the war was over. When he'd come into the barn to tell them so.

– And what do I do with you now – you children?

Yeva had looked up at him,

– You let us go where our mother is.

She'd said the same to the English soldiers who'd brought them here. And now she'd said it this afternoon, to the *Ofitserka*; Sasha had heard her.

– Our Mama will find us – or we will find her.

His sister was so sure, it made Sasha certain. Even when the Red Cross woman had looked at both of them, careful.

– It is best that you stay here, though. For now, at least.

Yeva had whispered to Sasha afterwards:

– Until our Mama comes only. Or until we can go to her.

She'd told him there were mothers at the camp here, looking for their children; she'd worked out that much. So there would be more mothers just like them – *just like ours* – still all over Germany. They could be so near.

11

A Town Boy on the Heide

Freya

She'd seen a letter come – the first since war's end.

Freya been riding the lane ruts, out on her own for once, when a jeep stopped at the lane mouth. It had pulled up at the box there; a soldier had climbed out with an envelope, and Freya had felt the heat in her cheeks rising, despite herself. A letter – after all these months – and she was the one to see it arriving!

But it was just from the army clerks at the Rathaus: a sheet of paper giving the order for Herr Brandt to go labouring.

– He's been assigned to a work detail.

Freya's Mama told her afterwards.

– It'll be at the rail line.

The tracks across the heathland had been hit last

winter – after one of the last Hamburg air raids. The same night they'd bombed the harbour refinery, the English had taken out the bridge too, at the old ford across the Heide brook. One of the pilots had dropped the end of his load as he flew over, to save on fuel on the homeward turn for London, and those bombs hit the heath line and the rail bridge.

Freya's Mama told her, tight-mouthed:

– So they've made trouble for themselves now, haven't they?

The English had to carry supplies by road, driving them out here from Hamburg, and this meant taking the long route to skirt the Heide, or using the ford as a short cut. Their trucks lumbered down the embankment and through the brook waters, before lurching – precarious – up the other side, wheels churning in the sandy bank soil. Freya had seen them when she was out and riding with Ursel; she'd taken her sister to the brook one hot afternoon, thinking to play in the cool under the bridge ruins – except a truck had tipped onto its side there, stranded on the far bank, so they'd stopped at a distance to watch the aftermath. The embankment collapsed, the truck's axle broken, the ration crates tipped out across the rubble and water. All the week's flour sacks for Heinrich's bakery lay split open in the shallows – and the English soldiers stood around the stranded vehicle, hands on heads and laughing in bewilderment.

So now Herr Brandt had been called upon, along with a group of old townsmen – *old remnants*, he called them. His days were spent back-filling the craters, and Freya saw his evening returns: stiff-backed and slow down the yard lane.

In the mornings, though, he was up and waiting for the English works truck at the lane corner – and when Freya's

Mama saw him heading out there at the end of his first week's toiling, she'd sent Freya running after him with an offering.

– Take this – quick.

The meals her Mama made were all the same now: bread and margarine, and never enough. But Herr Brandt had brought a gift to the schoolhouse, just the day before; just after returning from his new labours.

– I've got extra rations for my pains – look.

He'd stood at the front door, stiff-shouldered, and handed it to Freya: his first new ration loaf.

– From the English. From me to you, child.

So her Mama had cut two good slices – so thick, it made Herr Brandt snort when Freya held them out to him in their napkin parcel.

– That'll last me through the workday and beyond!

Except, when Freya glanced back, he'd already taken out the first slice. He was breaking it in half at the lane mouth, eating it while he was waiting for the soldiers.

They still had the heel left the next afternoon.

So Freya rode out with it to the Heide brook, thinking Herr Brandt might be there.

The house and garden chores completed, their Mama had retreated to the sofa, as always, and Ursel had lain down beside her. So Freya had gone into the larder. She'd unwrapped the bread heel from the paper, spreading it with margarine; she'd sprinkled it with sugar too – crumbling one of the ration cubes – before sliding it into her apron. When she got to the bridge, though, the men must have been sent to another stretch, because the brook was empty.

Freya stopped a while anyway. Wading in the calf-deep waters, enjoying the cool damp on her skirt hems, and the way her splashes echoed under the bridge shadows. The sun fell through the bomb gaps in shafts, and she sat on a boulder between them, her feet in the water, chewing the bread heel. Freya tasted the sugar-sweet, enjoying the crunch of it between her teeth – and she thought she was alone too, the whole time. But when she climbed back up the far side of the embankment, she found a boy there. A town son.

Benno?

He was one of the youngest; he'd been at school with Freya the longest: until just last year. Benno had gone off to the grammar school just like his brother; he'd put on his new shirt and neckerchief, just like all the others, and Freya hadn't seen him in she didn't know how long. She hadn't even thought of him in months now – only of Udo – only of his brother, and if he still rode around the Rathausplatz now the English were patrolling.

But here was Benno, sudden and awkward, stopped on his bicycle, as though she'd surprised him. He had heath sand on his palms and in his hairline, as though he'd been out here all day somehow. It was strange to find a town boy on the Heide. And to see him grown rough and sunburned under the blue sky, in a hand-me-down shirt too large for him.

– Hey Freya.

Benno was the first to speak: shy, while she brushed at the crumbs on her chin and her apron.

– Hey yourself.

– I've seen you on the heath paths.

Now Freya felt herself frowning; how often had Benno been out here?

It still didn't feel right to her: a town boy on the Heide, and maybe Benno saw that, because he plucked at the grass heads beside him, a little tongue-tied, while Freya picked up her bicycle. But then he went on anyway:

– I've been coming out this way. So I've seen you with your sister. When you ride with her.

Freya wasn't sure she liked this, either – being seen without knowing it. She started wheeling her bicycle; Freya started thinking about Udo too: his loose way of riding, his satchel slung across his handlebars. Had he seen her also? And the rest of those town sons? She thought of how he laughed – and how this set off all of them – and then Freya felt the heat rush to her cheeks again, so fast, she had to throw a checking glance behind herself, to see if Benno saw this. But he was still caught up in talking, falling into stride beside her.

– I came here already once this morning.

Freya could see from his palms that he'd been climbing.

– I went up the viewpoint – the dolmens – remember?

Benno pointed up towards the high slopes, to where her Papa used to take them with his classes, to see the shrubs and sand paths, and where the Heide folk of old lived and died and wandered.

– I was up there early.

Benno kept on. His shirtsleeves rolled over his forearms, their bicycle wheels clicking between them, he told Freya more too, about all the other places he went to; it sounded like he'd been ranging all over. And Freya thought it sounded like he came alone here, because he made no mention of Udo, or any of the other boys.

– The high track is the best. You know?

Benno offered a small smile, a little proud maybe, that he knew this about the Heide.

– Right up at the top there: where the sheep are sent for summer grazing? Well, I see them graze up there without the shepherds now, like they still know where to go without them.

He said all this a little shy still, a little rushed, like he knew this was odd for a town son. And then he asked:

– I could take you? It's not too far.

Benno pointed to assure her, and Freya found herself irked again – as if she didn't know the Heide!

– Or we could go tomorrow – maybe?

He tried another time. But Freya walked faster, too annoyed to answer.

When they reached the lane, Benno was still just behind her.

Her Mama was leaning on the yard gate, talking to Herr Brandt, and Freya saw how she straightened at the sight of this town son.

– You've brought our Freya home to us?

Her Mama nodded in her school wife way, upright and formal, surprised at a town visitor. Still, Freya could feel she was pleased somehow.

– So long since we've seen you. What brings you out here?

Herr Brandt didn't look too certain, though.

His palms still dirt-caked, just back from labouring for the English, he rested them on the top gate rung as though to get a better look at this caller, this policeman's boy in old shorts and Sunday shirtsleeves. What did he want?

Freya didn't know either. She only wanted him gone again.

– Well at least you've changed your shirt, *Junge*.

This was what Herr Brandt told him – gruff enough that Benno flushed before he rode away town-wards – abrupt enough that even Freya felt it dig at her. Especially when she heard her Mama murmuring to the yard man.

– You know his Vati is with the English, Brandt?

– I do, yes.

– How long before they let him out again?

– *Pfft!* How long before the Amis give us back our school-master – that's what I want to know.

Before, while they were still walking, Benno had asked after her Papa.

– Your father.

He'd said it just like that, without any lead up:

– He's not coming back yet, is he?

That's how it was here: her Papa was the schoolmaster and everyone knew she was his daughter; they felt they knew all about her. So Freya didn't answer.

But then Benno shook his head.

– Mine either.

His Vati was the police sergeant, so everyone knew he was in prison now; Benno didn't need to say more. The way he spoke, it was like they were the same somehow, the two of them with their fathers: both known to all, and both held by the Allies. It had annoyed Freya at the time. Or, she knew it would annoy her Papa.

– Won't you come up to the Heide flocks?

Benno had asked again.

– I would like that, Freya.

He'd spoken in a rush again, the words spilling out of him:

– Or we could just go riding?

Benno had wanted her to say yes; she'd seen it in his face: bright and nervous – and Freya had felt this dig at her also. She just couldn't think what he wanted.

Now she'd heard her Mama and the yard man, it made her feel a little softer towards him. It made Freya curious in any case – because wouldn't that annoy her Papa too?

Especially when Benno came along the lane again the next afternoon. He came right to the door this time, and when her Mama answered, Freya saw how he stood up tall to ask her:

– With your permission, please!

Benno stood so upright, his chin held high on the doorstep, Freya felt the heat rush into her cheeks again. She only hoped her Mama wouldn't laugh at him, his parade-ground bearing. Her Papa would have laughed out loud and sent him on his way again.

But her Mama took in Benno's face first, and then his hand-me-down shirt cuffs, and then she told Freya:

– Well. You can go if you're back before curfew. You can go if you take Ursel.

12

The Men of the Back Enclave

Sasha

In the new hut, there were five women he and Yeva had to share with.

Pani Josefa and Pani Natalia were at the far end. They were Polish, and they seemed old like grandmothers to Sasha, and always sad and serious, staying behind their blanket curtains.

The other three were younger; more like Yeva. More like three big sisters in the cot beds around his. They were all Ukrainian also, and Yeva said it was good they were among their own again.

His sister liked their talking; she liked going off with them about the duckboards. To the mess tent for bread rolls – to chat and laugh with the soldiers there – or off to the meadows, to lie in the grass a while. They went to the millrace in the mornings too, with their arms full of camp laundry; all the women did that, even the oldest. Then the younger ones sat together afterwards, whiling away the drying time with cigarettes and playing cards.

Sasha thought it was good when they unpicked the OST patch from his jerkin.

– Hold still there.

They stood him in the meadow grass, holding his shoulders, ripping at the stitching, and then they stuffed the cloth into Yeva's pocket for burning.

– We don't need that now, do we?

Sasha thought it was good, too, when they let him play in the millrace.

Yeva talked and talked with them at the water's edge, and they combed her hair for her, plaiting it in new styles, smiling about the freckles on her nape, her shoulders. And all that while, Sasha could watch the fish dart; he could kick his boots off and wade in barefoot, crouching in the cool waters, filling his pockets with all the best stones.

The rest of the time, though, all the hut women annoyed him.

They thought it was their place to order him: what time to go to bed, what time to get up in the morning; when to wipe his face clean; where to leave the soap when he'd finished, with the wash-cloth underneath it – how to fold his clothes, even. Although it was Yeva who did that for both of them anyway.

All the women in the hut rows took it upon themselves to be like aunties. They even took to watching him when he played at the millrace.

Sasha dropped his stones into the waters, just to hear the smack of them landing, just to see the splashes they sent up – and then, when he looked up for Yeva, to see if she'd seen that, it was one of the women he'd find there: one of the mothers come to watch over him, sitting at the banks with her mending and her meddling.

– Don't go too far now.

– Don't get your boots wet.

Or it would be the Red Cross *Ofitserka*, come to take him to be checked by the doctors, the nurses, striding ahead of him with her long legs, sharp shoulders.

– *Khodimo.*

Let's go, she said.

The medics shone torches into his mouth, and then into his eyes – and when the *Ofitserka* brought him back to the millrace, the mother-aunties checked him over a second time.

– Is he really fine?

If Sasha scowled, Yeva told him:

– Play nice – why don't you?

So Sasha played while the mothers watched him; he went with the *Ofitserka*; he ate the plates the sister-aunties set before him. He stacked up the bowls, too, when the eating was done with.

But he didn't want their soap-and-wash-cloth attentions. Soon, he didn't even stay in the hut after breakfast to wait for the day's chores to be decided, or for the *Ofitserka* to come and find him. Sasha didn't see that he should have to. Once the dishes were piled up, and the women and Yeva were busy with talking, or busy with hair-brushing and curling, he slipped out through the doorway and beyond.

Sasha didn't stick to the duckboard paths, slipping instead along the grass and dirt between the hut rows; he put distance between himself and the new hut that was home now.

The women would call for him when they noticed; Sasha knew they were bound to. The older ones like Pani Josefa would sit up in their beds and pull back the blanket curtains, and send Yeva to come and find him, or the *Ofitserka* would do that. But he made the most first, searching out new corners of this new place they'd been brought to.

Mostly, Sasha made for the Back Enclave: the one furthest from the old machine sheds. It was not too close to the mill-race and the meadows where the women might see him; the ground there was sandy underfoot, dusty from the summer heat – and the men's huts were there too.

Three rows back from where they started, there was a fire pit. It was fed with branches from the town woods, boughs fallen from the pine trunks and gathered from the low slopes. And even early in the mornings, when no fire was lit yet in the ashes, men came to sit and smoke and talk there. To whittle and play cards. To shake hands with the other men passing. There was always someone coming, someone going along the duckboards, someone lingering a moment.

When the men spoke, it was low and murmured, but Sasha heard they were Ukrainians, mostly. Even if he didn't catch half of what they spoke about, he liked the slow way they talked in the sunshine, caps pulled to shade their features; the way they stood and sat, easy and comfortable, or lay in the grass with their boots up on the duckboards.

Sasha lay down also, in the grass just beyond them.

In his own hut, there would be sweeping and folding; the washing would soon be piled up and carried to the water. Here, though, he could lie in the warm and the women didn't know where he was yet.

The men knew he watched them; Sasha saw how they threw him glances. He saw, too, how they ignored him. Sasha didn't know if he wanted to be noticed by them or not.

Jaro and *Dmytro*; he got to know their names just from listening. There were two *Osips,* or maybe more. And also a *Mirko.* He was younger than the rest of them, his hair a red blaze under his cap brim. Mirko was Polish, and he talked to all the Poles that came past, but he also spoke Ukrainian.

Then there was *Pan Artem.*

Men came from all the rows just to shake hands with him.

He did not stand to receive them. He sat in his folding chair, offering up his large palm, his wrist reaching long from his shirt sleeve. Pan Artem was hard-browed, with grey in his dark hair. He shaved with soap and an open razor, there at the fire pit each morning, a rag thrown across his shoulder, an old hand mirror propped up on the chair back in front of him. Still, his chin and his cheeks always had a blue cast; the lines in his palms also, and the skin around his eyes. When he smiled, Sasha saw how the skin there folded; he saw that even Pan Artem's smiles were serious. Even so: all the other men grinned when he did.

Women came to him as well, but not to sit or shake hands. They came with cartons, with half packets of this and of that saved from their ration parcels. They weren't the women from his own hut, but Sasha slipped into the shade when they came to barter. He saw the small morsels, though, that they pulled from their sleeves and their aprons to offer up to Pan Artem: soup tins for cotton thread, sardines for cigarettes, or cakes of laundry soap.

Pan Artem looked at what they laid out; he listened to what they asked for; then he sent one of the other men inside – lifting his chin to Jaro or Osip or Dmytro. Sasha could see that Mirko was Pan Artem's favourite, because he was the one who finished the bargaining. Mirko took the big soap cakes from the ration boxes, cutting them in half with a bread knife, and the women held palms out to catch the shavings, tipping them into their handkerchiefs, knotting them tightly.

Pan Artem had chocolate bars.

He kept one in his shirt pocket, always, and he took it out once the women were gone again. Breaking off a square while the other men were talking, Pan Artem sat with that chocolate in his cheek, sitting with his own thoughts. He stirred the embers with a fire iron, as though turning over new plans – and Sasha watched all of this. He could have watched Pan Artem for hours – and Sasha wanted that chocolate so badly, it made his throat hurt.

It had him pocketing the soap bar from his own hut one morning.

Slipping it from the windowsill where it sat, in its washcloth bed, and hurrying to Pan Artem, presenting himself in front of the fire pit.

– Here!

Sasha was there early: it was only Pan Artem and Mirko in the folding chairs. One dark, one blond, both wide-legged, wide-shouldered. They sat, looking up at him and waiting.

But then, the soap Sasha had brought to trade, it seemed so paltry. It was stolen also – and wouldn't the women notice? Sasha felt hot, just thinking about it, pressing his fingers around the bar now to hide it.

– *Co mas?*

Mirko said words Sasha didn't understand, lifting his chin at what Sasha held.

– You have something show us?

Now he spoke in Ukrainian, the words in a mixed-up order; his eyes sharp and wanting to know:

– What have you?

Then Pan Artem leaned forward; he grinned at Sasha:

– You can trust us, can't you? Come on, little brother. You can just hand it over.

But when Sasha only held the soap more tightly, Pan Artem laughed.

– All right, all right.

His teeth wet and smiling, the big man stood up and came to bend over him. And when he spoke, it was as though for Sasha only:

– At home, I have three boys – just like you.

Pan Artem lifted three fingers, stretching his arm out to squint at them: one for each of his sons, so far away.

He gave Sasha no chocolate. But Pan Artem rested his hand on Sasha's forehead. His palm was heavy and warm there, and even afterwards, lying in the grass while the other men came and went, Sasha could still feel the good weight of it.

*

It was Mirko who came for him the next morning.

When Sasha woke, he was there in the doorway; all the women were asleep still, even Yeva. Only just light outside.

His finger to his lips, Mirko helped Sasha into his boots first, tying his laces for him on the hut step. Then, laying an arm across his shoulders, Mirko steered him along the empty duckboards. The camp around them silent, dawn just a glow still across the horizon, they cut through the Ukrainian quarter, arriving at the millrace and the back boundary to find Pan Artem waiting there, his long morning shadow thrown ahead of him along the bankside.

Mirko swung Sasha over the water, and the two men led him onwards, through the meadow grass to the Poststrasse. When they crossed there at the corner, Sasha's boots were already soaked with dewfall, the bottoms of his trousers, but Pan Artem cut ahead still further. Slipping down a gully flanked by brambles, with Mirko ducking along after, as though they both already knew this route, had walked it already many times.

Sasha had to pick up his pace, now trotting, now jogging, not to be left behind. Still, the two men did not slow for him; they did not even stop once along the narrow path, until they came to a garden wall, all tumbledown, and on the other side an orchard.

– *Here.*

Pan Artem pointed.

Mirko lifted him over.

And then Sasha was alone there – under the old trees and spreading branches.

Beyond the orchard was a lawn; beyond that a house, tall and grand with flaking paintwork, all the curtains still drawn tightly. And the early light here was startling: blue and gold and sparkling; it was falling over everything.

– *Come, boy!*

Pan Artem pulled him onwards. He'd climbed the wall, and now Mirko came following, both men ducking low under the orchard branches, from one tree to the next, turning under each to peer up, scouting for the best fruit.

– *Come now!*

They urged Sasha to follow on. The apples still too small to bother with, they left them; and then the pears too; the walnuts. But in the last row there were plums: purple and ripening – and so many, the boughs were bending under the weight of them all; early wasps hovering at the sticky juice, clustering where the stem met the fruit.

– *There – look.*

Mirko put his hands under Sasha's armpits, lifting him high, pushing him up into the tree crown.

– *Make a grab, boy!*

He kept one palm pressed to Sasha's shoulder blades, whispering and pushing him further, until Sasha found a foothold.

– *Good, brother. Yes, good.*

The branches were twisted, speckled with lichen; thick with leaves, bright with morning. The first plums Sasha reached for were so large they filled his palms. Down below him, Pan Artem worked swiftly, unfolding a bedsheet from his knapsack, and a blanket, spreading both over the damp grass.

– *You don't let them fall – no.*

Mirko whispered his warning; the fruit shouldn't be bruised, he cautioned.

So Sasha was careful, picking and handing them down; picking and placing them into Mirko's waiting hold – with Pan Artem beckoning all the while: *faster, faster.* Soon there was a heap on the blanket at Pan Artem's feet. Once it was full enough, he knotted it at the corners, spreading out a second, and after that a third one.

Pan Artem smiled and nodded all the while they were working. But he threw glances to the house, too, and glances to the path; Sasha saw that Mirko did likewise. Still, they did not see the figure until the shout came:

– *Halt!*

A voice, hoarse and croaking.

– *Sofort!*

It was Sasha saw her first, through the branches. The woman was old, standing on the lawn with her arms raised. Thin and grey, like her skirts, like the plaits around her forehead; her voice was angry, but her old chin trembled – was she frightened? Behind her, there were footsteps in the dew, and Sasha saw she was barefoot. Then he saw she was coming for them.

– *Sofort, ich sage!*

He scrambled down the branches. Half falling, into the grass, Sasha landed hard, on knees and elbows, the shock of it jarring his insides – but Pan Artem was there. He lifted Sasha into his arms and ran with him.

– *Go! Go!*

Plum bundles already slung across his shoulders, he went

crashing through the branches, passing Sasha over the wall to Mirko, and then scrambling after them.

– *Go now!*

The two men pelted onwards, passing Sasha between them. His cheeks hot, his stomach jolted, the men kept hold of him; their running heads ducked, their path helter-skelter through the knee-high grass and brambles.

At the gully, they tumbled into the undergrowth, and there they stopped. Sudden and still and crouching. Mirko's face was close. Sasha could hear his breathing; he could see him blinking, feel him listening. Pan Artem held Sasha in both arms, holding tight and listening also.

Both men were so quiet, Sasha knew he had to hold still. But at the same time, Pan Artem held him so hard, Sasha could feel that the man was shaking with laughter.

Back inside Pan Artem's hut walls, they emptied the bundles onto the table. The plum smell filled the room, dark and sharp, and Pan Artem handed a large one to Sasha.

– Your reward, brother-mine.

Mirko grinned at him. His eyes glinting, he took hold of Sasha's shirt hem, making a sling to hold more fruit, leaning forward to whisper.

– These ones are for your sister. Your pretty sister only.

– Oh ho!

The other men jeered him. But Mirko only grinned more, loading Sasha with more plums for Yeva.

– The one with the freckles, yes? You be sure she gets the ripest.

Then Pan Artem turned Sasha by the shoulders, shoving

him out through the doorway, sending him running with his small and precious burden.

It made Yeva's eyes wide when Sasha whispered the story. His cheeks still hot, his chest still full of Pan Artem's laughter, he sat side by side with her between their blanket walls.

Yeva ate the plums he'd brought, and Sasha ate more too, and all the while his sister made him say again: where the path was, what the house was like, the orchard.

– Did you see any others like it?

Yeva laughed about Pan Artem laughing. And she wanted to know about Mirko.

– He said I was pretty? So?

That sent her eyebrows high, as though she might like it; and then her lids and lips narrowing, sharp with interest.

– And he's the one with the red hair?

But she made Sasha promise he would not tell anyone where he went this morning.

– You swear it?

Yeva told him it would be best if he didn't say a word of who he went with, either. Because the women in their hut had already done more than enough frowning when they found Sasha gone at breakfast.

– I was worried – but Pani Josefa, she was frightened. You know she wanted to come out and search with me? Through all the hut rows?

His sister hissed this, leaning forward; she tapped at his forehead and tugged at his earlobes, for making her search, and for making her nervous.

But the plums he'd brought back for her – and the story

of Mirko – the story of the morning – they were so good, they made up for all that. Both their chins sticky with juice, they grinned and sucked the stones dry, and spat them into Yeva's palms.

Only then came the Red Cross *Ofitserka*.

She pulled back the blanket curtains – and there she was, tall and sharp-shouldered and looking down at them.

– I have to talk to you.

She spoke in Ukrainian. This time there was no grey-haired Pole with her to get more words from, but it was like she didn't need him, not for what she'd come to say.

– Someone came.

She told them.

– From one of the houses. It was a lady from the town here.

The *Ofitserka* pointed – towards the road, towards the villas and their gardens, and the wall that Sasha had been lifted over – as though she already knew what he'd been up to.

– This lady. She saw someone stealing from her fruit trees. It was a boy, she said. In a grey shirt, grey trousers.

The *Ofitserka* looked straight at Sasha while she was talking, at him sitting in his trousers and his shirt in front of her; his boots underneath the bed still damp, blades of orchard grass still caught between the laces.

Next to him, Yeva closed her fingers over the plum stones. Sasha just caught this small movement: how his sister slipped them into her shirt cuffs, swift and calm. Did the *Ofitserka* see that?

Yeva told her:

– My brother. He has been here. With me. All morning.

The woman nodded, short, when Yeva had finished

talking. Then she looked again at Sasha, at the grass stains on his knees, and the plum smears on his shirt front.

The *Ofitserka* looked right through them; Sasha could feel her. But it felt like she might be laughing too.

13

A Town Boy Secret

Freya

When Benno saw Ursel had no bicycle, he lifted her onto the saddle behind him, and then they rode together like that, out along the Heide paths: Benno ahead, Freya following, Ursel holding tight to his shirt back, delighted.

The first bilberries were ripening; they were green-black and sour still, but good enough to stop and pick a while, each of them eating their own small palmful.

They did this all without talking, still awkward, and then they skirted along the slopes a while, back on their bicycles, not climbing yet, just riding. But when they got to where the track rose, taking them still further from the schoolhouse, Benno turned onto a new route that Freya hadn't taken before, and she had to pedal hard to keep up.

Soon the track became a path, and then the path all but petered out, and the rise grew so steep, too, Freya had to climb off her bicycle. Benno kept Ursel on the saddle, though, her fat plaits dangling, fingers gripped to his shoulders. He stood on the pedals, pressing onwards, up and over to the high pass.

By the time Freya had caught up, Benno had already stowed his bicycle, pushing it into a stand of junipers. He looked around himself, although there was no one for miles – certainly no English patrol cars – but still, he motioned for Freya to lean her bicycle in the brush beside his before he led them along the sand paths.

They followed the smaller tracks here, worn by the sheep. The herds grazed in small and grey clusters, keeping their shy and stubborn distance. Ursel found their wool tufts on low gorse branches so Freya twisted them around her fingers, into rings and bracelets while they wandered. And then Benno lay on his stomach to show them both; if they lay still and quiet enough among the heather scrub, the sheep would graze their way towards them.

It made Ursel giggle to lie down, to hear the sound of their cropping and nickering. They came up so close, she laughed out loud – and the sheep lifted their grey heads in surprise, scattering along the high pass.

– *Da!*

Benno still hadn't said where he was leading. But Ursel whispered to Freya as they lay there, excited:

– He said we mustn't tell anyone he brought us.

Freya threw a glance at him. Why not? Did he think it would get back to the English? Or would it shame him – maybe – if it got back to Udo that he had been out with the schoolhouse daughters?

But Benno only stood up.

– We're nearly there now.

He strode on further, keeping ahead of them, taking a bend along the high track. There, he ducked into the gorse brush and – sliding down a gully slope – seemed to disappear entirely.

– *Come!*

Freya heard him whisper.

– *Come further!*

She and Ursel crouched at the gully edge, peering hard into the undergrowth – but it still took a moment before Freya could make him out among the branches.

– Can you see now?

She could see a pair of wooden wheels beside him, and flaking paintwork. Freya saw wooden walls next, old and lodged in the gorse brush – she saw it was a shepherd's hut.

Since the shepherds had been called up, their huts had stood parked on the lower Heide – but this one looked abandoned. The wheel rims were cracked, axles broken, spokes falling out of their fixings; there was a rip in the tar roof, and the gorse had grown so thick around the walls, it must have been a good year or more since any of the shepherd kin had come to check.

– I found it empty.

Benno smiled up at her from the doorway, half proud, half nervous.

Inside, though, Freya thought that someone had been there. Someone else – and not too long back. Because the hut smelled of sun and earth and something sharper. Ashes lay spilled across the floorboards.

– There was a fire here.

Benno told them:

– Someone burned things.

The stove door lay open, leaning on its hinges, and inside were wisps of burned bark, knots of charred gorse wood. The walls above were soot-marked and flame-licked – Freya thought there must have been a blaze here. She saw the fire had been doused too; someone had thrown water, perhaps the flare of it too frightening. Because the ash had dried in crusts now, but under her boots, she could see it had run in rivulets first, under the bunk, between the wooden floorboards.

Freya stood between the low walls with Ursel, while Benno went ducking and crouching, showing them what he'd found here.

The shepherd's tinderbox, thrown under the back bunk; a charred cloth scrap that fell apart between his fingers, and three small and blackened shirt buttons.

– They were in the stove here. I need to clean them. I still need to clean everything. But I've found the shepherd's kettle now – look.

He lifted it from the stove top to show them: the enamel was chipped and rusted, but it was good and large, and still watertight.

– It was outside, flung into the undergrowth after the fire maybe. But I've been using it to fetch water. Because the brook starts not far from here, and so now I can scrub the floor – see?

He gestured to the ashy boards, to show them where

he'd started, a cleanish line running from the doorway to the bunk.

They sat on the slats there, on the shepherd's thin bedroll, the three of them shoulder to shoulder, with the door propped open. Looking at the view of the gully from the one dusty window, eating the bilberries Ursel had saved from earlier, Benno explaining what he wanted to do to the hut next.

– After I've cleaned up, I'll fix the catch on the window; I'll lay in plenty of kindling. The gaps in the walls will need to be caulked before the autumn. I don't know how to do that yet. But I need to find a bucket first in any case, or a milk can – something for storing more water. For when I wake up in the mornings.

– You've been sleeping out here?

Freya turned to him.

– All on your own?

Ursel joined in.

– Not when I wake up.

Benno gave them both a shy grin.

– The sheep are outside then – the whole flock!

He said the animals gathered there at nightfall.

– They sleep under the gully branches. They don't even scatter when I open the door. I can sit with them here most of the morning.

Then Benno lay down along the back wall, stretching his legs, folding his hands behind his head, and Freya looked around the hut again.

She saw the large task Benno had set himself. Freya saw the shepherd's mark by the doorframe also. The shepherd kin were all Heide folk, and Freya wasn't sure they'd like this: one of their huts being taken over, even if it was an abandoned one. But at least Benno was taking care of it, cleaning the few things left by the hut's last occupant: the flint and tinder, a tin mug, this musty bedroll – even the soot-black shirt buttons. He'd set these on the windowsill, and already Ursel's fingers had gone reaching, lining them up more neatly. Now she was adding a gorse pod, a twist of sheep's wool; her sister was digging things out of her pocket corners, arranging them in a row there.

– I need to find a way of storing food.

Benno told them.

– I need to get myself used to this. Making do and making good.

Freya glanced at him stretched out long behind her. Was he planning on camping out here for longer? Benno didn't say, though. He just asked if they would come again.

– You can help me. If you'd like to? You can come here – whenever you want.

He blinked at Freya, hopeful.

– Tomorrow – yes?

Benno was back the next day, waiting for her and Ursel.

It was the same on each afternoon that followed: after morning chores were done with, Benno would be at the school gate.

– There you are.

Freya's Mama began smiling when he turned up, already meeting her approval.

He still took the long route to the high pass, and Benno still insisted they stash away their bicycles. But once they were at the hut, under the gully branches, he didn't seem to worry about being found here.

They fetched water from the brook, Benno took out the rag cloths he'd smuggled from home – *out from under my Mutti's nose* – and he and Freya scrubbed the walls and floorboards while Ursel played in the undergrowth.

Freya's sister looked for seed pods and grass stalks; she found a bird's skull, tiny and delicate, and placed it carefully on the hut steps, along with the rest of her findings. Her hair caught in the gorse, and each time she came back her plaits were more tousled while she emptied more from her pockets to add to her step piles.

She left Freya and Benno to their cleaning, to their stop and start conversations.

– I used to see you too, you know?

Freya told him this, while they were scrubbing the floor one afternoon.

– I used to see Udo, anyway, and all the others. Klaus and Niklas and Thomas. When they were riding homewards. And when they were at the Rathausplatz.

She'd wanted Benno to hear that she'd ridden behind them – that she'd known how they stared at her – just to see what he'd say to that. But Benno only shrugged at first, keeping on with his scrubbing. And then Freya found herself wondering: had Benno been among them then?

– You didn't see me then?

Benno shrugged again in answer:

– I wasn't with those boys so much; I used to go home before them.

Freya saw that she'd embarrassed him; he'd been too

young to be included, and he didn't like to say so. Except then Benno told her:

– I used to go to the millstream, though. I used to go with them to the bathing spot. To the circle.

Freya knew the one. Not that she'd been there: it was a town boy place, and only for the oldest. Benno said:

– It was for other boys before us – before they went to the Front, yes? They spent whole nights out there before they went to the Wehrmacht.

But after they were called up, the spot fell to Udo and his classmates. Benno said they swam there on warm days; and in the winter, when the water froze, they went to slide on their boot soles.

– They used to stay on late too. Until after dark, you know?

Freya nodded: those were the days before the curfew.

– They'd take their torches.

Benno blinked now.

– Sometimes they'd invite me.

He paused at his wiping.

– Around the circle, that was the best part. Because Udo and the others, they used to talk about the fighting. When it would be our turn. Who would go first, where we might serve.

Benno said all this quiet, as though that talk had been exciting. Then he looked away again, going back to his wiping, like it had made him shy to say all this.

Freya felt shy herself then, rubbing at the floorboard beside him. She hadn't expected Benno to say so much. And also – she didn't know too much about being a soldier. In the schoolyard, the boys had talked about regiments and postings, but that had been child talk and she didn't want to repeat it here, in case she sounded childish. The girls at her grammar school had written to the Front. But that was to brothers and cousins, or to older boys they were in love with – and Freya couldn't say that, in case it sounded worse still. She could see, though, how it had been for Benno: with his brother and all the town boys, gathered at the millstream, looking into their futures, out into the wide world.

Benno told her,

– My Vati. When he spoke about the Front, he told us about the Steppe lands. The Don and the Dnieper. The Black Sea.

– He told you about the fighting there?

Freya's Papa had never done that, although he'd been at the West Front, or near to it. Her Papa hadn't even sent drawings – not of the places where he was posted, only the Heide.

Benno said:

– My Vati told us where the troops passed through; when we listened to the news, he had the atlas open, and he taught us all the place names and the new German ones they'd be given now. But he spoke more about afterwards – when the war would be over. My Vati said that fighting was hard, but we had to get it done with, because then all those new lands would be German. They'd be ours for always.

Benno had stopped wiping now. He was just crouching on the hut floor, his arms clasped around his knees, looking out of the hut doorway.

– He said when Udo went east, he should stay there. He should find himself a posting. Or Udo could find himself some land, even. My Vati told him it would be the making of a young man.

Benno squinted, his eyes narrowed against the sun's rays, and Freya squinted also. She tried to picture the East Lands, finding herself thinking of grass and pasture; a sky and riverscape, dotted with farmsteads. Had Benno's Vati meant Udo to have a Hof there? It seemed unlikely. So then Freya thought of towns out east, with town halls and men to take charge of postings, to be given police caps and uniforms; in her mind's eye, Freya tried to picture Udo as one of them. But all she saw was a town boy, his shorn nape. So Freya blinked at Benno. His face was hard to read, though: his eyes still narrowed against the sunshine, his chin on his forearms, his hair grown long across his forehead.

– Did your Vati say you should go east too?

Benno shook his head.

– Not to fight, no. Not like Udo. My Vati said the war would be over before I was old enough.

Then he blinked at Freya.

– He said that fighting wouldn't be right for me in any case. He said I wouldn't make a soldier. I wasn't made for that life.

Benno flushed as he said this, sudden and red, his face tightening.

– My Vati. He said there were other ways to serve. He said I could play my part in the life that came after.

It sounded like Benno had taken it hard, though, not being made for the soldier life. And so Freya found herself picturing this also: Benno and his Vati in their town villa parlour. Benno downcast by the radio, the atlas open between them.

Benno's Vati had thought the fighting was important; he'd said all that land out there would be German; and Freya could see that Benno had liked the thought of this, just as much as the other boys. But when she tried to picture him as a soldier, she found she couldn't do that – and this made his Vati right somehow, so then she didn't know what to think, or what to say next.

She wiped at the hut floorboards.

A pair of Ursel's grass heads lay on the hut steps, and Freya straightened up to look for her through the window: her sister had been wandering a long time.

– What about your Papa, then?

Benno spoke into the silence.

– What about him?

Freya's answer came faster than she intended.

– Well, he went to the front line – so where did he serve?

Benno lifted his chin to hear her answer, but Freya kept on wiping. Her father had been in France somewhere; he was still there now, across the border, in a camp for POWs – but that's all she knew about it. Benno had been told so much more about war and soldiering, she knew if she said that, she'd only sound stupid; or it wouldn't be nearly enough for him. Already he was waiting for her to say more.

– Your Papa was a good schoolmaster. My Vati said so.

His Vati? Freya tried not to let her surprise show.

– He was, though – wasn't he?

Benno kept asking.

– Except he was the one who didn't let you wear the uniform.

Freya wiped harder. She didn't want to answer. She thought

Benno's Vati must have told him that as well. Everyone must have guessed as much.

– It's true, though – isn't it?

Benno insisted, like it was town gospel.

– Because your Papa didn't want to go to the war either.

This was not the kind of thing you were supposed to say. Not out loud, not to someone you didn't know too well. Even now the war was over, it didn't feel right somehow. Strange to hear it from a town boy. Freya wasn't sure she trusted it either – because now it occurred to her: would Benno tell Udo what they spoke about? And then would Udo tell all the others?

Still, Benno kept on:

– Your Papa is being held by the Americans. And you want your Papa to come back now. Don't you?

– And you don't want your Vati?

The words were out before Freya had thought, before she'd heard how sharp they were, and heartless. She saw Benno's eyes darken.

Except then he blinked.

– My Vati?

Benno said this, half-frowning – like a question, or like there was no of course about it. His chin back on his forearms, his shirt cuffs grubby from wearing, he sat as though thinking, as though distracted.

He stowed his cloth soon after, taking the kettle to the hut steps and pouring out the dirty water – and then Freya thought perhaps that was that now: the afternoon was over. She didn't like how this smarted. Or the thought that came after: perhaps the next time she saw Benno, he would be back with Udo and the other boys.

– Do we have to go?

Now Ursel was calling her.

Freya turned to find her sister trotting along the gully towards the hut steps, holding out her handfuls to show them both.

– I've gathered so much today!

All afternoon, Ursel had been making two piles of her findings: one to decorate the hut sill, the hut walls; the others to take home. Now she scooped these last into her pockets.

– For my Papa.

She told Benno:

– We collect Heide things to send to him. I've done the gathering, so now Freya can write, you see? She can tell him where we found them all.

Benno had been standing quiet this whole time, still caught half in thought. Mention of their Papa, of a letter, had him blinking, though, and frowning – and Ursel saw that.

– Oh – but we don't have to tell our Papa about the hut here.

She told him, low and hurried, to reassure him.

– Not if you don't want that. We don't have to tell him anything. Isn't that right, Freya?

Still, all down the Heide slopes, Freya was sure she'd spoiled things, and Ursel had made it worse yet.

But then, when their ways parted, and Benno lifted Ursel from his saddle and onto Freya's handlebars, he smiled at both of them.

– Tomorrow, yes?

*

He still went wandering in the mornings; Freya knew this, because when he called for them he smelled of gorse and of grass and of hours spent outside. She thought he must stay over at the hut too, getting more work done – patching and hammering, or clearing the stove out – because he came with soot on his sleeves some afternoons, his knees all rough from crawling over the tar roof. They fetched water from the brook; Freya smuggled more rags from the schoolhouse kitchen, and she and Ursel cleaned the hut steps and the window.

And then a day came when all the work was done with.

They took the bedroll outside, spreading it out among the gully grasses, and then they lay there, grubby and contented, and like they'd done this always. The sun on Benno's shoulder blades, his hand-me-down shirt discarded, Freya beside him while Ursel tended to her gatherings.

Once her sister was off on her searches, though, Freya asked:

– Your brother. Where does he go now?

Because she hadn't seen Udo in so long, not since the winter or even before that.

– Or what about the other boys?

– They go riding.

Benno shrugged like it didn't matter what they did. But Freya pushed further.

– But they can't go to the bathing spot any longer.

That was too near the munition works, surely; too near the English soldiers.

– And they can't go the school route because of the curfew.

If the boys were stuck with the town streets, the lanes and the villa gardens, Freya felt that would only be right somehow: those were town son places, and they could stay there. But still, without school, without HY duties, they had so much time now. What did they do all day?

– I mean, they used to ride to the millstream; they used to ride all over.

Freya knew they used to swim and skate and talk about when they were grown up. But now the war was over – the war was lost, too – did they have nothing left to talk about?

Benno had listened all the while she was talking, lying on his back beside her with his eyes closed, but he didn't answer. Instead he asked:

– Don't you ever wonder what it would be like to be far from here?

Freya shook her head. She never had.

– I would like to go far away.

Benno said this matter-of-factly, like it was decided.

But Freya looked at him for more – why ask about this? Why leave the Heide? This gully felt enough to her: the hut walls they'd scrubbed clean, this sun falling through the branches; all the heath beyond them. And besides, Benno had been working on the hut for weeks now, making it warm and weathertight, did he really want to leave it? Why should he go anywhere?

– I just think it would be better that way. Just to be away from here.

His eyes were still shut, and his shoulders half-shrugged. But then he shifted, as though thinking further; Benno rolled over, towards her, and he lifted his chin to throw a checking glance behind himself.

– You know before? When Udo used to go to the

millstream with the others? They didn't just stay at the bathing spot – they used to go further.

Benno lifted his chin again, a little nervous. And then he asked:

– You know the old mill in the town woods?

Freya nodded, although she didn't, not really. She could only picture it faintly.

– You know you can see the works from there?

Freya nodded again – although she hadn't known this; it would never have occurred to her. Freya knew next to nothing about the munition works, just like she knew next to nothing about the front lines – so she kept quiet while he continued:

– You can stand at the top of the millrace; if you stand at the right place, you can see all down the slope there. In the winter, when half the trees are bare, you can see right over the factory wall and inside.

Freya felt herself tighten.

She didn't like the sound of this. Or of the boys going to look in the first place. They'd meant to look down into the munition works? She blinked at Benno, hoping this wasn't true now.

– Udo used to do that?

Benno nodded.

– When they were still making armaments?

Benno squinted his answer, a little uncomfortable.

– And all the other boys?

Freya had to ask, and he squinted his yes another time. So then she saw – Benno must have gone too.

– Udo was the first to find it. He went to look. Just to see, you know? He wanted to see the munitions they made there, or to try at least. Then he dared the rest. The time they took me, we saw works guards – so then I didn't dare to look for workers.

Benno shook his head, as though the workers had frightened him, and maybe as much as the guards had.

– The other boys, though: they didn't want to go home yet. So they waited for nightfall. When it got dark, they said the Werkschutz wouldn't be any the wiser. You see, the guards and the labourers; they worked right through the night there – did you know that? Udo saw the lights in the machine sheds.

Benno took a breath there, and Freya had to take a breath also. What the boys had done was wrong and frightening – they had gone to see things they shouldn't have. Now Benno learned in closer.

– My Vati.

His Vati? Freya blinked, a little confused. They'd been talking about Udo and the town works, and now Benno was switching to his father?

– He was called out there. At night-time.

Freya had to blink again – but still Benno kept talking.

– You remember when the snows came? Last winter?

He spoke faster now, like he had to get the words out.

– Well, there were labourers brought past here; they were driven in truckloads, in convoys. But they were marched also – in the snow time – I know because I saw that. Not from up in the woods: I saw them on my home route. I was coming home from school and there were workers marching. A column of labourers – women, too, in work clothes – right there on the Poststrasse. And then I saw my Vati called out that night.

He looked at Freya to see if she'd heard him; had she been listening? But Freya was more confused now.

– Your Vati was called to the Poststrasse?

– No, he was called to the munition works. That same night. Udo saw him also. My brother watched him, from the window. We both saw him coming home again afterwards.

Benno said all this with emphasis, as though to assure Freya this was all true – about the snow night and the women workers, about his father – as though having Udo there might prove it for her.

– Those workers I saw marched here – the women, out on the Poststrasse – I think my Vati saw them also. He must have. You understand me?

Benno spoke to her, sharp, frustrated. But then he stopped, just as sharply, like he'd caught himself.

His Vati had been called to the munition works; had he seen something he shouldn't have? Freya blinked at Benno, but he shut his eyes now, like he might be angry. Or like he thought Udo would be, if he knew how much he'd just told her.

Freya tried to think back to the snow time, but all she knew was it had fallen thick across the Heide. And then she watched Benno while she waited, unsure if he would say more. The winter felt like such a long time ago now.

Benno lay so close, she could see his lashes and his eyebrows, she could smell the sun and Heide on his forearms. And then it was so quiet here, just the two of them, just the hut walls and the gully silence, Freya closed her eyes also – because this felt better than talking about the town works. Or his father. Or about workers on a snow night.

When she opened her eyes again, Benno was watching her. His face close, his eyes level with her own, he asked:

– You won't say, will you?

Was he talking about his Vati? The snow time? The women workers?

Freya shook her head. Who would she tell? She didn't even know what Benno had said, not exactly: he'd started so fast, and then he'd just broken off. But he was watching her so intently, Freya had to shake her head another time so he'd believe her.

– I swear it.

And then Benno leaned forward; he pressed his mouth against hers, hurried and earnest.

Ursel frowned when she saw them.

She'd come back from her gathering and caught them – and now she was standing at the hut steps, her small cheeks flushed with shock.

Ursel threw her twigs at them, angry, along with the handfuls of leaves she'd collected – she ran off through the gorse brush. So then Freya had to chase her; she had to run after her up the gully slope and into the open. Catching hold of her sister's skirt hems, holding her down in the long grass, Freya had to tickle her and tickle her, until she promised not to tell.

– Not a word to our Mama – you hear me?

But then, all the way home, winding slow behind Benno, with Ursel on her handlebars, it was the kiss that Freya thought about. The kiss and the promise that had come before it. The press of her belly against the bedroll, the hush under the branches; her own new secrets about Benno.

August

14

Trespassers

Ruth

She saw what was happening. Ever since the plum theft, when Yeva and Sasha were at the millrace in the mornings, one of the Back Enclave lads had taken to stopping by there.

This Mirko. Ruth didn't think he was all bad.

He played with Sasha, bending with him and crouching, picking up stones from the stream bed. He taught the boy to how to skim too, not just throw them, helping him choose the flattest and the smoothest, and so now when Ruth passed along the duckboards she often heard Sasha call out to her.

– *Hey! Hey, Ofitserka!*

The boy held a stone high to show her, before sending it skipping across the surface.

But Mirko. He was the one who'd taken Sasha to the orchard – that much was obvious.

And he didn't stop by just to see the boy, either: he came for Yeva. Ruth saw the talk flashing between them. Come the afternoon, he'd be there again, too. Once the washing was dry again and folded, and the women went to gather kindling from the lower slopes, along would come Mirko, through the first of the pines there, as though just out for a wander.

He worked alongside Yeva, gathering fallen branches. Mirko found pine cones and made a new game for Sasha – sending the boy running to the millrace, higher up the slope this time, behind the camp boundary. The boy dropped the cone into the water there, and then, as soon as the flow caught it, Sasha ran hot-foot and downhill, to stay alongside the floating progress.

Of course he fell sometimes, pell-mell; of course he came away with grazes. Yeva was old enough to be responsible: just a short year or so from adulthood, she watched her brother's playing with the wary patience of a mother's eye already. She was just as guarded with Mirko, keeping him at smiling arm's length. But still, Ruth saw enough in that smile to leave her grateful the older women were there also. That there were more eyes on Sasha's antics – and Mirko's. What was his game here?

She was glad of the mothers especially. Josefa gathered kindling each afternoon, Ana and Natalia sat talking and darning in the meadow grass – and they called out to Sasha when he'd gone too far. These mothers without their children, they took it in turns to watch over him – and it seemed to Ruth that they were only too glad.

*

They still came to Ruth's office, but not to cry any longer, just to ask:

– You have anything this morning?

None of her requests had been met with matches – not yet, in any case. Ruth had sent dispatches to further camps, on advice from the major, as well as to the Red Cross in Warsaw, in Kiev. She had included the women's descriptions, and her own of Sasha and Yeva, thinking their mother should know her children instantly: her daughter's freckled arms, her son's freckled ear tops. So far Ruth had heard back from a team near Brunswick, at a holding camp near the border to the Russian zone. They had set up a whole children's section – still small, but growing, they told her – and they would send the names and ages and any distinguishing features of all new arrivals brought to them.

So, the process had started.

And though the women asked – of course they did – they did not press Ruth further. They sat on her office steps afterwards, just to sit and talk there, or they sat in the meadow grass, clustered with their mending, with their rosaries – and Ruth heard that most of their talk was of Sasha and Yeva. Since these two children had been brought here, the mothers seemed to trust more: theirs could be also. They would find them yet: their sons, their daughters.

The women were there to play chaperone when Mirko called at Yeva's hut door with a small meadow bouquet one evening.

He'd asked to walk out with her, just along the duckboards, but he arrived with his shirt cuffs buttoned, his boots blackened – with ashes most likely; that's what Stanislaw reckoned – and then he strolled with Yeva like a young gentleman, arm in arm along the wooden paths.

The three mothers walked behind them, keeping the young pair in sight as they walked in the summer evening light. But the young Pole must have passed some kind of muster, Ruth thought, because the younger women had curled Yeva's hair first, tying it up in rags, and then teasing it out across her freckled nape, her forehead.

– That's a sight for sore eyes.

– Isn't it just?

The new auxiliaries smiled with Ruth in the mess tent, over late tea and biscuits, watching the young pair conduct their camp circuit.

It was only Stanislaw who didn't seem too sure. He sat quiet beside Ruth when mugs were clinked to this first camp romance.

– Sasha doesn't only play, you know?

He told Ruth this afterwards. When it was just the two of them in their mess tent corner.

– I see him out on errands – the boy is sent running between the hut rows. He's not running them for the women – no. It will be for that Pan Artem.

Stanislaw shook his head about this – a child trotting from row to row, in service of the black market.

– I'd say our boy there, he is becoming a regular little courier. And isn't this Mirko one of the Ukrainian's best lads?

Stanislaw had told Ruth about the expanding camp trade. He couldn't name the source; he said there could be any number because in his own hut alone, he saw all manner of everything brought out to barter. Along with cigarettes – ubiquitous – cough sweets were swapped for flour, buttons for elastic or sticking plasters. The DPs saved part of their rations, of course, and traded them between the hut nations: the Italians favoured the sardines; for the Ukrainians it was the pudding rice and powdered milk. But last week he'd been offered copper wire for his radios – and who knew where that came from? Ruth didn't, certainly. And then, just the other morning, she'd seen Josefa in the Polish quarter with a pair of brand-new second-hand lace-up shoes.

– I don't judge.

Stanislaw told Ruth across their mess table.

– As long as it's done in good faith.

As long as they didn't barter with Pan Artem.

– Next it will be schnapps.

The old Pole warned Ruth – he said all the camp talk was about this, and perhaps she should inform the major.

– The man is building a still in that back quarter.

Pan Artem was burning alcohol. Glass-clear and eye-watering. Sweetened with the plums he stole.

– Are you sure?

– You are not?

Sasha

When Mirko came to the millrace, that was the best part of Sasha's day now.

While Yeva wrung out the clothes and the women spread them across the grass, Sasha kept lookout until he saw him emerging from the hut rows.

Mirko brought packet soup and semolina, buttered bread rolls: things for Sasha to eat, and others for him to deliver along the duckboards. He found stones for Sasha also, and he stayed long enough to watch him skim the first few, crouching at the bankside, before slipping away across the meadows to the Poststrasse. Sasha knew he went to the villas there: Mirko had told him so. *You keep this to yourself, boy.* Mirko went into the town lanes, and then he came back in the afternoons with more packets in his jacket lining: dried apple rings and macaroni, and handfuls of cigarettes, like so much change to be counting. He traded with the women against stove wood, or whatever else they'd been gathering and saving, stashed in their apron pockets, ready to offer him.

Some days, though, Mirko didn't head for the town. He went the other way, following the millrace, high up into the pine trunks – higher than Sasha climbed for the cone game. And where Mirko went then, Sasha didn't know.

– Can't you take me?

– No, boy.

That was his answer. He said:

– I can't.

And he shook his head.

– You want me in trouble with your *Ofitserka*? With our sergeant?

Mirko smiled while he spoke, but he was firm too: unmovable. And Sasha didn't know why. He wasn't checking on Pan Artem's plum still, because Sasha had seen the men go in pairs to do that – sloping off among the lower trunks – *you keep this to yourself also.* Mirko went alone; he strode up into the pine trees, and he was gone for whole afternoons. What was he doing?

It was Yeva who got it out of him.

Mirko had turned up late that morning; the wash was dry and folded, they'd already carried it back to the women's quarters. They hadn't seen him for two days – neither at the millrace, nor at the firewood gathering – and so even before he arrived at their hut step, Yeva was sore at him: two whole days with no visit, no nothing? When Mirko showed up – *knock-knock* at their open hut doorway – Sasha was alone with her among the cot beds; all the women were at the ration queue and elsewhere. Still, Yeva turned her back instead of asking Mirko inside. She went to lie down, half behind their blanket curtain, leaving him to talk to Sasha.

– You going to the town now?

– No, boy.

That meant he was going up into the pine trunks; Sasha just knew he would be.

– Can't I come?

– No, child. I've already told you.

Mirko gave all his usual shake-of-the-head answers, his usual firm smiles, until Yeva spoke up:

– Why not, though?

She spoke from half behind the curtain, but it had Mirko sitting up taller. Sasha could see he was glad she was talking to him, finally; that she had turned to take him in.

– You could take both of us. If you wanted to.

Yeva narrowed her eyes now, testing – or was she teasing? Mirko smiled his answer:

– And what if we're caught there?

– And so what if we are?

She shot back at him, just as fast – but she was smiling too now, just like Mirko. It made Sasha squirm inside, suddenly hopeful.

– Who is here to notice?

His sister pointed at the empty bed rows.

– No one will miss us. Will they? Not for a good while.

So Mirko went ahead of them into the pine trunks, and Yeva made Sasha lie with her in the long grass until long enough had passed for them to follow on after.

When they found him, Mirko was crouched where the millrace grew steepest and the banks were all grown over – and as soon as he saw them, he stood and nodded them further, stealing away into the undergrowth.

Yeva had to pull her skirts high to keep up with his striding; Sasha had to duck under branches, around boulders, and he thought he might lose them both. Until they passed from pine trunks into birch trees and the woods got lighter; until they came into a clearing, and Yeva turned to him.

– Look!

Mirko had brought them all the way to the stream banks.

A flat rock jutted out into the water: perfect for diving. Below was a small strip of shingle, sloping into the water; behind this, a stand of birches – and Mirko too, grinning at both of them.

They swam there, stripped to their underwear.

Mirko jumping from the big rock, with Yeva jumping after him, and Sasha stepping out onto their shoulders until he got brave enough. Yeva swam to the other shore and back again, skinny arms pulling her through the water, while Mirko went diving for stones from the stream bed and Sasha piled them in the shallows.

Mirko swam him out too – to where the water ran deepest.

– Just to feel the current.

Sasha held on tight to Mirko's shoulders, while Mirko asked if he could feel it tugging – at his legs, his ankles.

– Good, no? You can feel the pull, boy?

And then, after they'd dressed again, their clothes sun-warm over wet skin, the three of them lay in the sunshine, on their bellies, among the cotton-grass tufts and silence.

The shoreline curved here, so they were hidden from the rest of the stream banks. They were hidden from the town in any case, but the camp was also far behind them. While he was in the water with Mirko, Sasha had seen the town woods: the way the pine trunks rose above the stream waters – so thick and crowded and towering, he didn't like to look at them. There was just so much more of those woods than he'd thought. Lying in this light, though, even the pines felt forgotten beyond the birch grove. So then Sasha thought maybe he knew why Mirko came here.

In the clearing, there was a circle: stones and logs and boulders. Someone must have dragged them out from the birches; Mirko reckoned it was someone from the town here.

– Or a whole group, most likely.

Because he'd found paths trodden from the old mill, and from the villas also, starting way down by the Poststrasse.

– And it's a good place to swim, no?

It must have been a good while since anyone had come,

though, because the paths were half grown over, and their circle of boulders was blurring into the grass now.

When Sasha got restless, Yeva sent him to pile up his stream stones around those edges.

– Go on. You go now.

So he went splashing into the shingle to fetch them; then into the birches, returning with twigs and catkins, and white curls of bark skin. He dropped these next to Mirko and Yeva, in hopes they might help him, or maybe agree to a campfire like Pan Artem's, but they lay with their backs to the sunshine, faces close in talking.

Mirko watched him, on and off, over his shoulder. He'd told them there wouldn't be patrols here, *not in these middle-of-the-day hours*, but you could never know about townsmen. *And if they find us, they might not take kindly.* But Sasha thought of the old woman he'd seen from the orchard branches – barefoot and scolding, pointing up at him in her plum trees – and then of Pan Artem laughing and holding him afterwards. And he found he liked this feeling: being in a town place without town licence.

He saw that Yeva liked it here also. There was no trace left of her earlier soreness. All the while Sasha went about his gathering and piling, his sister lay beside Mirko. The two of them curled the birch bark around their fingers, and they spoke to each other in murmurs.

Yeva spoke about home first, and the different places they were taken to work; she spoke about their Mama, too – Sasha heard her. He didn't mind, though, because it was with Mirko. And because it meant they could stay on a while among the birches. As long as his sister was smiling, lying in the sunshine, her legs stretched long against Mirko's.

When it got to be afternoon and time to go back to camp again, Mirko stood up from beside her and swam out to the middle one more time.

Sasha stood on the diving rock and watched, the way Mirko pulled out with strong strokes, and then let himself just drift there. His hair bright in the sunshine, a blaze of red against the water, he lay on his back, on the surface, with his chest up and his arms out, the current pulling him and turning. *Good, no? You can feel that?*

The way he floated, easy and familiar, it had Sasha thinking he must do this all the time here. He saw how Mirko let the water carry him away from the flat rock, and then further. Away from the birch grove, the town woods, the camp too, until he was small and distant. Until he was just a red dot against the green of the water – until Yeva had to stand up and call out to him,

– Hey! Hey – you, stop!

Mirko laughed then, from far off in the flow.

He lifted up his arms, like she'd caught him, like he had to surrender; Mirko turned and swam for shore again.

There, he rubbed his hair dry on his shirt back, and he winked at Sasha as he lifted him onto his shoulders.

– All rivers lead to others.

This is what he told them both, turning to the water – a last look before they walked back into the birches, back to gather kindling before anyone missed them.

Mirko said:

– When I swim in this stream here, I think how it flows into the Elbe. And the Elbe – now that's a proper flow – so I tell myself I can follow it far across Germany. From the Elbe to the Havel, and the Havel to the Oder – and so on, and so on – to my old Poland, see? All the way to the Vistula – to my own Warsaw.

Mirko squinted along the water, along the stream shoreline, and Sasha saw how Yeva squinted with him, uncertain now.

So how far to their home? Sasha didn't even know what it looked like, not any longer. Not even what the rivers and streams were called there.

Yeva said:

– You'll be swimming upstream, though. Won't you? All that way, against the flow?

She tilted her chin at Mirko, pointing out the flaw in his homebound plan – and Sasha felt how Mirko grinned again, shrugging his shoulders.

– Who said it would be easy? Not me, girl. But in my dreams, it can be, no? Or should I steal a jeep maybe? Will you steal a truck with me from the transport yard?

– Oh – no more talking.

Yeva pulled at Mirko's arm then, turning him away from the water, back towards the birches, like she didn't even want to think of him taking on that journey.

– I won't hear another word.

She said this like none of them would be going anywhere. Not today, certainly. Not for a while yet. And then Sasha thought as they walked: *not without our Mama here.*

15

Contraband

Ruth

The major had called her in for a meeting. About what, he hadn't said, but Ruth caught a lift in to the town hall – into the town streets for the first time – with a pair of supply lads, her palm on the seat beside her, on the charred factory record books that she'd been storing. The major had been passing on word for her, of holding camps and transit centres, places to send her dispatches. But he'd still not come back to her about the missing workers – all those names in the burned paperwork; all those nameless others driven past here last winter. Whatever he wanted to talk about this morning, she hoped to remind him.

The lads drove and she looked out of the windows, taking in the cobbles and gables, the high villas and townhouses, their long front gardens. One of them would be the old Fräulein's, Ruth thought. She didn't see the old girl who'd come complaining, though, just other townswomen. Mothers in mourning, bent over their gardens; children in old clothes too large for them.

In the streets nearer the centre, there were more women in war black, in the summer heat, turning to one another in the ration queues and asking, swapping parcels from basket to basket. But Ruth turned away from their bartering, lest she feel for them.

Again, again, this twinge of fellow-feeling – unasked for, unwanted.

– Officer Novak.

The major was already at his door as Ruth came up the stairs.

– I saw you arriving.

Capless and in shirtsleeves, he welcomed her in to his offices, asking after her registration work, and whether her new office room was serving its purpose.

– Couldn't have you sweltering in that tent of yours.

His own windows stood open, his desk pulled close to them, and the major drew up a chair for her, asking how the DPs were faring under canvas, and the women in the Nissen sheds. It was their first meeting without Farley there, without Stanislaw or anyone, and the major spoke more easily, asking after the children especially – *that young Sasha and his sister* – and then nodding his approval as Ruth reported on how they were settling. Perhaps the major was settling in too, getting accustomed to his peacetime and town hall duties, or maybe it was just the warmth of the summer's morning leaving him less hurried than usual, but Ruth took heart, taking this chance to push the record books across his desk towards him.

– I wonder if I can ask, sir? Before we get on to business.

His eyes turned downward towards the bindings, and he listened while she told him – again – about the transports, and the workers being taken: everything Stanislaw and his bunk mates had said in that first week. *All gone from here.* The major leafed through the burned pages too, reading, considering, leaving her to wait a moment in silence, in the breeze from the window behind him.

Ruth looked out there, her eye caught by movement on the town square: a lone town boy, pedalling across the stone flags, his head down, heading out towards the Poststrasse. Behind him, she saw a pair of figures too, under the shade of trees. Not townswomen this time, these looked like young men, just a few years older than the boy on the bicycle – but were they wearing soldier's boots? Ruth lifted her head to get a better view.

But now the major sighed, closing the record books.

– I do see your point, Officer Novak. I don't know what more we can do, though. Not at this juncture.

He pushed the burned pages back towards her.

– Sir?

Ruth had to resist the urge to shove them under his nose again; she had to try another time.

– The workers in those books, major, they could be close still. The Germans could have scattered them somewhere around here, and they ought to be registered – at the very least. They might need more than that. Food. Medical treatment. We have workers who were abandoned, DPs who had to run from their work details. You've seen the kind of state they were in.

But there, the major lifted a palm to stop her.

– Some may yet turn up. We have to hope for that, Officer Novak. I do, certainly. But as you know yourself, the workers in your records there, they are from Minsk and Kharkiv, from Warsaw. They are all from out east, just like the workers our patrols picked up on the heath roads at close of hostilities. And weren't they all heading homewards – striking out eastwards – almost to a man? Didn't you have quite some arguments, getting some of them into your camp here? I imagine that any we didn't find will have been heading for the border – you can count on that much. So I'd say your missing workers are already in the Russian zone.

He gestured beyond his office windows. The Heide out there was British, Hamburg also – but Brunswick only just. The eastern zone was not so far from here: where the Elbe curved, the river marked the new boundary line.

– Any workers who've crossed, Officer Novak. Well, I'm afraid they're Russian charges.

The major spoke his words carefully, circumspect. Was he warning her off asking further? Ruth wasn't sure. But she felt she'd stepped out of line somehow – stepped just a little too far for him. He sat across from her in his shirtsleeves, still listening, but his face a little more guarded.

– I've already had notice from our side in any case.

He looked away from her, moving the conversation on now.

– My Higher Ups have decided: the smaller camps like yours here are to be disbanded; they are to be merged into the larger. This is why I asked you here this morning. You and the sergeant need to know this. In all likelihood, all your eastern DPs are to be transferred across the border: all those Poles and Ukrainians in your hut rows. It may take some weeks yet, or longer, but you'll need to make preparations.

Ruth nodded – she had to, she was being given orders – and she'd been expecting something like this at some stage: all DPs ought to go home again, it was only right. But the major wasn't tasking her with anything immediate; he was still talking in weeks – or months – so she didn't see how this changed things. Why not keep looking in the meantime?

– With respect, sir. The workers in those record books – they weren't brought alone; they'll have come with cousins, with uncles, taken at the same time. They'll have brothers held in camps now, all over Germany.

He'd told her of holding camps run by their own forces, French transit centres at the eastern border; American postings up in Bremen. Ruth had sent dispatches to all the Red Cross offices – and she knew the major would have contact with the Russians; he'd have a counterpart, just across the Elbe. Couldn't he ask that they consult their registers?

– Our DPs, sir. They haven't seen their families in years, or heard from them. Won't it be the same in every zone, the Russian included? Couldn't we do more to find them, to reunite them?

– They may have to wait for that.

The major had heard her out, but now he stopped her.

– I'm afraid our DPs may have to wait until they go home again.

He sounded that warning note another time – a little wearier now – as he blinked at her:

– You've sent your lists of those workers to your Red Cross colleagues?

– I have, sir.

– And to their offices out east?

– Yes, sir.

– Well, you have done what you can for these people here.

Was that all? It couldn't be – surely.

Ruth thought of the record cards clipped together in her files, the words she'd typed – *location unknown* – beside each brother, each uncle she'd listed. And then of the nameless others in the ash piles.

The major must have seen it in her face too because she felt him relent a moment, she felt him drop his guard again.

– The way I see it, Officer Novak. Our allies out east, they fought just as hard as us. All these past years.

She heard in his voice – just how long those war years had felt; Ruth saw it in the creases around his eyelids, across his brow too, as he frowned and blinked, looking away from her to find the right words.

– And now? Well, they're asking for their people back – every soldier captured, every civilian taken, each DP and POW. So that's what we will do for them.

He made it sound so simple, so reasonable. All those seized in the fighting were to be returned in peacetime – a sad and straightforward truth. What was there to argue with?

Then he gestured to the books again.

– I am sorry, Officer Novak – truly. But tracing isn't our work. That's for your Red Cross colleagues in Kiev, in Warsaw. Getting the DPs moved on is our task here. That is our priority.

*

The supply lads had parked up at the town hall steps. Ruth walked down them, knowing she'd have a long wait until Farley's boys were done with their ration orders. But it was too hot to stand idle at the jeep doors, and Ruth was too disheartened, too disappointed by the major's answers. Record books still under her arm, she started walking.

The town square lay empty, the streets beyond were quieter, the queues of town wives had dispersed in the meanwhile. A few turnings on, though, Ruth heard voices; she caught sight of a huddle of people at a corner – a cluster in soldier's boots – was it the same young townsmen as earlier? It was a small crowd this time; Ruth took in their shorn napes, the stubble on their young chins: just old enough to have served the Führer. And now they were home again? It seemed too soon to her.

Something passed from palm to palm among the cluster; Ruth glimpsed something slipped from shirt cuff to shirt cuff between the returners. Were they counting out cigarettes?

One of the young men glanced round at her as she passed, clocking her uniform and then pocketing his offerings, all in one swift movement. Only just back, Ruth thought, and already dealing in contraband.

He'd have brought it home with him, most likely. They'd all have done the same, she told herself. There would be many young Germans just like them, in camps like her own, but for POWs. Bartering their rations, dealing and bargaining, holding out for a homebound transport across the occupation zones.

Keep them there, Ruth thought. This town should do some waiting. Its sons and cousins and uncles shouldn't be returned too swiftly.

*

When the Ukrainian brandy hit the camp market, it led to an upsurge in trading between the hut nations, and to much singing in the evenings. Ruth heard this first hard evidence while sitting outside the medical tent, playing cards by lamplight with the auxiliaries on call.

Drunken cheer came drifting across the duckboards in the warm dark, and the auxiliaries cast her glances.

– Here we go now.

Ruth found a bottle on her desk the following morning: there and waiting, so brazen, when she opened her office door.

– A show of appreciation?

Stanislaw raised an eyebrow when he arrived.

– A token of gratitude for all your hard work?

He was cool with Ruth – for not taking his distilling concerns seriously, for not passing on his warning to the major, or even just to Farley.

– Will you be starting your own supply network, *Ofitserka*? Might I find you bartering?

Ruth had to smile – even if his coolness annoyed her – because Stanislaw was right enough about that bottle. The thing was bribery. A softening up, or a thanks in advance for turning a blind eye.

So Ruth did tell Farley, that same day, when she saw him in the lunch queue. But the man barely nodded in mess-tent passing, as though he'd already heard about those bottles – more than enough about the Back Enclave distillery.

– I'll come and collect it. When I have a moment.

This was all he offered by way of acknowledgement.

And then:

– Get better at locking up your office door at night.

So Ruth locked the bottle in the bottom drawer of one of her filing cabinets to thwart him.

She knew it was childish. But she half-hoped Farley wouldn't find the still. Or at least that the Ukrainians would get to finish another batch before he did. The DPs were waiting and waiting – to hear word of their brothers, their cousins, not just to go home again, like the major thought – and without contact, without a transport date in sight yet, it was such a long meantime. Interminable. So Ruth was pretty certain a drink here and there might just make camp life more bearable.

Whatever measures Farley took, they were not enough to stop the alcohol burning, because Ruth heard more singing in the nights that followed. It seemed that none of the measures were held against her either, because a few days later, there was a lipstick on her front step, wrapped in brown paper, and – even better – a whole packet of American cigarettes.

Ruth smoked these in bed, defiant. Enjoying the red smears on the filters. *Such decadence!*

She wouldn't report this to Farley, she decided, lying back against her pillows, window open to the July night.

Ruth wouldn't bother the major with this either. She would write it to her brother, though, to Daniel, and in her very next letter home. Because wouldn't it make him grin?

Hanne

The day began warm, and grew only more so. Hanne's chickens spread their wings in the Hof dust, and Gustav frowned about having to get bread flour. The heat made him irritable, as well as the notion of the long walk back from town again with the flour sack across his shoulders, so Hanne told him,

– Let me go.

So long since she'd been anywhere.

As soon as the eggs were collected, and Ditte was down for her morning nap, she strode out along the Heide track. Cutting past the old oak at the school wall, and then across the rail lines, Hanne stuck to the shade of the back route, rather than along the Poststrasse, heading for the town lanes and turnings, coming eventually to Heinrich's.

Here, she found young Christa in the bakehouse courtyard, all the doors open, night ovens still cooling.

The girl was sitting on the bench there, her back against the stone wall; eyes closed and legs stretched long and plump before her. No sign of her father. Heinrich's van was there, the back doors open, empty crates unloaded. But it was Christa who had her sleeves rolled, her cheeks pink with working, hair tied under a handkerchief, so Hanne thought it must have been her who had done that shifting and piling, and now she was taking a short rest while she was able.

Christa stirred as Hanne stepped in through the gateposts, opening one eye to look at her.

– So, what's new?

– Oh, not much.

Hanne didn't want the girl standing – she knew what the girl would ask next in any case; that they just had to get this part over with.

– No word of Kurt, then?

Christa was direct – but Hanne didn't mind that about her. She'd always liked the girl's straight ways, always thought Kurt had made a fine choice in his courting – even if there was little chance of them marrying, not while Heinrich still had a say in things.

– Nothing yet, *Mädchen*.

Hanne shrugged, and the girl rubbed her plump cheeks in acknowledgement, nodding for Hanne to sit down.

– Sit a while, why don't you. Just let me keep my eyes closed a little longer.

Waiting was tiring, Hanne knew this. She felt it herself, often enough, especially come nightfall. It left you no rest, so instead of doing battle with night thoughts, Hanne had taken to sitting up late to mark time with the radio – with the new programme from Berlin. The signal was still best after dark fell, so once Ditte was sleeping and Gustav was dozing in the big bed beside her, Hanne listened for the music – to soothe her – but also for the messages they broadcast now.

For Tante Marta in Jena: Have you heard from Peter?

From Willi and Grete: We have found rooms now, in Pankow.

They were from people who were bombed out of Dresden and elsewhere. Or driven out of Prussia; chased back into the Old Reich by the Russians. There were so many now who couldn't write to their families, who didn't know where to find them.

Frau Ingrid Moser, last of Danzig: please send word to your sister.

Hans-Gunther Waageman. Dorle is safe and well. Where are you?

Hanne squinted at the girl on the bench beside her – did Christa listen also?

Kurt wasn't one for writing. Even if the post had started, he'd have to find someone to write for him. Back when he was the yard apprentice, Achim Brandt had done all his paperwork, the two of them sitting elbow to elbow at the workshop benches. Or, when Brandt ran out of patience, Kurt had taken his pages to the schoolmaster – and as soon as Hanne remembered this, she found her thoughts turning to that good man: another one still not home yet.

She and Gustav had spoken about their Heide neighbour only a few nights ago, as she lay and listened to the radio; once the announcements had turned to soldiers:

Kai is home again, and we have word that Otto will be following.

Uwe has made contact; the Red Cross found him, his whole unit!

These were the ones Hanne listened for – sons and brothers and husbands, coming back from the fighting; back to their families. And she knew that Gustav listened with her, also – for all his dozing – all the way to the close of broadcasts. Because, just the other night, on the late bulletin, the English had said the schools would be reopening – *first week of September* – and Gustav had lifted his head when he'd heard this, because that meant they'd be allowing the teachers home again.

– They must be. Or who will take all those classes? Perhaps we'll see our schoolmaster?

Hanne knew what he meant. If they allow the teachers, then they must allow more men – surely? And so wouldn't they allow Kurt too? He must come soon!

But it was hard to hope like that.

Exhausting.

So Hanne turned now to Christa, looking for town news to distract her.

– What's new yourself, then?

The girl lifted her head at first, as though thinking. Then she pulled out a cigarette – an American one, with a filter. The girl slipped it from her shirt cuff, lit it, and blew smoke to the blue sky, all while Hanne regarded her. Where had she got hold of that?

Christa told her:

– Some are back, you know.

– From the Front, child?

Hanne watched the girl nod – did she mean townsmen?

– Who, then?

Christa didn't say; her face gave nothing away. Instead, she pointed at the bakery van and murmured:

– I'll tell you what's new here. It's my father going off when there's work to do.

And then:

– You didn't happen to see him, did you? On your way here?

Hanne shook her head, and the girl blew out smoke again, impatient, before she gestured at the bread crates.

– We're meant to take three crate-loads to the English. To that new camp, every Friday. He lets himself get distracted, though. Or he lets himself be called away, like he was this morning. He goes to talk with the grocer, or with his bar pals. He'll go and talk with anyone – any back-table men that are still here. So then I have to take the bread to that camp there, don't I?

Christa and her father were known for their arguments. They'd fallen out over Kurt so many times. Heinrich hadn't wanted her courted by a Hof boy, a yard apprentice, and he'd put a stop to Christa climbing out of her window. He couldn't stop Kurt calling, though; only war had put paid to that. And now? Hanne found herself wondering, as she had done so often: had Kurt's war wound put paid to his Christa chances? If he came home to stand under her window, would she still lean out to smile with him like she used to?

Hanne blinked at the girl beside her, frowning with her cigarette, but her annoyance was hard to place somehow; Christa's gaze was too distracted – and now she was tapping the ash off and asking:

– You know Frau Paulsen?

– What about her?

It was Hanne's turn to frown now. What did the Rathaus wife have to do with this? Hanne would sooner hear more about the returners, or even talk more about Kurt, but Christa continued:

– Well, Frau Paulsen was here just two days ago, fetching bread with her Erna, and with Frau Klemens. Because you know that's where they're staying now – at the Klemenses', at the station road – since the English turfed them out of their residence. Well anyway: they stood and spoke for ages with my father; I saw them, out by the wall here. And then afterwards, my father told me Herr Paulsen might be released soon. Or they're working on it. Or, I don't know.

Christa pulled a face at the thought.

– I really don't know where they got this idea from.

Neither did Hanne.

She couldn't see how the Paulsens would have earned that for starters: one of their own, back from custody, before the schoolmaster was home again, or her Kurt; before the English were even done here! Perhaps the English had nothing on Paulsen. That Rathaus flunky, that second-order underling. But what use was Paulsen here – to anyone?

Hanne dug out her ration coupons, annoyed now. If there was no better news to glean here, she'd rather be on her way again.

– Oh – wait there.

Christa told her. And then:

– Wait, just a moment.

Pinching out her cigarette, she ducked inside the bakehouse, and when the girl came out again, it was with a good sack of flour, and two loaves besides, wrapped tight in paper.

Hanne raised her eyebrows at this parting bread gift, but Christa smiled at her, swift and secretive:

– I know you can use them. You've an extra mouth now – haven't you? Up at the Hof there.

The girl raised her eyebrows too; not like she was expecting an answer, though – more just to let Hanne know that she'd heard about Ditte.

– Gerda told me.

Of course, of course.

Hanne thought her daughter would have come straight down here with her empty egg baskets. She'd have sought Christa out – probably right here in this courtyard – half to ask about Kurt, more to be rid of her annoyance at her and Gustav. *Those old fools hid a worker! Can you believe it? They've taken in a worker girl!*

Now Christa asked:

– So it's true, yes? That woman ran away – just like the other workers?

And:

– How far do you think they got?

Hanne wasn't sure what to say to that.

She only knew about the woman at the Hof, not any others – and she felt herself growing chary too: where had Christa heard about more workers? It couldn't be from Gerda.

Hanne pictured the bakery mornings, queues of town wives here at the doorway: had one of them seen more runaways? Or had they seen the Werkschutz out to run them down again?

Hanne didn't like to think of that snow night. Or of so much town talk, either. She only hoped Christa had been alone when Gerda came calling, no townsfolk to overhear her spill all about the snow child. Just the thought of this made Hanne shrink inside. Because Ditte was her business, hers and Gustav's only: she didn't want town wives talking about her – or Heinrich, for that matter. He'd never had a good word to say about Kurt, her Hof son, and wouldn't harbouring runaways only confirm things in his eyes? Kurt's whole family revealing themselves as no-good Hof types. How much did he know about that winter night?

– What does your father say?

She had to ask. Although Hanne didn't want him knowing more about Ditte than she did.

But Christa handed over the flour sack instead of answering. She pulled a finger across her lips as she did so, zipping them shut again, as if in assurance – or was it just better not to ask more? Enough talk for one day.

The girl told Hanne, dry:

– If you see my father – tell him from me: he can sort out tomorrow's loaves on his own now.

She gave a short laugh, even.

– Tell him I've climbed out of my window. Tell him I've gone AWOL – and with an English soldier.

Hanne didn't see Heinrich on her homeward journey.

But she did see her first Front returners.

They were sitting on the Rathausplatz benches when she strode past: a huddle of young town sons under the shade trees. Lean and sleepless in the noonday quiet.

Hanne knew most of their faces. All were around Kurt's age, but no Kurt among them. The schoolmaster would have taught them; he would know all their names still, Hanne told herself. And she knew she ought to be glad, or at least relieved that they were back. But it was odd to see how they sat there, so listless. A cluster of young-old faces, unwashed, unshaven. Young soldiers no longer.

It was hard to see them and not have Kurt here.

When she got back to the Hof, Ditte was awake and Gustav was holding her. He'd come to stand squinting in the doorway, like he'd been sleeping himself, and only just woken up.

The child reached her arms out, half-shy, and Hanne slid the flour sack from her shoulders, only too glad to swap it for this prettier little burden.

She carried Ditte with the loaves into the larder. *Let's see what we can find for you, shall we?* And then, when Hanne lifted the first of them from her basket, she found two cigarettes falling from the paper.

That Christa.

An extra under-the-counter gift from her.

Hanne lifted them to show Ditte. *Seh's du?* Then she tucked the cigarettes away on the back shelf.

Keep them for Kurt, she thought. For when he comes home.

Or keep them for the meantime, for when they needed bread again.

16

The Mill Pool Depths

Sasha

Yeva said they couldn't go to the millstream too often; they couldn't draw attention. But Sasha saw how she waited for those afternoons just like he did. And when they got to the clearing with wet legs, wet shorts and skirt hems, his sister was first to pull off her sodden boots, to drop her clothes to dry among the boulders – she was always first into the water.

While Yeva swam, Sasha drifted with Mirko, feeling the cool of the current, the pull of the water. He crouched in the shallows too, looking for the best stones, smooth and stream-washed, to add to the circle. And then, when it was time to go, his sister helped him choose the smallest, the most perfect; Yeva slipped it into Sasha's palm for the slow walk down the slope again on Mirko's shoulders.

The hours between, though, in the clearing – while Mirko and Yeva just lay there, hand in hand and murmuring – they were long and slow, and just too hot.

Sasha lay on his tummy on the diving rock, dangling his fingers into the millstream, dropping in handfuls of shingle, watching them scattering and sinking. But the sun on the water was too much, and if Sasha lay on the grass like Yeva did, like Mirko, it made his legs itch, and his arms.

So he went exploring.

At first, he stuck to the birches, looking for bark curls and twigs for the circle, because Sasha still hoped for a fire there: for a day when they didn't need to worry if the smoke was seen by camp guards or by townsmen.

At first, Sasha kept near to the clearing too, where he could hear if his sister called him. But Yeva only ever called when she noticed him gone – and mostly that wasn't until it was time to go back to the camp – so Sasha took to wandering further.

Soon, the birches became pine trunks and the glade became cooler, and in that shade and dry pine smell, Sasha stopped minding the hours here so much.

He still had to watch where he was walking. Sasha mostly followed the run of the millstream so as not to lose himself; he tried to keep in sight of the water over one shoulder, or at least in hearing distance, so he could find his way back again between the tall pines. But now he was in the town woods – right in the thick of them – the slope down to the meadows was steeper; it dropped away in places too, sudden and deep. Fallen trunks hid gulches, and there were twisted root balls that formed overhangs, with hollows beneath them, so Sasha was careful as he strode. He grew curious also. Lying on his belly at the gully edges, just to look down them. Or on his back to look upwards, to watch the slow sway of the pine crowns. He listened to their stirring, like a far-off rain roar. And there was so much else to find here.

Crouching on the ground thick with needles, he could dig for cones with his fingers; Sasha could crawl under fallen branches and find more still in that soft ground. He turned over stones and set beetles scurrying. There were red-brown ants, too, hurrying in lines along the roots, up the bark grooves – more on each of the trunks that he passed.

Sometimes Sasha forgot himself – in that dry-dark, in among that bracken and bark – and when Yeva's call came, it was thin and distant. Sasha had to hurry then, scrambling back across the root and trunk and boulder – and much further than he'd remembered – arriving in the clearing to find his sister already lacing her boots, making to go.

But Yeva always had her head bent close with Mirko's; they were always still looking at each other only; and Sasha had never made them late back to the camp yet. They strolled down to the meadow grass in good time to gather kindling, or to help the women with the evening chores, and no one asked where they'd been hiding.

So when he got properly among the trees one afternoon, Sasha didn't think he had to worry too much. Even when he was long out of sight of the clearing, Sasha was certain that his sister wouldn't miss him.

He'd been looking for a pine cone – a good one to take back, to keep under his Nissen bed alongside the stream stones – and he'd found one that was a fair size: big enough to fill his palm. But then he'd wanted one for Yeva, and one for Mirko also, so he'd gone walking onwards, bending and picking up and discarding, until he'd found two – at long last – that were just about the same size. Both still tight and closed, just the way he liked them.

Now Sasha stood up straight and looked about himself.

The pines here were taller, the gaps between them filled with beech trees, beech leaves and branches – how long had he been walking?

He could hear something else now besides the high roar – there was a new rushing underneath the crowns here; it sounded like water. Sasha didn't have to walk too much further before he saw the millrace – and more too: he saw that he'd come to the head of it, right to where it started, and he'd never been so high among the trunks, or come so far into the woods here.

Above the millrace was a water wheel, an old water mill, and Sasha stood on tiptoes; he tried to look over the old roof for a sight of the meadows – of the camp too – because he thought they must be below here, right at the foot of the slope. But the summer leaves were thick on the branches; he wasn't even nearly tall enough.

Still, a path had been trodden here, through the bracken and leaf mould. The earth under his bare feet was summer hard; it had been smoothed over time, and Sasha thought of how many feet must have come here before him. He thought, too, of how they must be town feet. Because this mill spot was a town place – another one – wasn't it? – and then Sasha felt a swell of excitement that he was the one to find it. The roof beams sagged, and the trunks and branches leaned so close around the old walls, they let through only a shaft here and there of sunshine. That rare light was pretty, though: the way it cast across the mill windows, the few panes left in the leadwork glinting as the crowns moved.

There was a bridge here also, so he could cross. The planks were soft with moss. But the bridge led over a mill pool, and the railings were slippery and ancient, so Sasha had to dare himself. He had to edge his way forward, because the drop here was sharp: deeper than the pine hollows. The water beneath was green-dark and far-down, and the weir was so loud, too, the rushing surrounding him. Sasha's excitement sank away a little on the bridge spars, replaced by uncertainty – and just by the strangeness of finding himself alone here, looking down over the mill pool depths, cool and dark and private.

He pushed his fingers into his pockets for comfort; Sasha closed his palms over his pine cones: over Yeva's and Mirko's.

He threw the first one – Yeva's – he felt he had to – dropping it into the waters, just to break the stillness. The splash made him start, but the cone threw a ring of bright spatters around itself, and Sasha smiled to see that, and the ripples that came afterwards. He watched them lapping and purling; how the ripples went pooling across the surface, rolling across that darkness.

What now?

Yeva's cone floated and turned; it looked just like Mirko did when he went drifting along the millstream, so Sasha dropped Mirko's cone to join it. The second cone broke the surface lightly, bobbing up again straight afterwards, and then they both rolled so nicely, there in the waters, Sasha let his own fall from his fingers to be close to them.

He watched it falling, thinking it would make a fine splash and bob, and then float alongside the other two.

But instead, when his cone landed, it sliced into the mill pool, cutting into the darkness. And then it seemed to tumble there a moment, just under the surface, before the water swallowed it.

It gave Sasha such a lurch, the way the cone tumbled and turned, the way it was swallowed too – down into that deep – he had to crouch down; he had to look away, checking around himself. Too alone now in this town place.

Over the bridge, the path continued. But the ground there was damp: still wet like winter under the branches. The path had sunk deeper there and Sasha could see boot prints, even – more and still more of them, the longer he looked. When had so many been here? Sasha saw the place must have been crowded; the earth had been churned up under boot soles. Whoever had come here, they'd spilled off the path, stopping and turning; slipping and falling.

– Sasha!

He heard his name called.

– Sasha!

A voice came from behind him, and he turned sharp to find Mirko standing in the bracken with his arms raised.

– Come away from there!

Mirko was frowning; Sasha saw he must have come searching; he saw that Yeva must be looking for him also. And then this thought had Sasha standing. Would Yeva be angry?

– Come away, I said!

Mirko wasn't angry – or Sasha didn't think so: he was trying hard to keep his voice low. So then Sasha looked about himself for townsmen – were they not alone here? That thought had him frightened. He'd come to this town place – crowded with footprints – a trespasser among the high trunks. Had someone seen him throw the cones into their water?

And then there was so much shouting.

– *Dziecko!*

– *Dziecko – tutaj!*

Camp voices, crying out in Polish, Ukrainian.

– *De ty?*

They were rising up from the millrace, calling his name out.

– *Sasha! De Ty?*

– *Sasha!*

He saw Pani Josefa in the pink trunks, Pani Ana, Pani Natalia in their headscarves; he saw Osip and Jaroslav come splashing up the millrace – and even Pan Artem. And then Yeva was beside him and taking his elbows.

– Where did you go?

She shook at his shoulders.

– Where have you been all this time?

Sasha's tears came hard then, sobbing and gasping – he couldn't get the words out.

He couldn't tell Yeva about the pine hollows, or the mill pool, or about the cones and the dark water. He just shouldn't have come here; he shouldn't have done that.

He was lifted in strong arms – first Mirko's, then Pan Artem's – Sasha felt himself carried off and away again.

The pines gave way to bright sun, the loping turned to

striding, the meadow grass to duckboards, and he was back inside the camp boundary – and Sasha cried all the way there. Until he saw the sergeant at the head of a hut row, until he saw the *Ofitserka* behind him.

Sasha had to hide his tears then – or try to – while the sergeant threw his arms wide at the Back Enclave men; while he ordered them back to their quarter – *nothing to see here* – and the women back to their hut row – *go on, get going*; while the *Ofitserka* frowned at the scratches on Sasha's arms, and the grubby tear-streaks on his cheeks and palms.

– What's this about then?

Sasha pressed his face into Mirko's shoulder; he knew if he said anything then the *Ofitserka* would find out about the millstream – she'd find out all about their afternoons – wouldn't she? And if he said about the paths through the pine trunks – or the bridge and the footprints – or even just about the mill pool – then she'd know that he'd gone wandering. *You shouldn't have gone there. You shouldn't have done that.*

Inside her little office room, she gave him a wet cloth to wipe his cheeks, water to drink, a bread roll from the mess tent in silence. Sasha sat down with it, under her desk, between the chair legs, leaving Yeva and Mirko to their back and forth with her.

But then all Sasha could think was how he had thrown his cone into the water.

He saw it, in his mind's eye: how it had fallen into the deep there. *You shouldn't have done that.* And then such a quiet came over him, such a tiredness also, after all the crying, after feeling he'd done wrong somehow, Sasha had to lie down.

His eyes closed over, the cones tumbled into the dark waters, footprints slipping and sliding in the winter mud.

And even when Yeva woke him, the sleep and the quiet had swallowed all his words; they had swallowed up the afternoon.

17

Women and Children

Ruth

They shrugged off all questions.

– It doesn't matter.

– It doesn't matter now.

This is all Yeva would say, and Mirko, although Ruth tried for half the afternoon:

– It's better you tell me. It would be better if I know – really.

The two refused to explain, even in Polish or Ukrainian – even when Ruth called Stanislaw to translate for them.

– They say there is nothing to tell.

The old Pole could only lift his shoulders, and so Ruth could only let them go again.

She could see why they might be frightened, though. If

Yeva were told off by Farley, if a report went to the major, wouldn't she and Sasha be sent somewhere new again? The girl might be thinking that they'd be sent across the border, even, and before their mother could find them.

– It will be something like that.

Stanislaw nodded when he and Ruth talked it through afterwards, alone again in her office. But the whole thing had Stanislaw frowning. He told Ruth:

– It goes to show: DP camps are not for children.

This one wasn't, certainly: not in his eyes.

Then Fräulein Berger paid a second visit – and the very next morning.

This time, Hilde Berger came with her sister. One behind the other, the two old girls walked up to the camp gate, but no further, and when they spoke to the sentry, they made it sound so important, he had to come and fetch Ruth.

– They want to speak to someone in charge, ma'am. And I can't find the sergeant.

Where was Farley when you needed him?

– They won't set foot inside our gates here.

The sentry told her he couldn't persuade the Fräulein Bergers, not even as far as the courtyard.

– They're just refusing.

– Oh, for crying out loud!

Ruth had to go out to them at the roadside; she had to call Stanislaw to join her. She had to hear them out.

– *Es ist nicht zu glauben!*

That was the younger one – Hilde – who did all the talking, all the finger-pointing, her old knuckles quivering, affronted, while her sister stood behind her in listening silence, and Stanislaw murmured his translation.

– Fräulein Berger says we let children run wild here. She wants to know if we think it's the right thing.

Had the old girls heard the shouting? The commotion over Sasha, up on the lower slopes? With her quivering fingers, her sister's walking stick, it seemed unlikely that they strayed far from their villa orchard, but there had been quite a noise yesterday afternoon. If Hilde Berger hadn't heard it herself, she must have been told about it, because she kept talking about the children, her complaints turning back to the plum theft.

– *Die Pflaumen.*

– She wants compensation.

Stanislaw explained for Ruth.

– She says they were counting on their fruit trees to supplement their rations, but she's not heard back yet from the town hall.

– *Nicht zu glauben!*

– She says it is unbelievable. And she wants to know how it is that we can tolerate thievery.

– *So?*

Hilde was the worst of the two, Ruth decided: so righteous. The older one: at least she was quieter. At least she only watched the conversation, leaning on her stick, a good two paces back from her sister. Trude Berger stood looking from Ruth's face to Stanislaw's, and then in past the gate posts, as though she had come less to complain, more out of curiosity about the camp here.

A crowd of DPs had begun to gather now, drawn from the hut rows to the courtyard by the sound of voices. It was women, mostly: Josefa and Ana, and a few of the younger ones stepping forward to listen in. Trude looked at them, and they looked back at her, while her sister shook her finger at Ruth.

– *Nun? Was sagen Sie?*

She had a long list of grievances. Hilde hadn't just come about her plums being stolen, she'd begun shaking her finger at the tent rows, shaking her head about the camp as a whole.

– *Was soll das hier?*

She asks: what is this place for?

Stanislaw translated, patient.

– *Wie lange soll das nun bleiben?*

She wants to know how long the town must endure it. They have endured a lot, she says.

This last had Ruth raising her eyebrows. How much more of this was she supposed to bear before she could interrupt?

– *Und der Junge. Euer Dieb hier.*

Hilde turned her words back to the boy-thief – this is what she called Sasha:

– *Ein kleiner Gauner. Wie kann das sein?*

She turned her eyes on Ruth, clear that she thought this child-thief her fault.

– *Nun?*

She wants to know if you think it is right, the way we allow the children to behave here.

– *Und?*

Ruth shook her head to end this. She said to Stanislaw:

– Tell them to go to the town hall. Not to come to us again. If they want to talk about rations or curfews, that is not our work.

They should go to the major, she decided.

– Anything to do with townsfolk, it's town hall responsibility.

Ruth spoke loudly, over Hilde, and she turned away from her also, leaving her to Stanislaw and his translation. But now Trude Berger stepped forward; the older sister reached for her.

– Wait a moment.

Trude spoke in English – direct, but under her breath. Her fingers pointing through the camp gates, she leaned in closer, as though speaking for Ruth only.

– Those females?

She pointed at Josefa, at Ana:

– Are they from the winter?

Her question came out of nowhere, and Ruth could only blink at first, confused at being asked this – and in English.

– No.

Ruth shook her head, looking to Stanislaw, but he was still finishing with Hilde.

– They came after war's end.

Did the old girl understand her? Ruth tried another time.

– They came later.

Josefa and Ana, all these women here, had come after the surrender.

– After the fighting, yes? *Nach dem Krieg.*

– Oh?

Trude dropped her fingers.

She blinked through the camp gates, her forehead creasing. Then she took her sister's coat sleeve, decisive.

– *Komm.*

Hilde was still busy with Stanislaw, but Trude took her

arm – *komm nun* – linking it in her own, turning her back towards the villa streets.

– *Wir gehen nach Hause.*

Back in her office, Ruth made grudging note of Hilde's complaint for the record. Stanislaw lingered too, as if caught by the same irritation, not yet ready to return to his radios, so when Ruth found herself stalling about Trude – what had she wanted? – she lifted her head to ask.

– The older one? Did you catch what she said at the end there?

It had come after her sister's tirade, and Ruth wanted it on record too, except she wasn't even sure what Trude had been asking.

– She was looking at the women here – she was talking about the winter – did you catch any more than I did?

But Stanislaw had been talking – he'd been translating – so he lifted his shoulders.

– I only heard Hilde. I only know they were here about Sasha. About the plums he stole for the Ukrainian.

Then he stepped inside, though.

– Can I say something, Officer Novak?

The old Pole addressed her so formally, Ruth had to stop writing; she had to look up at him.

– I heard nothing about women or winter. But I did see young Sasha earlier.

Stanislaw told her he'd passed the boy, just as he was called to the camp gates and the Bergers.

– I'd just left my radios when I saw him. The boy was crouching in the grass between the hut rows – and with a good dozen cigarettes. You understand me? He was pulling his socks up high, slipping the cigarettes down the sides.

Stanislaw mimed it: how Sasha had counted them, furtive.

– It looked like the child was taking his cut – or even a little bit more.

The old Pole shook his head, short, as if to underline the point.

– I had to learn some tricks, I can tell you, when I was living here under the Germans.

He turned out his jacket pocket to show her, poking his finger through the corner: through a hole just large enough to drop a cigarette into the lining, or anything small and tradeable.

– But should a boy know about holes in pockets and how they come in useful? It can't be right – can it? – for a child to learn such things. Or for Pan Artem to allow himself such liberties: passing on black market practices.

Stanislaw spoke hurriedly, as though he had been wanting to say this for a good while. As though he were speaking his mind to Ruth – finally – now that the Berger complaint had given him licence.

– You think we are all good people here? Just because we were taken by the Germans? You think the years we've lived under them haven't done their worst?

The old Pole looked at her. He saw she had no answer.

– Well, that man is no good for the boy, I am telling you.

Ruth sat a while after he was gone. Still rattled by the Berger visit, and rattled further now by Stanislaw.

He wasn't wrong about Pan Artem: the Ukrainian was

at least as bad as he was good – for Sasha anyway. Still, Stanislaw's tone chafed at Ruth. She felt his disapproval, and a little too keenly.

She felt it was not needed.

Since when was it his place tell her the wrong and the right of things in this camp here?

A fight broke out – that same night – on the border between the Polish and Ukrainian quarters. It was only over a pair of blankets, but it was fuelled by plum brandy, and after the Back Enclave got involved, it turned properly nasty. Enough to land three men in the medical tent, and Pan Artem under guard.

Ruth found the big Ukrainian there – long past midnight – bloodied and brooding, with a cut on his lip and more on his knuckles. He was being watched over by an orderly: made to wait while the nurses attended to the injuries he'd inflicted on those around him. Most were cuts and bruises, but one man had a fractured jaw.

Worst of all: this had happened in the hut row just next to Sasha and Yeva's, and when Ruth stepped back outside the medical tent, she saw the children's faces among the watchers on the duckboards.

– Into bed – now!

In the morning, the major called her and Farley to the town hall.

Still shocked at the night's events, Ruth had to drive in with Stanislaw, with the sergeant, queasy with lack of sleep, and the prospect of this meeting.

– So what do we propose here?

The major started in with questions.

He already knew about the brawl from the medics. He even knew about the alcohol burning, although he didn't name his source. It was the complaints from locals he wanted to talk about first, though.

– There have been more sightings. I think it's your Back Enclave Ukrainians because I've had more than a dozen reports.

Most had come from his villa neighbours – as far as Ruth could tell in any case. The major didn't name them, but he spoke of claims that they'd seen DPs, in twos and threes, crossing through their gardens at dusk; or that they'd heard them at night, rattling at their cellar doors. Whoever these neighbours were, they hadn't come to the camp like the Fräulein Bergers; they'd called on him here at the town hall, or even at his residence. Reporting cracked windowpanes, scratches on doorframes. Telling of chicken coops raided, and tools going missing from outhouses. He said:

– Most are polite enough.

Which meant others must be less so, and Ruth could just imagine it: town fingers raised in complaint, pointing blame in the direction of the camp. The major looked from her to Farley, weary – tired of all of this – before he continued:

– I know a lot of what they say seems fantastical. But I don't think the stealing is. Do you? Sergeant? Officer?

Ruth thought of the plum juice on Sasha's shirt front; the plum stone slipped into Yeva's shirt cuff – could she tell the major? She thought he might sympathise; Ruth wasn't quite certain, though. And then the man picked up again:

– It's not as though we treat the DPs poorly. Their rations are far better than the locals'– do your people all know this?

– They do, sir.

Ruth had already charged Stanislaw with spreading the word, and he'd reported it was a source of satisfaction: a DP ration was worth 1,800, a German only 1,200 daily calories. Ruth had even sent this news home: *Make sure to tell the Herr Doktors.*

The major said:

– We'd all have them fed more – of course. But what else do they want?

Fun, perhaps? Ruth blinked at the major. Revenge, maybe?

The DPs had seen so much done to their countrymen, to their home countries, she thought the man must be able to guess at that, surely. He'd been in the fighting for so long and so recently; and he'd been speaking to his eastern counterparts – hadn't he said they fought just as hard? The man must have heard some stories. And then Ruth thought of the town returners: the young Germans she'd seen last time she came here. Had they been out east? What had they seen or done there in the name of front-line duty? And here they were now, just a stone's throw, just a short walk from the DPs' hut rows. She searched for words to say all this; only then Stanislaw offered the next best thing – polite and careful:

– Anything German, sir: the DPs see it as their right to take now.

Ruth glanced at him: was this only what his camp fellows said? Or did he feel the same way?

– All fair game, yes.

Now Farley nodded in agreement. The sergeant surprised

Ruth by speaking out to the major, speaking up for the DPs. He said:

– I'm not sure many would blame them, either – not among our troops here. Our Ukrainians are a rough lot, but with all due respect, sir: you weren't here to see the works when we arrived. The way the Germans here had treated these workers.

– The ones still left at the factory.

Ruth added this quietly: a small reminder to the major – workers were taken; workers were still missing.

The man nodded once, twice. He looked at them, tired-eyed.

But then he told them:

– It's still two fingers up at us, though. You do see that, don't you?

Their arguments only went so far.

– And the stealing is only part of it: I've had too many reports of DPs wandering. Not just in the villa gardens, but slipping along the town streets – even out along the Poststrasse. And what's to stop them going further? Your DPs will all have their grievances against the Germans. I have my own, I can assure you. But we can't go losing other countries' citizens. They are here on our watch – may I remind you all – until we can get them home again, and we can't let them get in trouble with the locals in the meantime. If last night's brawling is anything to go by, that could get dangerous. So I ask again: how do you propose to get the DPs in line?

– Well, sir.

Still Farley countered:

– Speaking frankly now. I don't see how we can, sir. Not really.

The sergeant shrugged his shoulders:

– We can patrol the curfew. But the DPs are not our prisoners. And if they are just out and about in the daylight, enjoying the sun and the countryside, then is it for us – sir – to tell them what they do in their free hours?

Ruth kept quiet. She couldn't meet the major's eye: he would see whose side she took.

The man stood and lit a cigarette. He stood and smoked at the window; he seemed to need to take a moment.

Then he asked her to stay on after Farley left.

– Just a short word. If I may, Officer.

And after the door closed, it was just the three of them in that silence. The major at the window, Stanislaw on the chair beside hers, and Ruth's last report lying just in her eyeline, on one of the major's desk piles.

She found herself casting her mind through what she'd written there. Her usual update on DP numbers; her last dispatches from Hannover and Brunswick – the visit from the Fräulein Bergers was the only outlier. Ruth thought of Trude's questions about the women in the courtyard, and how the major would know there had been no women working in the factory, no women's names in the records. So was this what he wanted to ask about? Or could this be her chance to raise it? Ruth wondered how to phrase it. *Women were brought here, sir, before the surrender.* She had a German's word for this; it had come from one of his villa neighbours to boot: proof that there could be women among the missing workers. Didn't that make the question of searching more urgent?

Now the major picked up her report, though, and told her:

– It's this last part I'd like to talk about.

He leafed through her pages, and this had Ruth cautious, because that last section was all about Sasha and Yeva.

– I have to say, Officer Novak: I would sooner they weren't in your camp there, those children.

Ruth didn't like what she was hearing. She thought the major could see that; the way he watched her as he sat down at his desk again, resting his cigarette in the ashtray.

– You think I do not do enough, Officer Novak.

It wasn't a question. Ruth watched him, still cautious as he continued.

– You'd have me do more for the DPs here. You'd do more yourself – I am sure – for the women in your charge. For those two children. Would I be right?

Ruth nodded – just enough for him to go on.

– Well. You tell me, Officer: how much would be adequate?

His tone wasn't unfriendly. She sensed no impatience behind it. Only his familiar weariness. The major was simply asking – could they ever do enough for the people here?

He let this sit between them.

– Everything has its limits. We all come up against them. I saw that in the fighting; I see it here too.

He gestured beyond himself, as if to the town and the camp and the border – as if to the war's aftermath; its holding camps and ration cards and bomb-damaged railway lines; the demands of the townsfolk, of his eastern counterparts, of his own occupation staff. The major closed his eyes – as if on all of that – just for a moment.

Then he leaned forward, coming to the point:

– You are not equipped for minors.

He said the camp was not right for children – and Ruth could hardly argue. Even if she didn't like to hear this; even if she didn't like it said out loud in front of Stanislaw. The old Pole was still quiet beside her, but she couldn't look at him for the moment. The two of them hadn't spoken about the brawl yet; Ruth hadn't felt able. The fight had given her pause, though. The furious noise of it in the dark; the sight of the cuts and blood, split lips, split knuckles – and Pan Artem's hard-eyed refusal to answer to Farley. The man was remorseless. And how much had Sasha and Yeva caught of that?

The major told her:

– That Brunswick camp in your report: I've made enquiries. They have Polish nurses; Czech Red Cross too, if I remember rightly. A whole section just for children.

Enough room, Ruth thought, enough personnel to take better care of their charges. The major said:

– They gave me word about another place, too. In Hamburg. It's a new one, run by us. I don't mean by the army: by the new civilian authorities.

Ruth nodded. She knew what he driving at: better the children were in civilian care.

She knew also that she couldn't bring up Trude Berger. Not now – not after all he'd said. She'd only be told – again – about the limits of her work here: the tasks to which she should confine herself. It was the children she should be thinking of: Sasha and Yeva, not last winter, or transports of workers, and certainly not the vague say-so of an elderly townswoman.

– So I'll send word to Hamburg that you'll be visiting – shall I?

He was brisk now: telling her rather than asking.

– You can take a jeep from the transport yard. You can take a driver, if that makes it easier – take Stanislaw, here. Only make it soon, Officer Novak. We need somewhere sensible to send those children.

The man was right about that last part, just like he'd been right about so much this morning. But Ruth felt his impatience return and it irked her. Sasha and Yeva ought to be somewhere better suited – they ought to be away from soldiers – but already she had begun to wonder: was it only their welfare, or might it also be the camp itself that bothered the major? Spilling over its boundaries, causing trouble with the townsfolk, pushing up against the limits of his operation here. The war was over; he was tired; the British occupation of the Heide would be easier without it.

– We have to step up our repatriation efforts.

The major stood, lifting an arm to show her and Stanislaw out.

– We have to get those Ukrainians moved on for starters – and in quick order. Camp life is too idle. All this waiting around, it's no good for them.

Ruth turned for the door, her eyes falling on Stanislaw. Did he feel annoyed just like her? His face was careful, expressionless – but she already knew his thoughts.

It's no good for those children.

18

Not Yet

Hanne

The Elbe was oily against the bows, the Hamburg piers crowded, and Hanne breathless in the morning heat.

She'd set out as soon as she was able. Leaving Gustav with his breakfast, she'd lifted Ditte into a shawl sling – *gut, mein Dirn* – settling her with a kiss onto her hip and carrying her out of the Hof gate, heading for the Poststrasse.

All week Hanne had been nervy: ever since she'd seen the Front returners. She needed to know now – with more urgency – where her Kurt was, and how soon he might be returned to them. Each night, on the radio, in all the announcements, she heard *Red Cross* this and *Red Cross* that, so she'd decided – she had to go to the Red Cross offices, the German one, in Hamburg.

The English only allowed one sailing there each day now, and Hanne had to half-walk, half-jog to make it. Hoping for a van to pass, or a car. *Just not an English patrol jeep – please.* At Buxtehude, she caught a lift from an orchard wife, the woman hoisting her into the cart with Ditte and groaning:

– You see how hard they make our lives? Our occupiers?

But they'd made it to the pier at Jork; Hanne had made it across the waters, and now she squinted in the quayside glare before steering with Ditte into the streets beyond it, weaving a path through all the wharf queues, and the stragglers.

Everywhere she looked, there were more of them: women standing in line along the St Pauli pavements, men crouching in the scant shade of doorways: all of them oddly silent. Hanne thought they'd come to trade perhaps – but what? The women lingered, uneasy, the men's eyes blank under their hat brims, their cheeks slick and grimy – and everywhere a sour smell: sweat, or heat, or something else. Hanne was relieved to leave them behind her; soon she was among the tenements.

But here the buildings were roofless, and she had to slow down. Because where there used to be walls and street signs and shop windows, she found rubble piled to shoulder height. Without familiar landmarks, Hanne couldn't be sure which road they were on now, which direction she should walk next.

She had to stop – again and again – at every corner; either to check and to look – shouldn't they be taking another turning? – or just to swap Ditte to the other hip before she pressed further. The grit got inside her shoes, and Ditte grew heavy in her old arms, the sun too strong and beating down on them. The heat only grew worse, the further they got from the water, and still they walked like that, and walked, for what felt like far too far: Hanne thirsty and Ditte unhappy at being hefted, her curls sticking damp to her forehead. Until they got to the Heiligengeistfeld.

Hanne arrived at the open ground half by accident; they'd come much further from the Elbe than she'd expected. But here – out in the open at last, blinking out across the dust and the grass – she could stop and get her bearings.

The city bunker stood at the far side: a vast hulk, concrete sides pock-marked, flak turrets empty now at all four corners. Hanne made for the shade it cast, and for the standpipe she knew she'd find beside it – and there she found another queue, this time of housewives. Tin buckets on their arms, rubble dust on their aprons, smeared into the sweat across their foreheads. One had a baby on her own hip; she lent Hanne a tin scoop for Ditte to drink from; she let Hanne splash her face, too, and cool her palms.

– First they bomb us, these English; now they leave us to queue as punishment.

Hanne didn't like the woman's hard laugh.

She pressed on for Altona, worrying as she walked at how much time she'd already wasted.

Wouldn't they have to trek all this way back again to get the one sailing home this afternoon? And even if she caught it, Hanne knew she'd be late back to the Heide; she'd be out after curfew, so Gustav would fret until he saw her – and likely for a good while afterwards. He hadn't liked her coming to Hamburg, and she was uncertain herself now: what might she find out?

And then she was there – in Altona, on the Hauptstrasse;

Hanne made the turning and found herself almost directly outside the Red Cross offices. She'd been so sunk in her own thoughts, holding Ditte pressed damp against her, Hanne might have passed it entirely – but for the queue outside on the pavement.

It was dim inside, and just as crowded.

Hanne saw people waiting on benches; each time the queue shifted forwards, she found more folk. They were sitting against the walls; they were standing too, and crouching – all along both sides of the entrance hall.

There were so many faces, Ditte had to hide her eyes against Hanne's shoulder; and above their heads were so many notices – a great mass of papers and posters – Hanne could hardly take them in at first.

At the front desk, the Red Cross officer barely raised his face to nod, passing Hanne a request form, and with it a pencil, stubby from sharpening.

She slid Ditte from her hip, to have her arms free for writing, but then the child clung so she had to bend down to settle her. Ditte wouldn't stand at her ankles; she wouldn't sit either, she just kept clinging to Hanne's sleeves and fingers – and she even hid her eyes from Hanne's own now, burying her small face in Hanne's skirt folds.

– Ach, Kind.

So Hanne had to lift her again and hold her.

She had to write with Ditte's face pressed hot to her shoulder. Hanne printed Kurt's full name, as best she could, his rank and unit and birth date, his war wound; copying, laborious, from his Wehrmacht papers that she'd brought with her – and all with the officer watching. And when she pushed it back across to him, his eyes skimmed her answers, but his face showed nothing at all, as if this process were all so normal. Mothers came in all the time, with children clinging to their shoulders; they put in queries for sons who were wounded. Who weren't missing in action, but missing anyway.

– Very well.

The man stepped into the office room behind his desk; he passed Hanne's form on to another, who took and skimmed it in turn, and began flicking through a long box of record cards.

Hanne stayed at the front desk to keep watching. But then Ditte grew restless, twisting against her; Ditte began to cry also – and Hanne didn't blame her. The child was so hot and tired after the long and strange morning; Hanne was tired herself, sticky and prickling with heat – and now with rocking and soothing. She shifted Ditte to her other hip, but still the child's cries grew louder. And when Hanne turned back to look for the officer, his door had swung closed, so now she couldn't see either man, or what might be happening.

– You just have to wait.

A voice came from behind her: from the woman at the bench end nearest.

Her face large and unfriendly, she motioned Hanne to take Ditte and her wailing, to go and find a seat somewhere far from her.

Hanne pressed her face to Ditte's cheek in answer.

Few of the others on the benches showed interest; none showed much sympathy; most were just waiting, though, their eyes on the floor, or on the office doorway. Ditte cried, and a man came out and called a number – but it wasn't the officer Hanne had spoken to. Ditte cried, while the man called another time, irritable. Finally, a woman stood and hurried towards him, and Hanne turned her eyes away. The child was so hot with tears now, and her wailing so pitiful, Hanne had to walk the corridor – not to find a seat, though, only to soothe the girl.

The walls were crowded with notices.

Hanne rocked Ditte as she walked, looking above the waiting heads at all the paperwork. She saw posters about rations and rules and curfews – but other scraps and notes too, of all kinds. Some were typed; more were handwritten; Hanne rocked and read them, leaning in closer to work through the words there. She found names first, then dates and places. Inked on cardboard, or on old postcards, on the backs of envelopes. There were pleas and queries, pinned to the boards, or stuck up there with tape at the corners – layer upon layer – so many, they spilled out onto the plasterwork.

Oskar Petersen, age 7, last seen 14 March
Brown hair, blue eyes, birthmark on his right shoulder. Separated from his family on the evacuation ship from Stralsund.

Family Krause of Hamm – missing sister Karin.
Please write. We are living with Anni, in Harburg.

People lost, people looking: all along the corridor.

Hanne found Hamburg folk who'd been bombed out of their apartments; folk from Danzig and Königsberg, who'd fled from the Red Army. All had lost touch with someone: a sister, an aunt, a grandfather. Hanne read brothers' names, and uncles'; places last sighted; pleas from loved ones.

Ditte was crying still, but lower now, her head growing heavy on Hanne's shoulder. The child's limbs were growing softer again, pressed against her, but still Hanne rocked and read on – because there were mothers on the walls here.

Hedwig Kaspers, last of Elbing – separated from her two sons, 27 February.
Please make contact.

Ilse Röhl, last seen 3 March, on the transport from Danzig.
Your children are safe, they are here in Stade. Please send word!

After these first ones, Hanne found so many more. Fleeing on transports, all through the final war weeks. Last seen at cross-roads, on quaysides, then lost in the tumult – in the winter cold.

Hanne held Ditte closer.

All the words had exhausted her; the child had stopped crying; she lay in her arms, sleep-heavy and quiet, but the cards had Hanne thinking back to the snow night and the woman who'd come holding her.

Shouldn't there be a card for that woman on a wall somewhere?

All the mothers on walls here were German. Still, Hanne found herself blinking and turning. Because all these weeks and months that Ditte had been with them, she had taken for granted that the woman would return someday. That love would drive her; she would have to come and find her child.

Now, though, Hanne thought of the woman crouched in

Gustav's woodshed corner, holding Ditte shawl-wrapped and half-frozen. Hanne thought, too, of the empty lane the next morning, the woman's footprints in the verges. She thought of how the woman must have run from them – headlong and snow-blind.

She'd have been brought in on a transport – across the Heide in the half light – in the hardest cold of winter – and the place would have been strange to her, no familiar sight to hold on to. The heath was wide, the woman had fled at night, and in the morning there was snowfall. What else could she be but lost now?

Hanne turned to the cards on the wall again.

If she had to write one for the woman in their woodshed – what could she even write about her?

That she was young; maybe she'd been nineteen, maybe twenty. That she'd been thin and cold, with a raw face, raw fingers. She was a girl with no name, only a worker's patch stitched to her blouse front. She was a young Pole – that's all Hanne knew about her – this young thief, who'd made off with Gustav's work coat.

The yard coat!

Hanne lifted her face when she thought of it. Because it had Brandt's yard name stitched to the pocket flap – of course it did! That coat was the one part she'd not thought of; Brandt's yard badge was the one marker.

– Frau Buchholz?

The Red Cross officer was back; he was standing at the front desk with a slip of paper.

Pulled from her thoughts – Ditte heavy with sleep now in her arms – Hanne had to hurry with her along the corridor.

– Our apologies.

The officer told her:

– This all takes longer than it ought to.

The man gestured to the walls, by way of explanation, and then to the office behind him, to all the record cards and paper files. But Hanne couldn't quite understand yet – why he was apologising, and why he didn't say any more than that. The slip of paper he passed to her had nothing on it but a set of numbers.

– You need to keep that.

The office pointed:

– It's your case number.

– You have no information?

She sounded shrill, even to her own ears, but the man only lifted his shoulders in further apology.

– So do the Russians have him?

Hanne hoped he knew that at least. Or couldn't he give her some assurance?

– Please?

– We cannot be certain.

The officer was guarded.

– But your son was on the East Front at the close of hostilities, so this is the assumption we will work on. This is where we will start our enquiries.

It was only just starting? Hanne stared at the man. She thought of all the time she might have to wait still. What she would have to say to Gustav. To Christa. *They don't know where our Kurt is. No one does.*

– But he is wounded.

Hanne whispered this.

– I wrote about his arm, yes? You saw that on the form – you must have.

The officer nodded – was that sympathy? Hanne didn't want it.

– The Russians shouldn't be holding him.

She told the man – too loudly – and Ditte shifted in her arms, as though she might wake and cry again, but Hanne couldn't stop herself.

– My boy is wounded. The Russians need to send him home to us.

She insisted, although the officer didn't even know – no one did – if Kurt was with the Russians at all. Hanne told him:

– The war is over. And he's my son – yes?

– Of course. Of course.

The officer held up his hands: he spoke as though to reassure.

But then he gestured to the walls again – to all the notices – and Hanne turned and saw all the people too, still waiting, some of their faces pulled into frowns now.

– You think you're the only one?

The large woman spoke again, scornful, behind her. So Hanne stopped talking; she picked up the receipt and turned away.

Outside, on the pavement, she couldn't walk yet.

She knew she should be making for the Elbe, for the sailing; but Hanne had nothing to bring home.

Ditte was heavy in slumbers. The child was heavy in her arms too, and Hanne crouched on the steps to ease the ache in her chest, her shoulders; just to sit a while and hold her.

She thought of Kurt. But she couldn't picture where he was now. Hanne thought of the cards on the walls too – she hadn't been able to stop yet, still thinking of the woman hiding, of her running in the dawn light.

The woman was lost now, like her Kurt was. But if she still had that yard coat, Hanne told herself, then someone could help her. Hanne knew it would only be right if someone helped her find her child.

Not yet, though.

Hanne asked, holding Ditte closer.

Let it not be for a while still.

19

A Better Place

Ruth

She was out early – on foot, too. Striding along the villa streets, along their leaf and green.

When she came to the Berger house, the curtains were open on the ground floor, but still drawn in the upper storeys. Ruth knocked anyway. Stepping back from the house after she'd done so – so if the old girls looked out, they would see her uniform: they would see they ought to be opening.

Ruth wanted the Bergers to see she was alone here. She had come without Stanislaw to translate for her – Ruth had come without telling anyone – armed only with what she hoped was enough German phrases.

Sie haben Frauen gesehen?

She wanted to ask about the women workers.

Ist es wahr?

Had Trude seen them, or only heard rumours?

Wann war das? Datum?

When was this? What day, what month?

Ruth wanted proof for the major: *there are more missing labourers.* So she had to get as much as possible out of these old sisters. What was on their patches? Were they farm girls, or dressed like factory workers? Who had been guarding them? There were no women when Ruth's convoy arrived: someone had taken them somewhere.

But she knocked, and then knocked again, and got no answer.

Backing down the front path, Ruth looked up and saw movement. There was someone – Hilde? Trude? – at one of the middle-floor windows. An old face glanced down at her – angry? anxious? – and then the curtain was drawn again.

– Fräulein Berger!

Ruth called out.

She kept her eyes turned up at the middle floor, backing further to call more loudly, annoyed at being ignored now. Her last step took her out of the front gate, onto the road – straight into the path of a town boy.

– *Lass da!*

He swerved on his bicycle. Ruth heard him more than she saw him: a rush of spokes, a sprawl of long limbs, a young mouth open and shouting.

– *Verdammt!*

The boy missed her – but only just – only by veering. His wheels skidded under him, and he almost fell too, letting go of his handlebars, the satchel he'd slung over them landing in the road dust. The boy wasn't a Front returner; at least Ruth didn't think so. He was tall but gangling, and the satchel made him seem too young for soldiering. It had opened as it landed, spilling its contents across the cobbles; Ruth saw soap bars – English coal tar – and sugar cubes. So he was not too young for the black market.

The boy only stopped a moment. Once he'd seen her uniform, he grabbed at his satchel and righted his handlebars, pushing off down a cut-through between the villa gardens.

So then the boy was gone too. The villa road silent, all the doors closed to Ruth.

Back in her offices, she found the morning's dispatches – a great stack of them – already on her desk.

Most were papers for Ruth to work through. But among the last was an envelope, the handwriting careful and addressed to Stanislaw.

– For you!

She held it out to him when he came from the mess tent, and he blinked with surprise, taking it with a small nod, courteous as always, even in his coolness.

Stanislaw looked at the handwriting, and Ruth waited for him to say something. But then he tucked it into his pocket without opening it – without even turning it over to look on the back flap.

This was the first thing Ruth had done: look for the sender. She'd seen his brother's name there – *Barthos* – and then gone searching through her dispatch list, leafing through the papers, running her finger down the pages, scanning the lists to find mention of Stanislaw. *Next of kin located.* There it was: the Red Cross confirmation, typed in black and white. They'd found Barthos! Ruth had hardly been able to grasp it. Barely able to work further, she'd kept the letter on her desk, watching for Stanislaw's arrival.

But he'd looked at the envelope, and then he'd pocketed it without further comment – and now he pulled up his chair, starting in on his morning's typing.

She had to leave him to his silence; Ruth knew this.

Stanislaw would need time, she told herself, peace and privacy for reading; she owed him that much. But still, it smarted. Stanislaw was just as punctual as he'd always been, and diligent too, working on with her into the afternoons – but always at one remove. And she didn't know what to do about that.

Her own dispatches were from Hamburg.

Ruth opened them while Stanislaw worked on. The first said the visit to the children's home had been confirmed; the second that a jeep had been approved for her by the major.

So now Ruth had to go looking for Yeva.

– It's a home for children. For children only.

Sitting between her blanket walls, Ruth laid it all out for her in English, and then Stanislaw did the same in Ukrainian, in that slow and careful gentleman's way of his: pausing between sentences to be sure everything was clear for the girl.

– Our *Ofitserka* Novak here, she will visit now, to see that it is suitable. That it is a better place for you both. I will visit at the same time. And then we can tell you afterwards – what the rooms are like, where you will sleep, where you will eat. Everything.

Yeva listened just as carefully; her expression even, her gaze also, she gave no sign that the prospect of a move surprised her. Ruth thought perhaps the girl had even been expecting this.

Since the fight in the Back Enclave, since Ruth's last visit to the major, Yeva had taken to passing by her office in the afternoons. The girl sat on the step, helping Josefa with her darning, listening to Natalia, to Ana murmuring. But Ruth saw how she made sure to sit herself closest to the doorway, so she could listen out for anything Ruth and Stanislaw might talk about: anything to do with her and Sasha – or with the mothers here.

Her own mother's whereabouts would still be uppermost for Yeva; this much was clear to Ruth. So now she told her:

– I've written to the Red Cross as well. To the one in Kiev. To say that you are here, yes?

And then Stanislaw explained while he translated:

– If your mother has already gone home again, the *Ofitserka* says the Red Cross in Kiev will be the best way to make contact.

But Yeva frowned at this, turning to face Ruth.

– So you haven't written to Herr Maas? To the farmer?

She asked in Ukrainian; she knew Ruth understood enough now: there was no pretending with this girl. Yeva went on, too:

– I have told you. Our mother is here still. In Germany. She would not go home without us.

Then she looked to Stanislaw, talking low to him:

– You tell the *Ofitserka*. You tell her properly.

He did as she insisted.

– Yeva says it is better to write to the farmer. She says it is better than writing to your Red Cross people. Herr Maas was there the day her mother was taken; Yeva thinks the man must know who else took workers; or he could give names, perhaps, of other farmers to call on. She says he might do that. She says he was a kind man, even if he was a German.

The girl must have been thinking all this through, turning over all the possibilities; and now she turned to Ruth as though something more had just occurred to her.

– You have to decide, yes? About me and Sasha. It's you who gets to say – if we stay here, if we go to Hamburg. Or if you send us back home across the borders.

Ruth nodded.

The girl did too, and then she told her:

– So then: better you let us stay where our mother can find us.

They drove in to Hamburg through the remains of the harbour. Stanislaw in the front seat, beside the major's driver; Ruth in the back, squinting out of the jeep windows.

The Elbe bridges were shored up, but the waters were still choked with ship carcases. In the harbour yards, the cranes lay blackened and twisted, listless on the slipways. In the city, they drove along streets that were burned-out, desolate, passing row upon row of charred tenements, the windows just holes in that black, with nothing behind them. Ruth saw tram stops with no trams, and a station that was hardly a station any longer, just a bomb crater with a façade, the high tracks beside it left buckled by the blast, sagging under their own weight.

Then the jeep had to stop at a junction – right by a hollowed-out tenement. The street door had been torn off – the whole front entry – and the insides were exposed to the sunlight. Ruth stared at the stone flights of the stairwell: all firestorm-black, but strangely intact, still leading up and up, but into nowhere.

Beyond this, in the back courtyard, a gable end stood propped up by buttresses – leaning, crumbling, as though ready to tumble in on itself. But right at the base, at the cellar entry, Ruth saw an open doorway. Washing was strung from post to post there: aprons hung up to dry, nappies beside them, and three small summer dresses.

Children were living in these cellars. In the midst of all these ruins.

The sight had Ruth looking to Stanislaw: should they transfer more children to this now?

The driver saw her discomfort.

– It's something to behold, isn't it?

He nodded to her in the rear-view mirror.

– It takes a good bit of getting used to; I see that every time I drive someone new here.

Then he glanced at Stanislaw:

– Your Lwów, though. And Warsaw. I've heard all sorts – I can tell you. Whatever our airmen did here, remember: the Germans did tenfold.

Beyond the centre, the streets grew wider, and then came pavements that were suddenly tree-lined. The building they stopped outside was a fine one: white, with a stucco frontage. It was the last in a row of good Hamburg houses, all untouched by air raids, all requisitioned by the army – and Ruth saw a young matron in the doorway, smiling at their surprise, waiting to greet them under the portico.

– Makes an odd fit as a children's home, doesn't it?

Brisk and Scottish, no nonsense, she shook both their hands:

– I'm Frances. I'm Fran. I'm to give you the tour here.

She led on through the ground floor, telling them the rooms here had been a German field hospital of sorts at the end of hostilities.

– Before that, it was a doctor's practice. A father's – and the family lived upstairs.

She showed them the small reception office, off the entrance hall: the desks clustered, everything makeshift, but making the best of it.

After this, they came to a consulting room – now a bunk-lined dorm – and then a second one – now a dining hall. The cabbage smell of lunch still lingered, but the floor was mopped clean, trestles pitched along the parquet.

– We've enough tables – just. Two sittings at mealtimes means we can feed forty at a squash. Though we have more here.

Fran told them they had eighteen girls, twenty-six boys.

– That's our current numbers anyway.

Ruth had read the report the major sent her; she knew most of those children would be Poles and Ukrainians. *If they have space*, he'd told her, *your two will fit right in.*

– We've just taken in two more.

Fran lifted her chin to the far end of the dining hall, and Ruth turned to see a pair of girls come through from the back scullery. Two sets of skirts and plaits and aprons; two young faces – the first she'd seen here. They stopped in the doorway, their murmuring hushed by the sight of visitors, and Fran smiled to reassure them.

– Up you go now. Join the others. *Na górę.*

She ushered them through the near door and upstairs, then turned to Ruth again:

– Our newest arrivals; they came just two days ago. And you'll be sending us more now?

– Most likely.

Ruth nodded. Although she was still uncertain how Yeva might take this – and still more uncertain now that she'd seen the two girls' wariness.

– Our major says we're not equipped.

– And he thinks we are?

Fran raised her eyebrows, leading Ruth and Stanislaw out again across the hall.

In the small infant dorm, she passed along the beds, tucking and straightening, swift about everything – and she apologised:

– These field cots here, they're temporary. Or they're meant to be anyway. The doctor's rooms here are good – and upstairs is homely – but finding proper bedsteads, proper mattresses; finding so many things – it isn't easy.

Except then they came to a window, tall and elegant, and a view – what a view! – across a lawn; Ruth had to stop a moment. She hadn't expected the place to have a garden, let alone trees and brick paths. The grounds were narrow and overgrown, but they were full of leaves and sunlight, and she could even see water. Were they at the riverside?

Ruth reached for Stanislaw to point this out to him – *will you look at that now!* – and she even found herself laughing, inside, despite herself, nodding to the view there:

– No lawns in our place – are there? Or walls like this. Or ceilings.

She nodded to the cornicing above the window frame and Stanislaw blinked with her in dry agreement.

– None in my hut anyway.

Somewhere up there, above their heads, Ruth heard chairs scraping; a call and answer; children's voices.

– That's the afternoon classes you're hearing.

Fran had stopped at her bending and folding and now she pointed upstairs.

– We've been putting in schoolrooms, up in the family's old apartments.

So then Ruth laughed again – out loud this time – could this place get any better? She thought how good school would be for Sasha.

– You already have teachers here?

Even Stanislaw joined in:

– Do you need another one?

– If you're offering?

Fran grinned at the two of them, turning to lead them on again.

– We need another one of everything – any number of shoulders to press to this creaky wheel of ours.

The quarters for the older children were on the top floor.

Fran showed them to a small room where she said they might fit another field cot – just enough room for Sasha.

It was under the eaves, and full of the afternoon sun. Fran opened the dormer, turned back the blanket on the bunk nearest:

– We'd make them comfy here, your two. As best we can.

Ruth smiled in response.

Although she knew full well: she could tell Yeva all about the house and the beds and the gardens, and even about the school for Sasha, but she'd still have to assure her their mother could find them here. And how to do that? Wouldn't every move make finding them harder?

Then doors were opened – downstairs – on the floor below them. Ruth heard calling coming from outside, a sudden and jostling commotion, while Fran beckoned them swiftly to the window.

– Lessons are over!

Down in the gardens, the children were being let out now, and Ruth leaned on the sill to watch as the first boys ran across the wide lawn.

– This is the best part.

Fran murmured, propping her elbows on the sill beside her.

– When you see them like this.

First it was just a handful, then more boys came tearing, girls starting games of run and jump across the wild grass. Most headed for the lawns, others gathered at the terrace edges. These last ones still had that war-child wariness Ruth had got to know from Sasha, from Yeva. She felt Stanislaw watching at her shoulder, so she turned to see if he saw that.

– They do get used to the routines here.

Fran told them it came slowly.

– Given patience; we have to give them time.

For a moment, Ruth saw a crack in her smile.

– It amazes me how they get used to us, the children. I'm sure you can imagine how it is with them.

All were fed, Ruth noted: their cheeks already filling out a little, the way the DPs' had in their first weeks. Each child had had new shoes provided, new shirts and shorts or dresses – all except the two girls they'd seen earlier in the dining hall. Still in their farm aprons, they both stood to one side, eyeing the other children from the safety of their own corner. And wouldn't Sasha and Yeva be like that?

– Yes, I know.

Fran saw her looking.

– It's hardest when they're new here. Those two are sisters, from Poland. At least they came as a pair – I'm glad of that much. We think they're nine and thirteen.

– They don't know themselves?

Fran shook her head and then she sighed.

– It's just hard to get words out of them. It took us a good while to get them here, even – a good bit of finding out. We know they were taken with their mother, and that they were sent to work with her on the farm where we found them.

– Their mother wasn't there any longer?

Ruth already knew the answer.

– Not when we got there. From what the girls remember, she was only with them for the first harvest.

Fran shook her head again, squinting down at the daughters.

– Their mother was moved on by the authorities. She had to leave her girls with the farmers – probably that was three years ago. I hear this kind of thing all the time, you know?

Ruth nodded; she could imagine how many reports Fran had typed. She knew what that felt like. Fran said:

– It's just by chance – pure chance – that one of our patrols found them. The girls were out on an errand after curfew, else they'd still be there now. When the patrol found the farm wife, she said they were her brother's daughters – she started to lie, in other words. But even after we'd searched the place – after the older girl told us how their mother was taken – everything – the wife didn't want to give the two of them over. She said she was too fond now.

Ruth felt herself frowning, baulking at that notion.

– Did she say where the mother had been moved to?

Fran shook her head.

– She claims she doesn't know. She might not be lying about that either. The girls don't know, certainly.

– Maybe the mother will find her way back, though?

Yeva was so sure her mother would do this, Ruth had to ask:

– If the mother knows where she last saw them – might she not go to find the girls?

Fran looked at her, doubtful. A woman on her own, crossing Germany, along bombed roads, and through curfews? Through occupation zones?

Ruth nodded; she felt the impossibility. Hadn't the major warned as much? The man was right; again, he was right. And Ruth would have to explain all this to Yeva, if she moved the children here. It didn't make her feel any easier.

Then Fran shook her head a last time about the farm wife:

– She showed us the bedroom she'd laid out for the girls; the aprons she'd sewn for them; how they ate with her at the family table, *like they are my own daughters*. The farm wife cried, even. She cried even more when the older girl asked to go with us – *please*. The child asked the farm wife for permission to leave – can you believe it? And you know the worst part? The younger one cried when we came to take them. She's cried both nights they've been here, asking to go back. The girl must have grown fond of the farm wife as well. Or – I don't know.

Fran made a helpless gesture, and Ruth watched the two children; the younger one especially: the way she stood, uncertain, half behind the older. Better she is here, Ruth told herself: still with her sister. Not on a farm with some old German wife.

Ruth still didn't know, though, about Sasha and Yeva. Was moving them the best idea?

The children's shadows were long across the lawn; Ruth saw their time here was passing; the driver would be waiting. But Stanislaw turned to Fran now, a little hesitant.

– May I ask, please?

He pointed to the water, glinting between the treetops:

– Is that the Elbe?

– It's the Alster.

Fran smiled, grateful to finish with something lighter.

– It's the other river here. But it flows into the Elbe. And you'll soon get your bearings – once you come and work with us.

She tried a grin again – teasing him.

– Not half bad, that view. Don't you think?

Stanislaw wrinkled his forehead in the sunlight, and Ruth looked at his old face, still looking past her. Did he really want to work here? She hadn't thought he was serious. Wasn't he thinking of home and Barthos? What had his brother written in that letter?

Ruth squinted with him across the water.

At the far shore, a few church spires stood odd and tall among the ruins: copper rooftops strangely upright, out of place above the wastes. But the river and the sky did make up for that: both so wide and elegant – and the view was a step up from the one beyond his Nissen doorway, certainly. He'd had a letter from Barthos, but Stanislaw had no transport date. So was he hoping for a better place to wait out the next months, before he could make the home-bound, brother-bound journey?

– You see our gardens here?

Fran was telling him more now:

– They lead down to the shoreline. There's a jetty, just beyond those trees there – look. We even have a boat shed. No boats, though. A pity, that, because it'd be a grand spot for rowing.

She pointed further for Stanislaw, to a set of willows a little way along the shoreline.

– I have my eye on a good few picnic spots, I can tell you. I want to take the children – you can come too – as soon as I wangle a boat for us.

– Well, let me know when you do.

Ruth murmured:

– I'll come and visit you both.

Stanislaw smiled at that – just about – while Fran laughed.

– Yes, do! Bring your bathers. Keep your fingers crossed this weather holds – or that we're still here when spring rolls round again.

– You might not be?

Stanislaw asked this, glancing sharp at Fran now, and Ruth couldn't tell: was he disappointed?

– Who knows?

Fran shrugged.

– There's talk about handovers, withdrawals – order having been restored, and all that. Our Higher Ups, they'll be making pacts now, won't they? Agreements behind closed doors and between themselves. Poland wants its people back – everyone who was taken. The Czechs and the French too – everyone is asking. So maybe scratch your plans to work here.

She smiled, regretful, at Stanislaw.

– My guess is we'll be told to get all these children home again. With the ones we've already got across the borders.

– Have you sent some already?

This was news to Ruth. Children, making their way homewards?

– Oh, yes.

Fran nodded, and Ruth felt herself straightening:

– So you found their families?

– Oh. Well, no.

Fran corrected herself:

– They have gone to homes there – Red Cross ones, church ones. Good places. I do hope so.

Ruth found herself hoping the same thing. But then she thought again of Yeva – of how certain she was that her mother was still in Germany. But if she and Sasha came to Hamburg, it might not stop them getting sent back across the border.

A bell sounded downstairs; a voice called up the stairway.

– Nurse!

Fran started, pushing herself back from the window.

– Oh – that'll be for me. If you need to know about anything else, we won't have it – guaranteed.

She grinned across her shoulder, heading for the doorway.

– But ask anyway – do.

– Thank you.

Ruth nodded her gratitude, still in half-thoughts of mothers and borders. She told Fran:

– It's a good room.

Because it was, and because she'd say the same to Sasha and Yeva, in hopes that Fran might yet squeeze them in here.

– It's a lovely fit as a children's home.

– It is, actually – isn't it?

Fran grinned again – proud, despite it all, of this make-do haven.

But then she turned and dropped her voice:

– It's just such a shame, though, about the family who lived here.

She leaned in through the doorframe, as though they should keep this between themselves:

– I mean the real owners, not the Nazi ones who took it from them.

She shook her head.

– At least some of them made it to London: the sons did. They got out, thanks be. Even if not the parents.

Fran stopped there.

She'd caught Ruth's eye, and then Stanislaw's. And now – suddenly flustered – she apologised.

– Oh. I shouldn't have said that. Oh, I didn't think, you know?

Ruth didn't know what to think now either.

What she'd just heard was just too stark – too familiar from the Herr Doktors – all those others who'd fled to London.

Fran was still looking at her, disconcerted, like she ought to say something further, but Ruth wasn't at all sure she wanted to hear more. She'd come to visit a children's home, to make plans for Sasha and Yeva, not thinking she'd find herself at the heart of such cruelty.

This country.

These people.

– Some of the family made it out, though?

Ruth asked that much. She needed to hear this confirmed.

Fran nodded.

– Three sons. Just before the war started. They were sent to Liverpool, taken in there by families.

Then she told Ruth:

– The oldest, he's nineteen now and with British forces. With a sappers unit, in Bremen. He came here last month on leave. Just to see the place again, maybe. He said he was glad it had landed in British hands. But then he took a chair out there.

Fran pointed to the window, down to the lawn again.

– He sat in the middle of the grass and looked out at the water – for hours. It was the saddest thing.

Ruth sat down on the bunk nearest. She stayed there after Fran was gone, too, absorbing all of this. Her surroundings, the weight of what she'd just been told about them.

– You still want to work here?

She asked Stanislaw, wanting only to be gone now, to shut her eyes and be elsewhere. How soon might she request a transfer? Could she go to the major? *Home please, at the nearest opportunity.* How would it be to admit defeat to the man? That she'd reached her limits here.

Ruth could still hear the children. They were outside and playing below the window – and she would have packed all their bags then, gladly. She would have gone striding out to gather them into as many jeeps as she could muster. Get them far from here and further. If that was the last thing she did at this posting, it might be the best thing.

But then she thought of the two young Polish sisters, down at the edge of the lawn, and of Sasha and Yeva in the hut rows. She imagined fetching them from the meadows, speeding them across the borders – only to find the German harm there was tenfold. And then what? And then what?

Ruth let out her breath – at a loss.

What to do, in the face of all of this?

– *Ofitserka?*

She looked up to find Stanislaw beside her. He had come to stand at her shoulder, and now he offered a hand to help her up.

– I should like to go back to our camp now. You?

September

20

Strangers

Freya

The bilberries were dark, ready for bottling, and her Mama rinsed out jars each morning, lining them up for her and Ursel.

– Bring them home full, girls. As much as you can pick.

Their Mama spent her days blanching and salting, filling one larder shelf, then the next. Ursel liked to go inside there, to look at the red of the currants, the green of the peas, fat behind the glass curves. But those stores were for the autumn, the winter – their Mama insisted – and that felt like a long and hungry time away.

So Freya rode out early, before Benno came calling; Ursel on her saddle, and the jars clanking and jangling in her basket. They rattled along the Heide track to where the slopes were widest; out beyond the Buchholz Hof, where the bilberries caught the best sun; and there, they gathered for their Mama, for the larder. But they ate first. Filling their palms, and then their mouths, and then their pockets for later, to take up to Benno.

Freya saw others there some mornings.

First it was just old Gustav Buchholz, bent among the bilberries, but soon there came a scattering of townsfolk. Frau Klemens and her twin girls, just old enough to be crouching and picking alongside her; Christa Heinrich, with her round calves and her round cheeks, and her sleeves rolled over her forearms. Freya liked to watch her; how she bent and picked with Gustav, and then went to sit at the Hof a while, joining old Hanne at the lean-to, on the bench beside the chicken coop, the two of them counting eggs into her basket, the new girl child crawling from lap to lap between them.

But there were other pickers also, whose faces Freya didn't know.

They weren't from the town, and they weren't Heide folk either, because they were women in good dresses, old men in hats and suits and shoes not meant for walking, and Freya wasn't sure about having strangers here. They came from the far paths, so she thought they must be from other towns across the heathland, and she saw they must have the same bread and margarine rations, too, because they brought jars with them, and baskets. The men's jackets flapping open, the women's dresses blown against their legs, they tramped the Heide, distracted, like they were lost or they were hungry, or they didn't know where the good picking was.

Let them look. Freya kept her head down, picking with

Ursel, and as soon as the jars were full, they rode away and up to the high pass. She was glad to leave her bicycle at the junipers, to tramp up to the hut and stay there – as long as they could.

Benno was often there before them, stepping out onto the hut steps to greet their arrival, and to show them the latest.

– Here – I've collected some more things.

So far, along with the shepherd's bedroll, he had a knapsack that he'd found in his attic, and a red wool blanket.

– My Mutti still hasn't noticed.

Freya had swiped a hasp too, from Herr Brandt's yard. Ursel had kept watch at the gatepost while she'd slipped inside the storehouse, rifling along the shelving; Benno had fixed it to the doorway, to stop it blowing open on nights he went home. He'd asked for a bolt too, so Freya had plans to swipe a small one to fix at the window – to stop it rattling, to stop the draughts on nights he spent out here, alone under the hut roof.

He'd already got the stove to work; Benno lit it with matches taken from his Mutti's parlour box. But those were running low now, and there were limits to what he could get away with, so he'd been teaching himself to use the shepherd's flint and tinder, keeping it on the windowsill, by the shepherd's buttons, all lined up in their small row.

He'd told Freya he'd need to swipe a knife next.

– A good and sharp one. That will always come in useful.

Freya knew what he meant. This knife, the flint and knapsack: they were all being stored for later; for when he left the Heide. Benno had told her there were sailings now for Hamburg; he'd found out where he could cross the Elbe. *And from there, I can go further.* He didn't say where, though. And the way Benno talked about the hut now – collecting and storing, making it warm and weathertight – Freya thought the high pass might be far enough for a good while.

He walked the gully with Ursel, taking her to the brook to fetch water; they collected stove wood on the way back, bending and gathering the gorse brush, climbing up the hut steps with armfuls. Benno said he wanted to fill the space under the bunk first, to let the kindling dry there, but he'd already started on another stash, under the hut itself, of proper firewood. So he often took Ursel out further, to find branches.

While they were gone, Freya swept the ashes from the stove, the spent matches from the floorboards, the leaves that blew into the corners. She lifted the shepherd's flint from the sill, the shepherd's buttons too, brushing away the ash, trying to rub them clean again, before replacing them among Ursel's stones and snail shells. As she dusted the cobwebs from the ceiling corners, Freya felt the wind through the gaps in the walls, she smelled the gorse and grass, and she tried pretending that this was their hut – hers and Benno's. Their own Heide place.

It was just the kind her Papa would like. High up and lonely. So Freya thought of him as she swept, too; she couldn't help that. She and Ursel were helping a town boy to make this hut his own, and she didn't think her Papa would want this.

If he saw this spot, though. Freya thought he could approve of that much. Because he would surely choose it for one of his drawings. She could even see the way he'd frame it: the gully slope sketched in lightly; same for the high pass through the window; and then a gorse branch forming a darker mark, curled along the edge of an envelope.

Her Papa would leave the sky empty, Freya decided, wide

and high above the rest – perhaps just a torn cloud, faint, in the top corner. He'd know just how to make the picture feel right, in any case: high and hidden away, and just exactly like this place was.

Alone with her sweeping thoughts one afternoon, Freya heard voices.

Not Benno's and Ursel's: these sounded like grown-ups, coming up along the high pass. She thought they'd be carrying jars, most likely; they'd have come from another town somewhere, to pick their fill of bilberries. So Freya let them pass, turning away from the voices, back to her sweeping, waiting for them to go again.

Except then she heard laughter.

Looking up through the gorse, Freya saw two men in old shirts, old trousers. They had work caps like the men at the Brandt yard; their faces were work-rough also. Had they come out here to pick?

They didn't look down at her; too intent on their striding. Freya knew she was well-hidden in any case; deep in the gully here, she was free enough to keep watching them.

One was younger and red-haired, the other taller, darker too, and broader. The two men were each leaning forward, each carrying something heavy on their shoulders. And both had their caps pulled to shade their eyes – but she could see their smiles; the easy way they walked, despite their burdens; Freya saw their nods, heard their talking.

Tak, tak.

Their words were not German.

The men were strangers; Freya knew as soon as she heard

this: those men were from the munition works. From the English camp. They had to be.

They didn't frighten her, not exactly: they were too like the workers at the Brandt yard. They had her watchful, though, these worker-strangers – because hadn't Benno been wary? The way he'd spoken about going to look at the town works, it was like the labourers there were dangerous, not just the Werkschutz with their rifles. So Freya kept her eyes fixed on the two men – and then she saw what they were carrying.

The first had a ewe – a ewe! Had he caught it from one of the heath flocks? He'd tied it at the hooves; he'd strung its muzzle too, and flung it across his shoulders.

The older one had a child on his back – a boy. Barefoot, in a grey shirt, and maybe the same age as Ursel. The boy had his eyes closed, his mouth open; Freya thought he might be sleeping; rocked by the big man's walk, arms flung about his broad neck, cheek pressed into his shoulder-blade. And then Freya didn't know which was the stranger thing – the sheep, or this child being carried on workers' shoulders. Were the men carrying both to the English?

They'd have a wide arc to walk yet: out to where the town woods started. Freya thought of the pines there, of the high wall, and then of the child being carried inside them.

This thought had her blinking.

It had Freya thinking of Benno, of Udo and all the other boys, looking down over the factory at nightfall.

It had Freya thinking of runaways also – because hadn't Benno said that workers had run from there? He'd seen women on one of the transports – Benno hadn't said anything about children – but Freya had just seen one with her own eyes: a worker's child. So there was at least one among the workers in the English camp.

When Freya looked up, the two men were gone. They'd carried the boy out of sight.

But she still had the quiet of the heath, and the wooden walls around her, and she could still see him in her mind's eye. His bare feet, his sleeping features; light as pencil marks, sharp as one of her Papa's drawings on his envelope corners.

When Benno came back with Ursel, it was already time to go again.

He stowed the twigs under the bunk and the kettle on the stove – full of water, ready for next time – busying himself with all the last-of-the-day tasks. And Freya had been waiting to tell him about the boy and the workers because it still seemed so strange to her; she'd wanted to ask if he knew about children at the works there: had he seen some last winter? But as Benno shut the hut door – flicking the hasp closed, checking the gully slope, leaning a branch across the wall as camouflage – Freya saw that mention of anyone up here might have him worrying. Those workers hadn't seen her, but they might yet see the hut here. Or someone else could. They might slide down the gully and open it, finding all Benno's hard work; all these things they'd swiped and borrowed and stolen.

So Freya carried her thoughts homeward.

The three of them riding down the slopes, the jars clanking in her basket, Benno peeling off where their ways parted, waving and waving, smiling and none-the-wiser.

*

And then, when she and Ursel got back to the schoolhouse, their Mama was at the gate and calling.

– Come, girls!

It was like she'd been keeping lookout. Freya thought they must be late, or her Mama must be annoyed somehow – perhaps they'd been found out? Had Herr Brandt noticed the hasp she'd stolen?

– Quick, quick, you two!

Their Mama hurried them – into the house, into the parlour.

But when they got inside there, Freya saw her Mama was smiling.

Her Mama had her hair combed; she had taken off her apron. It had got so rare to see her Mama like this, Freya could only stare at her for the moment, Ursel too, as they watched her step up to the mantelpiece.

– Look!

Post had come.

Their Mama was pointing at an envelope; it was addressed to both of them.

– Do you see, girls?

She must have seen the van arriving; Freya thought it must have been while they were at the high pass: a letter had been dropped into the postbox.

It was a Red Cross notice. The front half-covered in a drawing. A view of the schoolhouse, the old oak behind it, their two names inked at the centre – her Papa's handwriting.

– Your Papa is coming home to us!

21

Where Is Home Now?

Ruth

A sheep was stolen.

Two DPs were seen, up on the Heide, carrying the animal across their shoulders.

A townswoman called at the major's offices, up in arms and with her twin girls in tow; all of them witness to the poaching while they were out and picking bilberries.

It was embarrassing to have to search the huts.

Ruth was glad it didn't fall to her to give that order, and that it was one of Farley's lads who found the animal. Hidden behind blanket curtains, in one of the final Nissen sheds in the Back Enclave, being fattened up on ration scraps.

The sheep was returned to the heath in a curfew jeep, a

patrol soldier releasing it by the bridge across the Heide ford, where the roadworks had been completed. It made a dash along the verge grass, before running headlong for the high ground; Farley's lad told Ruth when he returned.

– Bet it won't be the last, though.

The next sheep was slaughtered promptly. It was sheared and then roasted, polished off within hours. When the watch conducted their search, all that was left was the aroma, the fatty ashes in the fire pit, and the spit on which the roast had turned, fashioned out of an old truck axle pilfered from the transport yard.

Ruth had to tip her hat to that part – to the sheer audacity – even if she could only do so inwardly, standing beside Farley in the Back Enclave, while he asked Pan Artem and the other men:

– Who took that? Which one of you?

The Ukrainians looked to one another, then they looked at the sergeant; each man cast a shrugging glance about himself.

Ruth would have liked someone to laugh with. She'd have liked it to be Stanislaw.

Since their return from Hamburg, he'd been working less with her, more on his radios.

His morning duties completed, he took his leave from Ruth with his small bow, small nod before returning along the duckboards to the work bench he'd laid out by his cot bed. He had a toolbox, a stool under the window, a small stack of radios lined up against the wall there, and spent the rest of each day unscrewing the back plates, exchanging parts, testing and trying them out.

His own hut had a working set. So far, he'd supplied two more to the Ukrainian quarter, and Ruth saw a further one while she was visiting Sasha and Yeva one afternoon. The set was just inside their doorway, and the hut filled with the buzz and murmur of faraway voices. Music from New York, news from London, all broadcast from Berlin. Sasha pointed at the radio:

– It was Mirko!

The boy told her, proud and in English:

– He fix that for us.

– Yes, he did it with your translator.

Yeva confirmed this, saying Mirko had only gone to watch Stanislaw working, but then the Pole had set him to unscrewing the back plates, cleaning the dust off. The girl told her:

– He said to Mirko that he couldn't just sit there.

Ruth could well imagine this. But Yeva conceded:

– He is not so bad – really. He is teaching my Mirko.

She said Stanislaw had laid all the radio parts out for him on a table, each of them labelled.

– He wrote all the names, and he told Mirko to remember them. It took a whole afternoon because he told him all the ways they work.

Yeva smiled at Ruth.

– Proper lessons, you see? From a proper teacher.

Since Stanislaw had taken on this apprentice, he and Mirko had finished three more working sets between them.

– Listen! You listen, *Ofitserka*.

Sasha rolled through the dial, through the hiss for Ruth, until he found Polish spoken.

– It's from Mirko's home – yes?

Then he dialled on again, until he found jazz played.

– That's from Chicago, maybe. From America.

Sasha said Mirko had taught him.

– Mirko wants to fix more. So everyone can hear their home now, and hear this music. He says there should be one radio for every hut row.

All the while her brother spoke, Ruth felt how Yeva watched her, as though trying to see in her face – would they still be here to see Mirko do this?

Ruth had told her about the home in Hamburg: that it was a good one, but at capacity.

So we can't move you there. Not yet anyway. This was a half-truth, and the girl's half-nod had been guarded, as though she knew she could not trust it.

Ruth had reported the same to the major. Although she knew he'd ask about her visit next meeting – he was bound to – and any questions would get awkward.

But the major had yet to summon her, and Ruth was grateful. Not just because of that half-truth, either, but because she still wanted to bring up the missing workers. She needed to press him about the women too, push at him to investigate, and if she were going to do that properly, with dates and sightings, she'd have to try calling again at the Berger place.

September had started in the midst of all of this, bringing new orders, all agreed at Potsdam: hashed out at the lakeside between Churchill and Truman and Stalin.

– A rush job, if you ask me, Miss.

The supply lads heard more than Ruth did. They were at the town hall more often; and they told her the English word.

– Our troops here will be scaled back, and soonish.

– The major is already trying to find a Bürgermeister.

– He's been told to find a townsman – someone to oversee this part of the Heide.

They said the officer had been taking soundings, conducting interviews, looking for the right man to entrust with the office. But every townsman had filled out a questionnaire, and no candidate had emerged yet.

– You try finding a reliable German.

That was the supply yard verdict.

Once the DPs got wind of English troops leaving the town hall – even just the possibility – the duckboard talk was of little else. They knew the camp would be wound up at the same time; it stood to reason.

– *Repatriatsiya.*

– *Tak.*

Re-pa-tri-ay-shon.

Potsdam had brought new maps: new place names for Ruth to memorise. Borders were being restored; others were being redrawn, all across the continent; and the DPs went from enclave to quarter, from hut row to hut row, looking to find one with a radio. Impatient for news of their home towns, their home districts. Which country would they land in? Which side would the border fall?

They came to ask Ruth:

– Where is my home now?

And:

– When do we go?

The Czechs and Italians were first.

They were sent southwards, to Nuremberg, to await further Red Cross convoys. Climbing into a truck back at dawn, reaching down handshakes for Stanislaw, for Farley, and kisses on both cheeks for Ruth.

– *Ahoj!*

– *Ahoj, Pani Novak!*

The three Belgians departed a few mornings after this.

They were going home directly, across the new-old border at Aachen, and they called their adieus from the jeep back, their handkerchiefs and homemade flags fluttering away along the Poststrasse.

The first of the Herr Doktors had already gone home too.

Albert Kowal.

Ruth heard this from Daniel. The post was still woeful: letters came not at all, and then a whole fortnight's worth in a bundle. Two came the same day from Ruth's parents; more from old friends at the Archway hospital – and Dan's letter was among them. He described how Doktor Kowal had set out for Warsaw, and no one could talk him out of it. *He's been away plenty long enough – this was what he told us. A Pole should be in Poland? Yes! A Jewish Pole especially.* The doctor's sister was still missing – three years since he'd heard from her. But she had last written from Warsaw, from her old apartment, so when news came of her next – whatever it is – he said he'd sooner be there to receive it.

The Poles in the camp, though.

Once they'd seen Farley take down the Czech tents, and then the Belgians', they began stopping Ruth on the duckboards and asking:

– We must go too?

– Won't you let us stay on?

– Even just a while still?

Ruth hadn't expected such questions – to meet with such reluctance. Why not go home, to their old home country?

– It is difficult. This is difficult, Officer.

At first she heard it only from the oldest, those who listened most carefully to the radios. But they all spoke among themselves, and soon they spoke to Ruth also: almost all of Stanislaw's hut row neighbours coming to knock at her office door, to talk in quiet and private.

Some had watched their villages burn under the Germans:

– So you see: my old home is ashes. You want me to go back to where that happened?

Others did not want to return alone.

– No. Not without my cousin. I have told you about him; I have said I have to find him.

All had heard the reports about the pacts sealed at Potsdam, and the handovers to new governments.

– Those pacts were sealed with Stalin. With *Stalin* – you understand us?

They feared where Poland's new borders would fall; they feared that Communists would be installed inside them. And so they asked – politely, urgently – that their transports be held off:

– We need time to decide.

– Will your major not let us wait first? Let us talk with him at least?

Could the man not do more – please – to help them?

Formal requests began coming from the Back Enclave, the men there asking for their own meetings. Pan Artem came to Ruth's office, late and alone one afternoon.

She had to call in Stanislaw, set up a clean page in her typewriter, pull out a chair for the Ukrainian.

The big man's knuckles only just healed from the fighting, he spread his fingers over the maps he'd asked for, bending across Ruth's desk as she folded them out. Blinking and frowning, he laid his palms across the territory now under Soviet rule.

– All of my country? All?

So painful, to see his face as he lifted it. To hear Stanislaw's murmured explanations:

– He hasn't seen his district in four years. His wife is still there – in Kherson. He hopes so, at least.

– My sons also.

Pan Artem cut across him.

– My three boys.

He looked at Ruth to make sure she understood enough of his words:

– I will only go back to bring them out – you hear?

Then he squinted, and he tried in English:

– Your Churchill, your Attlee – why do they draw lines with Stalin? Why with this bastard?

Pan Artem turned to Stanislaw abruptly:

– You talk. Yes? It is your job. You tell her – you tell the English major – so they understand us.

After he'd gone again, Stanislaw nodded about the man's anger. He told Ruth:

– We all argue now – we DPs, I mean – among ourselves. None of us can help that. We argue about your leaders, your Higher Ups. If we should accept the next home transport, or if we should wait it out first, here in Germany.

Stanislaw said no one could agree; all sought to convince others. Most wanted a move to a larger camp – still in the British zone, or the American, where there might be safety in greater numbers; where they might apply for passports and visas, for papers to start a new life elsewhere.

– People say they will go to America, to Australia. To anywhere there is no Stalin. Few – very few – speak in favour of returning. So your major, he will have a hard time to convince us.

The DPs formed a delegation. Stanislaw was charged with putting their request for more time in writing, and with taking it directly to the town hall. Ruth released him from his next morning's duties – *of course, of course* – and arranged for him to take the early jeep with the supply lads.

He came to Ruth after he returned, after the major had confirmed what he'd heard:

– Lwów has been conceded.

His home was in Ukraine now; it would be staying in Stalin's hands.

– The wrong side of the border.

Stanislaw sighed the words, angry.

He still said nothing about his brother – although Ruth saw Barthos would be on the wrong side too now.

– Beyond the Pale.

Stanislaw shook his head.

For three days after this, he was not at her office door in the mornings. Neither did he work on his radios. Instead, Stanislaw went out to the town woods with the supply troops. The evenings turning cooler, Farley had been recruiting DPs to help with the laying in of stove wood, and Ruth saw Stanislaw among the small teams who strode out to fell trees on the lower slopes. She heard the axe blows, the sawing; the rush as the crowns came falling.

They cut a swathe through the trunks there. When Ruth looked out of her guard block window in the mornings, she saw the clearing where the trees had been: a cut into the slope, the piney ground laid bare.

Out in the meadows, the air was sharp with pine sap, and when Ruth stood in the grass and looked for Stanislaw among the felling and sawing, the cut looked all the wider: the slope steep and exposed, all its gouges and hollows laid open.

But the work seemed to soothe him. He even raised a palm when he saw her.

The supply boys hauled out the felled trunks, and Stanislaw and his hut neighbours spent three further mornings at the foot of the slope, splitting the logs into cord, and the cord into kindling. The spoils were divided between the hut nations. Stanislaw stacked his share at his own hut entrance, high and dry under the overhang – as though he too were planning on waiting it out here a while yet.

Up at first light, on her way to the mess tent for a hurried breakfast, Ruth saw Yeva on the duckboards. The girl was not with Josefa and carrying laundry; she wasn't with her brother either; she was with Mirko, the two of them ducking between the hut rows.

In among all the meetings about borders, and the brooding over the DPs' choices – which didn't feel like choices at all – the matter of the children was still undecided. Yeva had been avoiding her; Ruth had been putting off a verdict herself, and the inevitable meeting with the major. How to find a solution when sending them home didn't feel like anything close?

Out on the duckboards, she saw the girl glance at her – like a question – but that was all, before she was gone again between the hut sides.

When Ruth got to her office, though, there was a packet of cigarettes on her doorstep, and a note scrawled onto the cardboard.

A Mirko cigarette bribe; Yeva's handwriting.

We want get married.

Married!

That girl. So full of surprises.

22

Let's Not Pretend

Emmy

They had so many visitors, she didn't know how to keep up.

First there was Achim Brandt. He came the afternoon of Arnold's return, and then stayed on after curfew, at Arno's insistence – *oh no, Brandt, you must* – long, long into the evening. Ursel telling him, excited – *that's our Papa, see?* – as though the neighbour might not remember him; Freya quieter, sitting in the garden chairs between the yard man and her father.

– *Ach, mein Mädchen.*

Arno sighed as he smiled at her.

– Here we are again, aren't we?

So tired and gaunt – what a sight he made!

Although no one would say that: who had the heart?

They sat on the veranda while Arnold walked through the

house, through the garden and back again, like he couldn't see it all enough times.

And then they ate outside, there on the terrace, all of them. Peas from the new rows, and a good pork knuckle to share between them. It took all Emmy's meat coupons for the next fortnight, but it was worth it. Freya had Ursel on her lap; the yard man was smiling, smiling, and so was Arno. And at twilight, it was still just about warm enough to stay out and talk.

– Listen!

Achim Brandt put his cup down and lifted a finger as a Hamburg train came rattling.

– Oh! Will you listen to that now?

It was the first evening freight train in however long – it seemed such an age since they'd heard one – since the English bombed the rail lines, although it was only last winter.

Achim Brandt been working on the tracks there. His small labour gang of heath men had been moved on from the road bridge; they'd been set to filling the craters near the station, hauling out the bombed rails and sleepers, and then replacing them – and Brandt had been so subdued since he'd started labouring for the English, Emmy had often worried for him. The way he sat on the yard bench in the dusk light after he came home, slow about unlacing his work boots.

That evening on the terrace, though, the sound of the train had him lifted.

– Oh – wait, wait!

Brandt raised his arms and hushed them all to listen to its passing – *you hear it?* Like a slow and shunting herald, like a clattering good omen. And then, as it rattled off towards

Hamburg and the harbour, the big man stood up to his full height, leaning across the table to Arno, taking him by both his shoulders:

– So good that you are here again, my neighbour.

This is what he told him. And then:

– It does us all good.

And even:

– This town has need of its schoolmaster!

And then – after all of that high and sudden emotion – Ursel turned on Freya's lap and whispered out loud to her sister:

– So will school have to start again?

Arnold tipped back his head and laughed:

– Oh, I do hope so, *Kind*! I do hope so! As soon as is humanly possible.

They lay in bed that night, Emmy and Arnold, hand in hand, and with the curtains open, so he could look out across the Heide shapes in the darkness. The school oak, the school wall; the familiar sky, the familiar horizon.

In the morning, he tried on his school suit, and his winter coat too. It hung from his shoulders: long and loose, the way all the men's coats had fallen, back in the hunger years after the last war. Arno stood and regarded himself in the wardrobe mirror before he hung the coat away again. But he laughed again as he did so.

– How good that it is only autumn yet!

Arnold wore shirtsleeves, his waistcoat open, his trousers belted. He hammered a new notch into the leather so it could be fastened tight enough, and one into Emmy's coat belt also.

– Will you look at us, *Dirn*? Slender as youths again.

In his time at the Front – in all his time away from her – Arno had found a new and dry humour.

The September days were cooler, but the Heide was still bright beyond the windows, the heather coming into bloom, softening all the slopes and gullies with its purple and blue.

Arno was up early each morning; Emmy found the bed empty beside her. When she went downstairs, he'd be in the parlour chairs with all the windows open; sitting reading and reading, his glasses propped on his brow, three or four botanical volumes open on the rug before him. Or she saw him out in the garden, bent over the vegetable rows, weeding and picking and watering.

Emmy let him; she let herself sleep in. Arnold was glad to be home again; she felt that. Emmy allowed herself to be glad too.

One morning, though, just as she was dressing, just as she was checking for Arno from the bedroom window, Emmy saw a man out there – a stranger.

His shoes dusty, as though from walking, his trouser cuffs also, and his shirt front just as grubby, he was standing right there in her bean rows!

Emmy hadn't seen anyone from the English camp yet; she'd only heard about the thieves in the Berger orchard, about the *Fremdarbeiter* roaming those villa gardens, even stealing from the Heide flocks. Now the sight of this man threw her. Would he come to the house? What did he want?

It took her a moment to see that Arnold was out there. That the strange man was talking, and that Arnold was listening to him. Arno was kneeling and looking up at him from his gardening.

The man held out his palms, Arnold handed over the beans

that he'd been harvesting, and when Emmy got downstairs, the stranger was already at the gate and on his way.

– What did he say to you?

Emmy watched him heading for the Poststrasse.

– Why did he come out this far?

She waited for the man to turn at the corner, for him to make for the English camp. But he crossed instead: he began heading for the station road.

– Where on earth does he think he's going?

– Back to Hamburg, I imagine.

Arnold told her, getting on again with the weeding.

The man was from Hamburg? Emmy was more confused now: why was a Hamburg man out here? Arno said:

– He told me he'd already been to three Heide farmers this morning, asking for eggs, mostly. The man had a good number, wrapped in a handkerchief. From Hanne Buchholz, I imagine. They cost him a silver fork; he told me so – and that he didn't have much left to barter.

Arno stopped there, turning to squint up at her:

– He offered me a pair of teaspoons, and asked if he could dig up some of our potatoes. But I said he should keep his cutlery. I told him: it's been so dry here, our potatoes are so small this year, he'll need his teaspoons to eat them.

This, too, seemed to amuse her Arno.

And Emmy couldn't be certain – but perhaps he was amused at her as well? That she had come out into the garden – outraged – to chase away a fellow hungry German.

In the days that came after, Emmy saw more: men and women both.

While she was walking home from the bakery, she heard an early train pass. This time, it was a passenger service, and when Emmy looked down through the birches to the rail line, she saw how the people had crowded the carriages. They were pressed into the aisles and the seat rows: women in headscarves, men in harbour caps. They even hung on to the outside: clinging to the doors, standing on the tailboards.

The train was still a good half mile from the station, but as soon as the engine slowed, the people began to jump down, leaping and tumbling – and how they ran then! Up the embankment and past her, they scattered along the Poststrasse. Housewives and harbour men making for the Heide, throwing glances over harried shoulders. Each looking to outrun the others.

The English were next to visit the schoolhouse. They drew up in a jeep: two soldiers along with the major and a driver.

It was Arnold who answered the door to them. Emmy stayed upstairs – although this felt cowardly on her part.

She sat on the edge of the bed and told herself – over and again – that Arno never wore the lapel pin, and this English major would know that. He'd have checked before he came here, looking for Arnold's name on the Party lists found at the town hall last April. (Already that felt so long ago! An eternity of ration cards and ration queues, of vegetable planting, of weeding and peeling and bottling, and waiting and waiting and waiting for Arnold.) Still, the major stayed for so long in the parlour, his driver sat for so long outside in the patrol jeep – right in her eyeline – Emmy could hardly bear it.

After they were gone, Arnold came upstairs.

He sat down, heavy, on the bed beside her.

– The major said they need men at the town hall. They need townsmen. They need a replacement for Paulsen.

Emmy raised her eyebrows.

– Did he ask you, my love?

She tried to imagine it: the English major calling Arno to Rathaus duty. She tried not to let this thought please her.

– Well.

Arno spoke slowly.

– Not exactly, no.

– So what did he ask, then?

Arnold pulled out papers from his waistcoat to show her: pages that he'd folded over. The man had given him a questionnaire. Arno had done some of it in his presence – had the major insisted? – but there were more blanks to fill in.

– If I pass muster, the major said there may be an opening.

An opening? Emmy felt a small hope rise again.

– And what did you say?

Arnold blinked at her:

– I said I would just like to teach again. I would like to start work again. If I may do that.

If I may.

How this chafed! The way Arnold spoke, it rubbed at Emmy for days afterwards, so uncomfortable. It did not seem right to her – not at all – that he should have to ask permission from the English. Her own Arno.

But after the major, more and more folk came calling.

Now it was Arno's former pupils. Young men: Front returners – or rather it was their mothers who turned up. Emmy opened the door to the grocer's wife, and then the dentist's; every few days, someone's Mama, someone's aunt came up the path. They came with Maggi cubes and Ersatzkaffee, or even real coffee – procured from who knows where. Or sometimes it was bread they brought, or bread coupons, and autumn blooms picked from their gardens. Something, anything to show how glad they were to see the schoolmaster here again.

– We were so grateful when we heard!

– Truly. So much: we can't tell you.

That warmth was real, too; Emmy felt it, when she invited them across the threshold – and she could see how Arnold's return might feel like a marker. According to the evening broadcasts, the schools in Lüneburg were reopening on half days; the same would happen too in Hamburg. So might a more normal life begin in the town here?

Once these mother-visitors were inside, though, the conversation would soon turn.

They'd change the subject to their eldest, or their middle son, who had survived his Wehrmacht service, and now that he was home again, he wanted to resume his apprenticeship in engineering, or his studies in medicine or pharmacy.

– As soon as the universities reopen.

This was the way they started.

– Do you know how soon that might be, perhaps?

The mothers spoke as though wondering out loud.

– We just thought, you know – you are the schoolmaster, after all. You were on the school board. So you might have heard?

And then – as though the idea had only just occurred to them – they asked:

– Oh! Actually. Might you consider a letter of recommendation?

Later, after they had long gone again, and she and Arnold lay hand in hand, looking out into the Heide night, Arnold said:

– I wish they would not do that.

Of course, the English visit will have been noticed. Word of it will have passed; Emmy knew this. The major had visited the schoolhouse; he went to call on the schoolmaster; and so – if you want a reference – who better to ask?

But while they lay awake and looked out at the Heide sky, Arnold told her:

– My POW camp. It was full of this kind of talk, you know.

Letters of referral, references of good character.

– My bunk neighbours, they said we'd all need a clean pass. They were sure of this, even before the war was over. *A clean record: the next best thing to a clean conscience, Herr Schoolmaster.*

Arnold told her there were jokes that did the bunk rounds. After lights out, before sleeping. And there were always men with new versions.

– Here's one.

He rolled over to face her.

– If you recruit ten new Party men, well, they will grant you permission to throw away your lapel badge. You can even burn your members' card. But if you recruit twenty – or more – now, that's really something. Then you can get a Dachau stamp in your passbook.

Arno gave a grim smile in the dark beside her. A Dachau

record, once so frightening, might get you a new job now with the Allies.

– With the occupiers.

Arnold corrected himself.

– With our new colonial masters.

Because that's what his bunk neighbours had called the English – half in jest, but all in earnest. Most had been from the Ruhr lands; miners from Bochum, from Wuppertal; and when they got their release notices – and found the English Zone stamp on their travel passes – they'd laughed.

– We're going home to New India!

Arno gave a small smile while he recalled this, and then he pointed, out of the open window to the autumn night.

– Our own Heide. The newest outpost of the English Empire.

Emmy didn't really know how he could smile at any of what he'd just told her, even if it was in grim humour. She didn't know, either, how he she felt about the jokes he'd learned.

– Here's another.

Arno told her to close her eyes and imagine. Take herself back in time, just a few years.

– You are on a day trip to Hamburg. You are down at the harbour, yes? At the waterside. And it just so happens that Hitler and Himmler and Goebbels are all visiting at the same time. This great trio are touring the city and the shipyards, and enjoying the crowds out to greet them. Then, at the dockside, in front of all the assembled workers, a sudden wind blows all three of them into the harbour. Splash! Splash! Splash! Who do you think would be saved?

Emmy didn't answer. She blinked at him: was he really smiling again in the dark there?

– Why – *Germany*!

Arnold blinked right back at her.

– Of course! *Germany.*

Then he turned onto his back again, looking up at the ceiling.

– The first time I heard that, I thought of writing it down for you. It must have been in the last war autumn. I thought of putting it in the envelope; I thought of the censor who'd open it; I knew they'd read what I'd written there – and I wasn't frightened.

Arnold spoke like he'd surprised himself. He said:

– You know, in the end, jokes like that even came in letters from home. People got really bold – at the last moment. Funny how we discovered our backbones, when it was already as good as over.

Was he angry now? Emmy couldn't tell any longer.

– Anyway.

Arno rolled over; he sounded more weary than anything.

– You know, I thought of home on all those bunk nights. I thought of our schoolrooms, the yard lane. And when the jokes came, I thought of Brandt's yard men. Of Brandt's cousin especially – in Hamburg – remember him?

Emmy nodded.

The man with the Gestapo stamp in his passbook. And on both his thumbs also. He would have found those late jokes laughable; those late jokers all the more so.

And then Emmy wondered: did Arno count himself among them?

– I'd have liked to have the yard men to laugh with.

This was all he told her.

– I would have given a lot to have had them there with me.

In the morning, Emmy saw a townswoman come up the path.

Opening the door, she found it was the police sergeant's young wife, her face pale above her blouses.

Emmy hadn't remembered her being quite so delicate: thin in the arms and shoulders. Everything about her slight and uncertain – and so like her youngest, it was striking.

She must have come about Benno, Emmy thought; to talk about his roaming with her daughters; to ask when the schools might re-open. The boy had had a full summer now with Freya and Ursel – playing at the stream banks, taking to the high paths – and Emmy thought all three could do with classes to occupy them. But once she'd called Arno in from the garden, once she'd settled Benno's mother into one of the parlour chairs, the woman told them:

– It's about my Udo.

She looked to Arnold:

– I've come for advice, please. I don't have his father here to ask, you see?

She held her slim neck bowed, long fingers folded; she must know that Arnold would have heard about her husband; that Emmy would have told him about every townsman arrested, or Achim Brandt would. But Benno's mother held Arnold's eye as she continued.

– My boys' father. He always found ways to encourage Udo. I would like to do that, but I just don't find myself able.

She shifted forwards to explain for him.

– My husband saw good prospects. Out in the East Lands – you understand me? He used to talk to Udo about different postings, different offices. He'd thought the boy would be called up – that the war might last that long yet – we both did. But even if Udo didn't end up serving, we'd hoped he might still find a posting afterwards. He might find a cadetship, out in the new territories.

Emmy could see this suiting the boy – stepping from HY into police uniform.

– But now that's all over.

His mother went on.

– And my husband – well, I am sure I don't need to say, Schoolmaster; I'm sure my news will have reached you. But Udo hardly says a word, you see? Days pass, and he barely speaks to me. I hardly know what to say to him either.

Emmy thought of her, in that tall house, out towards the villa gardens; she thought of the woman's youngest in his hand-me-down shirtsleeves; then she looked at this town wife in the parlour chair, her clothes all war-dark against her fairness. She hadn't been ready for defeat. Probably she still couldn't quite believe it: that the war and the Reich could just be over; her husband arrested – and at their own doorstep. Emmy couldn't feel for her – not exactly. She began to feel for Benno, though; she began to see it in a new light, why the boy roamed the Heide.

His mother told them:

– I do talk to Udo. I try to. I say he could still do police work – not out east of course, but here in the town, or here in Hamburg. I say he should hold out for a cadetship, because this occupation can't last always. The English are already looking for new people now, aren't they? I heard they will be handing over the Rathaus. And so my Udo could be useful to them – don't you think so?

She looked at Arnold – a brief and checking glance – and then she dropped her voice a moment:

– You know the English can't keep up with the black market? It's bad in Hamburg, but even here it is shameful. Even my neighbours aren't above trading. If they want butter beyond their ration; if they want coffee, perhaps.

Emmy heard her disapproval: that townsfolk should stoop to this under the English. But she thought maybe this was the woman's hope too: that the patrols would need police cadets to help them – and so her son might be recruited.

– I don't know who to ask, though.

Benno's mother shook her head.

– And my Udo – he won't put his name forward. He doesn't want to be on any lists looked over by English soldiers – that's what he told me. He avoids the patrols at all costs. He doesn't even like to set foot near the Rathaus.

She looked at them, despairing – but maybe proud too, somehow, of her eldest.

Then she turned back to Arnold:

– I just thought – if you could talk to him? Give him some encouragement? Or – if you could write something, even? Might you recommend him to the English?

So it had taken longer than usual, but here they were: they had arrived at the usual request.

– You taught our Udo. You could say you know our family?

My son – he had a whole career ahead of him. And now what does he have?

Arnold rubbed his forehead. He sat forward.

– The English do want to hand over the Rathaus. I mean: they are starting that process. But do you know that they are offering police work?

He stopped there, letting the point hang in the air between them – how soon would the English offer that kind of work to Germans?

– Well.

Benno's mother started, a little hesitant. She turned to Emmy, uncomfortable.

– I imagine he could do the same work as Herr Brandt here. Out on the roads and the railway lines.

Did she disapprove of that as well? Emmy couldn't quite tell. Her Udo was a town son, not a labourer – perhaps she disdained it? Benno's mother turned away again to continue.

– I have a nephew in Bremen. My sister's youngest. He is only just seventeen – not quite a year older than Udo – but he's employed on the crane barges. He carts the bomb rubble from the docks, clearing it from the waterways – to allow sailings to start again. My sister wrote to me that it is the same in Hamburg. She wrote that he gets extra rations for the work he does – and of course she is glad of them.

Benno's mother tilted her head. But then she let out her breath.

– But my nephew is clearing up after the English. Isn't he? This mess left by their bombers. And should our boys be doing that? Really? Should our people be doing that in Hamburg? Should our Herr Brandt here?

This all came out in a whisper: sudden and vehement – embarrassing.

Arno shifted, and Benno's mother saw this. For a moment, she looked uncertain. She could see she'd said the wrong thing – but what? She'd just said so much – which part? Her eyes flicked to Emmy, as if for help deciding, and Emmy saw her confusion: her boys adrift, her husband behind bars, her country defeated; and here she was, coming to the schoolmaster to plea-bargain.

Benno's mother tilted her head again.

– I'm just worried for my Udo.

She said this like an almost-apology.

– I'm worried for all our town sons, coming back from the Front. What's left for them? What's next for my Udo? Or even for my Benno? He drifts across the Heide. He will barely talk to me either; he's barely at home, you see? I wish the schools would start – when will they start again? What does he do all day?

So he hadn't told her about Freya and Ursel?

Emmy kept quiet about her girls, though.

Arno kept quiet, too, about the letter question – and then it wasn't too long before Benno's mother stood to go again.

– I've taken enough of your time, Schoolmaster.

She must have seen his thoughts; Emmy could see them without Arno saying a word. Udo ought to be clearing the craters, repairing the rail lines; that was the work which needed to be done here.

Strangest of all, though, was finding Erna Paulsen on the doorstep.

The Rathaus daughter came early, with the first sun of morning, while Emmy was still in her housecoat. When she opened the door, the girl was there on the threshold, turned out in a dress and headscarf, like a young town Fräulein.

– I've come here for my mother.

She offered no handshake, or other greeting, she only nodded at Emmy, awkward:

– I'm to speak with the schoolmaster.

The girl came without gifts: at least there was that. Emmy thought: at least the Paulsens wouldn't stoop to bargaining.

As soon as Arnold came downstairs – as soon as he saw it was Erna – he gave a short sigh:

– You know I don't work for the English, child? I have no sway there. I don't know what you've been told – or what your mother has – but I have no town hall appointment. Even if they were to offer, I wouldn't take it. So if you have requests to pass on – please, tell your mother: it is the English major she ought to talk to.

– She has tried that.

Erna cut in there, her voice tight. So her mother hadn't been given audience?

Had Frau Paulsen gone to the Rathaus? Emmy wondered. Or had she gone straight to the major's villa? Emmy could imagine her turning up at his doorstep – early.

Since the Bürgermeister's residence had been impounded, she and Erna had been living with Frau Klemens at the station road: crowded into that small apartment, with those twin daughters. Emmy thought how this must gall Frau Paulsen: did it gall Erna? When Emmy looked at the girl again, she just took a breath as though coming to the point here:

– The English have been felling trees. Out by the factory: in our town woods. My mother wants me to ask – did you know this?

– I did not.

Arnold measured out his words. He saw that Erna's mother had sent the girl here, to spare herself the indignity; to avoid another closed door: that much was clear enough. But what a strange question to arm her with! Why ask about the town woods?

Erna shifted:

– Well, they've been cutting for days. We've been told so. They've been sending out parties of soldiers.

The girl spoke in a hurry now, as though she had much to get through, and Emmy watched her: what was this leading up to?

– They even send out workers – all along the bottom of the slope there. They send *Fremdarbeiter* into our town woods. Soon they will go higher. My father has heard this.

Her father? Had Erna been sent by him as well? From his prison cell?

Emmy knew Paulsen would be allowed visitors. But now she found herself wondering: was it his wife who made that journey? Or his daughter? Or who else brought news to him? All the latest on the town and its trees.

Arnold leaned against the door post, as though already growing tired of this, while Erna asked on:

– Are they felling to expand the camp? My mother would like to know, please. Because the English are supposed to be handing over the Rathaus; she says they're supposed to be going, along with the workers they've been holding here. So why do they need to fell in our town woods?

Arnold scratched his forehead, polite still, but Emmy could feel his discomfort at having to interrupt his former pupil.

– With respect, child. Fräulein Paulsen.

He corrected himself: what was he to call her?

– With respect, please. These are not questions I can answer. I can imagine what the English might say though, as I'm sure your mother can also: what have the camp and the town woods to do with your parents?

Erna frowned; she looked down at her fingers.

For a moment, Emmy thought she saw embarrassment. The girl was stung at being dressed down – and by her old schoolmaster.

Still, Erna tried again, taking another tack:

– You know about Herr Heinrich? That he bakes bread for the English? When they could bake their own in their mess tent. When Heinrich could use the room in his ovens to bake more for the townsfolk?

Arno knew about the baker's arrangement; Emmy had told him all the town news she could muster.

– Well, child?

– Well.

Erna lifted her chin to continue:

– My mother says there will be more of that. For example – have you looked at your fuel rations for the winter?

– I haven't yet.

– So she says you ought to.

Erna looked at Emmy, too:

– She says you will find it hard to heat your rooms here. And when the schools re-open, she asks how will you heat the classrooms for the children?

In the winter at the end of the last war, when Emmy had done her teacher training in Lüneburg, the children had brought a lump of coal with them each morning – all those whose families could spare some – and still there had been ice on the classroom windows. Perhaps it would be the same this year, once the cold came: frost flowers blooming across the panes, children scratching red-fingered at their slates? Even so, even so – now that the girl had mentioned it – Emmy felt how much she wanted the classrooms re-opened.

– Erna.

Arnold rubbed again at his forehead.

– Fräulein Paulsen. Please – do continue.

He wanted to get the conversation over. So the girl took a small breath and pointed to the station road.

– You will have heard the trains pass, Schoolmaster. I mean the goods trains, after dark here. We hear them from our room at Frau Klemens's, bringing goods for the English – from ships at Bremen, at Cuxhafen. They come from the Ruhr too, with our good Ruhr coal – I have seen wagon loads. They run all through the night, you know? And my mother tells me all of this goes to our Hamburg warehouses, to our Hamburg coal stores on the Alster. Just like they always used to.

She paused there, waiting for Arnold to respond, but he just lifted his shoulders – *and?*

– Well, the British are stockpiling. They are withholding. Do you see, please? There is no need for anyone to be cold this winter, or for any German to be hungry. My mother says so. And my father. He says it is deliberate. My father says this is a punishment.

Arnold dropped his shoulders – because of course it was.

Of course! After this war? After Dachau? And these works here? What else did Paulsen expect?

Arnold told the girl, sharp:

– Your father would be the one to know.

Her father in his prison cell.

But Erna must have heard that response before; she must already know there were those who thought her father deserved it. Because the girl only blinked in the early light:

– Yes, do you know what my mother says? That my father never should have been arrested. She says he only did his duty; he only did what was needed. Even when everything was falling – even when others lost their backbones – it fell to my father to hold fast. To do his duty for the town here.

She still believed all that?

Emmy could have laughed – grim, like Arnold. What was this great duty Paulsen had done for the townsfolk? What exactly had fallen to her father here, in those end days, when everything around them was falling?

– In any case.

The Rathaus daughter gathered herself.

– My father may be in custody. But should others be punished alongside him? What about the children in your classes? What about your daughters, your Freya and Ursel?

Emmy had no response to that; Arnold either – nothing would come for the moment. And now that she had them silent, Erna turned the subject back to the works again:

– The English are supposed to be handing over the Rathaus, aren't they? So then, they should be emptying the works too, that camp of theirs. All those *Ostarbeiter,* all those Polacks. Why don't they send them back across the borders?

Erna paused there, as though rankled by their silence.

– Well, that camp is a punishment also. It is – I tell you so. The English should go, instead they house the Polacks here, thinking to make us an example.

Her young eyes turned dark now, angry with both of them.

– You ought to know this. You ought to have asked yourselves. But you don't, do you? And in the meantime, the English do as they like here. They bake their bread in our ovens, they fell our trees to keep their stoves warm. They'll fell more trees in our town woods – you just watch them. And then what? And then what?

But there, Arnold stopped her.

– Fräulein Paulsen.

He didn't wish to hear more.

– I think you have made your point now.

Her rage was out of place here, and out of all proportion, and Arno stood up straight to keep her from speaking further.

– If I have an audience with the English. Or if the major should consult my good opinion. I will be sure to pass your concerns on to them. Your mother's worries about the camp here, and the trees. And that your father – our former Bürgermeister – wishes the same thing: no more felling and cutting. The town woods are ours; the English should be told: our trees are out of bounds.

Erna flushed, well aware she was being mocked.

But the young woman stood up straight too:

– Just so. Just so, yes.

After she'd gone, Arnold walked straight across the yard and unlocked the schoolhouse. Emmy was surprised to see him lift the keys from the wall hooks and go striding; he hadn't been inside yet, not in all the time since he'd returned. But she followed on behind, and then she found him in his classroom, by his desk, staring up at the blank space on the wall.

– You took it down?

The portrait?

– Of course I did!

What did he think?

Emmy remembered the reaching – up and up; how hard it had been to dislodge! – and then the crack of the damn thing landing. She'd had Freya there that afternoon, and Ursel, but Emmy had wanted Arno – only Arno. She'd wanted him to know how that had felt: the portrait falling, the shock of its shattering, and then the sudden quiet afterwards. Emmy thought she should tell him: and that all those first days after the surrender had felt much the same too. They had been waiting and waiting and waiting, and then – crack! – it had all been over.

Except Arnold said nothing further. He was just standing, regarding the gap where the portrait had hung.

The wall was still a shade paler there; Emmy could see the tell-tale dust rim. It didn't help how the morning sunlight shone across it, coming in so sharp through the window. It had Emmy thinking of Erna, blinking on their front step. And also of Paulsen, in his confinement; the same sun falling outside his barred window as he brooded over his end-of-days duties, his to-the-bitter-end loyalty. Then Emmy thought how the sun would be falling now on the munition works also, just outside the town here. Between the pine trunks, across the felled ground. Bright and bare and open.

– We will have to paint that. Cover it over.

Emmy pointed to the wall. She'd be only too glad to do that. But Arnold made a small noise – was it a laugh? It was back of the throat and scornful, and it hurt her.

– Must you laugh so?

She turned to him. Neither of them had wanted that portrait. Arnold least of all. He had put it off, and put it off, just as long as he had dared, without causing a rift with the school board, without losing his post here.

– You risked enough.

She told him.

– Far more than most.

And then:

– What else could we have done?

He'd never approved, or spoken for the authorities. Those years were awful – just awful – but inside – inside – he'd stayed the same man as always.

Arno blinked at her. Emmy saw the scorn again.

– Oh, let's not pretend.

23

Arrangements

Ruth

The next days were fraught.

She had to bring notices to the Back Enclave. The Ukrainians were to be moved on – once October started. In only a week or two, they would be sent to another holding camp, at the border with the Russian zone.

– Oh no – please.

They shook their heads when they heard this.

– At the border?

Ruth arrived at their hut doorways; they came forward to read the papers she handed over; or they had them read out loud by Stanislaw – and then they looked at her, aghast.

– Why?

Some shouted from inside:

– Why you do this?

Others followed her as she moved on, calling as she went from hut to hut along the duckboards:

– Your major – please – he should not do this to us.

– You say to your major – I will not go back now. Not to Stalin!

When Ruth found Pan Artem, he was sitting outside his hut, stirring up his morning fire from last night's embers. Adding dry boughs from the felled pines, needles scooped from the soft ground, newly opened.

– I have these for you.

Ruth held out his papers.

– They are important.

But he wouldn't take them; Pan Artem didn't want them read out either.

– I know what they are.

He poked at the fire with his branch, and then he pointed to the grass beside it. And although Ruth put the papers down there, as asked, she was almost certain they would land in the ashes as soon as her back was turned.

– The children will stay?

This was all Pan Artem asked her. He said it in English, watching for her answer.

– The little brother and Mirko's girl, yes?

– They will stay for now.

This was all Ruth could answer.

*

Josefa came to see Ruth about them. Not to her office, but to her quarters, and just before lights out. She knocked softly at her door there; Ruth found her standing in the corridor.

– So sorry.

Josefa whispered.

– We are so sorry to call on you.

Behind her stood Ana, and behind her Natalia with her rosary: a small maternal delegation in the autumn evening light.

But they hadn't come about the transports, or to ask if Poles might be sent away next; they said:

– We are here for Yeva and Sasha.

– For Yeva and Mirko.

Josefa whispered their names, and their marriage request, and then she said:

– It is only you we can call on, *Ofitserka*.

Had they come to give the pair their blessing? Or to refuse it? All three mothers looked so awkward, Ruth couldn't work it out.

– We feel you should make the arrangements.

Josefa told her.

– Soon, please. We ask you – really.

The other women nodded their agreement.

Ruth had already guessed at Yeva's marriage calculation. If the girl had a husband, if she were a married woman, her word might count for more, perhaps, when it came to decisions over homes and camps and transports – and over Sasha especially. With Mirko, she would have a husband to speak for them: a head for their little household. Now Ruth looked at the mothers and wondered – had they worked all this out with Yeva? A picture came to her: all the women in the hut rows, sitting on the cot beds, talking over borders and home-goings, girl-to-mother, mother-to-girl – while Yeva's own was far from her. This last thought was a raw one. Ruth was sure it stung at these mothers too, driving them to pool women's knowledge, women's experience, finding ways to make their appeals watertight.

– Soon, yes?

Josefa whispered again.

– It would be best.

Ruth could feel how much it meant to her – that the children should be safe, taken care of, that she and the others should do this mother's task for them. But still, Ruth could see, also, that this urgency embarrassed her.

Glancing from mother to mother in the corridor, Ruth's eyes flicked from face to face, and their eyes flicked away from hers. Why this awkwardness?

– Get a permission from your major.

Josefa pressed her, soft and woman-to-woman. And then Ana did the same:

– Before too much longer – please.

Natalia stood nodding and nodding behind her.

And then Ruth knew what they meant: not before any notice of transport – but before Yeva falls pregnant.

The girl had come to see Ruth herself. Just a day or two after she and Mirko made their request. She'd turned up at her office doorway once Stanislaw had left for the afternoon, looking to catch her on her own.

– You are still going to move us.

This is how Yeva had started.

– You will move me and Sasha, won't you? To a place for children only?

She'd said this like she wasn't a child any longer. Still, the girl had spoken without her usual hardness, and she'd pulled up Stanislaw's chair straight afterwards, as though she wanted to talk now, not just to confront Ruth.

– I have been thinking.

Yeva even blushed then, shifting the chair closer.

– If Mirko can marry me, then maybe he can work too. You see?

But Ruth hadn't been able to work it out yet; what was she getting at?

– Well, your translator. He will be asking you for a pass, yes?

– A pass?

– Yes – so he can get a job with the English. So he can stay a while. Or go to London.

Ruth tried not to let her surprise show – but Stanislaw had said nothing of this plan to her. She'd never thought he might want that. Why had she not thought of it before?

Ruth tilted her head.

– Go on, now.

She would not betray Stanislaw; she would not lie to Yeva either – Ruth couldn't lie to this child having to step up into her mother's shoes. Instead, she asked her to continue.

– Go on, please.

– So – well – you can do the same for my Mirko? Maybe?

Not to come to London, though. I was just thinking – with a pass like your translator's, you can make it that we stay here. Because we do need to stay, yes?

The girl flushed again, hot and heartfelt, as she said this last part. She wanted so much for their mother to find them.

– Please, *Ofitserka*?

– Oh, Yeva.

Ruth didn't like to have to apologise.

– It's really not so easy. And it's really not only down to me, either.

But the girl kept on, regardless:

– You can try, though?

Yeva blushed one more time.

– Not just for me, but also for my Mirko. Because we have been thinking – so many things. That if he can work here, then we can stay longer. And if we can stay on, then we could even go back to Herr Maas?

– To the German farmer?

Ruth had to raise her eyebrows.

– You want that? To work again for a German?

Yeva shrugged.

– He wasn't so bad to us.

Then she looked again at Ruth. She said her *please?* again too, like she wasn't going to let go of this. The girl had even been planning what Ruth could do next:

– If you can write, I was thinking you can tell the farmer about Mirko – that he is strong and a worker. You can tell Herr Maas if he takes us, he can also have Mirko.

*

So Ruth had sent a letter.

And when she'd heard nothing since, it hadn't surprised her. She only hoped that Yeva might yet forget all about it.

Now, though, without warning, just the day after she'd issued the Ukrainian notices, Herr Maas turned up at the camp gates.

He came in his farm cart, with a young man beside him, in the first chill of autumn, in the first frost of a late September morning – but then he refused to come inside.

– *Tut mir Leid.*

The old farmer stood holding his horse, his face and fingers red with the cold, saying the same words, over and over.

– *Es tut mir so Leid, ja.*

– He is telling you he's sorry.

Stanislaw translated.

– He is saying he cannot take the children. He cannot take Mirko. Not even if he and Yeva are married.

Ruth waited while the man apologised – too many times – while he kept glancing nervously from Ruth to Stanislaw, as though he feared they might insist. As though this request from Yeva might be some sort of new occupation rule they could enforce.

– *Ich hab' meinen Sohn wieder – sehen Sie?*

The man pointed to the cart behind him, to the young man sitting up there, hunched inside his coat sleeves, and Stanislaw lifted his chin at the farm lad.

– He says that's his son – look. Back from the Front.

– *Sehen Sie?*

The farmer sounded like he was pleading, gesturing for Ruth to look another time, to where his son sat wordless and watching all of this. A young-old version of his father; his face just as long, but already harder.

– *Sagen Sie's das Mädchen?*

Herr Maas wants you to explain to Yeva.

– *Es tut mir so Leid, ja? Bitte sag es ihr.*

– He wants you to apologise to the girl. Please. On his behalf.

Herr Maas had brought buttermilk: a lidded pail full. He lifted it from the cart back and handed it to Ruth.

– For the two.

He spoke in English.

– For the two children who were with me in the wartime.

He nodded his old chin, holding the pail out to her, imploring, until she took it.

But then he refused to wait while she called for Yeva; he wouldn't even stay long enough for her to come to the gates here.

– *Nein, nein. nein, nein.*

Herr Maas backed away from Ruth, climbing onto his cart again, as though calling the girl was unreasonable – or even as though he were frightened.

When Ruth found Yeva, the girl was standing outside the women's huts, stone-faced, with a blanket around her shoulders. Camp word had already found her, even before Ruth placed the milk on the doorstep.

– It's from Herr Maas, child.

She passed on the farmer's apology.

– He sounded like he meant it.

Yeva looked at her; she looked at the buttermilk.

The girl put a toe out, tipping the pail into the grass.

October

24

A Front Returner

Freya

Ursel had to start back at lessons. It made her surly in the mornings, slow over lacing her boots at the kitchen doorstep, even with Freya sitting down to help her.

It was what their Mama wanted though; Freya knew this. And that she'd wanted the same for her, too.

– Just in our Heide classroom.

Freya had heard her, asking her Papa:

– Please? Just until we have word about the grammar school re-opening.

But her Papa said:

– Why, though?

And:

– Let the child have her days still.

He didn't seem to mind Freya missing classes. He didn't seem to mind about Benno either.

Freya's Papa didn't know about the hut – not yet anyway – and Ursel had been sworn to secrecy. But Freya's Mama must have told him about their roaming, that Freya spent her Heide days with the policeman's youngest, because when her Papa saw Freya lacing her own boots after Ursel's, he told her:

– Give that boy my best now.

Or:

– You both make the best of it.

Before he walked across the schoolyard to open his classrooms.

Freya didn't know what she made of this change in her father. But at least she only had her morning chores before she could ride out to find Benno.

He'd be at the Heide brook when she got there, or he'd be at the hut steps. Sometimes he'd have the stove lit; the days all started cooler now. But Freya liked that it was just the two of them, watching the flames dance, lying on the narrow bunk, between the narrow walls.

Benno still talked about leaving.

Since the weather turned, he'd been making new plans. He kept his bicycle in the gully now, in the gorse brush: to have it close to hand, he said. And in the small hut cabinet, he'd been gathering more things. Along with the kettle, there were two tin mugs for drinking, a bottle for storing water – and the knife that he'd been after.

Benno had arrived with that after sleeping at home one night.

Freya had been first to the hut that morning; she was sitting on the steps when Benno rode up, lifting his bicycle, sliding grinning down the slope towards her.

– Look!

He pulled the knife from his pocket.

– I took it from Udo's desk drawer. It was wrapped in a handkerchief, tucked inside an envelope; it was pushed all the way to the back too. But I found it anyway.

Benno grinned again, like the finding had pleased him, almost as much as the knife did. Freya, though: she'd already seen the HY sign on the handle; she'd already decided she'd swipe a different knife.

Freya preferred the rest of their findings. The shepherd's flint and tinder, the charred shirt buttons, still in their sill row; Ursel's stones and snail shells. The red wool blanket was the best, though. Each time she came here, Benno spread it on the bunk for them to lie down. They filled the stove, Freya pulled up her blouses, and Benno pulled the blanket around them. Hours they lay there, pressed close and all in secret, his mouth warm against hers.

Curled with her under the blanket, Benno told her his plans too.

Gazing up at the hut roof, he spoke them out loud for Freya.

– I'll go to Hamburg.

He said it like this was decided:

– I'll still have to wait a while. But once the English leave the Heide, I can go to the harbour; I can find work there, on the crane barges. You know they are clearing the water?

It didn't worry Freya like it used to. She had even grown

to like it, lying in the warm with Benno, listening while he spoke his future.

She could picture him on the docksides, shy among the harbour men. She liked it best when he dreamed his way further, though: as if imagining himself years from now.

– When the sailings start again – just think of it. Maybe I can find a working ship?

Benno blinked at the roof beams and told her about Hamburg liners; he spoke about shipping lanes and coast-lines, ports he'd looked up in his father's atlas. Not like the Steppe lands, with their rivers and pastures: these were far flung, and across the oceans: half the world away from here.

– Montevideo and Buenos Aires. Sierra Nevada.

Benno spoke the names, and he described the way he saw them, in his New World mind's eye. Plains wide enough to leave you lonely, mountains that were impassable, cities where so many lived, you could walk and walk and lose yourself.

Freya couldn't picture them – not really – only the Heide, and the Hamburg docksides. But she could listen to Benno; she could feel her legs stretched long against his.

Soon, he would damp the stove, Freya would fold the blanket, Benno would ride her down to the junipers to fetch her bicycle. And she looked forward to climbing onto his saddle behind him, bumping down the sand paths, her fingers hooked into his belt loops, her cheek pressed to his shoulder blades.

If only it could go on like this; if only that were possible. Lying and kissing and talking, and cycling home again.

But at least the English were still in the Rathaus; at least no ships were sailing yet from Hamburg. They had no school yet either: Freya hoped it would be weeks – months – before they had to go back to classes. And in the meantime, Benno could weave his plans for her like stories. Like wishes for a future that was still far off.

Except one afternoon, he told her:

– It's all just lies, though. Isn't it? It's all just stupid.

They'd only just got to the junipers, down to the low slopes where she left her bicycle. Freya was still holding on to his belt loops; she hadn't even climbed off the saddle behind him when Benno said:

– If I was going, I should go. I should leave for Hamburg. But I'm not, though. Am I?

He sounded so angry; Freya couldn't think why. Or what had started this. They'd just been kissing and dreaming, like they always did.

Benno told her:

– School will start soon.

But school didn't seem like enough of a reason.

– Soon it will get too cold for sleeping out here on the Heide.

But how could he be cold with all that gorse they'd gathered for burning? Freya went to speak, but Benno turned to her:

– Udo will go. He told me so.

Since when had he spoken to Udo?

Freya had to hold her tongue there, holding his belt loops tighter. She thought of Benno, of his brother, of them talking at home, on nights when Benno slept there; on mornings, when she wasn't there to hear them. And then Freya thought of Udo, striking out along the Poststrasse – or along the rail lines, where he wouldn't be spotted so easily. She said:

– Bet he won't though.

Although she could see him doing that; it would be just like Udo to try in any case. To wait on a goods train – a good and slow one – before jumping up to hold on. Freya looked at Benno and hoped he wouldn't try that:

– Say you won't. Please. Even if Udo does. You'd never get far. Not with the English patrolling.

– That's just it, though.

Benno told her:

– That's just what I think. All the time. Even when I talk at the hut here.

The way he spoke, it was as though all his dreams had just been fool's talk.

– I talk about the shipyards. About working at the harbour. But inside – all the time – I think about the roads and patrols, and how the trains aren't running yet, and how far it is to get to Hamburg. I think about the curfew. And about what if the English caught me?

He blinked at Freya, hot-faced – not just angry, but ashamed too. He wasn't like Udo. Benno hadn't been made for the soldier life; it looked like he wasn't made for this life afterwards either.

– You see now?

What could she answer? Freya didn't like the way he looked at her. She let go of his belt loops; sliding down from the saddle behind him. Because he was getting things all twisted; he was talking like his Vati would. Except Benno wasn't finished yet.

– The English are staying here anyway. Even if the clerks

leave the Rathaus, it looks like they're keeping that camp at the munition works. I know, because they're chopping trees for firewood, for the winter. They're chopping trees from the town woods. Udo says so.

– Oh, but what does your brother know?

Freya kicked at the sand path, frustrated, but Benno blinked at her, serious:

– Udo says half the town has seen the trees cut. He's been to look for himself too.

– Well, maybe he shouldn't look so much.

Freya was growing angry herself now. Because it didn't make sense to her – why Benno should leave the Heide – or why the felling should matter either, the English firewood. She said:

– Didn't Udo go before? To look at the town works and the workers?

He'd always gone where he shouldn't have – and now he went to look at the trees felled.

– What does it have to do with him?

But Benno didn't answer.

The shadows had come, and with them the curfew. The sky was still pale, and the sand paths, but the heather already blue-dark, so Freya picked up her bicycle.

– We should go home.

She wheeled it towards Benno.

– Come on, now. Before your Mutti notices. Or before my Papa does.

Except then Benno told her:

– Udo says your Papa used to laugh at us. He used to hear him, with the yard men. With Herr Brandt and the other yard workers.

He was hunched over his handlebars. He didn't look angry, though – not any longer – not accusing – at least Freya didn't think so. Benno was just serious.

– You know who laughs now, Freya? It's the Front returners. Udo says so. He says it's why he wants to go too. Because the Front Boys laugh at all of us in the town here. At how we fret over our rations, and over the English. We think this is hard? That's what they ask. Well, we should have seen the East Lands. If we think this is punishment, then we should have seen the Russians come.

Benno looked about himself at the empty slopes, the empty paths, leading out and away across the Heide.

– The Front boys laugh hard – you know?

He squinted, like this was hard to think about.

– They went to war talking like my Vati. They came back talking like this.

Then he told her:

– They say the English will stay too. They will keep the workers here. They will fell more trees before they're done with us.

Benno said this like Front boys might be right somehow. Or that the English might be right to do this.

It had got darker while they were talking. Freya had to go; they both did. But Benno looked so sad now, not just serious, she had to step forward. Hooking her fingers back into his belt loops, Freya pressed her mouth to his – a swift kiss. Because he should stay; he shouldn't think he had to leave the Heide. Benno shouldn't listen to Udo.

The next morning, Benno wasn't at the brook when she got there, he wasn't at the hut step, either. Freya found the door open – but someone else was inside.

A man was asleep on the bunk there, with a greatcoat flung over him. A soldier: a Front returner with his boots discarded. He was sleeping in his trousers, in his shirt too, the cloth all crumpled like his face was. One arm slung behind his head, his other sleeve lay dangling – and as soon as she saw it was a soldier, a stranger, Freya backed up, ready to go again. Except then he blinked his eyes open.

– Hey, *Mädchen*.

The returner spoke up.

– Hey – wait there.

He pushed himself up on his elbow.

– Freya?

He said her name too – and like it pleased him.

– It's *Freya*.

He repeated it. And then he grinned so – sudden and wide, and delighted – Freya saw who the soldier was.

– Oh!

His face grimy, he was thinner and older, and with his sleeve hanging loose from his shoulder. But he was Kurt Buchholz! Kurt was here again! And he was smiling – and all this had Freya smiling also; it made her forget Benno for the moment.

– Stay!

Kurt urged her, like he thought she wanted to go still.

– You can stay with me a short while, can't you?

He ran his fingers across his hair to flatten it, as if to make himself presentable, pushing off his coat, pulling himself up to standing – all one-handed – as he came grinning to the doorway.

– I've been away so long, you hardly know me. And here you are: almost a grown girl!

Kurt put his head aslant to get a better look, leaning forward, his shirt sleeve drooping and empty. Freya glanced at it; she glanced away again – she couldn't help herself. But Kurt had seen anyway:

– *Tja, Mädchen.*

He told her:

– It's quite some war wound. My retribution.

But then he grinned again, tipping his head aslant again.

– Better an arm lost than a life, though.

Kurt sat down on the hut step, in the sunshine, rubbing at his cheeks, his half-grown beard, a little drowsy, and he gestured for Freya to sit too, to make herself comfortable on the gully slope.

– I'll make tea – I will. For both of us. In a moment. Just let me wake up a bit.

Inside the hut, Freya could see his Front pack, and a bottle too, standing beneath the bunk slats. It was nearly empty, and when she looked again at Kurt's heavy eyelids, at the easy hang of his shoulders, Freya knew he was not just sleepy.

But he'd been her Papa's pupil; he'd been Herr Brandt's apprentice. When Freya was younger, Kurt had been her favourite among all the yard workers – and Ursel's also. So she wanted to stay with him a little longer yet.

Freya watched while he pulled out his haversack, rummaging out a packet of tea leaves, a packet of cigarettes, both of them crumpled. Kurt had bread inside there too: the end of a loaf, wrapped in paper, and he saw that Freya saw it:

– My Christa gave me that.

He nodded.

– Fresh from the bakery.

He motioned to the bottle and the tea leaves.

– Look: she gave me all of this. Last night, when I called at her window.

Kurt smiled at that a moment, and then he told her:

– She'll be coming later. I've said to meet me here. If you stay, she'd like that, Freya.

And Freya thought she'd like that herself – to wait here with Kurt – and to see Christa. Even if it made her shy at the same time, the idea of waiting for the older girl.

Except then Freya thought of Benno. She found herself glancing down the gully slope and back again, thinking she still had to find him. She told Kurt:

– I might have to go soon.

Freya hoped that didn't sound too much like making excuses.

– I have things to do.

– Of course you do.

Kurt nodded, mild, like he didn't mind too much either way.

But then he pointed, just over her shoulder:

– So is he with you?

Freya turned, abrupt, and saw Benno was behind her. He was up on the gully top with his bicycle and looking down at them.

Kurt told her:

– He's been here half the morning. So I had been wondering.

– Come down!

Freya called to him – because Benno was standing a little way back, and a little to one side, like he wasn't too sure.

– Come on!

She called another time, beckoning him closer, because it was only Kurt Buchholz, and Kurt was no one to worry about.

Still, Benno didn't move, and so Freya turned back to Kurt again, a little flustered:

– It's only Benno.

She thought he must know all the town boys in passing; he must know Benno's father. She wanted Kurt to see that Benno wasn't a stranger here. But Kurt only squinted, like he hadn't quite placed him – or he hadn't quite decided – and then he pulled out a cigarette.

The tobacco dry and falling from the paper, he pinched the end closed with his fingers.

– Best American quality.

Kurt grinned at Freya, hush-hush and furtive, as he opened the hut cabinet. He pulled out Benno's matches, making to strike one. Then he pulled out Udo's knife too, as an afterthought – as though he'd only just noticed it.

– That's mine.

Benno spoke for the first time.

He stayed at the gully top, but he reached his hand forward, gesturing for Kurt to throw it up to him. But Kurt only glanced at Benno's palm, ready and waiting; and then at Benno's face, as though still trying to place him.

– These are your things, are they?

Kurt glanced at the knife again, and then he put it down on the step beside him – on the side with his missing arm – like he was daring Benno to take it.

Kurt struck a match on the doorframe, lighting his cigarette, lifting his chin to the kettle, the red blanket.

– I thought someone had been making good in here.

– We've been taking care of the place.

Freya tried smiling, because she wanted Kurt to like it – she wanted him to like Benno – and Kurt did give a small nod in acknowledgement.

– Nice work – yes.

But then he flicked the spent match into the undergrowth and he said:

– The shepherd. The one who kept the flock up here: Frank. He went to the Wehrmacht about the same time as I did.

Kurt didn't look at them as he spoke, he just turned to open the stove, feeding it with kindling, all with his one hand, and then he told them:

– He's gone now, though. Frank's not coming back.

And then Freya understood: Kurt was telling them this was his place now. Or rather: he was telling Benno. Because when the flames caught, Kurt turned and smiled at her, but he didn't smile at Benno.

Instead, he took a draw on his cigarette and set out the mugs on the step beside him: one for himself, one for Freya – and then Kurt blinked at her, like he was thinking. He took the paper from the tea leaves, smoothing it out with his thumbnail, then folding it over and over. He looked at her while he sat and smoked and waited for the tea to brew, like he was working up to saying something.

Was he wondering about Benno? Kurt still had Udo's knife there, but Freya wasn't sure – Kurt was just ignoring him.

So was he wondering about her Papa? If he was back too?

Freya hoped Kurt might ask after her Mama instead. Or after Herr Brandt. Or that he might ask about Ursel. Because if Kurt asked after her Papa – or if her Papa knew about this hut here, this town son she spent her days with – then Freya wouldn't know what to say.

– I know your Papa is home again, *Mädchen*.

Kurt gave her a short look, like she didn't have to say anything.

– Christa told me.

Kurt said this kindly, his eyes soft and sleepy, so Freya nodded; at least she didn't have to try explaining. And then Kurt gave her the same look as he continued:

– I know about my Mama too: that she has a baby at home now.

So Freya nodded another time, because Christa must have told him that also, or perhaps he'd been to the Hof and seen the child? Kurt was smiling in any case.

Except now he raised his eyebrows:

– I thought the baby was my sister's. I thought: I am an uncle now. Finally. But it's a little Polack. Isn't it? I didn't believe that, not at first – a little worker girl! But it's right. Yes?

Freya couldn't nod – not this time – although Kurt was waiting for an answer.

She'd seen old Hanne with a new child, but Freya hadn't thought the girl was a worker's. Even now she'd heard this, Freya felt herself doubting. The girl must be a Heide child, surely; she must be from someone in Kurt's family? Freya thought he must be spinning tales now to divert her, sleepy and drunken. Still, his gaze held her – and the way he was talking to her also: his eyes soft with drink but curious – as though he really didn't know whose child she was.

– It's what people are saying – you know that?

Kurt smiled again.

– They say the baby was left at our Hof. She was left with my Mama in the snow time. She's a little winter child. That's what my Christa calls her.

Kurt paused there; he blinked at Freya, like he was expecting her to confirm this; to know more than he did.

But it was so strange that he was asking this at all – and about his own mother and father. And it began to feel even stranger to talk like this in front of Benno, still quiet up on the gully slope above them both. Benno had fallen even quieter now that talk had turned to the winter, to the Hof and the new child there. But Freya could feel that he was listening – and hard – waiting for something further.

– Or maybe it was my Papa who found her? Old Heide Gustav.

Kurt was still talking, he was leaning forward, telling Freya:

– Christa says that's how some tell this story. That my old father must have found her – in the Hof or on the Heide – on the night the workers ran here.

What was he saying now?

Freya wanted to look to Benno, because Kurt was talking about the snow time, about workers running on a winter night – and hadn't Benno seen them? Hadn't his Vati seen them also – that same night? Except Freya thought if she turned now, then Kurt might turn to him also – and she knew Benno would want that: Kurt looking at him and asking. Not about the snow time, that cold night. Benno wouldn't want anyone asking about his Vati.

– There are children at the English camp.

Freya spoke now. Too loudly – but she felt she had to say something.

She didn't know about the winter, or the girl at the Hof; all Freya knew was that she'd seen a boy from the camp here: a child on the high pass, carried like a lamb on workers' shoulders.

– I think there are, in any case.

She faltered. As soon as she'd heard herself, Freya wished she hadn't spoken. Because she hadn't told Benno about that boy, or those workers she'd seen coming past here, and now she thought he might be hurt – or angry – that she'd kept something from him.

Kurt only nodded though, as if he already knew this. As if half the town did.

– Yes, they say that also. The town wives. They say the English have worker children, and so my Mama should hand the girl over. Others, though, they say she should keep her. Not tell the English. That's the main thing: keep quiet until the English leave – no?

Freya couldn't keep up now. What was he asking?

– Isn't that right, though?

Kurt asked another time.

Except Freya didn't know which part he meant. The snow time? The English? Did Kurt want to know if the girl was a worker's? Or if old Hanne and Gustav should keep her?

Kurt stopped there; he waited for her to answer. Freya only hoped he wouldn't press her further – and then she hoped even more that he wouldn't ask Benno. The moments ticked past while she looked for words and found none. Kurt looked from her to Benno, and Freya felt her cheeks burn.

– *Ach, Mädchen.*

Kurt broke the silence. He waved a palm like he was sorry he'd asked.

– Don't listen to me, will you?

He tried laughing.

– I drink and talk too much. My Christa says so.

And also:

– Don't listen to town word either, about workers and children. That's what your Papa would say, no? Don't listen to townsfolk about anything.

Except now he looked again at Benno – up on the slope and waiting. And then Kurt turned back to Freya too, like he'd had second thoughts.

– Oh – but you'll be careful. Won't you?

He said it like a warning, still sleepy-eyed but serious.

– People will say all sorts now. You know this? They will say my old father did the right thing, my old mother also. Soon, they'll say your Papa was right, too, about the men in our Rathaus, about that crowd in Berlin. Or about the war, even. Like they've changed their minds. Or like they knew it all the time.

Kurt shook his head, slow and drunk and cautious.

– You know what my Christa said? She told me the English are angry.

He even laughed now, soft and under his breath.

– She said all the town thinks so. They are sure of it.

Kurt leaned in towards her.

– But I was out east – yes? And the things I saw there. Oh, the things I could tell the town here, *Mädchen*. Then they wouldn't talk so much.

Again, he spoke as if in warning.

– I could tell them about folk being angry too.

He lifted his shirt sleeve, as if to show her. Then he shook his head, and let it drop again.

– I won't tell you, though. These are not things for a child to know.

But already she felt Benno standing up behind her.

Freya stood up also – she couldn't help herself – except when she turned, Benno was holding his bicycle and he wouldn't even look at her.

– You leaving so soon?

Kurt raised his chin as he spoke, his eyes cool again, voice also:

– Don't you want your knife, *Junge*?'

But already Benno was riding.

He pushed off, hard, and he rode away, fast, without once looking back.

It was a long walk down the track without him. Freya's head blurry with words, her throat tight with confusion, she only wanted to be home again. For the first time in so long, Freya wanted to be with her Papa. But at the foot of the track, in the junipers, her bicycle wasn't where she'd left it.

Freya looked and she looked, but she couldn't find it anywhere.

25

Left to the Wolves

Ruth

The children were already out when Ruth started on her early rounds. She passed them on the open ground where the Czech tents had stood. The earth still bare, dry and sandy, Yeva was sitting at the near edge. She was watching over Sasha, who was out in the middle – the boy was chatting and grinning – he was on a bicycle of all things – with Mirko teaching him how to ride it.

– Who brought that here?

Yeva smiled up at Ruth's question. Then she cast a shrugging glance about herself. So there was no point asking further; Ruth could see she'd get no more from her.

She could see, too, that Sasha was enjoying himself. It was a girl's bike, and a good size too large, but he was already getting the hang of riding, standing on the pedals, turning in wobbling circles, while Mirko applauded him.

– *Brawo!*

Farley would be out soon, preparing for the Ukrainian departure, and Ruth looked each way along the duckboards, then down at Yeva, and where she'd placed herself. Was she keeping watch for the sergeant?

When Ruth passed the bare spot again on her way to the offices, they still had the bicycle in any case. Mirko was teaching Yeva by that time, while Sasha had taken his sister's lookout place at the corner. The girl was on the saddle, with the young Pole walking next to her; Mirko was steering with one hand, the other arm held around her waist, and Yeva was leaning into this embrace, both of them laughing.

The trucks came for the Ukrainians the next afternoon.

None of them refused. They'd all read and re-read their notices, spending the past days packing up their few possessions, stripping their beds, sweeping their hut floors. Leaving everything clean; right and proper and proud.

But still, their leaving was angry. The courtyard was full of their shouting.

– *Vidmovleno!*

– *Zrada!*

Sent away! they called. Abandoned! Their voices echoing along the Poststrasse as they walked out of the camp gates, along the convoy that had come to take them.

The trucks had their tailgates open, benches set out inside, troops waiting. But the DPs refused all hands to help them, throwing their bundles into the truck backs, calling and shouting.

– *Do bisa!*

– Go to hell!

They hurled their worst words at the convoy soldiers who had come to drive them.

– To the devil with all of you!

They even turned their faces away from the supply lads who'd brought out the boxes of rations for the journey.

– Should we be grateful?

– *Zrada!*

– Should we be left to the wolves across that border?

Pan Artem was among the last out, although his truck was among the first in the convoy. He only came when the drivers were already starting up the engines, and instead of climbing inside, he stood at the tailgate, declaiming.

– It is not right!

He spoke loud above the truck roars, and directly at Ruth, at Farley.

– What you do to us here, it is not right, I say.

The convoy was ready for departure, but he continued.

– You say our country wants us back now? It is not our country under the Russians.

He pointed to his Back Enclave companions, his fellow Ukrainians, angry and fearful in the truck backs.

– You see what you do – yes? You should not do this. Your major at the town hall – he should not obey such orders. And where is he now?

The man had come earlier to greet the convoy, to see that all was running as ordered, but then he'd been radioed away to Lüneburg, to a meeting there about mayors and handovers. None of which was his doing, of course. But still, Ruth would have had him stay to hear this, to be here as Pan Artem let his scorn loose.

– Your Higher Ups. They are cowards. They should not send us to Stalin.

The soldiers had to take his arms; he had to be pulled up and inside by his countrymen – rough and awkward and undignified.

And the worst of it? Sasha saw this departure.

He came to the camp gates, although Ruth had hoped he would not do that. She'd hoped Yeva would keep him among the women's huts, or even that Mirko might take him off on his new bicycle, long enough until the trucks had departed. But then he came riding out onto the Poststrasse.

– Hey! Hey!

Ruth only saw him once he'd passed her.

– *Chekay!*

Stanislaw broke into a run after him, but the boy was faster. He kept looking as he pedalled, peering into each truck he passed, searching the faces under the tarpaulins. He searched the next and the next – until he found Pan Artem's.

The Ukrainian was inside now, and silent; he looked out and saw the boy too.

Did he raise a palm, or nod as his truck pulled out? Ruth didn't see what passed between them. Only how Sasha dropped his bicycle as the trucks pulled away from him, kicking it into the verge grass.

*

All of that made sleeping impossible.

Hours later, in her guard-block bedroom, Ruth lay and looked out at the night sky and the tree crowns, her mind still full of that anger, all of that shouting. And when she gave up on resting and went to the mess tent, seeking tea to distract her, she found Stanislaw in their usual corner.

He was alone there and just as sleepless. He gave her a nod as she took the seat opposite, and then another as she asked him:

– Might all the departures be like that?

Stanislaw considered this a moment. Ruth thought he must have considered this before too, because he said:

– I can tell you some Poles who will object. If you like, I could give you a whole list.

– And you?

Ruth asked:

– Might your name be on there?

They had never talked about Stanislaw's homegoing, and the old Pole looked up at her as though this hadn't escaped him.

– Me?

He paused a moment.

– You know I lived under Stalin. I lived like that two years – only two years, before the Germans came. But it was long enough, you see? To make me think twice. To make me think three, four, five times.

He waved his fingers – uneasy, undecided. Then he told her:

– Your Red Cross, they found Barthos. They found my brother; you know this.

Ruth nodded; Stanislaw did too, before he continued:

– Well, I am old now, but he is older. Since they found him, I say to myself: I must go back to my brother. We have lost so many years, he and I. So I should at least try.

Stanislaw sighed.

– But if I go back, I would go back to live under Stalin – under those who bow to him.

He blinked at Ruth.

– You have to see: this is the worst for me. I remember how it was. I lost so much. Friends were first. I just lost them – gone! Students I had taught for years, just lost one day from my classes. I heard how some were gone from their apartments.

He told her that he lost his job too, while others kept theirs.

– I was told from one day to the next – *you are out now* – and by men I'd worked with for so long. You understand me? I'd known them half my working life. Some I'd known since childhood.

Stanislaw said there were some who apologised.

– There were others – a few – who offered help and condolences. But I had more who closed their doors. They crossed the road if they saw me.

– And your brother?

– Barthos?

– He worked with you. At the same university.

– He did, yes.

Stanislaw sat back again. Did Barthos lose his job too? The old Pole blinked at Ruth.

– We were brother-colleagues. We were brother-neighbours also. We had our offices just across the same courtyard. All my life, I knew I could look to him for guidance. When I was thrown out, he came to my apartment. He was one of the first – of course. What brother wouldn't do that?

Stanislaw squinted.

– Barthos came more times. But you know. The last time, it was after dark and through the back door, up the back stairs. It was to tell me he could not come again. He would not be able.

Even saying that was painful.

– I know he was frightened. I saw that. Who wasn't?

Stanislaw looked at Ruth; he looked out of the window. She saw the lost trust, though; the years lost to this.

– I don't know what he told himself. If I go home, I don't know what Barthos would say now. But – you know – when I look at these Germans here. That baker. Those old Fräuleins with their orchard. Really: when I look all of them, I ask myself: so was that you too?

He sat and thought a while.

– It makes you small, no?

Then Stanislaw corrected himself:

– It makes you pitiful. Maybe even in your own eyes.

Beyond the mess tent, the duckboards were grey in the lamplight, the tea in their mugs grown cold.

– And if you don't go home?

Ruth had to ask.

Stanislaw took a breath: a long one.

– I don't know. I don't know and that's the truth.

He tried a smile now, rueful:

– You will forgive an old man for not knowing?

Then he blinked at her, a little shy, all of a sudden:

– Or you will laugh at me – maybe – when I say this?

– Oh!

Ruth shook her head.

– No, I won't. I promise.

How could she laugh at Stanislaw?

– Go on – please.

– Well, I watch our Mirko here. While he's dialling through the stations on our radios. I listen with him to Warsaw; I notice how he listens to New York, to Chicago. I see a young Pole and his young dreams – you know? – of the life to come after this. And then I think how your father left Poland. He will have had his own reasons – I am sure – but he made a new life, yes?

Ruth nodded; she smiled too, finding herself warmed by these new thoughts.

Then she found herself shifting forward, because perhaps she could arrange a pass for Stanislaw? Here was something she could do – at last.

– Do you want me to check about papers? I don't know about London sailings, if there are any planned yet from Hamburg, from Bremen, but I could investigate. I would look into that – gladly. If you would you like me to.

Stanislaw lifted his head.

– Sometimes, I think I would like that. Sometimes, I think: a visa. A London visa is not too much to ask, in lieu of my translation services.

But then he gave her that same wry smile again, that same sigh also, his fingers wrapped around his tin mug.

– But is it right for an old man? I don't know. I am not a Mirko. Much as I like his New World – it sounds so much better than the old, no? And I know there are many others here who think so. But sometimes – even London – it seems very far to go. And then. When I think about that, and about the years I have left me, I just want to work again. Maybe to see Barthos. Just not to think too much.

He smiled one more time. Stanislaw looked tired, though.

– I just want to go on. You know? That's all.

Yeva and Mirko were married a few days later.

Ruth had found a Polish Army chaplain: he was stationed in Aachen with the British forces and the major had him brought in to conduct the service.

They held it out in the open, on the grass outside the mess tent. The women went gathering in the meadows that morning, bringing in the first autumn seed heads, the last of the summer blooms to festoon the entrance, to weave crowns for the bride and groom. The men brought out the remains of the Back Enclave plum brandy, hidden half-bottles that they'd been saving, pouring it into tin mugs and raising it skywards.

There were toasts to the couple first, and then to the departed. And then there were tears also: Yeva's hands clasped in Josefa's, holding tight to this mother standing in for her own one; Sasha's fingers clenched into fists, his eyes rubbed red.

But the day was happy – miraculous – for all that.

The younger women fussing over Yeva's hair and freckles and skirt hems; all the men in the Polish quarter coming to shake Mirko's hand, to clap him on the back. There was jazz from Berlin on the camp radios, and dancing to the accordion. Mirko waltzed his Yeva across the summer-dry grass, wearing their flower crowns, encircled by DPs and camp staff, by singing and smiles, while Sasha ate the chocolate slipped to him by the supply lads – the boy's tears dried again.

That night, the young couple were moved into married quarters: into one of the newly empty Nissen huts at the start of the Back Enclave, with a plywood partition at the far end for Sasha's bedroom.

It was the hut opposite Pan Artem's, and Ruth saw the three of them around the man's old fire pit the morning after. Yeva brewing tea, Mirko attending to Sasha's bicycle. He'd lifted it from the verge where the boy had thrown it; now he was straightening the bent spokes with Sasha leaning sleepy against his shoulder.

The rains started not long afterwards.

A first autumn downpour came pelting against Ruth's windows, waking her in the small hours. It swept through the pines; she lay and listened to it tumbling. And when she woke next, it was dawn and the water was roaring down the millrace.

The rain slowed over the next days, but it stayed. The grass turned marshy under the duckboards; the earth puddled where there had been dancing; the remaining DPs huddled inside their Nissen rows.

Above them stood the trees, their crowns shrouded, the felled ground lying open. The clouds laden: more to come.

November

26

A Hof Visitor

Hanne

It didn't happen at all as she'd imagined it.

When Kurt came home to them, it was dark out, already well past curfew hour, and the first Hanne saw of him was his shadow at the Hof gate: his bag slung across one shoulder, his other still turned to the Heide, as though still deciding.

Hanne dropped the pillowcase she'd been folding.

– Gustav!

All in a rush, she called out to his father.

– *Seh doch!*

And then she arrived downstairs to find Gustav already pulling their dear son inside.

– Hanne – *schau mal!*

*

They sat him down in the kitchen corner.

Hanne placed a bowl in front of him, and then another one; she cut bread slice after bread slice – to the end of the loaf – watching as he ate, unable to do otherwise. They could only stare, she and Gustav, at their boy returned to them: grimy and stubble-chinned, his hair grown long over his ear tops. It stood out at all angles, stuck in a band around his forehead where his cap had held it.

Kurt leaned over his soup bowl, holding it close with his elbow, spooning with his one hand. His left sleeve rolled up, empty and folded in on itself – for all her gazing, Hanne found she couldn't look at that.

He smelled of earth and rain and wet wool. His coat sodden, he'd dumped it at the stoveside, and the steam rose from the collar and shoulders – and then the rain started up again while he was eating. Kurt turned to the door when he heard it, as though he'd been thinking to go again, but now he'd have to think that over.

He looked at Hanne and Gustav a good moment, then he turned his eyes to look upstairs.

– So is she up there?

Ditte had been asleep all this while.

She looked so small in the bed when Hanne showed him. Sleeping as only a child can sleep.

– *Ach.*

Kurt sighed, looking at her from the doorway. He asked:

– It's all true, then? About the winter?

What else had he heard?

Hanne threw a look at his father. How many must know

about Ditte? What did they know about the woman who had left her?

Gustav said:

– The woman ran, son. She left the child with us. We didn't know what else to do.

But Kurt only rubbed his forehead.

– *Ach.*

He sighed again, shook his head over the child again. Over the winter and the workers. Or maybe it was over her and Gustav – Hanne couldn't be certain.

He slept downstairs in any case.

Kurt took the blankets Hanne brought him and he made himself a bed by the kitchen stove. His knapsack for a pillow, his boots propped at the doorway to dry out.

They were gone when Hanne woke up.

She saw the empty space there when she came downstairs, Ditte in her arms. She'd meant to show the child to Kurt again – properly, and in the light this time – this dear thing left with them, in all her sleepy morning loveliness. Except when Hanne looked to the stoveside, she found no Kurt there.

27

The Woods

Farley

The morning rose cold. His fingers ached with it, and he hadn't even covered his first camp circuit; the trees high around him as he walked, drips falling from the branches, although the last fall had stopped an hour ago.

Farley had started at the back boundary, by the town woods. He'd sent three lads along that bottom route, to scout the remains of the back wall and the low slopes, before they returned along the Poststrasse.

– Mind you make a thorough job of it.

A track had been worn there: first by DPs out and trading, and then by patrols coming after them. All summer they'd done that, and into the autumn, but even now the Ukrainians were gone, there was still bartering between the camp rows, among the townsfolk, and none had been caught yet. So the patrol lads had looked at Farley, doubtful – feeling the cold no doubt. Until he told them:

– Yes, well. I'd sooner not have to do this myself. I'd sooner be leaving too. But here we are, boys. Until we're stationed elsewhere.

Farley followed the path up the millrace in the meantime, making for the top path through the pine trunks. It ran parallel with the back boundary, all the way along the factory compound, and he'd be able to catch sight of the patrol boys from up there. Once he got high enough up the slope – or once he got to the felled ground at the latest – Farley knew he could look down, check they'd taken the full route as ordered.

He listened for them, off and on as he was climbing, hearing only the millrace, the drips from the branches. He followed his own boot prints from last time – on top of those made by other patrols – on top of those made by DPs, or even by townsfolk.

The sergeant found a shoelace in the mud and discarded it, and then the foil from a chocolate bar, which he held onto. It had been smoothed out and folded over itself, into a ring of sorts, and Farley pushed it into his pocket as he strode onwards, up and up the steep banks.

When he got to the old mill, he was breathless. He stopped to peer between the pine trunks; to take a first look for the patrol boys. Farley found the camp roofs, the high wall, the road beyond it. He saw a jeep there – was it the major's? – departing for Lüneburg, most likely, in search of a mayor.

Below, the Nissen stoves sent up their thin smoke, but there was no sign yet of his soldiers.

The millrace roared on. The mill pool was still, though; the trees huddled around it, and Farley didn't much like the place. Dank and mouldering. Like this town here, like these people.

Below the old bridge where he'd have to walk next, the ground was churned up: a mess of boot prints from patrols, and boot prints from DPs, and yet more prints from god knows who before that. Farley's own boots slid once, twice. Each time, he reached for pine bark, putting out an arm to right himself, and cursing.

Out on the top path, he still had to watch himself, the earth firmer but slick with rainfall. Farley kept his head up as best he could, glancing down for tree roots, looking up and out for his patrol lads. Soon, soon, he told himself.

Catching sight of the town roofs, wet between the winter branches, he spied the turn of the Poststrasse – and then he found himself thinking as he walked: how he'd drive along there; it couldn't be too long now. Soon would come the day when he'd leave this place behind.

But even when he got above the felled ground, there was still no trace of his soldiers. Where had they got to?

Annoyed now, Farley stepped off the path, cutting down the slope, into the needles. He began to stride faster, moving downhill at a diagonal, meaning to cut down to the clearing – to get a clearer sightline. Except the further he trod, the softer the ground grew: thick with needles, sodden beneath that. And after Farley slid a third time, he decided this was a fool's errand – it was getting treacherous – so he turned to double back again.

But although he followed what he thought were his own sliding boot prints, Farley couldn't seem to find the top path again. And then, instead of taking him upwards, the prints began splitting first, then scattering – and after that, he lost them entirely.

The rain had washed through the trees here, sluicing away the leaf and needle, exposing root balls and boulders. There were fallen trunks before him, too: lying right across his path, where he hadn't seen them on the way down. Thinking himself lost now, Farley made for the first of them, but found himself stumbling. The sergeant reached, only for his boots to slide out.

– Christ!

The man went tumbling.

Head over foot over elbow, unable to right himself.

When he landed, it was hard and sudden. It took him a moment to register that he'd stopped again; that he was caught on an overhang: on the lip of a further drop.

The roots had caught him, but his left leg was jarred, trapped at an angle. The pain was sharp: his ankle twisted under him – was it broken?

His limbs cold, his stomach also, Farley tried lifting his foot, only for his guts to churn.

– Man down!

He tried calling – but the bile rose again.

– Here!

He called a further time – but then he had to catch himself. Stomach lurching, he had to lie back; Farley had to take a breath and hold it.

He thought he would just keep his head down, just a

moment – just to stop the churning – stop that nausea – and it worked too. Farley closed his eyes. But when he opened them, he saw what was below him.

Limbs and skirt folds among the tree roots.

Wrists and bare feet under the needles.

Farley saw ankles and shoulders; elbows in torn sleeves; the skin blue-pale, grey-blue and mud-smeared.

This godforsaken shithole.
These godforsaken people.

28

Winter Transport

The Woman Who Ran

Who had thought to run first?

She couldn't remember.

She could only feel how the thought flitted among them – constant – now that they had reached the heathland. Eyes darting from one to the next along their small column of workers – all the while they were walking – all the while she held her girl.

They were so few here. The heathland was wide; they had reached it at half-light, and perhaps it was the coming dark that had made running thinkable. The dark and the feeling that they might be the last now.

*

How many days had they been on this transport?

She couldn't remember that either.

But when it had started, there had been so many more of them: a whole convoy.

She'd been with women from her dormitory, from the same machine works, and from others also. They'd been driven from barracks to barns to workshops, and at each stop and roll call there had been new trucks and workers. Women from assembly lines, men from prison camps, girls from garment works: all crowded into lorries guarded by Werkschutz, and into others driven by Wehrmacht.

Why soldiers?

How much further?

No one knew where the Germans were taking them – who dared ask? – or which stop might be the last. They weren't put to work any longer, only left to wait out the night hours before they were driven on again. The women's eyes sunken, the girls limp with exhaustion, they lay down each night where they were ordered. And then – as soon as they were among themselves – they picked at the patches on their shirt fronts; they spoke of *where?* – of *what for?* – and of *how far now?* They slept and woke, slept and woke.

She fed her own girl under her blouses, wrapping her shawl around her. Fearful of the guards. Fearful that her milk wouldn't last.

She'd been fearful of that since the first.

When her child was born, she'd cried. Her girl was a warm mouth, damp curls, clenched toes and fingers. She was born in the barracks, and at night, and with only the women from the bunk rows to be there. You didn't call the Germans – not if you could help it – and at least this meant she got to hold her girl; she got to feed her.

That machine works was a large one. Not just one factory, but four: all fenced off, and all on the same compound. So many workers – so many overseers – and so many desk men up in their offices.

Those desk men kept the children apart: across on the far side of the compound. There, the factory managers had a ward for the sick workers, and another next to it: narrow and bare, with a few cots for the few children.

Before each shift and after, she walked the pathways, hurrying between the barracks and the office blocks, to hold her girl and feed her. She did the same when she got her lunch pail, cramming her mouth first as she went striding. But she never knew who fed her girl between times. What did they feed her? Bottles of thin milk? Sugar water? Her child was always so hungry.

The other mothers were few and older; she hardly saw them. And the nurses? They mostly worked in the sick bay, and if they came onto the children's ward, she didn't recognise their faces, they came so quick and went again.

She saw, though, that children were moved. A cot that had a boy child in the morning was empty when she came at shift end. She heard, too, that mothers were taken to work elsewhere, and their children left here. She tried not to think of this: of her child crying without answer.

None of the children cried like her girl did.

The noise woke her in the small hours – she was sure she'd heard her; she was sure her girl was just beside her, and she put out her arms only to find herself alone among the bunk rows, among all the women sleeping. And then, although it was night still, she got up and walked out, in her night shirt, to find her daughter.

There was one orderly who opened the door to her.

– *Es ist nicht erlaubt!*

He said it was not allowed.

– *Nein, ich sage!*

He shook his head each time, flustered by her arrival.

– *Du bist ja Kind selber.*

He said she was just a child herself, as though being young could be her fault. Or as though she came just to put him in danger. The man fretted while he let her through the side door, while she sat and fed her daughter, and she didn't like his hurry, or his fear either; she couldn't trust him, always so anxious to be rid of her.

If he wasn't on duty, though, no one came to that side entry. None of the nurses or the other orderlies. It didn't matter how long she knocked. Her cheeks hot, throat sore with yearning, her milk soaking through her blouses.

Already then, she would have run with her daughter. But for the guards and the fence wire. But for the dread thought that there was nowhere to run to. Only more of this cold country.

From the convoy, from the women's truck, she'd seen Germans at road junctions, at bus stops, in ration lines. All the women had seen them; all the girls from the garment works. They'd seen the schools and churches, and the villages they passed through – and there was no talk of running out to those closed doors. They'd had no chance to run in any case.

Too many Werkschutz at the tailgates; too many Wehrmacht carrying rifles.

On the third morning – or was it the fourth? – the Wehrmacht had driven away without them.

All the trucks had driven off after roll call, roaring away from the barn where they'd been sheltering, carrying most of the other workers. They'd left the weakest; mostly it was just women left on the wet concrete, and a few old prisoners.

The remaining soldiers had looked them over, before turning to the damp heathland they'd arrived at, all the wind-blown miles to the horizon. And then those Wehrmacht had divided them further.

– *Mach nun.*

They'd pulled rank on the last few Werkschutz, taking their choice of labourers, selecting all those they thought could work still: almost all the menfolk and only the women who were youngest, hauling them into rough lines. A soldier had grabbed at her. But then he'd seen her bundle, her girl-child, and pushed her to one side again.

– *Und den Rest?*

The Werkschutz corporal was dismayed by this.

– *Was soll das?*

His tunic sleep-rumpled, half undone in his confusion, he'd gestured helpless to the leftovers he'd been charged with: the ill and the frail and the female.

– *Was soll ich mit den bloß?*

What on Earth should he do with them?

But the Wehrmacht shrugged their shoulders:

– *Was auch immer.*

They only told him to get marching.

– *Weg hier!*

– *Los!*

On the heathland now, already the light was failing. Maybe they were only fifteen – she'd tried counting, glancing up and down the line, finding they were only twenty left marching. And with only two guardsmen.

She didn't look at them too often. The few times she'd dared, the few times a car or a van came past, she'd glanced behind herself to see the two of them lit by the headlights. Did these men know where they were marching? The rumpled corporal had taken up the rear post, pressing the line forward along with another in the same uniform, the two men keeping their heads close all the while, mulling over their orders. Or were they arguing? And the workers – the women and the few men – they dragged themselves onwards in the low light, their heads bent against the heath wind, shawls and jerkins pulled tight around their shoulders.

Her own shoulders ached with the weight of her daughter – and with the worry that she was too quiet now. Too cold? Too hungry? She'd already knotted the girl into her shawl folds to ease the carrying, now she pressed her close to keep her warmer, buttoning her blouses around her, as best as she could manage this. She wasn't at all sure that she could march much further – let alone run with her – or that this last was even possible But at every stop and turn she found herself glancing.

Here?

Here?

She felt others do the same too.

A man in prison jacket, prison trousers, restive behind her; a girl from the garment works near the head of their rough line.

That garment girl was a thin one, but dogged in her striding. They'd all picked at their patches, but the garment girl had started this. Already on the first night, while they were still in the convoy, she'd begun working away at the corners, fleet, with her garment worker's fingers; first the blouse on top, then the blouse beneath. Already then, she'd shown her daring – and it was there again now as they were marching: an urgency that rippled down from her, along the straggle of workers.

Still. They had to be wary. Careful – not to let it show to the two corporals.

The Wehrmacht might be gone, along with their rifles, but one of those guards had a truncheon. Neither of them wanted to be here.

The road they were on now was narrower, and she didn't know where the men were driving them: if they meant to find another convoy, or just the next place to shelter. Somewhere – anywhere – to be rid of them.

One car passed, then a post van, a schoolboy on a bicycle. And each time the guards pressed them to the verges – *Mach schon!* – ordering them to stand – *Stehenbleiben!* – while they cast sharp glances about themselves. She saw they were anxious and this didn't help her. They didn't seem to know where to turn next. Did they even know where they were now?

Then the corporals even ordered them off the road entirely:

– *Rast!*

– *Halt, halt!*

– *An-hal-ten!*

The men herded them into the grass – into a ditch there.

– *Runter, ich sage!*

Ordering them to crouch low to be able to stand over them. And then the rumpled man stood guard with his truncheon while the other went scouting. He strode all along the road and back again, and then further, and she didn't know how long they were made to crouch down there.

It was out of the wind, but the air alone chilled her, and all she could think was that her child was too still against her. She tried to rouse her, but she could hardly rouse herself; fingers weak with cold, useless against the shawl knots, she could barely get them loosened. She hardly dared to move much – not with the guard so close. Because who could trust in Germans? Not when they were nervous. And all this while her girl was so very quiet, she had to press her cheek to her curled head, rubbing her curled back, just to feel her moving, just to feel her breathing; then she wrapped herself tight around her, falling into a doze of sorts.

It was the garment girl who pulled her up again. The man in prison rags.

Go, go.

Up, up.

One fleet, the other raw-boned, they took her by the elbows. Her legs were numb with crouching, feet stiff and swollen, but the way they urged her, she felt it might be time soon: that they both thought so.

It was dark around them. Night had fallen, and with it a new cold – she felt it at her shoulders. If they ran now, they would not have shelter – so was it better to wait still? Let the corporals find somewhere to sleep first? Or wasn't it far better to run in this darkness? Away from these corporals and their nervousness. Their mistrust of their own orders. She looked to the garment girl, the prisoner, both thinking the same thoughts.

Her daughter shifted inside her blouse-and-shawl binding. She felt the child slip too: the knots she'd picked at loosening. She had to grab at the shawl ends to lift her. But now the prisoner gave a tug again – and when she glanced towards him, she saw what he saw.

There were lights here. Were those houses?

There were window-shapes, bright and beyond them. She felt the road turn from dirt to cobbles beneath her; she knew that they'd come to a place where there were people.

There were fence posts and gardens, and street signs. There were trees here also: more of them the further they walked, their pine shapes tall, darker against the dark sky. Had these corporals found somewhere?

Her daughter slipped again and she lifted her, because they had to be ready to run soon. She knew this, and she feared it – and she kept throwing glances to the garment girl.

Here?

Here?

With a town and Germans so near to them?

Then came a siren.

All heads turned at the noise of it. The line of bent backs twisting; each woman reaching for the next. What did that noise mean? She reached for the garment girl, holding her daughter closer: didn't that siren mean danger? It came from among the pine trees; from a lantern-lit pinpoint ahead in the darkness.

– *Weiter!*

The sound was loud enough to have the corporals hound them. The siren rising and falling as the men drove them with a new and hard urgency.

– *Weiter! Weiter!*

Her daughter slipped again, slipping further, the button-threads loosening as they were marched on. She had to duck each time to lift her, arms cramping as she held on. The next time she looked up, the siren had died down but the lantern light was close now.

She saw they had come to a guard post – high gates at the roadside with men standing behind them.

Their faces were shaded, their caps and uniforms, but already she felt they must be Werkschutz like the corporals. Their lantern light fell across a high wall beside them, and this wall and wire only confirmed it: they'd come to a works here among the pine trunks.

– *Halt!*

The first of the new men called out, still inside the closed gates, and the two corporals echoed his order – *Halt! Halt* – pulling the line of workers to a stop at the wall there. But when the rumpled one stepped up towards him, the new man ordered him to stop too.

– *Nicht hier.*

The new man shook his head.

– *Nicht hier.*

Not here, he said, turning and gesturing them onwards – did he mean to keep them marching?

– *Doch!*

The rumpled corporal called back, disbelieving, demanding to be let inside.

– *Doch!! Doch!*

The other corporal joined in, his nervousness spilling into anger, and then all the Werkschutz began raising their arms and their voices, while she held tight to her daughter, trying to keep track of the orders. All the words thrown out from the gates and along the road here; all the guards' voices suddenly furious, and their faces too, shadowed in the lantern light.

– *Wo, denn?*

The rumpled corporal persisted, pointing to the pine trees, the road ahead and behind them – too dark to be marching – and then the other one stepped forward, flinging an arm along the line of workers clustered behind them both.

– *Die Scheissarbeiter.*

He said they would take them no further.

– *Nicht heute.*

Not tonight. Not tomorrow, even.

– *Die Scheissfremden.*

And now the prisoner tugged at her shawl again.

As soon as the corporals' backs were turned, she felt him: the garment girl also – each of them nudging her and shifting. Best not be pressed inside that works wall. Best to keep out of sight now, especially of those new guards. The Werkschutz were still angry and still calling out orders, but she saw what the prisoner and the garment girl wanted – if they could keep out of reach of those lanterns, then this dark and this shouting, it might just help them. It might just be time now.

Except when she glanced behind herself, she saw a new light – was it moving?

She saw a torch beam, and more men. More Germans, but not in uniform.

A small crowd had come; she could make out the shapes of them at the bend in the road there. Men in hats and jackets and trousers – all of them ordinary. A crowd dressed like desk clerks, shopkeepers, or drinkers at a town bar. There was even a boy or two among these watchers: she saw their shorts, their narrow boy shoulders. They were town sons and fathers – what had they come for?

The Werkschutz were still shouting, and the prisoner put out a hand to hold her – not as if to stop her, though, more just to pause. He'd seen these corner men. He was looking from one to the next, as though weighing them up: just a desk man with a torch; just a handful of others, come to see about the siren, now brought up short by the sound of arguing.

So did the prisoner mean to run still? Did the garment girl?

She didn't dare look at her. Only at these new men, these corner Germans – her eye caught by the tallest. He wore a cap, but not Werkschutz; he wore a tunic, but she couldn't see what kind it was. He held a cigarette. It was bent into his palm, but she saw the glow there and how it trembled. Had this tall German seen them?

The prisoner ducked, sharp.

She heard him more than she saw him – seizing his chance while the Werkschutz were arguing. The man broke for the pine trees, dropping away from her, from the garment girl, making off into that darkness.

– Los! Los!

But now the desk man was calling and the tall man was making after him.

She heard this also: two strides, three strides, a scuffle and a blow; a short cry. She saw nothing more, though, until the Werkschutz stopped their shouting to turn to them.

– *Wer ist da?*

– *Was ist los hier?*

Stepping out from the gates and into the road, their lanterns found the tall man standing, the prisoner crumpled, cigarette fallen beside him. The tall man's fists were raised still, they were shaking, and the prisoner lay there.

– *Verdammt!*

– *Verdammt nochmal!*

That's when the running started.

– No!

– No!

The cries for help too.

– Help us!

– *Pomóż nam!*

There was no thought, no plan, only a scattering and wailing. Only a sudden will to get away – far away – fast – from all these Germans.

The guards pulled out whistles and blew them, but this only made it worse still. Women ran for the road sides, taking flight from the noise and the lanterns. They ran from the tall man, from the corner Germans, dashing in panic along the high wall. The corner boys ran also, peeling off from the turmoil, the Werkschutz throwing curses after them and their fathers: most of the corner men turning tail now, back to wherever they'd come from.

– *Anhalten!*

– *Scheissarbeiter!*

The corporals pulled out their truncheons, swinging at

the labourers. The Werkschutz joined them, pulling out their hand guns, flinging out their arms to herd the workers. The wails only grew louder, though, women crying out as all the guards turned on them – furious – trying to hound them into line again.

Only the tall man stayed rooted, and the desk man with the torch; both standing over the prisoner, as though standing guard; as though taking this duty upon themselves.

– Run!

– Run!

This shouting was Polish. *Now!* Was it an order? She tried to see who was calling, but the whistling was all around now. The women were being pushed and pulled and hounded – how soon before they were rounded up again? She wanted to flee like the voices told her; she wanted the garment girl. All she could feel, though, was the Werkschutz; their shrilling and circling. And she couldn't take her eyes off the tall German; he was right there before her with his fists raised. Soon she'd be surrounded – and she couldn't have that, she couldn't let them come for her daughter.

– *Sheissgören!*

She ran because she had to: bent forward, away from the whistles and truncheons.

First she felt the verge grass, then twig and bark as she tore into the pine trunks, away from the guns and lanterns. Her daughter slipped and she held her, but her child only slipped further, branches snagging at her blouse sleeves.

Roots sent her stumbling, and she felt herself gasping – too loud – the fear bursting out of her. A choke and a sob, with each jolt and scramble. With each blind step she took, she felt the ground rise – was there someone ahead, was that someone behind her? On and on, up and up she pushed, her body so cold, her child too silent – the trees all around now, the whistles growing fainter – but where were the other workers?

A roar of water halted her – but only for a moment. Where was the garment girl?

She groped her way higher yet, deeper into the pine wood. Because the pines might hide her – because the garment girl might find them – the girl might know where to run next.

The roar was closer when a flare of light startled her – bright and from below. It was a torch beam, she was almost sure of it: was it the tall man? But how high had she scrambled?

She heard boots on the slope; whistles drawing closer. Breath and cries down there among the roaring; the trees too full of movement. The women were being chased down – she couldn't stop now – but she couldn't run much further, her legs weakening, child weighing heavy against her.

One arm around her daughter, she tried to push onwards, only to find her other arm, her shoulder, up against a root and earth wall. Her flight was blocked – she could feel no way to climb further and below her only fear and danger. The earth was steep and high and solid: she was in a gully of some kind – and how could she get out of here?

The light flared up again; it was there and then gone this time; but still, she saw a shifting: a flick of something beyond her. A skirt, a shawl-wrapped face, just beside a fallen trunk there.

– Oh!

She cried for help – *please* – because it must be the garment girl.

– Help us!

This time she whispered it – *help me* – escape this fear, this gulch, those boots, that torch beam.

– Please!

Her breath pushed the words out, but her knees gave way at the same time, sinking to the root and mud. All her bindings coming loose, arms useless, blouses ripping open, she felt her child drop into her skirt folds.

She couldn't lift her. She couldn't lift herself even. But she felt the garment girl was just there.

Help us.

Palms out, she reached towards her as the light flared up a third time. She didn't know if it was the torch now, or a lantern; if it was carried by works guards or by townsmen; it made no difference. She heard their footfalls, their fear and fury; they were on their way now. Soon they'd be here, and they mustn't find her daughter.

This tangle in her lap, this weight she'd carried for so long; she asked the garment girl to take her – shawl and blouse and child – *please.*

The girl made a noise. Was it refusal?

It was too dark to see her.

The girl was close – so close. Then the girl was gone – she was gone – and so was her daughter.

She reached out her arms, but already she felt it: her skirts were empty.

It wasn't long before the lights came. Close enough to blind her.

She closed her eyes and thought only of her daughter. Of the garment girl running her far from here.

29

Afterwards

The major

A shallow grave; nineteen bodies, dumped inside and covered over.

Forced workers, all of them, shot in the town woods and buried there.

Women labourers: this was the hardest part for the major. Women had been killed here, left among the winter trees in their thin workers' skirts and blouses. Their bodies had been right there, all this time. Just on the camp doorstep. Within striking distance of his town hall offices.

As soon as the news of the discovery reached him, he returned from Lüneburg.

The major arrived in the trees to find his troops already

lifting the workers from the leaf and mud. His men were laying them out, careful, and under Ruth Novak's instruction. She was bending over each in turn, taking a moment first, before noting their patches, collecting the few scraps and cards from their pockets. Finding any names still readable, any works numbers. Gathering lockets, rings still on fingers, earrings in earlobes: anything that might yet identify them.

His men spoke few words among themselves. Only looking to him to acknowledge his arrival, and then to lift their chins towards the town roofs.

These people here.

These Germans.

The major knew what they meant. That the townsfolk should be ordered from their houses. The Rathausplatz gatherers, and the queueing town wives, his villa neighbours: they should all come and see this.

Ruth Novak was of the same mind. Except she wanted more too.

After each body was wrapped in its own tarpaulin, which would have to do until coffins were ordered, the major stepped up beside her.

– I'm sorry it had to be you.

– Me too.

She nodded – brief and blunt – tall and angry – before she turned her face town-wards.

– How many of them knew?

She asked – and then:

– Who will say that we've found them out?

She spoke out loud and in front of everyone:
– Will it be you, major?

He made the rounds with the new man at the town hall – only just installed, only just brought in from Lüneburg.
A veteran of the last war, he was old to be taking office, and aged further by his time in Gestapo confinement. He'd been persuaded out of retirement; the major had tried by letter first, and then – three times this past autumn – he'd gone to visit the man in his cramped apartment. To appeal to his sense of duty, his sense of pride, even – to those last few shreds his jailers had left him. And now the major saw how he had to steel himself for this first of his new Bürgermeister's duties, going house to house, telling all the key people.
– Who can I look in the eye here? This what I am wondering, major.
The two of them sat in the jeep before they set out that morning. Both old hands, both unprepared; wrapped in their coats against the chill beyond the jeep doors.
– What will I see there?

The schoolmaster's house was among their first ports of call.
The major did not know which was worse: the school wife sitting down abrupt when she heard, legs folding under her into her parlour chairs; or turning to find the eldest of the schoolhouse daughters, her child face hard, listening to all of this from the doorway.

And then, just a morning, two mornings later, the first army clerk to arrive at the town hall found a local on the town square. A Heide smallholder, out early. Sitting alone on the benches, seemingly waiting for someone to trade with.

When he saw the sentry approach, though, the old man stood up. He took off his cap, and then held up both his arms.

30

The Child

Ruth

Gustav Buchholz showed them the empty stores, the empty larder, opening all his doors, opening his palms.

– *Sehen Sie doch?*

His shoulders stooped before Ruth, before the major; the old man told her no workers had been assigned to him.

– *Keine.*

He asked them to believe it, too.

– *Bitte?*

The major had his soldiers search anyway, and Ruth was grateful.

She stood at the Hof gate while they looked all around the outhouses, the woodshed, the lean-to; until it was certain the man was keeping nothing from them. No other workers' children.

– *Nur das eine.*

Only the one, he said. *Only the one*, he repeated – as though this might help him, or make the whole thing more understandable.

Ruth sat to one side while the major put his questions, while Stanislaw translated at the Hof kitchen table. The man pressed his big hands up to his face, and he said he knew nothing,

– *Nichts.*

Of the woman he'd hidden that one night. Or of the transport that must have brought her. The man said he saw nothing,

– *Nichts.*

Of all those workers who'd been brought that same night – nor of any others who might have run at the same time. The Hof man claimed he'd heard nothing that winter evening.

– *Nur die Sirene.*

Only the siren.

He'd known nothing of the grave, either.

– *Gar nichts.*

No word of it had passed among the townsmen – none that he'd heard in any case.

Ruth had already been warned about this by the major. He'd taken her to one side before they came out here and said he'd been told much the same by all the townsfolk he'd called on since the grave was found. *Even the arrested ones.* The Werkschutz commander; the former Bürgermeister in his prison cell. *I am sorry*, he told her. *Even the police sergeant was silent.*

– *Die Heide ist breit.*

The heath is wide, the Hof man told them now, gesturing beyond his window, as though that might explain this.

But still – a small town like this one, and not a word fallen? Ruth could hardly credit that.

The wife had brought the child downstairs by this time – a babe in arms still, a blanket-wrapped bundle – and the smallholder turned to point at her, saying he had nothing.

– *Nur das Kind hier.*

Just the child who'd been left there.

The woman's face creased when she saw Ruth, not just soldiers; she saw she'd have to hand the girl over.

– *Seine Jacke.*

The wife spoke instead, and pointed to her husband. She began talking about a work coat, urgent, or a patch on the front of it.

– *Die Jacke, ja?*

She said a jacket had been stolen. But the child was already crying by this time, and Ruth had already heard enough at this place to last her.

– Enough, please.

The girl cried more when Ruth lifted her out of the Hof woman's arms. Proper and loud – her small body stiffening in protest – he small fists balling, reaching for the old wife – all her blankets falling.

She cried on and on too.

In the jeep, while Ruth held her; in the courtyard as she carried her; and all the way along the duckboards. Ruth thought she'd never stop.

Under the Nissen roof, her cries seemed even louder while

the women passed her from arm to arm. Josefa to Natalia, to Ana and back again. Patient, persistent, rocking and soothing. Rocking and singing too. Polish lullabies, verse after verse, humming and murmuring. And when the child quietened – when her tears turned to sobs, to sleep, finally – they laid her between Sasha and Yeva. This new camp daughter.

Later, once a cot had been made up and blankets found, gauze squares folded into nappies, Ruth got Pan Artem's brandy out of her filing cabinet. She poured it into mugs for her and Stanislaw.

– But for those children.

He nodded.

– Yes. Yes, I know.

But for the children, Ruth knew she would be done here.

December

31

Winter Departure

Ruth

The snow was thick underfoot the day the camp was disbanded. All the tents packed up, most of the huts already empty, the duckboard paths dismantled.

There had been no more requests to stay; no further delegations, not since the grave was found. The younger DPs had gone westward in convoy, heading to a larger camp near Münster, to wait out their visas there, their paperwork for New Brunswick, New Zealand, Nova Scotia. When Ruth received word that a train had been chartered to take all those remaining across the eastern border, she waited for objections, but none came.

Smoke rose only from the last rows of the Polish quarter on the morning the train was due, the DPs inside them subdued.

Each had been issued with ten days' rations, and when Ruth called in on her final round, she found them sitting on their cots, wrapped in their coats, their food crates beside them, their few belongings knotted into blankets.

There had been a hard frost overnight, and the train's arrival was delayed; even at midday the mercury was barely above freezing. Ruth cleared her desk, packing up her files, all the index cards, labelling the boxes for their onward journey to Hannover – away from her. And by the time the train whistle sounded, mournful across the frozen millrace and the meadows, the sun was pale.

The Poles made a sombre crowd, tramping down the Poststrasse. They were laden, ration crates swaying between them, bundles slung across their shoulders. Their breath came in clouds and they sang as they walked in the winter light. Not like they had that May night at the bonfire, the night of the German surrender, or when they were drunk on Pan Artem's brandy. These were songs of home: low and melancholic, ceremonious, their voices a solemn chorus. Dampened by the snowdrifts, and by the closed doors, curtained windows of the few German houses on the station road.

The train had no carriages, only box cars. Ruth had been warned, but the sight of them at the platform still shook her – for all the voices raised in song.

Inside each, though, was a small stove, and the army clerks from the town hall had been there and back all morning, carting the remaining firewood from the hut rows to the railway line. Still singing, the Poles hefted the stove-wood inside, then their food crates and bundles, and still more crates to sit on.

– *Ofitserka!*

Josefa leaned out from the first car, beckoning Ruth over. Together with Ana and Natalia, she'd laid out blankets to make the crates comfortable; now all the women were inside, arranging their bundles along the wooden walls that would be home to them on the long roll eastwards.

In the second car, the men were already setting out a card game, their singing accompanied by the camp accordion. Inside the third, Ruth found Stanislaw.

He was with his hut neighbours, frowning over his boxes, all crammed with parts and shells of his radios. But his face cleared when she climbed in; he stood and took her by the elbows.

– So?

– So.

Ruth had secured a roll of copper wire; she slipped it from her pocket into his.

– To keep on with your mending, yes?

Stanislaw had already been gifted his toolkit by the supply lads, and a spare soldering iron, Farley looking the other way while they'd packed up the camp stores.

The sergeant had set off for the border this morning; he and the supply boys heading for a Rotterdam troop ship; the medics were already in Hannover, awaiting new orders.

– And you?

Stanislaw asked now.

– Oh – I don't know.

Ruth told him.

– Not yet anyway. I'm still here, aren't I?

She smiled – a little – and Stanislaw did too, his nodding

gentle, understanding. Then he held out his hand to shake hers, homebound and grateful, and wishing her the same soon.

Still, as the doors began slamming on the other cars, and the shouts of farewell started, Ruth saw the uncertainty in his features.

– You will write?

– Yes.

– I will write to you.

They both made their promises as she climbed down.

The song rose again, and the accordion notes, and the wheels began to roll, and then Ruth stood and watched while the train departed.

What now?

Northern Germany

Spring 1946

32

A Home for Children

Ursel

When Freya started back at the girls' school, Ursel was lonely.

Freya only started on half days, but she had to be out early for the postbus, and even when she came back, she didn't play. She sat with their Papa instead. In his classroom, bent over her schoolbooks, like she used to.

Their Papa drew and Freya wrote out equations, Latin verbs on the school slates he set before her – *just so, yes, just so* – and their Mama told Ursel she should leave them to it, not bother them by lingering among the desk rows. Her own lessons were over, and the afternoons were growing lighter; she should go out into the lane and the garden, or over to the Brandt yard; she could go roaming. Her Papa looked up from his pages and told her:

– You can go up to the slopes, child. Come back and show me what you find there.

Ursel wanted her sister, though.

All winter, she'd had Freya to herself – all the months since Benno left – and Ursel had liked this.

Sweeping a path through the morning snow with her across the schoolyard; stoking the stove in their Papa's classroom before lessons started; collecting off-cuts and wood curls from Herr Brandt's yard to fill the kindling baskets; trekking out along the frost crusts to the Buchholz Hof, carrying jars from their Mama's larder.

Old Hanne didn't like to leave the house, not since the English took the child she'd found.

The English were gone now, and all the workers, but Hanne sat in her blankets by the stoveside, tired and slow and sad, and when she took the jars that Freya handed over, she looked at the peas and the pear halves and said things like:

– Oh, your Mama.

Or:

– Oh. She shouldn't have.

In the chicken coop, the hens sat with their beaks tucked, feathers fluffed, and old Hanne went from one to the next, bending and searching, bending and murmuring. Ursel knew her Mama would sigh when they brought eggs home. Her Mama would say old Hanne shouldn't have done that either. *She really didn't need to.*

The eggs were few but warm. They fitted into Ursel's palms. Hanne lifted them, careful, out from under the hen's wings, before she passed them over, and Ursel liked to hold them inside her pockets on the cold trek homeward.

Freya walked with her fingers bare, her coat blown open.

Ursel saw her walk to school the same way.

Their Mama had sewn her a new pinafore. Wool and in navy blue. She'd saved up coupons so Freya would be smart among the town girls. She said: *you'll meet so many new ones.* The first morning Freya wore it, she got up before Ursel, brushing out her plaits at the bed foot, braiding them herself at the window, and when she walked out, it was alone and with no coat at all.

But at night, Freya climbed into bed beside her. If Ursel lay quiet enough, as if she were sleeping, then Freya slotted herself against her.

She hadn't said anything about Benno leaving.

The first Ursel heard was from the girls in the bench rows in her Papa's classroom. They said how Benno's house was emptied.

– Just after the English left, no?

– Yes, I saw that. All the furniture – it was carried out onto the pavement.

– I saw the gramophone, and the parlour chairs.

– Well, I saw it all loaded.

The town daughters told Ursel how a van had come to drive it all to Bremen, but Udo and Benno hadn't been there.

– They went by train, stupid.

– You didn't know that?

– Their Mutti already took them to the station.

*

Benno's house was home to new folk now. Two families. Two mothers and two lots of children. One from Breslau, one from Danzig – both from the East Lands that were no longer German.

The daughter from Danzig sat at the same bench as Ursel. She ate with her too at playtime: ration bread from Heinrich's, under the old oak branches.

She told Ursel:

– You know the Vati in the house before us? My Mutti says he is a prisoner. He's with the English. But my Mutti says they will release him; they should release all the men.

When Ursel went to tell her Mama, though, in the schoolhouse kitchen, her Mama pulled her mouth tight:

– People shouldn't talk so much.

And then she went on peeling the lunch potatoes.

Most people didn't talk enough for Ursel. Or not when she could hear them.

When Herr Paulsen came back at Easter, Ursel heard it from Herr Brandt. Or rather, she overheard him, when he came striding to the classroom to find her Papa one afternoon.

Ursel was lingering in the desk rows, waiting for Freya to come home from the girls' school, and then the yard man slapped his hat down on her Papa's desk.

– So that's that, then?

He said he'd just heard from one of his yard men.

– From my joiner, just back from war hospital.

His man had gone for a glass at the town bar – a first home glass to celebrate – and there was Paulsen.

– Right there! With all his back table usuals. Sitting and smoking and talking, as though nothing has passed here.

Herr Brandt sounded so angry, his talk all spilling out of him.

– Can you believe the English? That they let that bastard out again?

But Ursel's Papa stood to close the door then, shooing Ursel away across the schoolyard – *off you go now!* – so that was all she heard.

A letter came for Freya not long after.

Their Papa brought it from the postbox when Freya was trying to get the stove lit. Ursel was with her in the classroom, rummaging through the kindling basket, looking for off-cuts or dry bark when their Papa came inside.

– For you, *mein Mädchen*.

He dropped the letter on the school bench nearest, so Ursel saw the ship drawn by the stamp, and Freya's name written in a boy's hand.

It had come from Bremen. It had come from Benno; Ursel thought it must have. Was his Vati home too?

Freya wiped her hands on her apron – dark soot marks – and Ursel saw how she looked at the envelope. But her sister didn't open it. Instead, Freya turned back to her stove task, sending Ursel out to look for plane curls in Herr Brandt's workshop. And when Ursel returned, the stove was lit, the envelope gone, flames dancing.

She wasn't supposed to ask; Ursel could feel this. Since the English had left with all the workers, she wasn't supposed to ask about them either. It was like she was supposed to forget all about them.

Ursel didn't see why. Or how Freya could want to forget about Benno. It made her sad – no – it made her angry. Did Freya want to forget all those months also? When it was just the three of them out on the Heide.

The day after, Ursel watched for her coming from the postbus, and Freya slowed in the lane ruts when she saw her; her sister blinked at her like a question mark.

They walked up to the high pass.

It took much longer than when they used to ride there, but Freya found the way all right. The wind blew them along the sand paths. It blew the fleeces of the sheep too, sending them nestling in the hollows, and it sent the spring birds swirling above the junipers, darting in pairs among the gorse brush.

In the gully, the twigs were in bud. The days were too chilly for the gold to be open, but at least they could see the hut through the branches.

– *Schau mal!*

Ursel slid down the slope, excited – only to find a board had been nailed across the doorway: she couldn't get it open.

– Why?

She rattled the handle, disappointed. Annoyed, too, because Freya took her time about following. Her sister edged her way along the gully slope, reluctant, stopping just short of the hut steps. But then she bent down and straightened.

– Look!

She'd found a curl of paper – silver, from a cigarette

packet – smoothed and folded. Freya held it out, her face suddenly brighter:

– Guess who?

Kurt had been at the Brandt yard just one time when they turned up with their kindling baskets.

– *Na?*

He'd grinned at them, rummaging in his knapsack, pulling out an English chocolate bar. It was only a half one, but he'd divided it between them anyway, and then Kurt had taken the foil while they were eating, folding two rings out of that purple, smoothing them between the fingers of his one hand, before winding them around Ursel's plait ends and admiring her.

– Fine, girl.

Just like she remembered him.

He'd been at the Hof once also. When they brought their Mama's jars to old Hanne, Kurt was sitting on the bench there with Christa, his knapsack beside him like he'd only just arrived, or he was ready to go again.

Ursel didn't know what he did between times. Freya said only Christa did, most likely. Christa didn't mind about his wandering and bartering like her father said she should. Kurt drifted along the Elbe, carting his rucksack between here and Hamburg and elsewhere, and Freya said Christa didn't care any longer, whether her father liked it or not.

– Kurt does what he likes, no?

Freya said it like she approved too.

In any case, it seemed like her sister was sure it was Kurt who'd been at the hut here, and that he was the one who'd done the boarding. It seemed like she was happy about it also, because Freya walked all around the hut sides, as though looking for more signs.

– Come!

She beckoned Ursel, showing her another two planks across the window. They'd been nailed at a diagonal, so there was a gap at the bottom of the pane, and Freya smiled as though she'd already peeked through there. She held out her arms to lift Ursel, but Ursel had grown just tall enough over the winter months to peer inside.

The bed slats were empty, and the floorboards bare and ash grey. Still, once her eyes adjusted, Ursel saw the kettle was on the stove top, and the bedroll stowed neatly. And – best of all – the burnt shirt buttons were there in their sill row, along with her snail shells, her Heide stones.

So then Ursel was glad too, because everything was there still. She was even glad about the boards. Glad about Kurt, keeping everything safe and inside: not forgotten after all.

Ursel carried that feeling home with her, swaying down the gully on Freya's shoulders. The birds swooped above the gorse and the hut roof, and Ursel turned to watch them. She thought how Kurt must watch them also, when he came to check on the hut here. And how Freya might bring her back again, if she asked her.

If she held her breath until the next one landed – this is what Ursel told herself – then the next time might come faster.

Sasha

Mirko mowed the lawn at the children's home.

Once the days grew warmer, the grass began to grow again, so Mirko went door to door, all along the townhouses, taking Sasha with him. They went to all the army-requisitioned places, asking to look in their cellars, until they found a mower, and then they rolled it back to the children's home, clattering it along the paving stones.

Mirko sharpened the blades and oiled the workings. He showed Sasha how to do that, and how to rake the grass: all the cuttings into piles. Mirko told Sasha all the things he did – jobs and chores and fixings.

At the home, he swept the paths clear, and the front steps, emptied wastepaper baskets and replaced typewriter ribbons. He fixed the cot legs that wobbled, and the chair legs in the dining hall. He found a radio and placed it in the corner, so the children could have music to eat by. It made Miss Fran smile that he did that, and the *Ofitserka* also.

Every morning, Mirko went to find her in her new office here – *good day to you* – and he asked for chores to do. She had a proper room now, but it was just as full as her camp one: walls lined with files, shelves full of clipboards and work lists; she and Miss Fran always had more work for Mirko. But even when he'd worked through her day's tasks, he went to the next house and the next, knocking at all the English offices. The *Ofitserka* said he must have mown the grass now in half the English army gardens along the shoreline.

– Making myself indispensable.

This is what he called it.

The *Ofitserka* said Sasha had to go to lessons, though – straight after breakfast – so he missed out on all of this.

Some mornings, he couldn't listen for missing Mirko. Sasha sat in the schoolroom in the upper storey and watched for him from the windows: Mirko's back as walked away along the pavement; the top of his curled head when he returned. Now that spring was here, Mirko went capless, with his sleeves rolled. And at least once lessons were done with, Sasha knew they'd spend the next hours outside.

The *Ofitserka* had loaded his bicycle on the truck back when they came here. Now Mirko kept the tyres pumped and the brakes tight, and Sasha slipped down from the schoolroom to find him, pocketing his lunch roll to be faster, joining him on the front path. Then Mirko rode with him, up and down the villa roads. Or he sat on the kerbside and smoked, watching while Sasha taught the other boys. Some afternoons, they filled the pavement: all the children waiting on their turn.

Sasha taught them to sit on the saddle while he did the riding. Or he lifted the youngest ones onto his handlebars, showing them where and how to hold on. *Tight – yes? Tighter.* Sasha rode them slow to the corner so they'd get used to it – and then around the whole block. The first time he did that, he came back to a hero's return. When Sasha rounded the corner, he found himself surrounded.

And then he wished that Yeva liked it here as much as he did.

Yeva had cried and cried in the winter.

While they were still at the camp as it emptied, when they came to the home here with the *Ofitserka*. His sister cried too much for Sasha to know what she made of the place. Or if she thought their Mama could find them here.

She'd stopped, though, since her belly started growing.

Yeva was slower now, and softer and rounder. When she came out to watch him riding, she walked carefully down the front steps to sit with Mirko.

Most often she came with Ditte, too. Slow and hand in hand, while Ditte wobbled on her small legs.

The *Ofitserka* had brought Ditte with her.

Now Yeva was the one who lifted her from her cot in the mornings. She sat with her at mealtimes: Ditte on her lap, at the table corner by the radio, humming while she spooned the oatmeal, the mashed potatoes. And when it was time to sleep, Yeva rocked her.

Sasha couldn't tell, though, how long Yeva meant them to stay here.

When the days got properly warm again, Mirko took him to the jetty.

He had a key from Miss Fran, and he opened the boat shed. It was dark inside and the smell was cool and green, and then the light came flooding inside – so surprising – when Mirko opened the doors to the water.

Mirko cleared the weeds from under the moorings, cutting back the willow branches that hung in from the doorway. He fixed the hinges, and then – he and Miss Fran between them – they found a boat from somewhere.

– Look!

Sasha was up in the schoolroom when he saw them. He

pointed for the other boys, all of them calling and leaning out of the window as Mirko came rowing it back along the shoreline.

With these warmer days, the *Ofitserka* brought a visitor: an English soldier who spoke like a German.

The two of them shook hands on the doorstep. Palms clasped, they stood there. Then they talked and talked while she took him from room to room, showing him everything – or was he showing her?

The boys in the dorm, they told Sasha that this was the soldier's house.

– That's what he thinks.

– He's here to take it back.

– Yes – he'll do it, too. You just watch.

But Mirko said it used to be his family's.

– So you boys should find other things to talk about.

The soldier looked the whole house over. Kitchen to dorm rooms to parlour. Then he took a chair from the dining hall, carrying it out across the lawn. He sat down at the jetty, gazing and gazing out across the water.

Sasha saw him from the schoolroom window, and the soldier was still there while he raked the grass behind Mirko's mowing.

For a while, he came every day. Calling in on the *Ofitserka* to talk first, then taking his place down at the water. He brought a notebook and a pencil; the soldier drew pictures, page after page of them. The house and the trees and the gardens, and then the water and the spires.

– Do you see those tall ones?

He saw Sasha come to watch him, beckoning him over.

– Copper blue, yes?

The soldier said one spire was a church, the other was called the Rathaus.

– I'm drawing for my brothers. In England. So they can remember.

He said that the pictures were for his children also.

– For when I have some. Or just for myself. To remember it all.

He drew the home children, on the lawns and the pavements, running shoeless and bare-armed.

He drew the *Ofitserka* in her office room, at her typewriter, with her lists and her letters.

He drew Mirko in his boat, teaching himself to use the oars, pulling out along the shoreline. And because Yeva came to watch Mirko, the soldier drew her also, holding Ditte on the jetty planks. And then Yeva lifted Ditte high to make her laugh, pulling her little socks off, dipping her feet into the water.

When the soldier came to draw Sasha, he stood him by the front steps, holding his bicycle, bare toes on the pedals.

– Just so. Yes.

The soldier smiled while he sketched, drawing a first picture fast, and then another, a little more carefully. He tore that second one out of his notebook and handed it over, and Sasha pinned it on his bunk slats – so even after the soldier was gone again, he remembered him.

When he looked up, it was the last thing he saw before lights out, and the first thing in the morning.

*

It got so warm then, the *Ofitserka* took to sitting on the jetty too. On the same chair the soldier had used, but with a folding table in front of her. She brought out her index cards and papers, tapping away at them on her typewriter.

Yeva sat with her there, and the two of them murmured. They wrote letters too, Yeva and the *Ofitserka*. To the Red Cross in Hannover, in Berlin; at home in Dnipro; to places all over where the Russians were in charge now.

They didn't know where his Mama was.

Yeva didn't say this. Or the *Ofitserka*. But Sasha knew anyway.

He could hardly remember her. When he tried – lying on his bunk bed, picturing their Mama searching, or coming to Hamburg; coming along the pavement here, across the garden – he couldn't think what she looked like. Even when he closed his eyes, he mostly just saw Yeva. Folding his clothes, scolding and holding him, wiping his face with a wash-cloth.

His sister didn't speak about staying in Germany, not any longer. She didn't say how soon until the baby, how long they would stay here. Or even how long before the *Ofitserka* went back to England.

– Well I'm here now, young Sasha.

This was all the *Ofitserka* said herself.

But she sat each evening, on the jetty planks with Yeva, writing and nodding and murmuring. Tall on her chair, Yeva smaller beside her, Ditte smallest of all of them, dozing in Yeva's skirt folds.

Mirko rowed all the while.

He said he was scouting. Looking for bathing places, picnic spots, all along the Alster shore.

– Fine places. Just you wait.

But all rivers ran into other rivers, Sasha knew this – because hadn't Mirko told him so?

While Sasha watched him from the jetty planks, he thought how Mirko could row from the Alster here to the Elbe. From the Elbe to the Havel. Havel to Oder, Oder to Vistula. *And so on, and so on.* And so perhaps – perhaps – Mirko meant to row them away from here: upstream and home again.

When Mirko helped Sasha into the boat, though, he said all rivers run into the oceans.

– And the oceans, now. They can take you further, boy.

One oar each, Mirko taught him how to scull; how to steer; how to turn.

And then they rowed out across the Alster, all the way to the harbour.

– You know that ships used to sail from here to New York?

Mirko said there used to be cargo ships – *so many* – and ocean liners, and that they sailed from Hamburg docksides all over the New World. So then Sasha saw Mirko might have other plans – or why else would he bring him here?

When they got to the quayside, the water smelled of salt and rust.

The tide slapped at the boat sides, and the yards seemed empty to Sasha. No ships in sight, or liners. The boat sheds were huge and old and echoing; spooky too, with their burned walls and bombed roofs.

But then men came from inside.

Sasha only saw a few at first, coming to catch the rope from Mirko, and the bag he threw. But soon there was a whole crowd, reaching down their palms, slapping handshakes and grinning their greetings. All of them Germans.

These men were young like Mirko, but with war wounds. Missing eyes, missing fingers. One stood propped on crutches, another with his sleeve rolled and pinned to his shoulder. Mirko crouched with his bag and opened it; the men hunkered down to trade and bargain. English tea for German candles, English soap for American coffee grounds. The goods passed from hand to hand, from pocket to knapsack, on and back through the circle – and then Sasha saw boys come also. Barefoot, like he was, they slipped across the dockside to crouch among the menfolk. Knees grimy with rubble dust, cigarettes tucked into their hat bands – watching and learning.

When Mirko rowed them back with their new bargains, Yeva was waiting, sitting with Ditte in her skirts.

– So are they sailing yet?

She smiled and Mirko did also, tying up the small boat.

– We'll see.

The sun on the jetty planks, Mirko lifted Ditte from Yeva's arms and held her, and Sasha dangled his toes into the water.

In 1948, three years after war's end, the United Nations sought to collate the records of all displaced children still in Germany into one register. They surveyed orphanages, hospitals, care homes and foster homes across the English, French and American zones, and the western sectors of Berlin, finding a total of 347,057 children. 191,199 were in institutions, 130,682 in German foster homes, and 21,176 had been adopted by German families.

For adults, too, displacement continued well into peacetime. Holocaust survivors sought to leave Europe for safe haven elsewhere; alongside them, over one million Polish and Ukrainian forced workers refused to be repatriated from Germany, most because they feared life under Soviet rule. Housed in camps across the western zones of occupation, people waited years for their fate to be decided, marrying, starting families, all while living in uncertainty. Only once their legal status as refugees was agreed were they able to begin new lives, migrating to Britain, Australia, Palestine, North and South America.

I hope this book pays them some small tribute.

With grateful thanks to:

Dan Stone, who started me off on this book, and whose own I highly recommend. Christine Schmidt, Elise Barth, and all the staff at the Wiener Holocaust Library in London, for their expert guidance and the access they afforded me to the International Tracing Service holdings. Every Name Counts.

Veronique Baxter, agent and friend. Lennie Goodings, editor of wisdom and patience. Toby Litt for dropping round at exactly the right moment. Clare Cohen for listening while I talked myself back in to writing. Ida Bova for her kindness in checking my Ukrainian. My mother, Gretchen Seiffert, for our conversation-without-end. Michael, Edie and Finlay for love and support.

The research was greatly assisted by a grant from the Society of Authors.

Readers may be wondering about the spelling of place names in this novel, especially those in territories that have been (or are currently) contested – Kiev rather than Kyiv, for example, or Donbass rather than Donbas. I chose to go with the spelling in common usage in English at the time.

Rachel Seiffert's novels have been shortlisted for the Booker Prize and the Dublin/IMPAC Award, and longlisted three times for the Women's Prize for Fiction. She has received awards from the American Society of Arts and Letters and the Association of Jewish Libraries, and was named one of Granta's Best of Young British Novelists. Now a Royal Literary Fund Fellow and Writer in Residence with First Story, she lives in London with her family.